Gathering Storm

by Alexa Land

The Firsts and Forever Series
Book Four

Books by Alexa Land

Feral (prequel to Tinder)

The Tinder Chronicles

The Firsts and Forever Series

(as of October, 2016)

Way Off Plan

All In

In Pieces

Gathering Storm

Salvation

Skye Blue

Against the Wall

Belonging

Coming Home

All I Believe

Hitman's Holiday (novella)

The Distance

Who I Used to Be

Dedicated to R.L.M.
With much love and gratitude

Contents

Chapter One

"Say my name, baby."

Crap, what was his name again? I should probably know that, given the fact that I was riding him like I was racing to the finish line of the Kentucky Derby. Since I actually had no clue, I went with a diversion. "Your big cock feels *so good*," I purred, bouncing a little harder and faster. He reached up and twisted both my nipples like he was trying to tune in his favorite radio station, and I fought the urge to roll my eyes.

"Say my name, Hunter."

Gah! I stepped up my diversion tactics and moaned, "Oh God, I'm so close."

"Yeah babe, cum for me," he said as he thrust up into me. The fact that I wasn't even remotely hard seemed completely lost on this guy. I took hold of my cock and began to stroke it for all I was worth.

"Oh shit, oh *shit*," I gasped, closing my eyes and throwing my head back as I rode him feverishly. Who says men can't fake orgasms? It's totally doable, especially if your sex partner is too self-absorbed to realize you aren't actually jizzing on his six-pack.

"Oh fuck baby, yeah." He thrust wildly, then let out a long, loud, "MMMMNNNNNNFFFFGGGGGGGG" as he came. I almost asked him if he wanted to buy a vowel, but didn't think he'd get it.

When he finally stopped twitching like he'd just taken ten thousand volts to the nut sack, I reached underneath me and held the condom in place as I eased off of him. "That was fucking incredible," he said, once he'd caught his breath.

"Yes it was, sweetheart." I snuggled up beside him and slipped my arm around his waist. "You're welcome to spend the night if you want to."

But he untangled himself from me and swung out of bed, saying, "Thanks babe, but I gotta be up early." He sauntered into the bathroom and turned on the shower.

Brushing off my disappointment, I muttered under my breath, "Sure, use my shower. Make sure to use a ton of my Bulgari body wash while you're at it."

I got up and wandered into the living room, looking around for my briefs. I finally found them dangling from the top corner of the mirror in the entryway. That had been a nice shot. I probably couldn't have done that intentionally if I tried. Just to test it out, I flung the little black underwear at the corner of the mirror. Nope, missed. I retrieved them again and pulled them on, then wandered around gathering up the rest of my clothes, which I carried to the walk-in closet.

When Mr. Tall-Dark-and-Whoever was dressed, I walked him to the door (he'd used so much body wash that I could practically see a cloud of fragrance around him, like in a cartoon). He turned toward me, and I thought I was going to get a goodnight kiss. But instead, he whipped out his iPhone and asked, "Mind if I get a picture? My friends are never gonna believe I banged Hunter Storm." Before I could answer, he blinded me with the flash and said, "Awesome."

That right there sums up the glamorous life of a porn star. Jealous?

"Okay. Well, see ya," I said as I held the door open for him.

He paused right in front of me on his way out. "You don't have a clue what my name is, do you?"

"Nope."

He considered that for a beat, then said, "I don't care. You're smokin' hot," before disappearing down the hall.

I locked the door behind him, then went into the living room and sprawled out on my couch, still in just my briefs. According to the silver clock on the end table, it was only ten-thirty. Ugh. I considered getting dressed and going back out to the bars, but was feeling highly unmotivated right then.

So instead, I reached for my phone and shot a text to my friend Christopher. It said: *I have terrible taste in men. And also, I think you should come over so we can play Madden. Your winning streak must end, I fear it's going to your pretty blond head.*

I didn't really expect him to come over. He was engaged to a hot cop named Kieran with huge biceps that must tear through shirts like the Incredible Hulk. Why would he leave that to come play videogames with his home-alone-at-ten-thirty-on-a-Friday loser of a friend?

He texted back: *You* do *have terrible taste in men, I keep trying to tell you that. It'll take me twenty minutes to get there, I'm going to walk over. See you soon.*

The hot cop must be working. I texted *Yay!* and reached for my game controller, so I could practice before he arrived. After a few minutes though, I glanced out the floor-to-ceiling windows comprising one wall of my living room and noticed it had started raining heavily. I dropped the controller and went to retrieve my friend, throwing on a black overcoat and stuffing my feet into a pair of boots before grabbing my keys and an umbrella.

Once outside, I started jogging toward Christopher's apartment, along his usual route. By the time he and I crossed paths, he was soaked, his cotton sweatshirt providing no protection from the rain. I threw my arm around his shoulders and held the umbrella over both of us, and he kissed my cheek as he slipped his arm around my waist. "Hi, Hunter. What are you doing out here?"

"It wasn't raining when you started walking over, so I figured you could use an umbrella."

"That was very sweet of you, but you probably shouldn't be out here by yourself."

I sighed at that. "I'm not going to let fear rule my life, Christopher." I had a stalker, another super fab perk of being a porn star. In the past few weeks, his threats had gone from harmless loser in his mom's basement to unholy spawn of Norman Bates and Hannibal Lecter. It was special.

When we got back to my apartment, I dropped my umbrella in the entryway and flung my arms around my friend, who held me for a good long time. He was a great hugger. "Thanks for coming over," I said.

He rubbed my back. "I'm glad you texted. I thought about calling you earlier, but figured you'd be out having fun on a Friday night."

When I finally let go of him, I asked, "Is Kieran working?"

"No. There was some kind of plumbing crisis at the house. His brother Brian called a couple hours ago and had a screaming fit over the phone."

"So naturally, Kieran dropped everything and ran right over."

"Well, the house does belong to both of them."

I took his hand and towed Christopher into the master bathroom. My earlier 'guest' had left damp towels (three of them. Really?) all over the floor. After I handed Christopher a clean towel from the cupboard to use on his damp curls, I scooped up the wet ones and deposited them in the laundry hamper that was *right there in the corner*, but apparently invisible to anyone but me. Then I unbuttoned my dripping overcoat and hung it on a hook as I used my foot to push off one of my boots.

"Wow, that's quite a look," he said with a little grin, rubbing his hair vigorously. "A trench coat, galoshes, and see-through underwear. And you went out in public like that."

I looked down at myself. I'd forgotten I was wearing nothing but the sheer black briefs. "The coat was completely buttoned up. And I was on a mercy mission," I said with a grin, pushing off the other boot. "I knew you'd be out there looking like a sad little half-drowned kitten, so I didn't have time to plan my wardrobe."

Christopher's blue eyes flickered down to the briefs one more time. He had zero interest in me sexually (trust me: *zero*. I couldn't believe it at first, either), so that extra glance was nothing more than incredulity at what I was wearing. I decided to tease him about it anyway, and wiggled my eyebrows at him. "You totally just checked out my package. Don't think I didn't notice."

He threw his towel at my head and grinned at me. "I did not. Get dressed, Hunter."

I pretended to be disappointed. "You're the only person that's immune to my porn star superpowers," I said, then turned and trudged from the bathroom.

Christopher followed me, peeling off his soaked sweatshirt. "The only one, huh?"

"Well, straight guys are immune, too. But they don't count."

I went through to my walk-in closet and pulled some things from the shelves as Christopher said, "Man, it's like Johnny Cash came by and hijacked your wardrobe. Why do you wear nothing but black?"

I handed him some clothes and said with mock seriousness, "It matches my soul."

"Uh huh."

"Actually, you wouldn't know this because, as I said, you're immune to my superpowers, but I happen to look damn hot in black. That's not all I own, though. Look, there's a blue shirt right over there."

I pulled on a pair of jeans and a T-shirt while Christopher changed into the sweats I'd given him. Next, I put his wet things in the dryer, which was tucked away in a little closet off the kitchen, grabbed two bottles of water from the fridge, and found a packet of weird peanut butter-filled crackers in the cabinet. Christopher ate them almost exclusively, because he had an odd eating disorder. Well okay, technically, it was a, what did he call it? Trauma-based phobia involving food. He'd been getting help at some kind of specialized clinic and was able to eat a couple more things these days, but those gross little crackers were still the mainstay of his diet.

He was a couple pounds heavier than when I'd met him four months ago, but still looked fragile as a little porcelain doll. His appearance was deceiving though, because Christopher was tough as nails. He'd survived things in his life that would have killed lesser men, and I admired the hell out of him for being so strong.

We went to the living room and settled in on the sofa, and after I handed him his game controller and the snack, I draped my legs over his lap. That was another of the many great things about my best friend: he accepted my incessant need for physical contact without judging. I actually might have sat on his lap if I didn't outweigh him, and I really believed he would have let me do that without making me feel like a freak.

As the game loaded, I asked, "Why didn't he just call a plumber?"

"What?"

"Kieran's brother, Brian. Why didn't he just get a plumber to come to the house, instead of calling up your honey and harassing him?"

"Because it's more fun to harass Kieran."

"Brian sounds like a total douchebag."

"Yeah, he kind of is, but I feel bad saying that."

"Why, because he's in a wheelchair? People in wheelchairs can be douches, too, you know. It's not just a term reserved for the ambulatory."

Christopher smiled at that. "I know. But I still feel like a jerk when I think badly of him."

"The guy treats his brother like his own, personal butt monkey and trashes the house they grew up in faster than Kieran can repair it. Somebody seriously needs to tell him that losing his legs in Afghanistan didn't actually earn him a get-out-of-nice-free card."

He grinned and said, "I believe you're misusing the term butt monkey."

"Doesn't it mean, like, personal servant or something?"

"I'm pretty sure it means ass-kisser."

"Perhaps there are nuances to the term butt monkey that you aren't taking into consideration."

"Well, I never claimed to be an expert."

I smiled as I clicked through the on-screen menu. "I'm glad you're here, Christopher."

"Me too." After a pause, he ventured, "So, who was Mr. Damp Towel?"

"How do you know I didn't leave wet towels all over the bathroom myself?"

"He missed the trash can when he threw out the condom."

"Ugh, I hadn't noticed that. And I literally don't know who he was. Right in the middle of sex, he was all—" I lowered my voice several octaves, "— say my name, baby." In my normal tone of voice, I continued, "And I completely drew a blank."

"Oh man, that's awkward. What did you do?"

"I faked an orgasm to distract him."

"You did not. Men can't fake orgasms."

"Sure we can." I shot Christopher a bright smile. "If you need evidence, I can pop in one of my films."

"Porn stars always finish on camera. The movie doesn't end until there's a money shot."

"Yeah, but the bottom's cum shot is usually spliced in at the end, after about twenty minutes of wanking that are edited way down." I glanced at my friend and asked, "Didn't you ever fake an orgasm when you worked as a prostitute?" He'd been a teenage runaway and supported himself the only way he could for five years. But he'd finally been able to quit the business and was a rising star in the art world after a smash-hit debut show. He was even about to open his own gallery. Christopher was a total success story, another reason why I admired him so much.

"I faked everything *but* that. People tend to notice if you don't ejaculate."

"The guy tonight didn't. And that sounded very professorly, by the way."

"What did?"

"*Ejaculate.* I usually just go with jizz, splooge, bust a nut, cream…I could go on, for about a day and a half. But you get the idea."

"I do," he said with a grin.

I rubbed my eye and muttered, "Hang on, my contacts are killing me. I'll be right back," as I jumped off the couch and headed for the bathroom.

When I returned a couple minutes later, I said, "Okay, promise not to laugh."

"At what?"

"I needed to take my contacts out, and I'm completely blind without them, so I had to resort to these." I stuck a pair of thick, black-framed glasses on my face and said,

"When I picked them out, I was shooting for a retro-hipster vibe. But I kind of ended up with mathlete."

Christopher shot me a wide smile. "You look so cute."

I rolled my eyes. "I look like I'm here to fix your computer." I dropped back onto the couch, draped my legs across his lap again, and picked up my controller.

"I'm serious, you look adorable. I can't believe I haven't seen these before."

"I'm getting far too comfortable with you. The romance is dead. Next time you come over, my hair will be in curlers and I'll be sporting a green face mask and a ratty housecoat."

He laughed and said, "I'm totally picturing that."

"Well, stop it." I was smiling too, and never happier than when I was hanging out with Christopher. I would have said he was like the brother I never had, but I actually had *three* brothers and they were all complete tools.

We played the football videogame for a while, and every so often, Christopher snuck a look at me. Finally I said, "Out with it. What is it that you're thinking about saying to me?" Before answering, he executed a game-winning move that made me collapse in a heap and yell, "Holy crap, not again!"

He balanced his controller on the arm of the couch and said, obviously choosing his words carefully, "Hunter…do you really think it's the best idea to bring strange men back to your apartment? It just seems so risky. I mean, that stalker's out there somewhere. We even know he's local, since he hand-delivered a threat letter to your production company."

"My taste in men isn't *that* bad. I'm not going to pick out a total psychopath and bring him home with me."

"But this guy's not going to be wearing a tag that says, 'hi, I'm psychotic.' In all likelihood, he's going to blend in with everyone else. Remember what I told you about the man who attacked me? He seemed completely harmless. I didn't have a clue what he really was until it was way too late."

A little over a year and a half ago, when my friend was still working as a prostitute, he'd been drugged, raped, and almost beaten to death by one of his customers. That incident was at the root of his food phobia, since the drugs had been hidden in a sandwich.

The assailant was still at large. When the police ran out of leads and let the case go cold, Christopher took matters into his own hands and began distributing sketches of his attacker all over the city. He'd learned a couple homeless boys had disappeared around the same time he was assaulted and were presumed dead. A pattern linked Christopher's attacker to those disappearances, which could mean that man was even more dangerous than anyone had imagined.

But Christopher didn't worry about his own safety, or about drawing the attention of a possible serial killer. He was determined to bring his attacker to justice, and was still out there every week with his sketches. I thought he was incredibly brave.

I leaned in and gave him a hug as I told him, "I know you're concerned, and I appreciate that. I really do. But like I said, I'm not going to let fear dictate how I live my life.

Besides, it's just a bunch of letters. I don't think there's much to worry about."

Christopher pulled back to look at me with a crease of concern between his eyebrows, and he reached out and tucked a strand of my shoulder-length blond hair behind my ear. "It's more than that. You know that as well as I do, which is why you went to the police with those letters. It's just not safe to bring strangers home with you, or to go home with them. Actually, that's risky with or without a stalker out there somewhere."

"I know. But what am I supposed to do, put myself under house arrest?"

"I think you're in denial, Hunter, and that's why you haven't really changed your behavior since all of this began. Making changes would mean admitting the threat is real." He was probably right, but I just looked away and shrugged noncommittally. My friend watched me for a long moment, then asked, "What happened to the idea of hiring a bodyguard? Are you still looking into that?"

"I interviewed a few applicants."

"And none of them were good enough?"

"None of them were *gay* enough," I said with a little grin. "That line of work tends to draw a lot of hetero alpha douchebags. If I'm going to be stuck with someone 24/7, I need to be able to stand them."

"Is that really the issue?"

"Well, no. Actually, I've been thinking about it, and I decided a bodyguard is overkill. I know those letters are pretty unnerving, but this person hasn't actually done anything."

"He's threatened your life, Hunter."

"But that's all it is, a threat. I don't think he'll ever act on anything in his letters."

Christopher looked like he had a lot more to say on the subject, but I was spared a lecture by his phone buzzing on the end table. The worry line between his brows got deeper as he read his screen. I asked what was wrong as he got up.

"Kieran hurt his back trying to fix that plumbing problem. He asked me to take a cab to the house, so I can drive him home in his car. It must be pretty serious if he can't drive."

I jumped up too, and said. "I'll come with you. If it's that bad, you might need my help to get him to a hospital."

*****

Maybe fifteen minutes later, our cab pulled to the curb on a quiet street in Noe Valley. It was the first time I'd seen the compact Victorian that Kieran and his brother had inherited after their dad died. Two people were on the little front porch, one in a wheelchair, the other flat on his back. After he paid the cab driver, Christopher ran up to the prone figure. I trailed after him, eyeing Brian suspiciously as I turned up my collar against the heavy rain.

Like his brother, Brian was a big guy with broad shoulders. He was also a double amputee. Both legs ended somewhere below the knee, but that was obscured by his baggy sweatpants. He was also dressed in a grubby T-shirt and had a bandana tied around his head. His arms were crossed over his chest, and a thick beard and long, brown hair made him look like a Hell's Angels wanna-be. From everything I'd heard about that guy, he was a homophobic asshole and most definitely on my shit list.

"Kier, are you okay?" Christopher asked as he dropped to his knees and rested a hand on his fiancé's forehead.

"I will be, baby," Kieran said with a little smile.

"What happened?"

"Well, turns out I'm not much of a plumber."

"Ya think?" Brian muttered.

I glared at him as I came up the stairs and said, "Wow, way to instantly live up to your douchey reputation."

"Who the hell are you?" Brian asked, raising an eyebrow at me. "Because I don't remember calling anyone to fix my computer."

"Bite me, Duck Dynasty," I said with a sneer. Then I shot Christopher a look and tapped my thick black glasses with a fingertip. "Told you."

"What happened?" Christopher asked Kieran.

"I dropped the toilet I was trying to replace, and wrenched my back trying to catch it," he said.

Brian added, "Don't forget the part about it falling all the way through to the basement and rupturing the main sewer line in the process."

"Turns out, the toilet had a slow leak, which rotted out the wood beneath the tiles," Kieran said. "It's surprising the floor didn't collapse sooner."

"Fucking awesome," Brian muttered.

"God, you're ungrateful," I told him, hands on my hips. "Your brother was trying to fix things for you."

"My brother just caused a crater in our only downstairs bathroom!" Brian exclaimed.

"He was still trying to help, and he doesn't deserve your shitty attitude."

"Screw you," Brian said.

"Wow, clever comeback."

"Who the hell are you?" he repeated.

"I'm your very favorite thing, yet another gay guy. You're totally outnumbered."

"Yeah, because I really needed you to tell me you're gay," he said.

I narrowed my eyes at him. "And I didn't need to be told you're a rude, homophobic dickhead."

Christopher interrupted us, asking his fiancé, "Why are you out on the porch?"

"Well," Kieran said, "turns out when you rupture a main sewer line, your entire house reeks of shit. It's totally uninhabitable, and the plumber I called can't get replacement parts until tomorrow."

"Come on," Christopher said, sliding his arm behind Kieran's shoulders. "Let's get you to the emergency room."

Kieran sat up slowly, wincing with pain. "That might be an idea. I don't know what I did to my back, but it's definitely not good."

"What're you going to do with Grizzly Adams over there?" I asked, tilting my head toward Brian.

"They don't need to *do* anything with me," he snapped.

"Oh really?" I asked. "Because last I checked, it's pissing down rain and you're stuck on the tiny porch of a poop-scented house." That earned me a hard glare.

"Brian will need someplace to stay for the next few days, until I can get that bathroom floor rebuilt," Kieran said, his face contorting with pain as he stood very, very slowly.

My friend chewed his lip as he helped his fiancé to his feet, then said, "Well, I'd suggest dropping him off at our apartment, but there's no elevator. The gallery downstairs is accessible, but other than four walls, it doesn't have much to offer." Kieran tried to straighten up a bit, but doubled over with a grunt, and Christopher tightened his grip on him and spoke to him soothingly.

"I'll make sure Cro-Magnon Man gets situated somewhere," I said. "You just worry about Kieran, he's not looking so good." All the color had drained from his face. He'd also broken out in a light sweat and was breathing quickly and shallowly to try to manage the pain that standing up had caused.

"That seems like a really bad idea," my friend said, glancing from Brian to me.

"It'll be fine," I told him. "I'm not going to roll him off the Bay Bridge or anything, no matter how tempting that is. Now go on, get Kieran to the hospital and hooked up with some painkillers, stat."

Christopher weighed his options for a few moments, but came up empty. "Well, okay. I'll check in with you as soon as I can," he said, and focused on his injured partner. They started down the wheelchair ramp, moving at a snail's pace, and I tugged off my overcoat and draped it over Kieran's slumped form to keep the rain off him.

"Thanks," he murmured.

"You're welcome. Feel better, Kier," I called as I ducked back under the roof of the porch. When they reached Kieran's rusty old Ford Mustang, Christopher helped him into the passenger seat before jogging around to the driver's side. He started it up, and the car lurched away from the curb. I'd never seen my friend drive before, and I wondered if he actually had a license.

"What are you still doing here?" Brian wanted to know. "Aren't they expecting you back at Geek Squad headquarters?"

I pointed a finger at him. "Don't think I won't bitch slap you, Chewbacca. Now, who do you want me to call to come get your sweatpants-wearing ass?"

"Just go away."

"Gladly. As soon as you tell me who to call." I pulled my phone from my pocket and waved it in the air.

"I can dial a damn phone, nerdboy. Leave."

"Is your phone on you?"

"No, it's inside." He rolled over to the door and tried the handle, then dragged a hand over his face.

"Did you lock yourself out?" I asked, and he sighed and glared at me. "Here, use mine." I held the phone out to him, and he looked at it and then looked away.

"Don't tell me, let me guess. You've alienated all of your friends and family with this angry-at-the-world pity party you've had going on for God knows how long, and now there's no one to call. Am I right?"

"Eat me."

"I'm exactly right, aren't I?"

That pissed him off, and he yelled, "Just go to hell, you fucking f—"

I cut him off, getting right in his face and yelling back, "I swear to God, if you say faggot I will force feed you your nasty-ass ZZ Top beard!"

22

Surprisingly, he grinned, just a little. Then he said, "I was going to say fucker."

"You were going to call me a fucking fucker?"

"Yeah, I was." When I shot him a look, he added, "What? It's not like I rehearsed it." That tiny grin still lingered.

"Do I amuse you?" I asked, straightening up and putting my hands on my hips again.

"You just threatened to force feed me my beard. Was that not supposed to be amusing?"

"I'm colorful. So sue me." I waved the phone again and said, "Really? There's not a single person you want to call?"

"I was going to call a cab and have it take me to a motel, except that my wallet's locked inside, too."

"Okay. So, I'll take you to a hotel and check you in, and you can pay me back later."

He glanced at me suspiciously, one eyebrow raised. "Why would you do that?"

"Because I promised Christopher I'd look after you, and he and Kieran have enough to worry about right now. I want to be able to report that you're safe and sound."

"I'm not a child. I don't need you *looking after me*."

"Like hell you don't."

"Fuck you."

"Wow, another damn fine comeback. And you know you need my help, Brian. That probably hurts your big, stupid, hetero ego, but I really don't give a shit."

"Stop acting like you know a damn thing about me."

"I know plenty," I said. "For example, I know that a while back, you didn't like what your brother made you for dinner, so you threw a plate through the living room window."

"That wasn't about dinner. I was having a bad day."

"Were you also having a bad day when you met my best friend for the first time and called your own brother a faggot?" I held my hand up and said, "Don't answer that. I don't care what kind of day you were having, because that was *not okay!* That's your kid brother, you jerk! And here you are, calling him names and acting like a schoolyard bully. How dare you treat Kieran like that? I mean, what the hell is wrong with you?"

"I'd assume that would be pretty fucking obvious!"

I stared at him incredulously. "Are you seriously trying to tell me it's okay to treat your brother like shit because you lost your legs and ended up in a wheelchair? Are you *kidding* me?"

"No, that's not at all what I'm saying! Shit!" Brian grabbed the metal rims on the wheels of his chair and propelled himself forward, gliding quickly down the ramp.

"Where are you going?" I called. He didn't respond, so I ran after him, the rain immediately soaking through my T-shirt. When we reached the sidewalk, I jumped in front of him and acted like a human brake, stopping his momentum with a palm on each armrest of his wheelchair.

"Move," he growled.

"No. I'm serious about not letting anything happen to you, for Christopher and Kieran's sake."

"God, you're a pain!"

"Look who's talking! Just let me get us a cab and get you checked in to a hotel, and then you never have to see me again."

He sighed and pushed a strand of wet hair out of his face, glaring up at me for several long moments. Like Christopher had, he too was obviously weighing his options and coming up empty. Finally he admitted defeat and muttered, "Fine."

I let go of his chair and watched him for a beat to make sure he didn't take off down the sidewalk. Then I ducked under a tree and dialed a cab company. When I disconnected, I called over to him, "They said ten minutes." He was giving me the silent treatment, which was a plus, as far as I was concerned.

When the taxi finally arrived, he rolled up beside it and tugged the back door open, then positioned himself as close to the side of the cab as he could get. He hesitated for a long moment, then glanced up at me. For the first time, I saw a hint of vulnerability in his blue eyes. But then he pulled up his veneer of anger and said, "I don't need a fucking audience for this."

I half-turned away from him and pulled out my phone, scrolling through a few texts. Out of the corner of my eye, I watched as Brian struggled out of his chair and into the taxi, awkwardly pulling himself onto the back seat. He then reached out the open door, flipped a couple levers on his chair and folded it flat, and tried to pull it into the cab with him. It was never going to fit. I went over to him and took the chair from his hands, called to the driver to pop the trunk, and deposited it in the back for him without discussion.

When I got in the taxi, I directed the driver to the nearest hotel I could think of. As we pulled away from the curb, Brian muttered, "I didn't need your help with that chair. I had it."

"No, you didn't. And I can't believe anyone would be stubborn enough to refuse basic mobility training. I mean, what the hell, Brian? Not only that, but you're supposedly an excellent candidate for prostheses, but you refuse to go to the clinic and find out about your options! What are you trying to prove?"

He stared at me, his eyes blazing with anger as he growled, "I can't believe my brother's been blabbing to strangers about my personal business."

"He's not *blabbing to strangers*. He was talking to his fiancé about it once and I happened to be there, since your future brother-in-law is my best friend. My name's Hunter, by the way. Not that you asked."

"This is none of your damn business, *Hunter*."

"Of course it is, because I care about Christopher. He loves your brother, you make Kieran miserable, and in turn, that makes my best friend unhappy. Oh look! Now it's my business."

"You're a real piece of work. You know that?"

We bickered all the way to the hotel, and when the cab pulled up before the big glass doors of the Marriot, I patted my pockets and murmured, "Shit." My wallet must have been in my overcoat, which I'd lent to Kieran. I pulled a few crumpled bills from the pockets of my jeans and chewed a nail for a moment, thinking through my alternatives. Then I told the cab driver, "Change of plans," and recited my address.

As the taxi pulled out of the circular driveway, Brian asked, "What are you doing?" After I explained the whereabouts of my wallet, he muttered, "Fucking awesome. So, where are you taking me now?"

"My apartment."

"Why?"

"Why do you think? No hotel is going to let you check in without a credit card, and neither of us has access to one at the moment," I told him. "This is the only alternative I can come up with, unless you can give me another address to take you to. I know you have a huge family, surely all of them can't hate you."

"I have no idea if they hate me. All I know is, I don't want to see any of them."

"My apartment it is then, just for one night. In the morning, you're back to being Kieran's problem. Hopefully by then, he'll be hopped up on enough painkillers to make you tolerable."

He shot me a look and said, "Why don't we go back to my house and break a window? Then you can climb in and get my wallet."

"Oh yeah, because I really want to experience the fascinating aroma of raw sewage. Plus, can't sewer gas blow up?"

"Kieran had the sense to shut off all the pilot lights, it's not going to ignite."

"Well, I still don't want to go in there."

"Wimp."

"Neanderthal."

"Bite me."

"You first."

After a pause, he suggested, "We could go to the hospital and retrieve your wallet from Kieran."

"Let's just leave your poor brother in peace tonight. This'll be fine. I have a big apartment, you and I will barely see each other. Plus," I admitted, "I'm not positive the wallet's in my coat, I might have left it at home." He rolled his eyes and fell silent during the remainder of the ride to my place.

After I retrieved the wheelchair from the trunk and gave the cab driver all the cash I had on me, apologizing profusely for the measly tip, I unlocked the door to the lobby. Brian rolled ahead of me, and we rode the elevator wordlessly to the top floor.

Once inside my apartment, I said, "I'll get you some bedding for the couch, it's pretty comfortable. I fall asleep on it all the time." I locked the door behind us as I muttered, "What's that smell?" Something sharp hung in the air.

Brian preceded me into the living room and glanced around. "It's paint," he said. "How do you not know that?"

"I just couldn't place it for a minute, and I don't see why it would smell like paint in here. I haven't had any work done." I shrugged it off and said, "Must be coming from one of my neighbors' apartments. I'll get you a blanket and pillows."

At the door to my bedroom, I stopped short. It took a moment to process exactly what I was seeing, as fear trickled like ice water down my spine. Someone had spray-painted a single word in four-foot high red letters on the wall above my bed. It said: *Whore*.

Chapter Two

I hadn't heard Brian come up behind me, and when he muttered, "What the hell?" I jumped. "What's going on? Who did that?"

I was way too stunned to reply. I just kept standing there dumbly, staring at that word, watching the red paint slowly run down the wall. It was surreal. All I could hear was my heartbeat thudding in my ears as the smell of spray paint overwhelmed my senses.

"Hunter, who did that?" he repeated, his tone a little more forceful.

"I...I don't know. I have a stalker. Maybe...maybe he did this. I don't know how he'd get in here, though."

"Do you own a gun?" I raised my hand and pointed into the room. "In the nightstand?" Brian asked, and I nodded. He quickly rolled over to the little bedside table and yanked open the drawer, then pulled out my Beretta and checked the clip. He stuck his head in the bathroom and looked all around, then said, "Get in the bathroom and lock the door behind you, then dial 911. Do you hear me?"

"I have to get out of here," I whispered.

"Get in the bathroom, Hunter, and call the police. It's safe, I checked. Do it now."

Abruptly, the 'flight' end of a fight-or-flight response kicked in, and I repeated, "I have to get out of here." I turned and bolted, and Brian cursed vividly and came after me. I ran out of my apartment and pounded the button for the elevator again and again, then rushed into the enclosed space when the doors slid open. Brian was right beside me with the gun on his lap, and he hit the button for the ground floor.

"What if he's still in my apartment?" My voice sounded like a child's, high and frightened.

"All the more reason to call the police. Give me your phone." I tugged it out of my pocket and handed it to him, and Brian dialed 911. Moments later, he began speaking to the dispatcher. When we reached the lobby, I ran to the big glass door, but then I hesitated. Suddenly, the darkness looked sinister, foreboding.

"Stay in here!" Brian yelled, grabbing my wrist with his free hand. He concluded the 911 call, then towed me away from the door. "The police are on their way. We just need to stay right here and wait for them. Do you hear me, Hunter?" I backed myself into a corner, and glanced nervously all around the obviously empty lobby. When I turned to look at Brian, his brows were knit in concern. "You're going to be okay," he told me. "I promise." I nodded automatically.

What happened after that was a blur. The police arrived and searched my apartment, but they didn't find anyone. The building manager was roused from bed, and footage from the security cameras was taken as evidence. The officers asked me a million questions, which I tried to answer coherently.

They also asked Brian a bunch of questions. I was too distracted to pay attention to his answers. After a while, he disappeared. I assumed he'd had enough of my drama and figured out someplace to go. But a few minutes later, he appeared beside me and said simply, "Here." He was holding out one of my T-shirts and a jacket, and I realized he must have gone upstairs and retrieved them for me. Only then did I notice I was rain-soaked and trembling violently.

"Thanks." I pulled off my wet shirt and put on the dry clothes, all while answering the questions the police officer kept lobbing at me about my job, my social life, my acquaintances. He had a lot of questions about the man I'd brought home earlier that night and whether he could have come back and done this. The cop was doing a decent job of pretending he wasn't a raging homophobe. But occasionally, a little smirk gave him away.

Eventually, the police ran out of questions, declared my apartment safe, and took off with the tapes from the security cameras. I chewed my fingernails as I sat in one of the upholstered chairs in the lobby with my knees drawn to my chest. Brian was a few feet away, watching me closely. Finally, he asked, "Are you really a gay porn star?" When I nodded, he looked skeptical.

That made me knit my brows at him. "Is that really so unbelievable?"

"You look like you belong in a computer lab."

"You're completely judging me by the glasses. That's pretty shallow."

"No I'm not. I'm also judging you by the dorky haircut."

My hair was all one length and grazed the top of my shoulders. "This from a man who got his last haircut during the Bush administration."

We sat there for several long moments, frowning at each other. Finally he said, "So, what are you waiting for?"

"What do you mean?"

"Officer Keller told you the apartment is safe, they searched every inch of it. Why are you still sitting here in the lobby?"

"I'm afraid to go back in there," I admitted.

"Come on," he said, tilting his head toward the elevator. "I'll go with you. I still have your gun, by the way."

But I shook my head. "I don't feel safe there. Not tonight, anyway." I pulled my phone out and started scrolling through my list of contacts. "I'm going to stay with a friend, you can come too if you want. Sorry to hitch you to the crazy train, by the way. I know this is a hell of a lot of drama."

He grinned, just a little. "This is actually the most interesting night I've had in years."

I scowled at that. "I'm glad my personal crisis has entertainment value."

"I didn't mean it that way. I just meant that I'd planned to go into law enforcement after the Marines, and I…never mind."

I sighed and returned my attention to the phone. There were dozens of names in my contact list, but most were little more than fuck buddies, people I could call when I wanted to party or get laid, but not when I actually needed something. I started chewing on the nail of my right ring finger.

"You don't have anyone to call either, do you?"

I hit Brian with a hard glare. Surprisingly, he looked sympathetic instead of smug. Not that I wanted his sympathy. "I have plenty of people to call," I lied. "It's late though, so maybe I shouldn't disturb them."

"Uh huh."

I chewed on the nail of my index finger for a while, then sent a text to Christopher, asking how Kieran was and asking him to check the pockets of my coat for my wallet.

The phone rang in my hand, and I answered it with, "Hey."

"Hi, Hunter," Christopher said. "We're still waiting to see a doctor. The emergency room is apparently the happening place to be on a Friday night. Nana Dombruso and her grandson Vincent are here too, coincidentally, because her maid was having chest pains." Christopher was friends with another of the little old lady's grandsons, and she'd taken a liking to both of us. Apparently she had a tendency to adopt every stray gay guy she came across.

"How's Kieran?"

"Not so good. He can't even sit up, so he's flat on his back on the floor of the waiting room."

"I'm sorry he's in pain, and even sorrier he's on that gross, germy floor. You're going to have to dip him in hand sanitizer when you leave there."

"I know. Oh hey, here's your wallet. It was in an inside pocket of your coat. Want me to bring it to you?"

"No, you have your hands full."

Christopher must have heard something in my voice, because he asked, "Hunter, are you okay?"

Before I could answer him, a shrill, familiar voice in the background yelled, "Is something wrong with Hunter? Give me the phone!"

Nana got on the line and exclaimed, "What a night! First Marta thinks she's having a heart attack. I think it's gas, but better safe than sorry, I always say. So here we are in the emergency room, and then who should come through the doors but Christopher Robin and his hottie! And now something's wrong with you, too? What is it? Do I need to send an ambulance?"

"No, Nana, it's nothing like that. I just…well, someone broke into my apartment tonight."

"*What?* Jesus, Mary and Joseph! What did those scumbags take? They didn't get the painting that Christopher made of you, did they? Or your gun? Tell me they didn't steal your gun, because you and me got a date at the shooting range tomorrow!"

"Um, I don't know if anything was taken. I haven't been back in there yet to find out, actually."

"Wait a minute. Don't tell me it was that stalker bastard!"

"Maybe."

"He got in your apartment? But how?"

"I have no idea. This building is really secure."

I could hear Christopher in the background, asking, "What's going on?"

"Where are you now?" Nana asked me.

"In the lobby of my building."

"That's no place to be, not with that psycho on the loose! Tell me you at least have your gun with you."

"I do, actually." I glanced at Brian. He was relaxed in his chair, watching me like I was a TV show.

"Well, thank heavens for that," Nana said. Then she held the phone away from her ear and exclaimed, "Marta! They let you out already? Vincent, go help Marta. It was gas, wasn't it?" Her maid must have nodded, because Nana said, "See, I told you! But it's good we came to the hospital just to make sure. You can't mess around with your heart. Trust me, I know. Vincent, bring the car around, and Marta, come and sit down. You look exhausted." Just when I thought she'd forgotten I was on the line, she said into the phone, "Hunter, sit tight, I'm on my way. We're just going to drop Marta off at her house and then we're coming right over. What did you say, Christopher Robin?" I could hear my friend in the background. After a moment, Nana told me, "I'll bring your wallet, and Christopher wants to talk to you. I'm gonna go see what's keeping Vincent and that car. We'll be there soon!"

"Wait, Nana, you don't have to—"

"She's gone," Christopher said. "Are you okay?"

"I'm fine."

"What happened?"

"Someone broke into my apartment and spray-painted the word 'whore' above my bed. It was all very slasher film."

"But your building is always locked! How could they get in?"

"No idea."

"Ask Nana to bring you here to the hospital when she arrives. You can wait with us, then come home to our apartment. I'm sure you don't want to be alone after something like that."

"I'm not alone, actually. Brian's still with me."

"He is?"

"Long story."

"I'm so sorry, I shouldn't have burdened you with him. You have enough to deal with right now."

"It's fine. I'm actually glad he was with me," I admitted. "If I'd discovered the break-in when I was alone, I would have completely lost it."

I glanced at Brian again, who was still watching me. His head was tilted to the side, and he looked a little perplexed. I wondered what he was thinking about. When Christopher and I hung up, I pointed myself toward the front door and waited for our mutual friend to arrive.

"Stop it," Brian said after a while.

I turned my head to look at him and raised an eyebrow. "Stop what?"

"Stop biting your nails. You're making yourself bleed."

I glanced at my hands. I hadn't even realized what I'd been doing, and I really had drawn blood, more than once. "I can't help it. I used to be a compulsive nail-biter when I was a kid. I've mostly stopped now, but when I get stressed, I revert right back to it." I folded my hands in my lap and went back to watching for Nana's car.

A couple minutes later, Brian muttered, "Christ." He wheeled right in front of me and grabbed my wrists. "You have to stop doing this. It's giving me the willies." Again, I hadn't realized that I'd gone back to biting my nails, and a couple more were bleeding.

"I don't have control over it."

"Sure you do." He let go of me and said, "You only lapse into it when you're idle, so talk to me about something."

"What could I possibly have to say to you?"

"Lecture me some more about what an asshole I am." There was that tiny grin again, almost hidden by the big, nasty beard and mustache.

"You *are* an asshole."

"I know."

"And you're okay with that? Are you just planning to be an asshole forever? To spend the rest of your life being miserable and making everyone around you miserable in return?" He frowned at me, and I said, "You got home from Afghanistan three years ago. Isn't there some kind of expiration date on taking your frustration out on the people that love you?"

He knit his brows. "You know I was kidding when I told you to lecture me about being an asshole, right?"

I ignored that and said, "I get that some really shitty things have happened to you, but right now, you're letting them define you. I know your life hasn't gone the way you planned. So maybe what you need is a new plan, a new direction."

"You're such a hypocrite."

"Excuse me?"

"You're spouting off about needing to make changes," Brian said, "but look at your life. You work in porn, for Christ's sake! I'm guessing that wasn't your dream growing up, any more than mine was to end up in a fucking wheelchair. If it's so damn easy to change your life, why haven't *you* done it?"

"We're not talking about me right now, we're talking about you."

"But why not talk about your problems? Your life's just as fucked up as mine, only in a different way."

"My life is not fucked up!" I exclaimed. "And you know what you're doing? You're deflecting. I learned all about that in therapy. Something you should seriously look into, by the way."

"Because it did you so much good."

"You met me less than two hours ago. Do you really think you know me well enough to judge me?"

"You've known me the same length of time," Brian said, "and you've been judging the shit out of me."

"Yeah, well, your reputation preceded you."

"All you've ever heard about me has come from my brother, who, granted, has every reason to think the worst of me. But maybe consider the fact that his perspective is kind of skewed."

"I don't think it's skewed at all. He sees you for exactly what you are."

"And what am I?"

"You're an angry, frustrated man who feels like life royally cheated him. But you're more than that too, Brian," I said. "You're also scared out of your mind."

"That's what Kieran thinks, that I'm scared? That's bullshit."

"Actually no, he's never said that. But it's so damn obvious."

"I am *so* fucking done talking to you," Brian hissed, and swung his chair around, barreling for the door.

"You're just making my point for me," I called after him. "You can't even talk about this, that's how scared you are."

He swung back around to face me. "Of what? What do you think I'm afraid of?"

"You're afraid of letting people get close to you. You're afraid that if you let anyone in, they'll see how hurt and vulnerable you are, and they'll judge you for it."

"You have no idea what you're talking about."

"I know from hearing Kieran talk about his life that you were both raised by a macho cop father in a macho cop family. You were probably expected to behave a certain way, to be strong and tough. But, Brian," I said, "that's all bullshit. It's okay to be vulnerable. You really don't have to keep pushing everyone away and hiding behind your anger."

"You don't understand any of this," he muttered, and turned from me again.

"I do, actually, because I was raised the same way. In my house, I was expected to 'act like a man', and if I didn't, there was hell to pay. I remember this one time, I must have been about ten years old. I was crying, and when my father saw that, he beat the shit out of me. I'm not telling you that to get sympathy, by the way. I'm telling you so you know I really can relate."

"That's a pretty extreme reaction."

"I know. My father is a raging alcoholic. Most of his reactions were totally out of proportion like that."

Brian stared at me for a long moment. When he finally said something, it was, "What made you cry?"

"My dog got run over."

He knit his brows. I half-expected him to make some sort of wisecrack. But what he said was, "It's surprising to me that you and I would have the first thing in common."

"Why? Because I'm queer?"

"No," he said, "because you're a scrawny little geek with a stupid haircut." I was about to get mad at him when I saw that little, teasing grin again. It was always so unexpected, like sunshine right in the middle of a thunderstorm.

Sudden pounding on the main door of the building made me jump. Nana's face was pressed up to the glass, her hands cupped around it. "Hunter, lemme in," she yelled. "It's raining like a bastard out here!"

I rushed over to the door and swung it open, and my 'adopted grandmother' came bustling in. She was all of five-foot-nothing, but make no mistake, Stana Dombruso was a powerhouse. She was also colorful as all get-out, literally and figuratively. Apparently, her maid's faux heart attack had gotten Nana out of the house in a hurry, because she was wearing bright floral pajamas, a purple raincoat, bulky red snow boots, and a huge yellow sun hat. Though she had to be about eighty, she was still the type of woman who never went out without her lipstick. That evening she'd clearly applied it on the fly, and had misjudged the location of her mouth by a good inch.

Trailing behind Nana was her grandson Vincent, holding an umbrella that was obviously hers, because it was bright yellow with black and white daisies all over it. I had to grin at that. It was just such a wonderful contrast to his dark, brooding persona.

Vincent looked a lot like his older brother Dante, who was an acquaintance of mine. That meant he was about six-four with shoulders that Atlas would have envied, slightly long black hair, and chiseled features. Unlike Dante, he wore a pair of silver, wire-rimmed glasses. And also unlike his brother, he never smiled. Never. That was a real shame, because he was a beautiful man.

I glanced at him as Nana fussed over me and hugged me about half a dozen times. He was alert as a sentry, very nearly standing at attention, his dark eyes taking in everything. When his gaze landed on me, he didn't react at all. He just looked at me for a long moment, then went back to scanning the room.

"I can't believe you're here in the lobby," Nana exclaimed. "Doesn't it make you nervous to be in this building?"

I said, "It's not so bad down here. I like the fact that the lobby's wide open, no hiding places. And I just can't quite make myself go back to my apartment."

"Well, I can certainly understand that," she said. "Your home's been violated, it's going to take time for you to feel safe there again. You know, my friend Glenda Meier's granddaughter, she's one of them, what do you call it? Witchens. We should have her come out and do this cleansing ritual Glenda was talking about. It'll rid your home of all the bad juju that this psycho scumbag brought in with him."

"Wiccans," Vincent said.

"What?"

He explained, "Mrs. Meier's granddaughter is a Wiccan."

Nana raised her eyebrows at him. "That's what I said, Witchens." To me she said, "I'll arrange the cleansing ceremony, just leave everything to me."

"That I would love to see," Brian murmured. He was actually smiling.

"Who's your friend?" Nana asked, apparently noticing Brian for the first time.

"That's Kieran's brother, Brian."

"The asshole?"

"Yup," I said with a grin.

"You're not dating him, are you?" she asked me.

In unison, Brian and I said, "Oh, hell no."

I told her, "I was supposed to take him to a hotel after Kieran got injured, because their house is temporarily out of commission. But we didn't quite make it that far."

She frowned at Brian for a long moment. And then she told him, "If you promise to behave, I guess you can spend tonight at my house." Then she shook a bony finger at him and added, "But be forewarned, Fuzzy: my grandson Dante is a gay homosexual, and other people I love are too, so I won't tolerate hateful language in my home. You got that?"

"Yes, ma'am," he said embarrassedly, and I flashed her a huge smile.

She linked her arm with mine and said, "Come on, I'll escort you upstairs so you can grab a few things." With her free hand, Nana reached into the pocket of her raincoat and pulled out a .44 Magnum. The coat must have had *really* deep pockets. "Don't worry, I got us covered."

Both Vincent and Brian looked absolutely stricken. "Nana, give me that," Vincent said, stepping forward and holding out his hand.

"No way, Sonny, you got your own piece. Now come on, let's all go upstairs and make sure Hunter's apartment is secure while he packs an overnight bag."

I felt pretty safe when we got upstairs, since my entire entourage was packing. Brian retrieved my gun from a pouch on the side of his wheelchair, and Vincent pulled a freaking cannon *with a silencer* from inside his black overcoat. Okay, I knew Nana's family was old-school mafia and all, but *damn*.

While Vincent and Brian did yet another sweep of the entire apartment (for no real reason, since the cops had been thorough), Nana stayed by my side. I quickly shoved some random clothes into a suitcase, then took a satchel into the bathroom and threw in some toiletries. When I happened to glance in the mirror, I frowned at my reflection. God, what a mess. I ignored it and kept packing.

As we cut through the bedroom, I made a point of not looking at the graffiti above my bed, and Nana clicked her tongue and muttered under her breath, "I'd love to get my hands on that sick son of a bitch and shove that can of paint right where the sun don't shine." To me she said, "I'm going to send Vincent over here tomorrow to clean this up, replace your locks, and add an alarm system. He's got my house wired up better than Fort Knox, he'll do the same for this place."

"He doesn't have to do that, Nana. I can hire someone."

"Nonsense! For a job this important, you only trust family." I didn't bother pointing out that we weren't actually related.

All of us were quiet on the ride to Nana's house, even her, which was really out of character. She was obviously worried about me. I was worried, too, since this person, whoever he was, had really stepped up his game.

For the past few months, I'd been receiving letters at the production company that employed me. They'd started

43

out harmless enough, though this man was clearly delusional. He began by declaring his undying love for me and talking about the wonderful future he had planned for the two of us. Soon, that gave way to anger and frustration over the fact that we weren't together. According to Ramon Sanchez, the not-overly-concerned cop that had been assigned to my case, it was all pretty textbook.

Calling me a whore was part of the stalker's latest rage package, so I had little doubt the graffiti and the letters were from the same man. Not that I still read the letters he sent, because they were deeply disturbing. My manager just forwarded them directly to Detective Sanchez, and he relayed the gist of them to me. Apparently, my stalker's latest twist was to talk about my movies as if they were real life, and then accuse me of cheating on him. Sanchez was very uptight and very straight, and he must have loved the detailed descriptions of every one of my films, scene by buck-naked, sweaty scene, that the letters apparently contained.

Christopher had said he thought I was in denial about the whole thing, and yeah, I probably was. I mean, how the hell was I supposed to deal with something like that, with knowing a clearly unhinged person had me in his sights? It had been bad enough before that person broke into my home. Now it was completely nightmarish. That was actually the perfect way to describe it, because, like a nightmare, it didn't quite feel real. Was that still the denial talking?

"Hunter, sweetheart, we're here," Nana said, snapping me back to the present. I turned away from the window of the limo that she'd bought herself a few months ago and

44

looked into her concerned brown eyes. "Come on, I'll tuck you into my grandson Dante's old room. You'll like it, it's cozy. Brian can have that crappy extra bedroom on the ground floor, the one that smells a little like cat pee. I don't know why. I've never had a cat." I had to grin at that, and glanced out the door of the limo at him. He and Vincent were already out on the sidewalk, waiting for us and eyeing each other suspiciously.

I leaned in underneath the big brim of her hat and gave her a hug. "Thanks, Nana. I'd be lost without you."

"Damn right," she said, "and don't you forget it. But you got nothing to worry about now. Your Nana's got this all under control."

Chapter Three

I'd been completely exhausted when I dropped into the narrow twin bed that had been Dante's as a child. Despite that, I spent the next couple hours staring at the ceiling. I occasionally had bouts of insomnia, and that night's events had brought it back in a big way. I couldn't even make myself turn the lights off, which told me just how deeply it had affected me.

Eventually, I gave up on ever falling asleep and swung out of bed. I had a favorite place in Nana's palatial Queen Anne Victorian and decided that was where I wanted to be. I climbed the wide staircase to the third floor, wandered down the hall to the back of the building, and stepped into a little slice of heaven.

I closed my eyes and took a deep breath. The room smelled rich and earthy, like soil and dampness and moss. It was calming, and it centered me somehow.

Since I'd grown up on a big, ugly potato farm, I despised anything to do with plants. But the whimsical, built-in greenhouse spanning the entire width of the mansion was most definitely an exception. The intricate glass panels lining the back wall and part of the high ceiling were slightly wavy, made back when the molten glass would have been rolled out by hand, without mechanical uniformity. Hundreds of orchids thrived in that little ecosystem, some commonplace, some incredibly rare and exotic, but all maintained with obvious love and devotion.

I'd asked Nana once if she was the one who took care of them, and she'd said, "Hell no. I'm way too busy for that crap." So, I assumed their caretaker was the same person who maintained her backyard, which was a wonderland of sculpted shrubs and bright flowers. If I ever ran into her gardener, I planned to thank him or her for creating something so magical.

I took my favorite seat, an ornate Victorian 'fainting couch' right beside the wall of windows. There was a small, round table beside it, and every time I visited, a different orchid was on display on the mosaic tabletop. That night's specimen was particularly tiny and delicate, its yellow flowers less than a quarter-inch across. It wasn't very impressive, until you leaned in and really looked at it. When I did that, I decided it was the most perfect thing I'd ever seen.

"You've had a trying night," a deep voice said, "so I want to make sure you know I'm here. I don't want to startle you."

That, of course, startled me so much that I almost knocked the little plant off the table, but caught it before I did any real damage. As I scooped up the bark that I'd knocked out of the little terra cotta pot and put it back in its place, I said, "Damn, Vincent, you almost made me squash this precious little thing." I leaned over and took a look at him around the shelves of plants. He was seated on a bench toward the back of the greenhouse, dressed in a form-fitting black T-shirt and black sleep pants. It was the first time I'd seen him in anything other than a dark suit. His bare feet were up on the bench and a book rested on his bent knees. The lighting was very subdued, and I wondered how he could read by it.

"I'll leave you alone. I imagine you could use a little peace." He had a way of making everything he said sound so formal.

Vincent started to get up, but I said, "No, don't go. This is your home, I'll just go back to my room."

I headed for the door, but he intercepted me, detaining me with a light touch on my forearm. "Stay, I insist. You need this place far more than I do tonight."

I looked up at him. He was ever-serious. I found myself wishing I could see him laugh, just once. It must be a wonderful sight to behold.

Impulsively, I reached up and brushed his black hair off his forehead, and for just a moment, desire flared behind his glasses. But it was gone in the next instant, and he took a step back from me, knitting his brows.

That look intrigued me though, and I took a step forward. Again he retreated, so I caught his arms lightly and said, "Hold still a minute. I need to see something."

"See what?"

I got up on my tip-toes and kissed him gently. Fortunately, he cooperated and bent down a bit. He was so tall that at five-foot-nine, I never would have been able to reach otherwise. I closed my eyes and sank into it, and his big hands came up to circle my waist as he returned and deepened the kiss.

But a moment later, he seemed to remember himself and stepped back from me again, his hands falling to his sides. "Why did you do that?" he asked.

"Because I suspected it was what we both wanted. Obviously, I was right."

"You've had a rough night, Hunter, and what you're doing right now is the very definition of 'any port in a storm.' But believe me when I say, in no way am I what you need."

"Why not?"

He frowned and said, "Don't you get what I am?"

"Um, a really hot guy?"

He sighed in frustration. "Families like this one need someone to do the dirty work, so the rest of them can keep their hands clean. They need someone brutal, and ruthless, because that's what keeps families like mine safe."

"And that's what you are? The family pit bull?"

"Pit bull would be a huge step up." He turned and left the greenhouse, and I sighed and sank onto the bench he'd vacated.

I mulled that over for a while. It certainly explained the giant concealed weapon with a silencer…it explained a lot about Vincent, actually, including why he always seemed so burdened. Apparently the dark side of the Dombruso mafia rested firmly on his shoulders.

Eventually, I picked up his book. It was an old, dog-eared copy of The Picture of Dorian Gray, and I flipped randomly to a point in the middle and started reading. I'd liked the book in high school and was immediately drawn in.

I'd made it through a couple chapters when Vincent reappeared in the greenhouse. I hoped he'd had a change of heart and had come back to finish what we started. But all he said before ducking out again was, "You may want to check on your friend downstairs. It sounds like he's having a hell of a nightmare." I returned the book to the bench and headed for the stairs.

Before I even reached the ground floor, I could hear Brian yelling. It was the sound of raw agony. I hesitated outside his bedroom door, hoping he'd wake himself up, but the yelling just kept going, so I knocked loudly. There was no response. I tried the handle and found it was unlocked, so I slipped inside the little room, shut the door behind me and turned on a lamp. Brian was tangled in his sheets, a sheen of sweat on his skin, his features contorted as he thrashed around.

I was kind of afraid to intervene, since I was pretty sure he'd wake up swinging, but I felt like I needed to do something. I leaned back as far as I could, hopefully out of punching range, then shook his shoulder. "Brian," I said loudly. "Hey."

He gasped and immediately sat bolt upright, his eyes wild and terrified. He looked all around him, then stared at me for a long moment, totally disoriented as he asked, "Where am I?"

"It'll come back to you in a minute," I said gently, sitting down on the edge of the mattress. He was still staring at me, looking younger and more vulnerable than I'd have imagined possible.

After a while, he came back to himself and murmured, "Hunter."

I nodded and he relaxed a bit, falling back against the pillows as I turned the light off again. "Scoot over." There was no place else to sit in there, so I propped myself up against the headboard and pulled the covers over my legs.

Brian did as I said, then asked, "What are you doing?"

"Keeping you company while you calm down a bit."

He was quiet for a while before murmuring, "Thanks."

"You're welcome." After a pause, I asked, "Do you have nightmares a lot?"

He was flat on his back, staring up at the ceiling. "Yeah. I hadn't had one in almost a week though, I think that was some kind of record. But it figures that sleeping someplace unfamiliar would trigger them again. Sorry I woke you."

"You didn't."

"Really?" He turned his head to look at the clock on the nightstand, then said, "It's three a.m."

"Sleep and I don't really get along well."

His next pause in the conversation lasted so long that I was pretty sure he'd fallen asleep. Finally he said, "I'm sorry about your dog."

"What?"

"You told me earlier tonight that your dog got run over when you were a kid. I didn't get a chance to say I was sorry that happened before your friends showed up."

"Ah."

After another pause, he said, "It's bizarre that you're friends with an eighty-year-old woman."

"I know, but she's awesome."

"Is her last name Dombruso?"

"It is."

"So, you know her family's in the mafia, right?"

"Don't judge," I murmured, settling in and letting my eyes slide shut.

"How do you know her?"

"Well, let's see. Her grandson Dante married a guy named Charlie, who's Christopher's best friend, and I met Nana through Christopher. She has a habit of taking in strays, and she latched onto me right away. I'm really glad she did that."

He was quiet again for a couple minutes before saying, "I can't believe I'm sharing a bed with a gay porn star."

"You're judging again."

"That's not judging. I'm just expressing surprise at the incredibly bizarre day I've had." He tucked a hand behind his head.

"I can go back to my room if I'm making you uncomfortable."

"You're not. I'm grateful for the company, but don't feel like you have to babysit me."

"This isn't babysitting. And honestly, I really don't want to be alone tonight either," I admitted.

"I wish I could have caught the guy that broke into your apartment," he said quietly. "I really wanted to help, but I'm not much use."

"You *did* help. You not only had the sense to grab my gun and call the police, but you stayed by my side throughout all of that. If you hadn't been with me tonight, I don't know what I would have done."

"You would have handled it."

"Doubtful. When I saw the graffiti and realized someone had been in my home, I froze up. And after that, all I could think to do was run. I'd really hoped I was better than that in a crisis, but apparently I totally suck."

Brian turned his head toward me in the semi-darkness. "You should really think about getting a bodyguard until your stalker's behind bars."

"Yeah, I already looked into that." A thought occurred to me, and I asked, "Do you want the job?"

Brian scowled at me. "That's hilarious."

"I'm serious."

He stared at me for a long moment, then said, "Okay, A, you hate my guts. And B, how do you envision that working? Because a bodyguard that can't even climb a set of stairs would be super useful."

"Tonight you did exactly what needed to be done. You were there for me, and you were calm, competent, and totally in control of the situation. What more do I need in a bodyguard?"

"Legs."

I sighed and said, "If you don't want the job, that's fine. I know you can't stand me, either. But don't make excuses, because I know you can do this. I think you'd enjoy it, too. You came to life when all of that was happening. You stopped being this hurt, angry guy, and you became something else. It felt good, didn't it?"

Brian narrowed his eyes. "This is a pity thing, isn't it?"

"Oh, come on. I'm not nearly that nice."

"It has to be pity."

"If you don't take the job, then I'm all alone."

"No you're not. Just call a security firm and go with whoever they send over."

"I've already interviewed several candidates that way, and I didn't like any of them."

"You don't like me, either," he pointed out.

"Yeah, but at least I know what I'm getting with you."

"This is the second worst idea you've ever had."

"What was the first?" I asked.

"Getting a job in pornography." I sighed at that, and he added, "See? I'm a total pain in the ass. Even if I could do the job, *and I can't*, you'd fire me in two seconds anyway for pissing you off."

I swung out of bed. "Look, just think about my job offer. It's only temporary, of course, just until the police catch that guy."

"Where are you going?"

"Back to bed."

"I thought you didn't want to be alone tonight."

"I *never* want to be alone, but that's beside the point. I was just staying until I knew you'd put that nightmare behind you, and obviously you have. I'll see you in the morning." He opened his mouth like he was going to say something else, but then he closed it again and nodded.

*****

Brian was gone by the time I got up the next morning. Nana told me he'd asked her to call a cab and a locksmith, and had taken off bright and early. She also told me Vincent was already at my apartment, installing a security system. Man, everyone was being productive so early. A productive morning to me usually just consisted of making it to the coffee pot and hitting the on button.

I visited with Nana for a while over coffee, then she and I headed out to our prearranged date at the gun range. When the whole thing with my stalker had started, she'd bought me a gun and told me I needed to learn to shoot. I didn't like guns and had never planned to own one, even though I'd grown up around them. But I had to agree with her about needing to be able to defend myself in an absolute worst-case scenario.

After the gun range, she went off to an appointment and I kept myself busy for as long as possible by working out at the gym and running errands. It was early afternoon when I returned to my apartment. Vincent was still there, suit jacket off and shirtsleeves rolled back. A couple workmen were there, too. Apparently they'd torn a few holes in my walls to install the new security system and were patching it back up. They'd also done some repainting, including the bedroom wall.

"The system is operational," Vincent said in lieu of a greeting. He reached into the pocket of his black pants and pulled out a slip of paper, which he handed to me. "This is your temporary access code. Be sure to change it right away. I can show you how to do that, if you'd like."

"What I'd like," I said quietly, taking a step closer to him, "is for you to stay after the workers go home, so I can thank you properly for the new alarm." I ran my hand down his big arm, and for just a moment, Vincent's lips parted slightly.

But then he remembered his self-imposed no-fun-at-all rule and withdrew from me. "You shouldn't use your body as currency," he said. That stung, more than a little. "I was glad to do this as a favor to Nana, who cares quite a bit for you. Nothing more is required."

I frowned at him. "I wasn't offering myself in payment, but thanks for making me sound like a prostitute.

I just thought we could have a little fun. We obviously find each other attractive, so why not act on it?"

"My attraction to you is irrelevant. I would never take advantage of your current state of vulnerability." He turned and walked away from me.

"Well, awesome, Mr. Spock," I muttered.

He and the workers cleared out maybe half an hour later. Once they were gone, I sat on my couch and tapped my foot rapidly. I tried to take a few calming, deep breaths. A minute later, I began to chew off what was left of my fingernails.

Okay, no, I couldn't do this.

I launched myself from the couch and grabbed the overnight bag that I'd dropped beside the front door earlier, set the alarm with the passcode I'd been given, and headed for the elevator. I knew I was being irrational. The apartment was perfectly safe, now that Vincent had installed a security system worthy of the Louvre. But I still felt vulnerable there.

I flagged down a cab, and when the driver asked, "Where to?" I had to think for a moment. Finally, I recited Brian's address. I'd probably spend the night at Christopher's place, since he and I had been texting throughout the day and I had a standing invitation. But Kieran was currently sleeping off some hardcore painkillers, and I wanted to give him a chance to rest. That gave me plenty of time to check on Brian. I had a vision of him stubbornly trying to live in his sewage-scented, bathroomless house.

As it turned out, I wasn't very far off. He answered his front door with knit brows and asked, "What're you doing here?"

"Checking up on you. Why aren't you at a hotel?"

Brian's frown deepened. "Because I don't want to be."

"Did the plumber fix the main sewer line?"

"Yes."

"But your bathroom still has a huge hole in the floor, right?"

"Yeah, but it's fine. I figured out a solution."

"I'll bet. What did you do, put a five gallon bucket in your hallway and call that a toilet?"

He looked surprised, then quickly broke eye contact and muttered, "No, of course not."

"You did, didn't you?"

"No."

"Oh man, you totally did!"

"Maybe. But so what? And do I really need to remind you that this is none of your business?"

"You can't live like that, Brian. Come with me, let's get you to a nice, comfy hotel."

"I'm telling you, I don't want to go to a hotel."

"You were willing to go to one last night."

"I was desperate and too tired to think straight."

"Why don't you want to go? Give me one good reason."

He surprised me by admitting, "I don't want to go someplace where everyone's staring at me."

"What do you mean?"

"I feel like a freak when I'm out in public. People seem to think it's okay to stare and make comments, like because I don't have legs, I'm somehow exempt from common courtesy."

"Wow, that sucks," I said. "But why don't you just give them the finger and tell them they're being assholes?"

"I do sometimes. But then they just think I'm even more of a freak."

"Well, fuck them. There are always going to be dipshits in the world. The trick is learning to hold our heads high no matter what they come up with and refusing to let them get to us."

Brian rolled his eyes and said, "Don't pretend you have a clue what I'm going through. If anyone stared at you, it would just be because you're cute. And that is *not* the same thing."

"You think I'm cute?" I said with a grin.

He knit his brows again. "Now that you've combed your hair and lost the nerd specs, you're obviously an attractive, if highly annoying, individual."

"Thanks. Kind of. But I do know what it's like to be singled out, talked about, and made to feel like a freak."

"How could you possibly know what that's like?"

"I grew up in a town of eight hundred and sixty-seven people in rural Idaho, and never fit in, not even a little. I was called a fag before I reached middle school, before I even knew what that meant. For the first eighteen years of my life, I didn't know anyone else that was gay, not until I met my boyfriend Cole during our senior year of high school."

"That's a terrible example."

"Why?"

"Because," Brian said, "once you grew up, you had the option of leaving that rural shithole and going someplace accepting of gay people. What am I supposed to do, move to Planet Legless?"

"Eleven days."

"What?"

"That's how long it's been since I was called a faggot by some punk-ass jerk. Even living here, in one of the most tolerant cities in America, I still face prejudice all the fucking time. Does that mean I know what life is like for you in that chair? Of course not. But I sure as hell know what it's like to have to deal with rude assholes."

Brian considered that for a long moment. Then he said, "I still don't want to go to a hotel."

"So don't. Let me help you move in with one of your friends or relatives until the bathroom floor's fixed. Which one do you hate least?"

"I don't *hate* any of them."

"Why are you avoiding them, then?"

"Because," he told me, "I'm so sick of their good intentions and their oh-so-helpful words of advice. As if it hadn't occurred to me that I need to get on with my life! Worst of all, though, is the pity in their eyes. I don't hate them, but I *do* hate that, so fucking much."

"Okay. So, of all the people you know, who's least bad?"

"Kieran. He's too busy being annoyed with me to pity me," he said with a faint grin. Then he added, "But even if his apartment was accessible, I still wouldn't want to stay there. I don't want to be around those two."

I snapped, "Oh no, of course not. God forbid you'd have to watch a happy and in love *gay couple*."

That really flustered him, and he exclaimed, "I didn't mean it that way! At all!"

"How did you mean it, then?"

"I mean I fucking hate your friend for taking my brother away from me!" Brian obviously regretted that confession as soon as the words were out of his mouth. He looked away, fighting back some sort of strong emotion, and muttered, "Christ, why am I telling you this shit?"

His admission struck a chord with me, and I felt bad for jumping to conclusions. I kept my tone gentle as I said, "Probably because you really need someone to talk to, Brian, and I'm better than nothing."

After a while, he glanced at me and his tense shoulders relaxed slightly. "You're way better than nothing. Hell, you're better than therapy."

"Have you actually been to therapy?"

"Of course. The Corps required me to go for a full year, when I first got back from Afghanistan. But it was really useless."

"Why?"

"Because every session went like this: 'Talk about your feelings, Brian.' To which I'd reply, 'I'm fucking pissed!' There was nothing to say beyond that."

I grinned a little. "Yeah, that doesn't sound terribly productive."

He knit his brows and watched me for a moment, then asked, "Aren't you going to lecture me about the fact that I need to give therapy another try? Because everyone just *loves* pointing that out to me."

"You already know that. Why would you need me to harp on it?" He seemed surprised. I said, "So, back to my original question. Aside from Kieran, which of your friends or relatives is the least objectionable?"

"My cousin Jamie, I guess. There's always a hint of pity in his eyes, but at least he manages to keep the lectures and 'helpful' suggestions to a minimum."

"Well, great! So I'll text him and let him know you'll be staying with him for a few days while you pack a few things."

"You know my cousin?"

"Indirectly. Christopher knows him, since he's best friends with Jamie's ex, Charlie."

"Suddenly everyone I know is gay," he muttered. When he saw my expression, he added, "I'm just saying."

"Are you okay with the idea of staying with Jamie?"

"I guess, but I'll text him myself. I am actually capable of working a phone, you know."

"I was just trying to save some time so you can go pack. I wasn't implying that the phone's too difficult for poor lil ol' you." We both rolled our eyes, and he went off to find his phone. While he did that, I took a couple steps into the interior of his house. All the curtains were drawn, so it was fairly dark. It was also really cluttered, with all kinds of crap shoved up against the walls and piled on every surface.

I was a bit too anal to let it go, so I went into the kitchen and found a garbage bag, then returned to the living room and began tossing empty pizza boxes, Chinese food containers, and other miscellaneous crap into it.

"What exactly are you doing?" Brian asked when he returned to the living room.

"Keeping the health department from seizing the premises," I said, using two fingers to gingerly pluck a pizza crust off the arm of what was probably the sofa (but who knew, since it was completely piled with crap).

"You really are the most intrusive person ever," he told me.

"And you take the term slob to a whole new level." I was still gathering trash, and the garbage bag was bulging by that point.

"I thought you were eager to deliver me to my cousin's apartment."

"That was before I got a look at your living room."

Brian grinned a little. "You can't help yourself, can you? You literally *have to* clean this up. It's just like your nail biting, you're completely compulsive."

"Yes."

"Really? You're actually agreeing with me? I thought you'd argue about how well-adjusted you are."

I stopped what I was doing for a moment and looked at him. "I'm pretty aware of my flaws. But this particular glitch is actually beneficial, especially in a case like this. If you let me, I'd have this living room spotless in twenty-four hours."

"There's no way. It'd take weeks to bulldoze through all this clutter."

"Please let me prove you wrong."

"Are you actually begging me to clean my house?" he asked. "Because that's really strange."

"This is a compulsive person's dream come true," I said with a grin. "And to be honest, I really need a project right now. I'd love a way to take my mind off the total nut job that's stalking me and breaking into my home."

Brian considered that for a long moment, then said, "I still think it's weird that you're just dying to clean my house, but I guess I get it. Besides, I'm pretty sick of it looking like this."

"So you'll let me clean?"

"Let's just make one thing clear: the house is the project, not me."

"What does that mean?"

"It means I don't want this to snowball from let's-fix-the-house to let's-fix-Brian. I totally get that I'm a fucked up mess, but I really have no interest in Mr. Clean Junior trying to inflict some big life makeover on me."

I took off my leather jacket and tossed it onto a coat rack near the door. "The only thing getting a makeover is this room. You won't even recognize it when you get back from Jamie's."

"Oh no, I'm not leaving you here unattended. You're liable to throw out everything I own in your cleaning frenzy."

"You can't stay here. There's no downstairs bathroom, and a bucket is *not* a solution."

"So, I'll figure something else out, but I'm staying."

"Fine."

*****

I'd always found cleaning really therapeutic. Given that, Brian's pigsty of a house was better than a week at a spa. I completely lost myself in the task at hand.

At first, Brian just hovered, occasionally exclaiming, "That's not trash," and taking things out of my hands. After my fiftieth 'I know' he finally relaxed a bit. Gradually, he joined in, focusing on the task of sorting through his mail. At least a year's worth of unopened envelopes, sales circulars, and random junk mail was piled on almost every surface. He started by gathering it all up and stacking it on the recently-unearthed table in what was once a formal dining room, but which had become little more than a junk-filled pass-through between the living room and kitchen. Then he began sorting it piece-by-piece. Most of it went into a bag for recycling. The few seemingly important envelopes went into a big shoebox.

While he was doing that, I concentrated on one particularly piled up corner to the left of the fireplace, sorting through layer after layer of junk. When I'd almost reached the wood floor, I carefully picked up a little stack of photos I'd uncovered.

The picture on top was of Brian, Kieran, a boy I didn't recognize, and Charlie, Jamie's ex, all in their high school football uniforms. Brian would have been totally unrecognizable, if it wasn't for his eyes. All four looked so happy, their arms around each other's big, padded shoulders.

The next photo was a posed portrait, probably taken at a prom. His date was a tall, pretty brunette whose long hair was curled into ringlets. Brian was so handsome in his tux.

He was laughing and looking at something off-camera. I wondered what it was.

The third and final photo really got to me. It was a picture of Brian and a couple other people at the beach. He was dressed only in baggy swim trunks, looking tan and fit, but most of all, totally full of life and carefree. I realized then just how much war had taken from him, far more than his legs. I glanced over my shoulder at him, through the arched doorway to the dining room. He was concentrating on his mail, an all-too-familiar frown line etched between his brows, his broad shoulders hunched. My heart broke for him.

Brian sighed and turned toward me with a raised eyebrow. "Okay, what did you find that's making you go all introspective?"

I dropped the photos like I'd been caught doing something wrong and said, "Nothing."

"It was obviously *something*, because you hadn't actually stopped moving in over two hours. Was it a picture of me before I ended up in this chair, and did that trip all your sympathy switches? Because just so you know, one of the only reasons I can stand you is because you look at me with contempt, not pity. If you're going to get all compassionate on me, I'm totally throwing you out on your ass."

I fixed a neutral expression on my face, stood up, and stretched my arms over my head. "No worries there, Sasquatch. The only things I feel pity for are the cockroaches that have to live in squalor with you."

His expression got downright alarmed, and he asked, "You didn't really find a roach, did you?"

I grinned at that. "Surprisingly, no. I think this place is below their standards. But look at you, all afraid of bugs."

"I'm not afraid of bugs, I just fucking detest cockroaches. They're the most disgusting things on the planet."

"Well, then it was a pretty dumb idea to let your house go to hell like this. It was probably about twenty seconds away from a major roach invasion."

He stared at me for a beat, then spun in his chair and headed for the kitchen, muttering, "I'm going to go load the dishwasher." I grinned at that. Once he was gone, I gathered up the pictures and stuck them inside an old, dusty photo album, which had been wedged haphazardly into the cluttered built-in bookshelves. Then I went back to work.

*****

Probably two hours later, Brian interrupted me. I had scaled the aforementioned floor-to-ceiling built-in shelves, taken everything off, and dusted thoroughly. Now I was putting things back, arranging them nicely as I went.

"That doesn't go there," he said, then took a sip from his can of beer. He'd been watching what I was doing for the last couple minutes, and I'd just put a little earthenware vase beside a glass candy dish.

"Given what this place looked like when I got here, are you really going to get weird about knickknack placement?"

"Yes. The vase goes one shelf up, and the glass bowl goes on the next one down, on the right side."

I glanced at him over my shoulder. His expression was grave. Since it was obviously important to him, I followed his instructions to the letter and put everything back exactly where it had been. When I finished, he looked a little embarrassed and murmured, "Thanks."

"You're welcome." I brushed my palms on the legs of my jeans, then ventured, "That stuff was your mom's, wasn't it?" I knew Brian and Kieran had grown up in that house, and that their mother had died over ten years ago. Maybe in some way, keeping things the way she'd had them was a little memorial to her.

Brian gave me a 'well, duh' look and said, "No. I'm just really partial to frilly little candy dishes."

"Okay, Sarcasmo. I was just wondering."

He changed the subject by saying, "So, you've been working like a maniac for about four hours straight. How about if you take a break, and I order us some dinner?"

"You don't have to do that."

He sighed and said, "Would you just let me do something nice, for Christ's sake? You're cleaning my house, and I want to be able to repay you in some way."

"Okay, fine." I picked up a dust rag, and he rolled forward and plucked it out of my hands.

"If you don't take a break, *I'm* going to collapse from exhaustion, just from watching you. Look," he said, pointing across the room. "You found the couch. Why don't you try sitting on it? I'll bring you a beer and my take-out menus."

"But I'm so close to finishing! And as soon as I do, I'm starting on that kitchen. It's horrifying."

"It's not that bad. Kieran gets totally repulsed by it periodically and gives it a thorough cleaning."

"When was the last time he did that?"

"I dunno. Three, four months ago?"

I shuddered dramatically and began to dash for the kitchen. "I should have done that room first. I can just imagine the salmonella growing in there. And botulism! Ebola. Dengue fever. The Black Plague!" I was joking, but only slightly.

He caught my arm and pulled me back. "Wow, you're hyper as a five-year-old. Do you ever actually stop moving?"

"Only when forcibly restrained."

"Literally. Go sit down, I'm bringing you a beer. Let's see if you can make it all the way through dinner without actually cleaning anything." Brian headed to the kitchen and I followed him, which elicited a big sigh.

"Not to sound ungrateful," I said, "but do you have anything besides beer?"

He looked over his shoulder at me and raised an eyebrow. "Seriously?"

"Seriously. The stuff's nasty."

"You're the first guy I ever met who doesn't like beer."

"Well, you don't get out much. I can't imagine you meet a lot of people."

"This is true." He looked in his liquor cabinet and said, "So, what do you like? Just FYI, I don't know how to make anything that requires an umbrella."

I rolled my eyes and said, "My drink of choice is a whiskey sour, hold the umbrella. Is that butch enough for you?"

Brian grinned and said, "Why yes. Yes it is. I finished off the whiskey a couple days ago, though." He reached into the cupboard and pulled out a square bottle. "How about tequila shots?"

"Are you trying to get me drunk?"

"I was *trying* to offer you a beer, but you shot it down. Now I'm looking for alternatives."

"I could do tequila, but just until dinner arrives. Where are your take-out menus?"

We ended up ordering pizza and salad. The guy on the phone sounded way too jovial, like maybe he, too, had been doing tequila shots. We carried the bottle and a couple glasses through to the living room, and I settled in on the couch.

Then we proceeded to get totally, ridiculously shitfaced.

It started with a challenge. Brian teased me, saying he was sure I couldn't hold my liquor. I, in turn, bet that I could match him shot for shot. He actually laughed at that. But as it turned out, big, beefy Brian didn't stand a chance against little ol' me.

We'd intended to stop drinking when the pizza arrived. Only, it never did. Maybe I hadn't been too far off in thinking the guy at the pizza parlor had also been drunk off his ass.

The more Brian drank, the more cheerful he became. I beamed at him and said, "I'm so glad you're a happy drunk and not an angry one. I would have put my money on angry."

"Nah." He waved his hand dismissively. "Angry is for when I'm sober." Then he said, "Hang on, I need to pee. Don't go anywhere. And don't start cleaning again."

"How are you going to go to the bathroom? It's all busted." I'd been using the one upstairs.

"I've been peeing on a bush in the backyard all day, like a Rottweiler or something," he said with a tipsy grin, then held a finger to his lips. "Shhh, don't tell anyone. It's gross, I know."

For some reason that struck me as hilarious, so apparently I was pretty drunk, too. As I fell back on the couch and laughed myself silly, he spun on his wheels and headed to the kitchen door.

He returned a couple minutes later and said, "Scoot over, I want to lie down." I moved to the end of the sofa and he slid out of the chair and onto his knees, then easily swung himself up beside me and reclined against the armrest. "Normally, I wouldn't want you to see that," he said. "It's so damn awkward when I try to maneuver myself out of that chair. But right now, I'm too drunk to give a shit."

"That wasn't awkward at all. It was actually pretty graceful."

"Oh yeah. Graceful is definitely the word for me." He grinned and picked up the tequila, then took a swig directly from the bottle before passing it to me. We'd given up on the formality of glasses somewhere along the way.

I took a drink and watched him for a while, the alcohol making me feel all fuzzy and relaxed, then told him,

"You're a pleasant surprise, Brian. You're so much nicer than I'd expected, given what I'd heard about you."

"That's 'cause I've been happier since I met you. You're like this cute, blond, little ball of sunshine. Even when you're being a total pain in the ass, it's still fun to be around you. Go figure."

I laughed at that as I handed the bottle back to him. "I can honestly say no one has ever called me a ball of sunshine."

He took another drink, then blurted, "I really wanted to take that job you offered me, even though I know it was a total pity thing. I really wanted to keep you safe. I can't be a bodyguard, though. I wish I could. But I'm not capable of that, and if something happened to you because I couldn't protect you, I'd never forgive myself."

"You could totally do the job. Right now, I feel safe because you're here with me." I then illustrated my level of drunkenness by climbing on top of him and resting my head on his chest. Surprisingly, his big arms wrapped around me and held me securely. I sighed with pleasure.

"Okay, maybe I'm slightly better than being alone," Brian conceded. "But only slightly." He nuzzled my hair and said, "Wow, this feels good. Do you know how long it's been since I held someone? Years."

"God, I would die. I can barely go five minutes without physical contact." After a while, I murmured, "I can't believe you're not freaking out right now. I mean, you're cuddling with a *guy*."

"You think I'm *such* a homophobe," he slurred. "You don't know."

"I don't know what?"

"You don't know this," he said, and tilted my face up with a finger under my chin. Brian's lips met mine, sweetly, tenderly. His kiss was so soft, so easy, like we'd been lovers for a hundred years and had done that a million times. I sank into it.

We kissed for a long time, and when he finally ended it, my heart was racing. I returned my head to his chest and murmured, "Why did you do that?"

"Just wanted to. Why'd you kiss me back?"

"Same reason."

Chapter Four

Brian woke up shortly after sunrise, blinking and stretching out on the couch. We'd both spent the night there, sort of tangled up together. He pressed a hand to his forehead and murmured, "Oh man. Has anyone ever died of a hangover?"

I'd been awake for at least an hour and was across the room, finishing the last of the cleaning. I said, "No. They just wished they were dead."

"What was I drinking?" he muttered, rubbing his forehead.

"Tequila." I crossed the room to him and picked up the bottle from the floor. "*Lots* of tequila." I gave the empty bottle a little shake to illustrate my point before setting it on the end table. "You don't remember?"

He shook his head and said, "Damn. It's been a long time since I drank enough to black out."

A sinking feeling settled in the pit of my stomach. I reached out tentatively and brushed the hair from Brian's eyes. As I predicted, he pulled back reflexively and glared at me as he muttered, "Dude. Personal space issues much?"

For some reason, I was struck with a sharp pang of disappointment. The comfortable camaraderie we'd shared the night before was completely gone. Forgotten.

It shouldn't matter to me. But somehow, it did.

I kept my tone light as I said, "I have somewhere I need to be. I'll see you later." He just nodded and went on rubbing his forehead.

As I hurried out of his house and in the general direction of my apartment, the disappointment lingered, and that was annoying. So what if Brian didn't remember what happened between us? That kiss hadn't meant anything. We'd both been drunk, and shit happened when tequila was involved.

I was so distracted that it took me a while to realize just how early it was. After walking two or three blocks, I stopped abruptly and looked around. No one was out yet, and fog hung thick in the air, making everything cold and gray and slightly foreboding. It was so heavy that I could only see a few feet in any direction.

A shiver snaked down my spine, more from fear than from the cold. I was all alone out there, in an unfamiliar neighborhood. And that man was out there somewhere, the stranger who had broken into my home. Suddenly, I felt so exposed. Vulnerable.

Oh shit.

Abruptly, my messed up little brain decided to make the situation so much worse by serving up a full-blown panic attack. Really? Now? I huddled against the façade of the apartment building beside me, hugging my knees to my chest.

I used to have them fairly often in my late teens, but they'd died down over the years. Apparently, it was like riding a bike, though. You never really forgot how to totally lose it.

My breathing was too quick, too shallow, and my heart was racing. A cold sweat broke out all over me. Oh God, this was bad. Really, really bad. I was close to hyperventilating. I didn't want to pass out. Not there, not out on the street, where I was already so alone, so vulnerable. "Oh God, oh God," I murmured.

The more I tried to talk myself down from the panic, the worse it became. "Breathe, breathe, breathe." It was almost a chant. I hugged my knees tighter and rocked back and forth instinctively, trying to soothe myself as it all just kept building. The panic felt like a tangible thing, pressing down on me, almost crushing me. Getting air into my lungs became a struggle. I wasn't getting enough. Not enough. Suffocating. Oh God. Please. No. *No.*

"Holy shit, what's going on?" The voice close beside me made me cry out, startled, and my hands flew up to shield myself.

"Hey. It's okay, Hunter. It's me, Brian. Look at me." I tilted my head up and focused on his blue eyes. "You're having a panic attack, aren't you?" All I could do was nod. "Take a slow, deep breath, you're hyperventilating." I did as he said, forcing air into my lungs. "Good. That's good."

I didn't even think about it, I just launched myself onto his lap, and his arms came up to hold me tightly. "Just keep breathing," he said gently, stroking my hair. "You're going to be fine, I promise."

It took a long time, but finally, my panic began to ebb and my breathing leveled out. "I didn't know where I was," I said after a while, as my heart rate gradually decreased. "I couldn't really see in this fog, and all of a sudden I got scared. Not that that's any reason to have a panic attack."

"You don't need a reason, panic attacks can come out of nowhere. I used to get them a lot, my first year back from Afghanistan," he said. "And you shouldn't have been out here alone, not with a stalker out there somewhere. It was careless to let you leave without a cab waiting for you, but I was so damn hung over that I wasn't thinking clearly." He pulled something out from under me, then draped it over my shoulders before hugging me again. "I brought you your jacket, that's why I followed you."

"I'm sorry," I managed. "I'm totally violating your personal space."

"I shouldn't have said that earlier, I was being a dick."

"No, you just don't like me touching you." I started to get off his lap, but he pulled me right back down.

Brian rubbed my back gently as he spoke to me, his tone low and soothing. "This isn't about me right now, it's about you. You're getting through that panic attack, but you're not completely out of the woods yet, so just stay put and relax."

"You're being so nice to me, even though you hate me."

"I hardly hate you."

"Sure you do."

"If I hated you, would I have allowed you into my home? Hell no. I'd have slammed the door in your face. In fact, I would have answered the door for the sole purpose of then slamming it."

I tilted my head back and grinned at him. "I can totally see you doing that."

He grinned a bit, too. Then he asked, "How often do you get these attacks?"

"This is the first one I've had in nearly three years. I was starting to think I'd outgrown them. Obviously, I was wrong."

"What was it like growing up in rural Idaho?" That was random, but I knew what Brian was doing. He was trying to get me to focus on something other than the panic attack. I thought he must have learned that technique when he was going through them himself. Either that, or he just had really good instincts.

"Idaho itself isn't bad, unless you grow up on a potato farm. Then it's the worst place *ever*."

He smiled at that. "You're the son of a potato farmer? I can't even imagine you in that kind of environment."

"I'm wondering how to take that," I said with a little smile, sliding off his lap and putting on my coat before self-consciously tucking my hair behind my ears.

"Well, look at you. You're about as cosmopolitan as they come. I'll bet every single thing you're wearing is designer this or name brand that. But you must have been raised very differently."

"Growing up, all my clothes were either hand-me-downs or from the thrift store," I said. "When I started making money, I decided I deserved better."

"Your parents were poor?"

"No. They were incredibly cheap and didn't think I needed nice things." I stuck my hands in my pockets. After a while, I said quietly, "They never thought I was worth anything. I'm not talking about giving me things, I mean in general. By the time I was five, they had their minds all made up about me. They'd already decided I wasn't smart, not like my oldest brother, Jer. And I was uncoordinated, so I'd never be a jock, not like Oliver, the second-oldest. I wasn't the one with good common sense, either, that was Arthur. And my sister Nina, well, she was the only girl, and that made her special. Me? I wasn't anything, just the 'H.' Beyond that, I served no purpose in my family, aside from free farm labor."

"Okay, if that's some kind of slang term, I've never heard it. What do you mean, you were just the H?"

"My siblings and I are as follows: Jerry, Oliver, Nina, Arthur, and Hunter. Notice a pattern?"

"No. Should I?"

"Our first initials spell 'Jonah.' My mother is really religious, and she thought she'd be clever. Instead of giving us all names from the Bible, she picked secular names, coming together to form a single Biblical one." Brian was staring at me like I was crazy, and I added, "Don't blame me. I didn't come up with that shit."

"That's insane."

"Welcome to my world."

"So, you must be the baby of the family, if you're the last letter of the word."

"Nope. I'm a middle child."

"Wait. They spelled a name, but did it out of order?"

"Well, no. They started out spelling a different name, John. It was meant to pay homage to my mother's favorite Bible verse. But then Arthur and Nina fucked it up by being twins, and my parents had to scramble for a plan B."

"Why didn't they just name their first born John? Why go through all of that?"

"Because," I explained, "my parents are idiots."

"Apparently." Brian mulled all of that over for a bit, then said, "So, I have to ask the obvious question. Do they know what you do for a living?"

"Nope. They don't even know if I'm alive or dead, and that's just the way they want it."

"What do you mean?"

"They disowned me when I moved here."

"Why?"

"It's kind of a long story. Do you want to hear it?"

"Yeah."

"After high school, it took my boyfriend Cole and me a couple years to save up enough money to move to California. That had always been our dream. Well, specifically, that was *my* dream. Cole's was simply to get the fuck out of Gomsburg, Idaho, he didn't really care where we went. But from the first time I ever heard of San Francisco, I knew this was where I wanted to be."

I leaned against the apartment building beside us and continued, "When the time finally came to move and I told my parents what I was doing, they gave me an ultimatum. They said, 'If you go, don't bother coming back, because you won't be welcome here anymore.' I thought they were bluffing, but they were so angry that I was running off with Cole that they really did disown me. I tried to reach out to them a couple times after I moved here, but they want nothing more to do with me."

"That's such an extreme reaction."

"Yeah, well, it was bad enough that I was moving in with a guy, and I'll spare you the horror stories of my family's efforts to 'cure' me of being gay when I was growing up. But they were doubly pissed that I was running off with Cole, of all people."

"Why?"

"Because he hit the trifecta of prejudice. Not only was he gay, he was also half African-American and half Jewish. My parents got to channel their homophobia, racism and anti-Semitism all into one person. So did a lot of other rednecks where we grew up, actually. He had it so rough as a kid."

"I can only imagine." Brian took in all I'd told him for a minute, then asked, "Are you two still together?"

"No."

"Where's Cole now?"

"Here in the city, waiting tables at your cousin Jamie's bar, actually."

"Small world."

"Yes and no. I actually met Christopher, your future brother-in-law, last Christmas Eve, when I crashed a party at your cousin's bar. I was there looking for Cole, but he was a no-show."

"So, you and your ex remained friends."

"Far from it," I said. "Cole hates me now, with the intensity of five million suns."

"Because you broke up with him?"

"Yeah. It's been two years, but he's never gotten over it."

"Why'd you dump him?"

"Because we were utterly wrong for each other. We kept trying to make it work, we tried for three years, but it was a constant struggle. I finally realized it just wasn't meant to be."

"If he hates you that much, why would you go to the bar looking for him?"

"Because being by yourself at the holidays can make people do stupid things. I was feeling so desperately lonely that I went there to beg Cole to take me back, as a friend, a lover, any way he'd have me. But that would have been such a huge mistake, and I was so glad later that he blew off the party."

His expression was sympathetic. "Thanks for being so candid with me."

"I've totally been up in your business, so why not let you be up in mine?" I smiled and said, "Thanks for faking an interest in my life, Brian. Mission accomplished: you distracted me long enough to get through the panic attack."

"I wasn't faking it. You're a legitimately interesting person."

As we'd been talking, the city had gradually been waking up around us, and a few people on the early shift had begun filtering past on their way to public transit. It was still really foggy, but it didn't seem sinister anymore. It just seemed like any other day in the city. Brian shielded a huge yawn with his arm, then asked, "Do you always get up this early?"

"Hell no, I hate mornings. I never really get going until about ten, and then only with about a gallon of coffee."

"So, come back to my house and let's work on some caffeination. Why'd you take off so abruptly, anyway?"

I shrugged and said, "Your personal space comment made me feel like I was intruding." There was more to it than that, but it would do for an explanation.

"I say a lot of dumb things, you shouldn't take it personally. Also, I'd like to point out that I was under the influence of a raging hangover, so you're lucky I didn't bite you when you put your hand near my face." He grinned as he said that.

I grinned, too. "You do seem kind of feral with all that hair and that huge beard, I wouldn't put biting past you.

What's with this look, anyway?" We both began meandering back in the direction of his house as we were talking.

"This is called total and utter failure to give a shit. I think it's going to catch on in a big way. Just watch, pretty soon all the hipsters will be sporting the full-on crumb catcher and locks of loveliness."

I laughed at that and said, "Hey look, you actually have a sense of humor."

"It's been known to happen. Okay, maybe not for like, the last three years, but it *has* happened."

"Well, I'm honored to be here for the rebirth of your shriveled up funny bone."

He chuckled and said, "Weird way to put that."

"Yup. By the way, next time you fall asleep in my presence, I'm attacking you with a weed-whacker. I hate to be the one to break it to you, but the locks of loveliness aren't so lovely."

"That seems to suggest you're planning on more sleepovers."

"If that ever happens again, I have an idea: let's *not* polish off an entire bottle of tequila."

"Oh, no problem there. Jose Cuervo and I are no longer on speaking terms. It's going to be a long time before tequila sounds like a good idea to me again."

When we reached his house and he worked his way up the ramp, Brian asked, "How come you weren't affected by all that drinking? Were you even a little hung over?"

"Not really. I was definitely buzzed last night, but I can hold my liquor. By-product of being raised in the country, where there was nothing else to do. Drink early and drink often, that's our unofficial motto."

"And yet you don't like beer, country boy."

"The one time I got sick enough to throw up, I'd been drinking beer. I was probably about sixteen. Once you experience beer both coming and going, it tends to lose its appeal."

He chuckled at that. "Just hearing it described that way is enough to make it lose its appeal."

When we reached his kitchen, he got the coffee pot going and I immediately started cleaning. "There's your compulsive side again," he commented, watching as I used a pair of salad tongs to pick up and throw away his kitchen sponge, then began rinsing dishes.

"Don't knock it, just enjoy the benefits of my compulsion."

"Wait, wasn't there someplace you needed to be?"

"I just said that to make my speedy exit."

"Ah." Brian glanced at me, then looked away.

When he did that again, I turned to him and said, "What? Just say it."

"I have something I need to do. Could you just, like, stay in the kitchen for a few minutes?"

"Are you going upstairs to use the restroom?" I guessed.

"Exactly."

"And you don't want an audience for your stair-climbing method," I guessed. He looked embarrassed, and nodded. "Believe me, I have more than enough to keep me occupied in this kitchen. Go do what you have to do."

He left without further comment, and I listened to his progress as I poured myself a cup of coffee. The building was at least eighty years old and creaked like a haunted house. I was concerned about him making it up the stairs safely, but wanted to respect his wishes, so I stayed where I was. It took him a while, but eventually he made it to the second floor, and I heard the floor creaking overhead.

Once I knew he'd made it up the stairs, I tossed my jacket over a barstool and rummaged around until I found a new sponge still in the wrapper and a packaged pair of yellow rubber gloves. They were a women's medium, stiff and flaking with age. It was pretty obvious who'd purchased them. There was something sad about the fact that so many, or maybe all, of his mother's things had been left in place, as if the family had never really let go after her death.

I put on the gloves and flexed my fingers a few times to loosen them up, then got to work scrubbing the sink. The kitchen wasn't quite the botulistic nightmare it could have been, maybe because Brian lived almost exclusively on take-out. It still needed a good cleaning, though.

A few minutes later, the floor above me creaked again, and then I heard Brian on the stairs, climbing down on his hands and knees. I stopped what I was doing to listen, just to make sure he made it down safely. His shout and the crash that followed made my heart leap. I took off running.

Brian was curled in a tight ball at the foot of the stairs. "Oh my God," I exclaimed, dropping to my knees beside him. "Please be okay!"

He was clutching his right hand to his chest, and drew in his breath sharply. "I think I broke my wrist." I helped

84

him sit up, and he winced as he tried moving his hand. "Shit, this is bad. How am I supposed to work my chair with only one hand? I'm going to be completely stuck."

"We can get you an electric wheelchair until you heal," I told him. "Those can be operated with just one hand."

That calmed him a bit, and he nodded. "Didn't think of that."

"Does anything else hurt?"

"I probably bruised the hell out of myself, but I don't think anything else is broken."

"Did you hit your head?"

"Yeah, but not that hard."

"We need to get you to a hospital, both for your wrist and to make sure you don't have a concussion." I peeled off the gloves and pulled out my phone. "Taxi or ambulance?"

"Taxi. I'm not that bad off."

"You sure?" He nodded, and I called for a cab. While I did that, he crawled over to his chair, locked the brake, and tried to pull himself up into the seat with one hand. It wasn't working very well. "Will you be insulted if I try to help you?" I asked when I disconnected the call.

He sat back and shot me a look. "How?"

"I could lift you into the chair."

"I think I literally weigh twice as much as you, so there's no way you could lift me."

I smirked at that and quipped, despite myself, "Judge me by my size, do you?"

Brian burst out laughing. "Oh my God, I knew it! You *are* a total nerd, with or without the glasses."

"What? I am not. Shut up."

"You just quoted Yoda. That's freaking hilarious."

"Yeah, well, you got the reference, so you're no less geeky." I went around behind him, then said, "Push up when I tell you to." I grasped him by his armpits, and he squirmed like he'd been hit with an electric shock. "Oh man, you're ticklish. And yet *you're* making fun of *me*." I grasped him again, despite his spastic gyrations, and said, "Push yourself up with your knees." When he did that, I used his momentum to lift him and swing him around in one fluid motion, and deposited him in his chair.

"I can't believe you just did that. How could you lift me?"

I told him, "I work out six days a week, sometimes twice a day."

"That's kind of insane."

"Another compulsion, I guess."

"But if you work out that much, why are you so slender?"

"I'm very careful not to add any bulk when I exercise."

"Why?"

"If I developed too much muscle mass, it would damage my career."

"Because muscular guys don't get roles in gay porn? Come on."

"Of course they do, but I'm too short and small-boned to pull off the muscle-bound jock look," I said as I leaned against the staircase's railing. "This thin, waifish thing is my claim to fame."

"And if you changed your physical appearance, you think you wouldn't get any work?"

"Well, I'm under contract, so I'd still get work, but the films wouldn't be as popular. I'm famous for a specific thing, and a lean body type lends itself best to that."

"A specific thing?"

It was embarrassing to admit to Brian, "Most of my films are domination fantasies."

"Meaning?"

"Well, a bigger, stronger man overpowering me, forcing me to do things…you get the idea. And my fans like that I'm kind of…you know. Fragile-looking, I guess." I felt the color rising in my cheeks and muttered, "How did we get on this subject?"

He stared at me for a few moments, brows knit. And then he asked, "Do your co-stars get rough with you during filming? Do they hurt you? Is that a part of the whole 'domination fantasy' thing?"

"Sometimes. But you know, just to whatever extent the director calls for."

He was still staring at me. "So, you don't just get fucked. You get, what? Tied up? Smacked around?"

"I think we should probably stop talking about this," I said, fidgeting uncomfortably.

"Really? You're too embarrassed to talk about it? Then maybe you *shouldn't be doing that for a living*, Hunter."

"It doesn't usually embarrass me. Most men I meet are gay and they've seen my films, so I don't have to describe any of this to them. It's just awkward trying to explain it to someone like you."

He frowned at that. "Someone like me. That's all you see me as, a homophobic bigot. Right?"

"No! Of course not. I just meant—"

"Oh, I know what you meant."

I sighed in frustration, then glimpsed the taxi pulling up out front and went to get my jacket. Brian was sulking when I returned and seemed to resent the fact that I had to push his chair down the ramp because of his injured hand. He got into the cab using his knees and elbows to hoist himself up, and I folded the chair and put it in the trunk.

When I started to get in the taxi, he held up his uninjured hand and said, "There's no reason for you to come with me. I've got this."

"Like hell you do."

"The nurses at the hospital will help me when I get there, that's their job."

I frowned at him. "Why are you suddenly so pissed off at me?"

Instead of answering, he said, "Can I please just go to the fucking hospital, Hunter?"

"Fine." I slammed the door to the cab, and it took off down the street. He was *such* a pain in the ass.

Chapter Five

For lack of a better idea, I went to the gym. I did two yoga classes, plus about an hour of cardio, which helped burn off some of my frustration. By the time I'd done all of that and showered and dressed, it was no longer obscenely early, so I texted Christopher.

He told me to come over, and answered the door to his apartment looking like he'd just gotten out of bed. His blond curls were rumpled, and he was dressed in a white T-shirt and plaid pajama pants. I said, "Please tell me I didn't wake you when I texted."

"No, I just haven't made it to the shower yet." Christopher gave me a big hug as soon as he shut the door, and as usual, I didn't let go for a really long time. "How are you, Hunter?" he asked.

"I have to think about my answer."

He pulled back to look at me, and brushed my hair from my eyes. "Did you spend last night at your apartment? Nana told me her grandson installed a new alarm system for you."

"She called to tell you that?"

"She's worried about you. So am I."

"I tried to go back to my apartment and just couldn't do it, so I actually spent last night cleaning Brian's living room."

"Really? Why?"

"I went over there to check on him, and one thing lead to another. And another."

"What does that mean?"

"Where's Kieran? What I'm about to tell you might freak him out."

"He's soaking in the tub, his back's still really sore."

"What did he do to it?"

"Strained a muscle. He's all drugged up on painkillers and a muscle relaxant."

"Poor guy."

Christopher led me by the hand to his sofa, and we settled in side-by-side. "So, let's hear this news that might freak him out," my friend said as he tucked his feet under him.

"I don't quite know what to make of this, and I should mention that *a lot* of tequila was involved." I hesitated before blurting, "Brian and I kind of made out last night."

Christopher flashed me a big smile and said, "That's hilarious."

"You totally think I'm kidding."

His blue eyes went wide. "You're not?"

"Nope."

"But…wait, are we talking about Brian *Nolan*?"

"Yup."

"There's no way! He's just not gay. And even if he was, there's not enough tequila in all the world to float him out of the depths of that deep, dark closet."

I shrugged and said, "And yet."

"How did it happen?"

"I don't know. I mean, there was a lot of drinking involved, like I said, and for some reason I was laying on top of him. Next thing I knew, he was kissing me." Christopher absorbed that for a few moments, and I added,

"He doesn't remember it, by the way. That's how drunk he was."

Christopher shook his head. "That's pretty much the very last thing I was expecting you to say. It was hate at first sight between the two of you. Never mind the fact that he's a rage-filled homophobe."

"Maybe the ones yelling the loudest have the most to hide."

"Maybe," he agreed. I shifted my position slightly and curled up right beside my friend, so close that our arms were touching. "Or...I mean, I don't know. Maybe he's not as bad as we think he is."

"Brian admitted he lashed out the first time he met you because he hated you for taking his brother away from him." I waved my hand and added, "Not that that excuses him from calling his brother names, or any of that hateful shit."

"He actually told you that?"

"Yeah."

"Wow. In addition to never thinking he'd kiss a guy, I also didn't believe he was capable of talking about his feelings. He just always seemed so angry and closed off."

"He's not always angry." I grinned a little. "He said he was happier because I was around."

"Oh wow," Christopher exclaimed. "You actually like him."

"No, I don't." I thought about that for a moment, and amended, "Okay, kind of. But not like, *a lot.*"

"Did you kiss him because you'd had too much to drink?"

"No. I was tipsy, but not drunk. I knew what I was doing."

"So, you must be attracted to him."

I mulled that over before saying, "I guess I *am* drawn to him on some level. There's something kind of appealing about Brian."

"If you say so."

Kieran came out of the bedroom then, wearing only a towel. He was bent forward slightly, a sure sign that his back was still bothering him. "Oh hey, Hunter, I didn't know you were here," he said amiably, and I gave him a little wave and a smile. I also tried like hell to maintain eye contact, even though I was tempted to let my gaze drift down to his killer abs. To Christopher he said, "Did you already invite him to brunch with us at Jamie and Dmitri's place?"

"I was just about to," Christopher said. "I got sidetracked when Hunter told me he and your brother locked lips last night."

Kieran stared at me for a long moment, then turned and headed to the bedroom. "I need to cut back on the pain meds," he muttered. "I'm starting to hallucinate. I could have sworn you said Hunter and Brian kissed."

Christopher stood up and patted my shoulder. "Make yourself comfortable. I'm going to give Kieran a hand, then take a quick shower. If you don't have other plans, I want you to come to brunch with us. We're expected at Jamie and Dmitri's place in about half an hour."

"Is Kieran up for that?"

"He says he is, but I'll still make sure he takes it easy. I'll drive us there, then all he has to do is find a comfy chair and relax."

"I shouldn't crash your family function."

"Sure you should. You know how Jamie's get-togethers are, everyone's welcome. There'll be a million people, way too much food, and general chaos, just like the night I met you. It'll be great."

"Yeah, okay. I'll be your third wheel."

"Good." Christopher kissed my forehead before heading to the bedroom.

*****

The word 'brunch' was kind of a stretch. The get-together on the rooftop of Jamie's building could better be described as a ruckus. Kids and dogs were running around, loud music was playing, people were dancing, and alcohol was flowing in abundance.

Jamie's husband Dmitri welcomed us with hugs all around. Someone had brought a big recliner up on the roof by way of the freight elevator and had roped it off with Kieran's name on it, so the injured Nolan could enjoy the party, too. Kieran settled in happily, and Christopher curled up on his lap. Oh yeah, third-wheel mode was fully engaged.

I stuck a smile on my face and said, "I'm going to mingle. See you in a bit," then worked my way into the crowd.

Being a gay porn star was the world's most effective form of 'gaydar.' It always took only a moment to determine a guy's sexual orientation, based on his reaction to me. The straight ones looked at me blankly, and the gay ones lit up like fireworks. A couple of the latter variety went into full Roman candle mode as I made my way through the crowd, one of them loudly exclaiming, "Oh mah gawd, it's Hunter Storm! Somebody pinch me!" I gave him a friendly smile and kept going.

Well okay, no, I wasn't so well-known that *every* gay guy lit up at the sight of me. But it sometimes felt that way. Often, my little ego found it flattering. On days like that, though, when I'd rather blend into the crowd, it was kind of a pain.

Jamie and I crossed paths halfway across the rooftop. He was carrying two cases of wine, which looked heavy, but he still paused to smile and say, "It's nice to see you again, Hunter, I'm glad you came."

"Thanks for letting me crash your shindig."

"Any time, you're always welcome. By the way, there's a big buffet set up downstairs in our apartment, please help yourself. Brunch was supposed to be in there, but somehow, it spilled out onto the roof."

He started to lose his grip on the boxes and I tried to lunge for them, but a big, hunky brunet swooped in and lifted a teetering crate off the stack. "Crisis averted," Charlie Connolly said with a grin. He was Jamie's ex-boyfriend, and also my best friend's best friend. I tried not to resent him too much for that last part.

"Awesome timing!" Jamie exclaimed.

"Well, my good deed's done for the day," Charlie said cheerfully. He leaned in and gave his ex a kiss on the cheek before saying, "And hi, Jamie. You know, only in the

Nolan universe would this free-for-all be called *brunch*."
He turned his perfect smile on me and said, "Hi Hunter, good to see you."

"You, too."

I excused myself after a minute of polite small-talk and left the two of them to catch up. Food seemed like a decent idea, so I headed in that direction. Down in the apartment, the noise from the party was still audible but muffled, and the space was almost empty, except for a couple people at the buffet. It suited my mood a lot better than the gala on the roof.

Feeling a bit nosy, I swung to the left when I entered the apartment instead of heading straight ahead to the food, and cut through the living room. I grinned when I took a look at the furnishings, which were such a perfect blend of Jamie and Dimitri's individual styles. A few sleek, modern pieces (Dmitri's influence, no doubt), shared space with some quirky details, like a river of vintage surfboards suspended from the high ceiling (that was pure Jamie). The whole thing came together in wonderful harmony somehow.

When I reached their fireplace mantel, I just had to pause. It was crammed with photos in a mishmash of frame styles. Both men had huge families, and I was pretty sure every single relative was represented in those pictures. There were plenty of photos of friends as well, and I recognized a few familiar faces.

A picture of Jamie and Charlie caught my attention, and I picked it up and looked at it closely. In the photo, the two of them were flanked by their husbands, the foursome all laughter and smiles. It made me a little sad, somehow.

I'd watched Jamie and Charlie together on a couple occasions and had heard their story from Christopher. Apparently, I was the only one who found it really bittersweet.

The two had been each other's first loves, together for something like eight years, beginning in high school. Then Charlie had panicked and fled the relationship. He'd been afraid to come out, especially to his parents, and tried briefly to live a straight lifestyle. By the time he'd realized what a terrible mistake he'd made, it was too late. Jamie had met and fallen madly in love with Dmitri.

Charlie's story ultimately had a happy ending as well. He'd met and married gorgeous Dante Dombruso, Vincent's brother. Charlie and Dante were deeply in love, and I should have been happy for all involved. But somehow, I couldn't help but think, what if?

What if things had gone slightly differently? What if Charlie had talked about his fears, instead of running from them? Would he and Jamie have gotten their happily ever after? From everything I'd heard, the love between them had been the real thing. Maybe it could have worked out between those two, if only life had taken a couple different turns.

Did that mean they'd ended up with the wrong men? Hell no. Both couples were wonderful together, the love between them so obviously strong and true and totally perfect. So maybe that meant there wasn't just one perfect person out there for us. I always heard people talking about finding their 'one true love,' but maybe that wasn't the way the universe worked. Maybe it was really all about second chances, and starting over.

I hoped that was true. When Cole and I first got together, I'd honestly (and naïvely) believed he was the only one for me, and that we'd be together forever. And when I ended our relationship, I felt like I was walking away from my one and only chance at happiness.

Despite loving him, I'd ended our relationship because of one huge flaw: the total inability to talk about anything serious without it turning into a giant argument. God did we argue, day after day after day, for three years. And it had to stop. It just *had to*. I couldn't keep living like that. So finally, when I was offered a way out, I took it. I'd still been in love with Cole when I left our relationship, but I knew it had to end. It had taken me a solid year to get over him, and there was a scar on my heart (a self-inflicted one, I understood that) which might never actually heal.

He'd loved me too, which made my leaving unforgivable as far as Cole was concerned. I'd tried to talk to him several times after I left, wanting to apologize for the abrupt way I'd ended it. But of course, instead of talking, we fought. Same as always. It had been a while since I'd last seen him. But from what I'd heard, Cole was still really hurt, and my guilt was sharp as ever.

I returned the photo to the mantel, cut through the remainder of the spacious living room and stepped through a wide, arched doorway. There was only one person at the buffet now, and as I watched, he looked around, though not in my direction, then quickly wrapped two cookies in a napkin and stuck them in the pocket of his cardigan.

It was obvious from the way he carried himself that this wasn't an act of greed, it was one of desperation. I stepped back so that I was partly concealed by the doorframe, and watched him for a moment. He was young, maybe nineteen or twenty, and thin, with pale skin and dark hair that hung into his face. His clothes were clean but faded with age, and the sweater had been stitched up in a couple places.

My heart went out to him. He began eating quickly, as if that was his first meal in days, picking up morsels with his long, delicate hands and bringing them to his lips. He kept looking down the hall to his right, almost directly across from me, as if he was waiting for someone, or maybe just waiting to get caught stuffing his face.

I made a decision, pulled out my wallet, and quickly counted my cash. I separated out all the big bills, four twenties, and folded them into a little rectangle, then palmed them in my right hand. As quietly as possible, I hurried back the way I'd come, through the living room. I stuck my head around the corner and watched him for another moment. He was wiping his mouth with the back of his hand, and he looked guilty.

The guy didn't notice me as I snuck out of the living room and cut across to the stairwell. I closed the door firmly so he'd know I was there, then started walking toward the buffet table. He glanced up at me and looked down quickly. He was on the far side of the table, so I circled around, coming up right beside him and saying, "Hi. Some party, huh? It feels more like a wedding reception than brunch." He smiled shyly and nodded, and I reached around him and grabbed an appetizer, steadying myself with a hand on his hip. I slipped the money into the pocket of his cardigan without him noticing. "What do you think this is?" I asked, holding up a little fried ball of something with two fingers.

"Um, I'm not sure what to call it, but it has some kind of fish inside," he said, a blush instantly rising in his cheeks.

"Are we talking sushi, or mystery fish balls?"

He smiled and said, "The second thing."

"Mystery fish balls?" His smile got a little bigger, and he nodded. "Well, damn," I said. "I've already picked this up, but now I'm afraid to eat it."

"I mean, it's not, like, bad or anything. It's just unusual."

"Really?" He nodded again. "Okay, here goes nothing." I popped the appetizer in my mouth and bit down. Not only was it odd, it was also insanely spicy. "Oh my God," I mumbled around the God-knows-what on my tongue, and looked around frantically. "Napkin," I exclaimed, fanning my mouth with my hand (as if that would help).

The guy leapt into action, accidentally knocking the stack of napkins all over the floor in his haste. "Oh crap," he exclaimed, and dove under the table to retrieve one for me. I dove under there with him and grabbed the napkin he offered me. I'd intended to spit out whatever the hell was in my mouth, but felt like an idiot doing that in front of this guy. So instead I forced myself to swallow it, then dabbed my watering eyes.

He looked mortified, but then I burst out laughing. After a moment, he started laughing, too, and dropped down so he was sitting cross-legged on the floor. When I caught my breath and wiped the tears from my eyes, I asked, "What's your name?"

"Trevor Dean."

"Well, Trevor Dean, you might have mentioned the fact that I was about to eat a flaming fish ball from hell. Holy crap, that was so freaking hot."

"It was?"

"Did you eat one?" He nodded, and I asked, "And you didn't think it was too spicy?"

"The one I had wasn't very hot."

"Ugh, that was torture."

"I'm sorry, I really didn't know yours would be so spicy. Are you alright?"

"I'm fine, just embarrassed," I said. "I totally made a fool of myself."

"No you didn't, and I really feel bad. I should have told you not to eat it."

"It's not your fault. Well, unless you're the caterer and concocted the flaming fish balls. In which case, it's totally your fault." I flashed him a big smile.

Trevor smiled too, then hesitantly reached up and ran his thumb over my cheek. It took me a moment to realize he'd brushed away a stray tear. He asked shyly, "What's your name?"

"Hunter. It's a pleasure to meet you."

"You too."

"Are you a friend of Jamie's or Dmitri's?" I asked.

"Neither. I mean, I work for them. I just started last week, as a busboy in the bar and grill downstairs, and I'm here on a first date."

I grinned at him and teased, "You brought a girl to your boss's house for a first date?"

"Actually, I'm here with a guy, someone I met at work. He brought me." He was watching me carefully from under his thick, dark lashes, probably waiting to see what I'd do with the revelation that he was gay.

"That's one lucky guy," I said, giving him a flirty smile to let him know I was more than fine with his sexual orientation. Trevor blushed yet again, lowering his head so his hair fell forward over his blue eyes. His bashfulness really was charming, and I started to consider hitting on him.

We heard footsteps, and he quickly scooped up the spilled napkins and got to his feet. "Oh, hi," he said to whoever had just come into the room. I got up, too, and pushed my hair back from my face as Trevor said, "Hunter, this is my date. Cole, this is Hunter."

Oh, *of course*. My ex-boyfriend and I locked eyes, and his jaw clenched as he ground his teeth together. His voice was a low growl when he said, "Is it not enough that you left me to go off and have sex with all of San Francisco, *and* get filmed while doing it? Did you really have to show up during my first date in for fucking ever and hit on Trevor, too?"

"Oh, come on! I was hardly hitting on Trevor!" I mulled that over for a beat, then admitted, "Okay, I was thinking about it. But how was I supposed to know he was your date?"

"You just know instinctively, Hunter," Cole snapped. "You're somehow hardwired to ruin my life. There must be eighty people at this party, so of course you show up and zoom in on the one person here that means something to me!"

"That's ridiculous, and also kind of paranoid."

"Paranoid? I just caught you blowing my date behind the buffet!"

"Blowing your date! I was picking up cocktail napkins, you ass!" I snatched a few napkins from Trevor's hands and tossed them in the air to illustrate my point.

"Yeah, well, you also just admitted you were thinking about hitting on him."

"Cole, *I didn't know he was your date!*"

"But you knew he was *someone's* date, right? He told you that, didn't he?" I shrugged, and Cole exclaimed, "You're such a slut, Hunter! You *knew* he was on a date, and you were still hitting on him! Absolutely nothing is sacred to you, is it?"

"I wasn't really hitting on him, and this isn't why you're mad," I said. "You're still pissed at me for breaking up with you, even after all this time, and you'll find any excuse to yell at me."

"So...you two are ex-boyfriends?" Trevor asked, fidgeting awkwardly.

I turned to him and put my hand on his arm to reassure him as I said, "Yeah, and I'm so sorry to put you in the middle of this."

"It's okay."

"Stop touching him!" Cole yelled. "Just get away from him, or so help me God, I'll—"

"You'll what?" I was getting mad now too, and stepped around the buffet table. My ex was taller than I was, but I still tried to get right in his face. A few people had begun to gather around when they heard the commotion, and they took a couple steps back as they watched our confrontation brewing. "What are you going to do? Beat me up for talking to a stranger at a party? Would that make you feel better, Cole?"

"It might!"

"Well, I'd like to see you try!"

All of a sudden, someone was right between us, pushing us apart. "Alright everyone, show's over. Go find something to do," a familiar voice said. Of course the crowd totally ignored him, and a few more people gathered around us.

I looked down into Brian's blue eyes. He was obviously amused, but was trying to look stern. "That's enough now, Hunter. You need to calm down."

"I'm perfectly calm! And by the way, I didn't start this, he did!" I tried to step around the wheelchair so I could get in Cole's face again, but Brian cut in front of me and pulled me onto his lap.

"I don't care who started it, you're walking away now." His right wrist was wrapped in an Ace bandage, but he still used that hand to flip a switch and propel his new electric wheelchair forward, while restraining me with his other arm.

"Well, technically *rolling* away," I muttered, then added, "Let go of me," as I struggled against his grip. He was surprisingly strong.

"Just let it go, Hunter. Be the bigger man."

"I don't want to be the bigger man. I want Cole to know he can't push me around." I looked back at the crowd. Jamie had appeared in the dining room and was trying to placate my ex. Brian punched the call button on the freight elevator as I caught sight of Trevor. The poor guy looked completely bewildered, and he was still clutching those damn napkins. I just wanted to give him a hug. "I'm so sorry, Trevor," I called. "It really was nice to meet you! I hope to see you again."

For some reason, that was the last straw. Cole growled and lunged forward, looking like he wanted to beat the shit out of me, and Jamie had to forcibly restrain him. Brian boarded the elevator, then did an odd eighteen-point turn and finally pulled up beside the panel of buttons, tapping the one for the ground floor. I raised an eyebrow at him as the door slid shut, and he said, "What? I've had this chair all of an hour. I'm not good at maneuvering it yet."

"What are you doing here, anyway?"

"You mean besides preventing you from getting beat up?"

"Oh, no. I could take Cole. He wouldn't be able to beat me up."

"You're high. He had three inches and thirty pounds on you."

"Did you forget that I was able to hoist your sweatpants-wearing ass up off the floor?" I looked at him closely, then said, "Hey, you're not wearing sweatpants." He was dressed in a plaid shirt over a T-shirt, and jeans. His hair even appeared to be combed...sort of.

He rolled his eyes. "Yeah, they just invented this new thing. It's called *changing your clothes*."

"I totally love it when you're sarcastic."

"Right back at ya."

The door slid open on the ground floor, and as Brian propelled us forward, I asked, "Is there some reason you still have me in a basket hold?"

"It's only a half-basket. I need the other arm to drive."

"Is there some reason you still have me in a *half-*basket?"

"You're faster than I am. If you decide to run back upstairs and get in that guy's face again, it'll take me a couple minutes to come after you on the elevator. By then, you will have been beaten to a pulp."

I sighed and said again, "I could have taken him."

"Is that what you want, to beat up your ex-boyfriend? That's who that was, right?"

"Yes, that was Cole. And no, I don't really want to beat him up. But I did want to yell at him some more."

"Were you really hitting on his date?"

"No. I was only *thinking* about hitting on his date. And I didn't even know that guy was there with Cole. I thought he was just some random cutie at a party." I looked at our surroundings as Brian sighed elaborately. We'd left the back of the building, and were rolling down an alley. I asked him, "Where exactly are you taking me?"

"I have no idea, other than *away.*"

I sighed too, then let myself relax a little. After a few moments, I rested my head on his shoulder. As soon as I did that, his hold on me relaxed too, but he kept his arm around me. A weird little tremor went through me as the adrenaline drained away, and he rubbed my arm reassuringly.

"What were you really doing there?" I asked.

"I'd decided to move in with Jamie until my downstairs bathroom was repaired. I think I illustrated pretty vividly this morning that I can't live in my house until that's done."

"Well, that's good."

"Yeah, but I'm not going back there."

"Why not?"

"When I texted my cousin after leaving the hospital, he told me he was having a few people over for brunch, although by 'a few people' he meant our entire family and half of San Francisco. He knows I've been trying to avoid my relatives, and I felt pretty blind-sided."

"I'm sure Jamie didn't blind-side you on purpose. I think brunch just sort of snowballed into a big party."

"Still." We'd left the alley and were travelling down a side street. He came to a stop in front of a hole-in-the-wall diner and asked, "Do you feel like a cup of coffee?"

"Always."

I hopped off his lap and went up the stairs, while he swung wide and took the ramp to the left of me. "I'm going to hold the door open for you," I announced, tugging on the door handle. "Just giving you fair warning, in case you somehow find that an insult to your masculinity or something."

Brian stopped right in front of me, a smirk on his full lips. "You're a pain even when you're doing something nice," he said, before heading into the coffee shop. I noticed there was a backpack slung over the back of his chair.

We each ordered coffee, and Brian got a slice of key lime pie. When it arrived, I picked up a fork, scooped up a little dollop of whipped cream, and stuck it in my mouth. "I thought you didn't want anything," he said.

"I don't." I scooped up a little more whipped cream and licked it off the tines.

"Why don't you order some pie?"

"I don't want any." A third dollop of cream found its way between my lips. He chuckled and doctored up his coffee. "Ugh, four packets of sugar," I observed.

"Be quiet and eat your pie."

"It's not my pie."

"Then *stop eating it*."

I knit my brows and said, "Sorry," as I put my fork down. A minute later, I poked my finger into the whipped cream, then sucked it clean. He grinned at that and pushed the plate to my side of the table.

"I'm not going to eat that," I told him. "I'm on a diet."

"And calories don't count when they're stolen?"

"I'm sorry. You just ordered my favorite dessert in the whole world, so it's hard to resist."

"Then eat more than just the whipped cream."

"I can't. And I usually have more willpower than this, I don't know what's wrong with me."

"You're rattled, and pie is comfort food."

"I know better than using food to comfort myself."

"What do you comfort yourself with, then?"

"Sex." I hadn't really planned on answering honestly, but there it was.

He took my answer in stride, saying simply, "That's a risky proposition in this day and age."

"I use condoms."

"For both business and pleasure?"

I frowned at him, but took a good look at Brian at the same time. He wasn't being flippant or insulting, he just really wanted to know.

"The production company that holds my contract is safe sex only. That's why I signed with them. I may be dumb, but I'm not stupid." I grinned at him a little.

"Well, thank God for that at least," he muttered, then took a sip of coffee. Meanwhile, I snuck another forkful of pie, this time dipping into the pale green filling. When I put it in my mouth, my eyes rolled back in my head.

"Good?" he asked.

"*So* damn good."

"You know, people that work out fifteen times a week can indulge occasionally."

"I don't work out *fifteen times a week*. And I indulge plenty. I had half a bottle of tequila last night, remember?"

"Ugh, don't say the 'T' word, I still have a headache."

I watched him for a long moment. He was fidgeting with his coffee cup, spinning it with one hand in a slow circle. After a while, I said, "So, your wrist just turned out to be sprained, I see."

"Yeah. A few days' recovery time, instead of a few weeks. That fall could have been a lot worse."

"Did they examine your head?"

He looked up at me and flashed a smile. "Yes. I had my head examined."

"And?"

"And, I have a mild concussion," he admitted.

"You're just telling me this now? We need to get you home! You should be in bed."

"I'm fine, a mild concussion is nothing. Besides, I don't currently have a home to go to."

"If you're totally put off by the idea of staying with Jamie now, come stay in my apartment."

"I thought you were uncomfortable there."

"I'm too uncomfortable to be there by myself. But if you're staying over, then hey, problem solved."

He mulled that over for a minute, then said, "I'll make a deal with you. Stop being so goofy and eat that piece of pie, and I'll agree to stay with you and be your extremely unofficial bodyguard, just until you find someone qualified to take over."

"Really? You'll do that?"

"Stalker or no stalker, you've proven that you're someone who really shouldn't be left unattended." He was obviously teasing, but I still found it annoying.

"Shut up!"

"You almost got in a fist-fight over brunch, Hunter."

"You should talk about being left unsupervised. You almost brained yourself while coming back from taking a crap."

Brian threw his head back and roared with laughter. It was a good thing the diner was empty, and the one waitress on duty was too apathetic to even glance our way. When he finally got himself under control again, he wiped his eyes with the back of his hand and said, "God, I love that about you."

"What?"

"That you're irreverent enough to razz me about falling down a flight of stairs. Every other person I know is always so damn careful about what they say to me, and I fucking *hate* that. They act like I'm an emotional cripple, like I have to be treated with kid gloves. 'Oh, poor little Brian, he doesn't have his legs anymore, so we'd better be extra, super nice to him.' Ugh. It's enough to make me want to swallow the working end of a Smith & Wesson."

He took a sip of coffee and added, "By the way, if I said that last sentence to anyone else I know, they'd already be speed-dialing the psych unit at the V.A." He looked from me to the piece of pie on the table, and back again. "So, are you going to eat that like a normal person, or what?"

I grinned at him and picked up my fork. "Yes, but order yourself another piece. I feel bad for hijacking this one."

He did as I asked, and when the second piece of pie arrived, he tucked into it with gusto.

"You know," I said as we enjoyed our dessert, "people also treat you with kid gloves because you have a terrible temper and occasionally throw plates through windows."

"This is true."

"I'm surprised you're just owning that, I expected you to argue."

"Why? You're absolutely right."

I mulled that over as I drank some coffee, then said, "Cole would have argued. Even if I was right."

"Was what I witnessed back there typical for the two of you?"

"Not really. We fought constantly, which is why I broke up with him, but it wasn't that intense and it never got physical. We just had to argue about absolutely everything, all the time."

"Kind of like you and I do?"

I shook my head. "Absolutely not. You and I bicker, we don't fight. It's totally different."

"Well, good. I'd hate for you to have relationship flashbacks while you're hanging out with me."

"No worries there."

His next words surprised me. "So, have the police considered Cole as a potential suspect in your stalker case?"

"Of course not. Cole would never do something like that."

"You sure about that?"

I nodded and said, "What you witnessed back there, that's not really who he is. He's actually kind and gentle. I just bring out the worst in him."

"Maybe the 'worst in him' is far worse than you'd imagined."

I frowned and told him, "I wish you hadn't said anything. Now I'm doubting Cole, and he doesn't deserve that. Sure, he's royally pissed off at me, but he's not a stalker."

"If you say so." Brian didn't look convinced, but he changed the subject slightly by saying, "I guess if I'm going to be your temporary, utterly useless bodyguard, maybe you should bring me up to speed on your case. What's the stalker done, and what are the police doing to catch him?"

I told him about the letters that had been showing up for months, some hand-delivered to my production company, and described the threats they contained. I also told him about my numerous conversations with the police.

When I finished, he said, "So, the threats are escalating, but the police aren't really doing anything."

"They've done some investigating."

"Not enough, obviously, since this nut job's still at large."

"They're doing what they can. And while they work on finding this person, I now have you to look after me. I feel better knowing I'm not going to be alone."

"You're going to hate having me around all the time. You really should place a few calls today and line up some bodyguard candidates ASAP."

"I don't know why you'd think that. I like being around you."

"Why?'

"Why?" I repeated. "Do I need a reason?"

"Yes."

"I just like you, Brian. You're interesting, and smart, and funny when you want to be. I even like bickering with you. I enjoy that give-and-take."

He grinned and said, "I like that, too. Which probably means we're both crazy."

Abruptly, I blurted, "You're also a really good kisser."

It bothered me that he didn't remember what had happened, so I decided on the spur of the moment to clue him in. I thought there was a fifty-fifty chance that little news flash would completely freak him out, send him into some kind of straight-guy denial spiral or something, but I just couldn't leave it hanging between us. I explained, "You kissed me last night, when you were completely drunk off your ass."

He took a sip of coffee, then put the cup on the table and said, "I know."

"You do?"

"Yup."

"Wait a minute. I thought you'd blacked out last night from all that alcohol."

"Yeah, so, I was lying about that," he said levelly, maintaining eye contact. "I apologize. That was a really childish thing to do, pretending I didn't remember what happened."

"Why were you pretending?"

"It was just easier. I figured it would generate this whole discussion about what it meant, and 'but I thought you were straight,' and so on and so forth, and I just really wanted to avoid all of that."

I considered that for a moment, then said, "Fair enough." After taking a sip of coffee, I picked up my fork and popped some pie in my mouth.

Brian looked surprised. "That's it? I was sure you'd make a big deal out of it."

"Why would I?"

He shrugged. "Maybe because you love to harp about me being a homophobic asshole, and an alleged bigot kissing another man seems discussion-worthy."

"Oh, I *do not* harp. I've merely mentioned it a couple times."

"More than a couple." Brian smiled and added, "At what point does it graduate from bickering to arguing? Because I'd like to avoid crossing that line, if at all possible."

"We're nowhere near the line. If we get within a mile of it, I'll let you know."

"Good."

We'd both finished our dessert by that point, and I asked, "Would you think less of me if I licked my plate?"

"Like this?" He picked up his plate and gave it a great, big lick, then grinned at me over the top of it.

I grinned too, and said, "Kind of. But I would have been classy enough not to wipe my nose in it." I reached across the table and ran a fingertip over the tip of his nose, then held it up to show him the dollop of whipped cream.

He surprised me by taking my finger between his lips and quickly sucking it clean, then beamed at me when I looked startled. "Betcha didn't expect the bigot to do that, either."

I leaned back in my seat and exclaimed, "Okay, so now I *have to* ask, you've left me no choice. *Are* you gay? Straight? Bi? None of the above? I'm at a total loss when it comes to you."

"And that," he said, flipping the controller on his chair and rolling back from the table, "is exactly why I wanted to pretend I didn't remember kissing you."

"Dude, you just sucked my finger in public. It begs the question."

He just smiled at me and crossed the restaurant to the waitress. They had a short discussion as he paid the bill, while I used the side of my fork to scrape up every last bit of my dessert. When he returned to the table and said, "Ready?" I noticed a plastic shopping bag in his lap.

"What's that?"

"An entire key lime pie."

"For what?"

"For eating, duh. Now you can stop trying to scrape every last molecule off that plate. You've cleaned it so thoroughly that they don't even have to wash it, they can just put it back on the shelf."

I rolled my eyes and started to reach for my wallet. "How much do I owe you?"

"In addition to not forgetting that I kissed you last night, I also didn't forget that I was going to buy you dinner. It was supposed to be a thank you for cleaning my house. Since the pizza never showed up, this is my do-over."

I was going to argue. But after a moment, I thought better of it, got up and pushed in my chair. "Thank you, Mr. Nolan."

"You're quite welcome, Mr. Jacobs."

As we headed for the door, I said, "I never actually told you my last name."

"I know. I Googled you last night, when you were in the midst of your cleaning frenzy. You have a really stupid stage name, by the way."

"I know. I didn't make it up, my manager did. Now I'm stuck with it." I held the door for him, then followed him outside.

"It doesn't make any sense. 'Hunter Storm.' What's that supposed to mean? If it was reversed, it'd at least refer to one of those idiots that armors up his car and goes chasing after tornadoes."

I chuckled at that and said, "Because those guys are a big draw in the porn industry."

"Well, sure. They're studs."

"How did you search for me without a last name?"

"I searched 'Hunter, gay porn, San Francisco.' You're all over the internet, by the way."

"I know," I said. "And it was that easy to find my real last name, huh?"

"Yup. Took me about ninety seconds."

"Figures. There's no such thing as privacy anymore."

"Apparently not."

Something occurred to me, and I stopped short. A few people on the sidewalk had to quickly adjust their trajectory to avoid crashing into me. "While you were Googling me, did you...you know?"

"Watch any of your films?"

"Yeah, that."

"Hell no. I wasn't even drunk at that point, so how could I? As if a total homophobe like me would be able to watch a bunch of nekkid guys humping." He faked a massive shudder, then took off down the sidewalk with a big grin on his face.

"That wasn't a real answer. Did you or didn't you?" I called after him. He just kept going. "Damn it, Brian!"

I jogged after him, and when I caught up, he said, "You know, if you're worried about people actually watching your films, you're in the wrong line of work."

"I'm not worried about *people* watching them, I'm worried about *you* watching them." He started to protest, but I cut him off by saying, "It doesn't have anything to do with the fact that you may or may not have a problem with gay people. And you didn't have to get all snippy this morning when I was trying to say this to you."

"So, what is it then?"

116

"I guess I like the fact that there's one guy in my life that hasn't watched me getting fucked," I told him. "You said I'm the only person you know who doesn't treat you differently just because you're in a wheelchair, and maybe it's kind of similar. If you'd ever seen me in action, maybe you'd treat me differently."

"I wouldn't."

"Maybe, maybe not. Still though, I like the fact that you only know Hunter Jacobs, and not Hunter Storm."

He grinned at me. "Is there a special effect that goes with that name? Does lightning flash and thunder rattle whenever you appear on screen?" He simulated the sound of thunder (badly) and waved his hands around.

I laughed at that and said, "Oh my God! Shut up about the name already!"

My phone rang and I pulled it out of my pocket, putting it on speaker and answering with a cheerful, "Hunter Storm here." I then made the sound of thunder, doing an even worse job than Brian had. He burst out laughing.

Christopher said, "Well, thank goodness you're alright, I've been worried. I heard what happened with Cole and sent you a million texts."

"Sorry. I haven't checked my messages."

"It sounds like you're having fun, I'm glad. I was worried that the run-in with your ex might have upset you. Who's that laughing in the background?"

"Brian."

"Man that's weird, you two palling around."

"Yeah, I know. It's like hanging out with a grizzly bear. Only a grizzly is less furry." I winked at Brian, and he pretended to try to bite me, which made me laugh.

"It's as if you know a different Brian, one from an alternate dimension."

"Maybe that explains it. You're on speaker, by the way. You know, just in case you're about to call him a visitor from the Planet Douchebag or something."

Christopher laughed at that. "I'll leave you and Invasion of the Body Snatchers Brian to your fun. I just wanted to make sure you were okay. Kieran and I will be home in about an hour, by the way, if you still want to stay with us."

"Actually, I think I'm going to return to my apartment after all. Thank you for the invitation, though."

"Oh! Well, good. I'm glad you're feeling better about that."

"Only because I won't be alone. Brian's agreed to guard my body." I wiggled my eyebrows at my companion, and he chuckled and rolled his eyes.

All Christopher said to that was, "Ah."

"That was kind of a loaded syllable. I take it you don't approve?"

"I never said that. Text me later, okay?"

"I will. Love you, honey." I made kissing sounds into the phone.

"Love you too, Hunter."

When we disconnected, Brian asked, "Are you having an affair with my brother's boyfriend?"

"Of course not. He's my best friend, nothing more."

"That's too bad. If you were going to try your hand at being a home-wrecker, that'd be a good place to start."

"Don't be an ass. Kieran's so damn lucky to have Christopher, and they're madly in love. You should be thrilled that your brother found such a sweet, beautiful, wonderful person."

"Wow. Did they give you a T-shirt when you became president of the Christopher fan club?"

"He's just a great guy. If you could stop being jealous for five minutes and get to know him, you'd see that for yourself."

"I'm not jealous, exactly. Just resentful."

"Well, at least you can admit that much." My phone rang in my hand, and I answered it by punching the speaker button again. "Hello?"

"Hi there, babydoll." The voice on the other end of the line was odd, distorted. It sounded mechanical, as if it was coming through a voice synthesizer.

"Who is this?"

"Good news, sweetheart. We're going to be together really soon. I've been making plans, everything's almost ready."

Fear trickled down my spine as my mouth went dry. "Is this the person that's been sending me those letters?"

Instead of answering, the stranger said, "You've been such a dirty little whore, letting all those men inside you, night after night. I'm going to have to punish you severely for that, you know. But then we can be together, just you and me, and no one will get to fuck my beautiful little babydoll ever again. No one but me."

"Who are you?"

"See you soon, Hunter."

The line went dead.

Chapter Six

I just stood there after the caller disconnected, staring at the phone in my hand as my heart raced. "Oh God," I whispered.

"Breathe, Hunter." Brian took the phone from me, then held both my hands in one of his.

"Oh God," I whispered again. "He's coming for me."

"Look at me." I tried to focus on Brian, staring into his eyes, and he said, "Take a deep breath." I did as he said, and it sounded ragged. "Again." I pulled more air into my lungs, and he said, "Good. That's good, Hunter. You're okay."

"I'm scared, Brian. I'm so scared."

"I know, but I'm not going to let anything happen to you. I promise." He let go of my hands for a moment and picked up the bag on his lap, then looped the handles over the arm of his wheelchair. "Come here," he said, holding his arms out to me.

I climbed onto his lap and buried my face in his shoulder, and he held me tightly. I was shaking all over. "We should get off the street," he said. "Where do you want me to take you?"

"I don't know."

"How about Christopher's apartment? Do you want to go there?"

I nodded, then said, "But they're not home yet."

He kept his right arm, the one with the injured wrist, around me as he pulled out his phone and dialed with his left hand. When someone answered, he said, "Kier, we have a bit of a situation. Hunter's stalker just called and threatened him, and he's really rattled. Can you and Christopher meet us at your apartment as soon as possible?" Kieran must have agreed, because Brian said, "Thanks," and ended the call.

It only took a few minutes to hail a taxi and travel to their apartment. My friends were already there when we pulled up, standing on the sidewalk waiting for us, and Christopher grabbed me in a huge hug as soon as I got out of the cab. The four of us went into the gallery on the main floor of their building, and once we were inside with the door locked behind us, I climbed back on Brian's lap as he repeated what the caller had said.

"Have you reported this yet?" Kieran wanted to know.

Brian shook his head. "We came straight here, Hunter's really upset. We'll call the police after he's had a chance to calm down a bit."

Christopher rubbed my back and said, "Let's go upstairs and get you nice and comfortable on the couch."

I nodded, but then remembered something and said, "There's no elevator to your apartment. Brian can't make it up there."

"Don't worry about me," he said. "Just go upstairs with your friends, they'll take care of you. I can wait down here."

"No. I want you with me."

"You do?" When I nodded, he said, "Okay, then I'll climb the stairs on my hands and knees. Well, elbows and knees," he amended, indicating his injured wrist.

"You can't. What if you fall again? You already have a concussion."

Kieran exclaimed, "Wait, what? Are you hurt, Brian?"

"I'm fine. Let's just worry about Hunter."

Kieran knit his brows and stared at his brother, who stared back levelly. Then he told me, "I can help Brian up the stairs. Go on up with Christopher, we'll be there in a minute."

"Just act as a spotter," Brian told Kieran, as Christopher took my hand and led me to the back of the building. "And if I start to fall, for God's sake, don't catch me. Your back's bad enough as it is."

When we were all finally in the apartment and his chair had been carried up the stairs, Brian rolled up to me and smiled a little, taking my hand. "Where do you want me?"

"What do you mean?"

"Assuming you want to keep sitting on my lap, would you be most comfortable if I was in my chair, or on the couch?"

"Couch. But you don't have to keep letting me do that. I know I'm being ridiculously needy, and—"

"Does it make you feel good? More secure?"

"Well, yes, but—"

"But nothing. And here's a newsflash: I like it, too. If I didn't, I really wouldn't be offering you my lap. I'm not nearly that self-sacrificing."

I grinned a little and let him lead me to the couch. He executed a graceful pivot, going down on one knee before swinging around onto the sofa, and I climbed on top of him. When his arms encircled me, I exhaled and relaxed.

Kieran didn't quite know what to make of that, and asked, "So, um, are you two...dating?"

123

"No. We're cuddling," Brian said, traces of a smirk tugging at the corners of his lips.

Kieran clearly had a million more questions, but decided to let it go for the time being. He and his fiancé settled in on the loveseat, and he offered to call the police officer assigned to my case for me. When I agreed, he dialed the station.

After a short cop-to-cop discussion involving various call numbers and jargon, he hung up and said, "Detective Sanchez is going to access your phone records and find out where the call originated. He's also pulled a couple officers to review the footage from your apartment building's surveillance cameras. He'll let us know what they find."

"Thanks, Kieran."

"You're welcome."

We were quiet for a few moments, and then I said, "I hate that I freeze up so badly whenever this guy does something. I'd always hoped I'd do okay in a crisis, but I'm just completely useless."

Brian held me a little more securely as he asked, "Have you ever taken self-defense classes?" When I shook my head, he said, "You should look into that. It might make you feel a little more confident."

"Plus, I'll need those skills when this psycho comes after me. And it is *when*, not if," I murmured, adding what he'd surely been thinking.

"If he does come after you, I'm going to do everything in my power to stop him," Brian said. "I want you to know that. You aren't in this alone."

Christopher chimed in, "I know someone who teaches self-defense classes. She works with the homeless women at the community center where I volunteer. Want me to get in touch with her, Hunter?" When I agreed, he immediately pulled out his phone and started texting, obviously glad to be doing something to help.

"If she's not available, I can teach you a few moves," Kieran said. "I learned a lot of self-defense during my police training."

"Thanks, Kier. Only when your back's better though," I said.

He shrugged, "It's not so bad."

"Let's see if Christopher's person is available first."

"Yeah, okay," Kieran said. Then he added, "So, the fact that this person disguised his voice makes me wonder if it's someone you know. Has Sanchez already asked for a list of people that might hold a grudge against you?"

"Like Cole," Brian chimed in, and Kieran nodded.

"Detective Sanchez did ask, but I couldn't think of any names to give him. Because like I said, no way is Cole capable of something like this."

"Just today, he called you a slut in front of a bunch of people, and almost beat you up for talking to his date," Brian said. "I think the police should at least ask him a few questions and find out if he has an alibi for the time that call was placed."

I shook my head. "I can't do that to him."

"But you're not a hundred percent certain of his innocence," Brian reminded me. "You told me that some doubts were creeping in."

"That's just because this whole thing is making me paranoid," I said. "I'd feel terrible sending the police to question him, he'd be so humiliated."

"What if I talk to him? I'll forego the uniform and just make it really low key," Kieran suggested.

I mulled that over for a while, then said, "Well, I guess that would be alright. Just please be nice to him."

"I will, I promise."

"Thanks, Kier." I settled back down on Brian's chest, and he began stroking my hair.

"I might as well go talk to him now." Kieran got up and stretched.

"You don't have to go right this minute, or even today," I said. "Your back's still bothering you."

"It's going to hurt whether I'm sitting here or having a conversation with your ex. I'll get his address from Jamie, and I'll take a cab over to his apartment since I'm taking muscle relaxants and shouldn't drive. It won't be strenuous," he said, "and you'll feel better if we can eliminate Cole as a suspect."

I glanced up at Brian. "What's with you Nolans acting like you're fine, even when you're injured? You're tooling around with a concussion, and your brother's hopped up on painkillers and acting like he could swim to Alcatraz."

"It's a *mild* concussion," Brian said with a half-smile. "And swimming the bay would probably be good for Kier's back, it'd loosen it right up."

"It must be a macho cop family thing," I said.

"Alright, I'm off to talk to Cole, I won't be long." Kieran kissed his fiancé goodbye, then left the apartment.

Christopher indicated his phone and told me, "Kaia is free in a couple hours, I asked her to meet us here. She's going to do an intensive version of her introductory self-defense class, just for starters. If you like it, she said we can do a series of private lessons."

"We?"

"Yeah. I thought I'd do them with you, if that's okay," Christopher said.

"I'd like that."

*****

Kaia Anderssen looked like any other thirty-something Yoga babe at first glance. She was short and compact, dressed in cropped leggings, a purple tank top and hoodie, and her light brown hair was pulled back in a ponytail. When she effortlessly flung me over her shoulder and then pantomimed driving her heel into my throat during the 'advanced techniques' demonstration I'd been dumb enough to ask for, I revised my opinion of her. The woman was a total badass.

"You okay?" she asked, hoisting me to my feet. "That exercise mat's not very well-padded."

"Fine," I lied, shaking off the impact. "Can we take a short break? I need some water." And an ambulance.

"Sure thing."

"I've never worked out that hard," Christopher said as he led us to the kitchen and grabbed some drinks from the fridge. Kaia's teaching method was all about muscle memory. She'd show us a basic defense move, then have us do rep after rep after rep. It also functioned as strength training, which was another goal of her classes.

"Thank you so much for doing this on short notice, Kaia," I said as we settled in around the kitchen table. "It's exactly what I needed today."

"You're welcome. I'm just glad I was able to shift my schedule around. When Christopher told me what you've been going through, I wanted to get started as soon as possible. I figured it'd be valuable for you to take a proactive approach like this."

"That's exactly why this is so good," I said. "I feel like I'm replacing helplessness with action."

She smiled and toasted me with her bottle. "That's what I like to hear."

Kaia left after another half hour of training, setting a time to meet the next day and assigning homework before she took off. Once she left, my friend fell onto the couch. "Man, was that strenuous. Am I totally ripped now? I feel like I should have the body of a Greek God after that." Christopher flashed me a smile.

"You totally do. I'm going to start calling you Zeus," I said with a wink, then began doing my homework. That particular move combined driving a heel into the top of an assailant's foot, bringing a knee up into the groin, and striking the nose with the fleshy part of the palm, all in rapid succession. I did it over and over again, trying to ingrain it so deeply that it would come to me automatically when I needed it.

"I can't believe you have the energy to do that now," Christopher said, sitting up and wiping the sweat off his forehead.

"Might as well get it done," I said, doing another rep.

My friend pushed himself off the couch. "I'm going to get a hot shower before all my muscles seize up," he said, and headed for the master bathroom.

Brian was watching me from the adjacent dining room. Once Kieran had returned from talking to Cole, the brothers had settled in around the table and begun drinking beer, while engaged in some sort of deep discussion. As I could have told them, Cole had solid alibis for the time of the phone call and the break-in, so he was on and off the suspect list in the blink of an eye.

Eventually, Kieran admitted defeat with his back pain and went to lay flat on his mattress, so his brother turned his attention to me. After a while, Brian came up behind me and said, "Take a break, Hunter."

"Just a few more." I repeated the exercise a couple more times. Heel, knee, palm. Heel, knee, palm.

"That's enough for now. Come here."

"I'm almost done." Heel, knee, palm.

"No you're not. Your compulsiveness is kicking in."

"It's not."

"Oh yes it is."

"Kaia told me I had to practice."

"She told you to do a hundred reps. You just passed two hundred and forty."

I raised an eyebrow at that. "Were you actually counting?"

"Yes."

"And you call me compulsive!"

"Because you are!"

Heel, knee, palm. "Just five more minutes." Heel, knee, palm.

"Do I need to forcibly restrain you?"

"Oh, *please* try. Then I can practice this move on you," I said, grinning over my shoulder at him.

"It wouldn't work on an assailant in a wheelchair."

"The last part would," I said, spinning around and tapping his nose lightly with the tip of my finger.

Brian flicked the switch on the armrest and spun his chair around quickly, bumping me with his knees, just enough to make me lose my balance. He scooped me into his lap and put an arm around me. "You were just looking for an excuse to cuddle me," I teased.

"Yup. That, and watching you be so manic was making me all twitchy."

He was cradling me the way someone would hold a child and reached up with the fingertips of his injured hand to gently brush the hair from my face. I watched him for a while, and had such an urge to kiss him, especially because there was so much longing in his eyes. But instead, I said quietly, "You confuse me, Brian. You're such a contradiction. I have absolutely no idea how someone could call his brother a faggot, and yet also be so sweet and tender with another man."

"I don't know what to tell you."

"You can tell me what's going on in that head of yours."

"Do you like what I'm doing right now?"

"Yes."

"Then just relax and enjoy it."

"But why are you doing it?"

Brian sighed as he swung me off his lap and onto my feet. "Because I like you. And I'm done talking about this now." He spun himself around and took off across the apartment, and I trailed after him.

That seemed to annoy him. When he ran out of apartment, ending up in Christopher's home studio at the end of the hall, he pivoted around to face me and said, "Just so you know, I'm not exactly the type of person who sits around talking about his feelings. I—"

"I like you too, Brian."

"What?"

I climbed onto his lap again, this time straddling him, and took his face in my hands. "I said I like you, too." I kissed him gently, and after a moment he returned the kiss as his arms encircled me.

Eventually he said, "You have terrible taste in men."

I smiled at that. "Yes and no. This time, I have a feeling I found a diamond in the rough."

"You didn't. You just found the rough."

"Scoff all you want, but this feels right. *You* feel right."

"How could I possibly feel right? Your instincts must be seriously out of whack. Like to the point where you need some sort of instinct intervention."

I kissed him once more, and again he responded, taking it a little deeper, his lips parting, his tongue gently sliding between my lips. After a while, he pulled back and said, "You have to stop kissing me."

"Me! You're the one that upgraded it to Frenching."

"That wasn't Frenching. That was just a little lick."

"Oh, it was Frenching."

"Please. *This* is Frenching." He tipped me back a little and proceeded to illustrate his point. He kissed me fiercely, deeply, his tongue claiming my mouth as his hand slid under my T-shirt, caressing my back. When he pulled me upright again, we were both more than a little overheated. But all he said was, "I think it's gross to call it Frenching, by the way. Makes it sound kinda nasty."

"What would you suggest?"

"Well, at the very least, French kissing. But it needs a better name."

"You're not wrong." I leaned in and kissed him again.

"Didn't I just say you have to stop kissing me?" His big hand was still on my back, holding me to him.

"So many mixed messages." My lips found his once more, and he returned the kiss passionately.

"Damn it," he muttered against my lips. "Why do you have to be so incredibly tempting?"

"There's no reason not to give in to temptation."

"There's *every* reason. In no way can I go where this is leading."

I reached down and rubbed his thick, swollen cock through his clothes, his erection straining the fabric of his jeans. "Parts of you beg to differ."

He plucked my hand off his crotch and held it. "I mean emotionally, not physically. It would be really unfair to you to even try."

"Why do you say that?" I draped my arms around his neck and rested my forehead against his.

"Because I'm a huge mess. I know I've seemed better these last couple days, but that's only because of you. This is going to be the single corniest thing I've ever said, and I can't believe I'm saying it, but…you brought light into my darkness, Hunter. When I said you were like sunshine, that wasn't just random. I've been in such a dark place for so long, and you've been a great distraction. The thing is though, my demons aren't gone. They're all still right there, waiting. And when they find their way out again, I don't want you to be anywhere near me."

I kissed his forehead, then said, "That was quite a speech, for someone who doesn't like to talk about his feelings."

Brian grinned a little. "It's ridiculous. You put my former therapist to shame with the stuff you get me to open up about."

"You know," I said, "This doesn't have to be a big deal. We can be fuck buddies if you want to keep it light and just have fun."

His grin broadened. "You say that so casually, *just be fuck buddies*. As if sleeping with another man is something I do every day."

"It could be," I said with a big smile. "Every. Single. Day. Three, four times a day, even."

He chuckled at that. "Stop making it sound so easy. It's not, you know."

"Oh, but it is." I kissed him again.

When he pulled back, he had one eyebrow raised and a skeptical look on his face. "Why are you trying so hard? You're obviously the type of guy who has men falling at his feet. It doesn't make sense that you'd pursue something with me."

"I told you Brian, I like you. I feel good when I'm with you. More than that. I feel safe, and that's kind of huge."

He reached up and tucked a strand of hair behind my ear. "So, that's what this is. You must be feeling really vulnerable right now, with that stalker making threats and breaking into your home, so you latched on to the first person who came along. I was just in the right place at the right time."

"Maybe I have latched on to you a bit. I tend to be kind of clingy anyway, I know this about myself. But Brian, what part of *I like you* aren't you hearing?"

"There's no way. I mean, look at me."

"Well, you are a couple years past due for a haircut," I teased. "But I won't hold that against you."

"That's just the start of what's wrong with this picture."

I narrowed my eyes at him. "You'd better not be saying what I think you're saying."

"What do you think I'm saying?"

"That I wouldn't want you because you're in a wheelchair."

"Not only because I'm in a chair, but because I'm half a man." I punched his arm, and he exclaimed, "Ow! What was that for?"

"That was for thinking I'm completely shallow," I said as I climbed off him.

"I didn't mean it that way."

"Sure you did!"

"All I meant was, there's just no way that you could be attracted to *this*. Even if by some huge miracle the chair and the fact that I'm a double amputee didn't bother you, there's everything else wrong with my appearance, the hair, the beard, the spare tire—"

"I have a newsflash for you, Brian. When I look at you, I don't see any of those things. I see *you*. I see a guy with beautiful eyes and a great smile, and a sense of humor that sneaks up in really unexpected ways. I see a guy who makes me happy."

"You can't expect me to believe that looks mean nothing to you. I mean, you're someone who works out constantly, colors his hair, wears designer clothes, and I'm pretty sure that tan came from a salon. You're all about physical appearance!"

"I'm all about physical appearance when it comes to *me!* I *do* constantly work on myself, and I *am* deeply concerned with how I look. You left out the regular facials, full body waxing, and tooth whitening in my list of vanities, by the way. And all of that is because this—" I waved my hand down the length of me, "— is all I am! The only way I make a living is by being a pretty face and a nice body, and the only reason anyone ever wants me is because of what they see on the outside."

His expression softened. "I'm sorry, Hunter, I didn't mean—"

"Yes, you did. You think I'm nothing but this shallow, self-absorbed little twink. But I know what it feels like to be valued only for my physical appearance, and I try not to do that to other people in return."

He knit his brows. "So, when you go out to the bars, you're not just looking for the buff guys with big biceps. Right."

"I'm not going to lie and say I don't admire a hot body. I mean, who doesn't? But it's not like big, muscular jocks are the only thing I find attractive."

"I'll bet that's who you seek out to take you home, though."

"Brian, I seek out *whoever will have me.*"

He seemed surprised at that admission, and I felt like an idiot for having been so candid with him. I started to leave the room, and he called after me, "Where are you going?"

"I don't know. All I know is, I'm so totally done having this conversation."

"Wait, come back." When I didn't respond, he added, "Please?"

I turned and looked at him. "Why?"

"Because we're not done."

"Sure we are."

"I don't think you're shallow, Hunter. I think you're too good for me."

I put my hands on my hips and studied him for a long moment. He held my gaze steadily. Eventually I said, "Well, that's just your lack of self-esteem talking."

He grinned at that, relaxing his posture a bit. "Pot calling the kettle much?"

"Yeah, it's not news to me that I have self-esteem issues. So sue me."

"I'd rather go back to kissing you."

"Ugh!" I exclaimed, throwing my hands in the air. "You're so damn frustrating! Either you want me or you don't. Which is it?"

"I want you. Even though I can't have you."

"Yes, you can! Well, unless you keep being such a colossal pain in the ass. I mean really, what do I have to do, gift wrap myself?"

He grinned at that. "You'd look cute with a bow on your head."

"You're driving me insane, Brian. You know that, right?"

"Sorry. I'm really not trying to play games. All I'm trying to say is, I'm attracted to you and love being with you, but I can't get involved with you. I can't get involved with *anybody*. I'm just way too damaged, inside and out." Then he added, "Also, holy shit, I can't believe I'm *still* talking about my feelings! Is this what gay men do? Now that I've gone over to the pink side, am I doomed to a life of *sharing* and *communicating*?"

I laughed at that. "I love how you make those sound like dirty words."

"They are. They're very, very dirty." A little grin played around his lips.

I took a few steps toward him, stopping when I was a couple feet away. "So, is that what you've been doing lately? Going over to the pink side?"

"Sorry. I didn't mean to sound derogatory."

"It didn't. I kind of like it, actually. But are you? Coming over to the pink side, I mean?"

"I can't answer that question right now."

"Why not?"

There was a sparkle in his eyes when he smirked at me. "Because if I share one more thing, I'm going to explode and die."

"I mean, you must be. Why else would you be making out with me at every opportunity?"

"Oh, I'm hardly *making out at every opportunity*."

"Okay, that's true. Half the time, you're telling me that you can't be with me, that you're too terrible and I can't possibly want you, yada yada yada."

137

He laughed at that. "Do you see what a pain you are?"

"Me! You're the one pulling me to you with one hand while pushing me away with the other."

"Oh man," he said, propelling himself forward, out of the studio and down the hall.

"What are you doing?"

"Running away from you, before you make me talk about my feelings again."

"How far are you running?"

"The living room."

I grinned at that and trailed after him.

*****

That afternoon, Brian and I hung out with Christopher and Kieran. We played Madden for a while, until all of us got sick of Christopher constantly beating the crap out of us. Then we switched to watching movies. We'd decided to do a Ridley Scott triple-header, but were only halfway through Blade Runner when Detective Sanchez called and asked to meet with me.

He volunteered to come to the apartment, and arrived twenty minutes later with a manila envelope and a grim expression. But then, he always had a grim expression. Ramon Sanchez was about sixty-two, paunchy, and fighting baldness with an epic comb-over. It started somewhere around his left earlobe, and looped all the way around his head. When that meager strip of hair wasn't slicked down, it must have been a foot long.

He accepted the offer of coffee as we all settled in around the dining room table, and Christopher played host,

138

bringing the pot to the table with a plate of cookies. The sight of those cookies suddenly made me think of Trevor.

I would have liked to visit him at work and apologize. I felt bad that he'd gotten caught in the crossfire between my ex and me, and it had obviously upset him. But then, Cole worked at the same restaurant, and if he caught me checking up on Trevor, he'd probably blow a gasket.

The police detective horked down several cookies and drained his coffee cup before turning his attention to the topic at hand. "As you know," he said, "I asked two officers to review the footage from the surveillance cameras in your apartment building, Mr. Jacobs. There were six cameras in operation at the time your home was vandalized. It appears the suspect knew the locations of five of these cameras, and was very careful to keep his face concealed when he passed them. This suggests he's been in your building before, and probably did some reconnaissance before staging the break-in."

"Wow," I murmured, "that's super comforting."

Christopher was seated right beside me, and he picked up my hand and gave it a reassuring squeeze. Sanchez frowned ever-so-slightly at our joined hands, but kept his tone professional as he said, "The sixth camera, though, the one the suspect seemed unaware of, captured some good images. It's in the lobby, concealed from view behind a grate. It was part of an enhanced security system that the property manager installed about four years ago, when there were a couple burglaries in the building."

He picked up the envelope and pulled out a thin stack of photos, sliding them over to me as he continued, "This is our suspect, another camera had a shot of him from behind, picking the lock to your apartment. Take a good look at these pictures, Mr. Jacobs, and let me know if you recognize this man."

The photos were black and white, fairly clear, and in chronological order. The first few showed a man with a goatee and mustache, dressed in dark clothes and a baseball cap, walking across the hotel lobby, toward the elevators. His profile didn't look familiar. The second half of the pictures had a time stamp eleven minutes later than the first and showed the same person headed toward the main door. Two of the pictures were flagged with yellow Post-It notes. When I reached the first of the two, I paused.

The man had happened to turn his head toward the camera at just the right moment, and it had captured a clear shot of his face. "There's a close-up of that same image, it's next in the stack," Sanchez told me. I flipped to the next photo and took a long look at the face of my stalker. There was something familiar about it, but only very slightly. I couldn't place when or where I'd ever seen him before.

I studied him carefully. He wasn't even close to what I'd expected. It was the face of a regular-looking guy in maybe his early thirties. If anything, he looked kind of…pleasant. He looked like the type of man you'd see coaching Little League. No one would ever look at him and think he was capable of something like this, not in a million years. To me, that made him terrifying.

As I returned the photo to the stack on the table, I said, "There's something vaguely familiar about him, but aside from that, I don't recognize this man."

"I do."

We all turned our attention to my best friend, who'd whispered those two words. All the color had drained from Christopher's face, and his eyes were haunted. "You do?" I asked him. "Who is it?"

His voice sounded thin as he said, "That's the man who raped me and left me for dead."

"Oh my God," I murmured. And all of a sudden, I realized where I'd seen that face before. It was the drawing on the flyers Christopher had been distributing around the city, just with the addition of facial hair.

Sanchez asked, "Mr. Andrews, can you elaborate?"

"Over a year and a half ago," Christopher said, still in that same hollow voice, "when I was working as a prostitute, I was drugged, raped and severely beaten by one of my customers, then left in a dumpster to die. The case went cold, until today."

Sanchez had pulled a notebook from his pocket and quickly scribbled a few notes as he said, "I'm going to need to access the records associated with your case, Mr. Andrews." Christopher nodded.

Brian murmured, "That's such a weird coincidence."

A cold, terrible feeling settled over me, and I shook my head. "No it isn't. It's not a coincidence. It's my fault."

"What are you talking about?" Brian asked.

I turned to Christopher and said, "You're a 'Hunter Storm type.' Remember? You said that the night we met. You said you used to get a lot of work from men calling up your escort service and asking for a Hunter Storm type."

"I wasn't working for the escort service at the time of my attack."

"No, I know. But still. I just have this terrible feeling that that's why this man targeted you, because he's obsessed with me, and you're the same physical type." His big blue eyes went wide, and my voice broke as I said, "Oh God, Christopher, I'm *so sorry*."

"No," he said, grabbing me in a fierce hug. "You have nothing to apologize for, Hunter. We don't know why that man targeted me, and even if it somehow was part of his obsession with you, in no possible way does that make it your fault!"

"But what if it is, though? What if that's exactly why he did those things to you? Because he was acting out a fantasy of what he wanted to do to me?" I felt absolutely nauseous.

"Hunter, *it's not your fault*," Kieran chimed in. "This man's obviously a sick individual, and that has nothing to do with you. It just means that he goes after thin, blue-eyed blond guys in their early twenties." He turned to Sanchez and said, "You'll see this when you read Christopher's case file, but you should know we suspect there may be other victims as well. We think he may have killed at least two people."

Sanchez looked surprised. "Wait a minute. If there's a multiple murder suspect running around San Francisco, why wasn't I and the entire police force made aware of it?"

"Because the evidence I uncovered was really flimsy," Christopher said, "and the police department didn't take it seriously."

"What was the evidence?" Sanchez asked.

"In the two weeks before my assault, two other boys disappeared from the Tenderloin. Both were young and

142

blond, like me, and both worked as prostitutes. They didn't have families, so no one missed them, except for a friend of mine who works at the community center," Christopher explained. "Oh, and both disappeared on Thursdays, which is the same day I was assaulted, so there's a pattern. But that's it, that's all the evidence I had."

Sanchez leaned back in his chair and mulled that over. Finally he said, "I'll do some digging, see if any missing persons might fit the pattern. I'll re-interview the employee at the community center, too, see if that turns up anything. I assume his contact information is in Christopher's file."

"It is," Kieran said.

"In the meantime, we have more to go on in Mr. Jacobs' case," Sanchez said. "We now know, based on Christopher's testimony, that this individual committed rape and assault. That makes him a lot more dangerous than a run-of-the-mill obsessed fan. I'll need to put some additional resources on this case."

"Were you able to trace the call to Hunter's cellphone?" Kieran asked.

"Yeah, but it was a dead end. It came from a payphone in the Richmond district. It's hard to find many of those these days, but our suspect managed it. I've asked an officer to take a look at security cameras in the vicinity of Finley and Marsden, where the payphone is located. She's going to try dusting for prints, too, but I don't expect that to yield much, not on a public phone."

"Finley and Marsden," Brian repeated. "That's...."

"Exactly where you and I were when I got the call," I finished for him, feeling like I'd just been punched in the stomach. "He was so close."

143

"Oh God," Christopher whispered.

I said, "I'm trying to remember where the phone booth is in relation to where we were when the call came in."

"Across the intersection, diagonally," Brian said as he wheeled himself around the dining room table. He could see the fear and panic building in me, and by the time he reached me, I was shaking.

I joined hands with both Brian and Christopher as I took a deep breath. It wasn't just about me anymore. It affected my best friend, and maybe other boys, too. Knowing that made me want to dig a little deeper within myself to find an untapped reserve of bravery. I hoped to God there was actually some to find.

I tried to keep my voice steady as I said, "I hate this, I hate waiting for this person to strike, not knowing when or how it'll happen." I took another deep breath and continued, "So, maybe we shouldn't wait. Maybe we should draw him out. We could set a trap, use me as bait and have the police waiting. I don't know how we'd lure him exactly, but I'll bet there's something I could do to make him come after me."

"Hunter, no," Christopher said. "That's too dangerous. We need to figure out how to keep this man far away from you, not bring him closer!"

I held my best friend's gaze. "He hurt you, and he might still be hurting other boys. He has to be stopped, but he's so elusive! His picture is all over town on your flyers, and yet he's still walking around, free as can be. I'm probably the police's best shot at finally bringing this person to justice."

Christopher started to protest again, but Sanchez interrupted him, pushing back from the table and saying, "I need to get back to the station, I have a meeting in half an hour. But the idea of a sting operation's not bad, let's give it some thought." To Kieran he said, "Officer Nolan, forward me Mr. Andrews' case number, and I'll give it a thorough review. And of course, call me right away when something else occurs."

When. Not if.

"I'm so sorry, Christopher," I said as Kieran walked the detective to the door. "I led the stalker right to your apartment. If he's been following me, now he knows where you live. He might recognize you as the person who survived his attack and could identify him for the police. I put you in danger by coming here." I felt ill.

"You had no idea your stalker and my attacker were one and the same."

"No, but even when I thought it was just some random guy, I still shouldn't have come here. I knew this person was unstable, and I should have led him away from my friends, not toward them."

"This is where you belong, Hunter, right here with people that love you and care about you." Christopher planted a kiss on my forehead and said, "And we're all going to get through this together."

Chapter Seven

It had to be well past midnight. I was stretched out on Christopher's couch, staring at the ceiling through the darkness. The apartment was perfectly still. But I was listening.

We're going to be together really soon. That's what my stalker had said. He was going to come after me. And do what? Hurt me? Abduct me? Knowing what this man had done to Christopher ratcheted up my fear exponentially. Part of me had been in denial before learning that my stalker and my friend's attacker were one and the same, clinging to the belief that this individual would never actually make good on his threats. But I'd learned what he was capable of, and it was so much worse than I'd ever imagined.

A creak sent me bolt-upright, the hair on the back of my neck prickling. The building had an alarm system, so I was being paranoid, I knew that. Still, I strained to listen, struggling to hold a tremor in check, to remain perfectly still, as if some prehistoric part of my brain remembered what it meant to be prey, to be hunted. *Stay still, stay invisible*, it said. It was the part of me that froze up whenever a threat presented itself, and I hated it.

After a minute or two, I relaxed a bit and exhaled slowly. The building was old, it was going to creak and settle. Sounds like that didn't mean anything. They didn't mean that man was coming to get me.

Another sound caught my attention, and I listened intently. After a few moments, it came again, just the tiniest cry. I was already so rattled that it was hard to process at first, to figure out just what I was hearing. When the scream came, I knew.

I pushed the blanket off me and swung my feet onto the floor as the scream came again. And again. It was the sound of pure terror and heartbreak, despair in its rawest form. Brian was having another nightmare.

I got up and padded across the living room, just as my friends' bedroom door swung open. Kieran, half-asleep and dressed only in a pair of pajama pants, was heading toward his brother on autopilot. He'd probably done that a million times before.

"I've got this, Kier," I said, halting him with a gentle hand on his arm.

He blinked at me and asked, "Are you sure?"

"Yeah. You can go back to bed."

Kieran looked skeptical, but after a moment he said, "Be careful. Brian often wakes up swinging, and he may try to fight you off. Sometimes, it's a solid minute before he remembers where he is. And once you calm him down, get out of there right away."

"Why?"

"Because he usually needs to cry after he's had one of his nightmares, and he can't stand doing that in front of anyone."

That broke my heart, as did Kieran's ongoing struggle to help his brother. "You've had a lot of experience with this."

Kieran nodded. "Just watch yourself. Like I said, expect him to throw a punch."

"Okay."

"Good luck," he said.

I started to head to the studio, where Brian's cries had become even more frantic. But then I turned back to Kieran, who was following me. "Aren't you going back to bed?"

"Soon as I know you're alright."

"I've actually already dealt with his nightmares once before. It'll be fine."

"You have?" When I nodded, he said, "Well, I'll still be right outside the door, in case you need backup."

I let myself into the makeshift bedroom, closing the door behind me, then turned on a little desk lamp. Brian was strewn across the futon in one corner of the art studio, tossing and turning. "*No,*" he screamed, one arm reaching out, fingers grasping. "No!"

"Brian," I said, leaning in and shaking his shoulder. "Hey. Wake up." He was lost to his dream and went right on thrashing. I shook him again, harder. His screams turned into desperate sobs, both hands reaching out, grasping desperately. I yelled his name, but it wasn't enough to cut through the terror that enveloped him.

Finally, I made a decision and disregarded Kieran's advice. I climbed right on top of Brian and hugged him to me. There was every chance it would result in me getting pummeled, but I just couldn't stand to see him like that. "It's okay, Brian, I'm here. You're not alone," I said, right into his ear.

His big arms closed around me, crushing me to him. "Hunter," he murmured, burying his face in my hair. "Hunter. I thought I lost you."

That didn't make sense to me at first, but then I realized he wasn't awake yet. I stroked his tangled dark

148

hair and said soothingly, "I'm right here. It's okay. It's all going to be just fine."

It was another few moments before Brian awoke with a gasp, his eyes wild and fearful. He was obviously completely disoriented, dream and reality hopelessly blurred. He looked all around at his unfamiliar surroundings, then focused on my face, blinking a few times. He released me from his grasp, but took my face in his hands. And then, unexpectedly, he kissed me passionately. I totally gave myself over to that kiss, my lips parting for him as he wound his fingers in my hair and tasted my mouth.

There was a knock on the door, and when it opened, we broke apart almost guiltily. "Oh God, I'm sorry," Kieran exclaimed embarrassedly. "It got so quiet, I didn't know what happened."

"We're fine," I murmured, sliding off Brian and sitting on the edge of the futon.

As he pulled the door shut again, Kieran repeated, "I really am sorry, I didn't mean to interrupt. I'm going back to bed."

"Good night, Kier," I called after him.

My heart was racing from that kiss, and when I stood up, I was a little unsteady. To Brian, I said, "Okay, so, I'm going back to the couch. Call me if you need anything."

"Wait," he said, before I'd even taken a step. He took my hand, interlacing his fingers with mine. "Stay with me. Please?"

When I turned to look at him, his eyes were still haunted, and he made no effort to hide his stark vulnerability. His need for me couldn't have been more obvious if he'd shouted it.

I returned to his bed and his arms, and he held me protectively against his chest. It was unclear which of us was comforting the other, given the way he held me, but maybe that really didn't matter. We both felt better, calmer.

After a long pause, Brian whispered, "I always used to have the same nightmare. I've relived the moment I lost my legs a thousand times, the sound and flash of the I.E.D., the feeling of the shrapnel tearing into my body, the sight of the two other soldiers I was with dying right before my eyes...." He paused and took a deep breath, then shook his head as if to free himself from the memory's grasp. After a while, he said, "But that's not what I was dreaming about this time."

"What was this nightmare about?"

"You. I was dreaming about losing you, Hunter. I dreamt that person came after you and I tried to stop him, but I couldn't. He snatched you up and ran away with you, and I couldn't catch him, no matter how hard I tried. I couldn't save you. I was so useless, so helpless. What a horrible feeling."

I leaned back and searched his face as I asked quietly, "Do you really care that much what happens to me?"

"Yes." No hesitation. A simple statement of fact.

"In that case," I said, settling against his chest again, "we really should start dating."

Brian grinned just a little at that, then slid a hand under my chin and tilted my head up. His lips brushed mine tenderly. Then he ran his fingers into my hair as the tip of his tongue lightly traced the curve of my neck, up to my earlobe. He surprised me when he bit my lobe, very lightly at first, sending a jolt of pleasure through me. When I drew in my breath and arched my back, pressing my cock against him, he bit down just a bit harder, and a moan escaped me.

When his mouth returned to mine, his kisses were hungrier, more demanding, and a tremor of desire shook me as he nipped my lower lip. I rolled onto my back and he climbed partially on top of me, his knee sliding between my thighs as he continued to claim my mouth.

Without giving it much thought, I put my hands above my head and crossed my wrists, remaining perfectly passive beneath him. He ran his big hands up my slender arms, and when he reached my wrists, he stopped kissing me and looked up at what I was doing. There was a question in his eyes as he met my gaze. "I like being bound," I admitted quietly. "I don't normally do it in my private life, because I usually have sex with strangers, and I would never trust someone I didn't know to tie me up. But if you wanted to…." I felt stupid and needy then, and stopped talking, breaking eye contact.

He took my face in his hand and turned it so that I was looking at him again. "Is that what you want, Hunter?" His voice was so gentle.

"I mean, it's up to you. This is probably already weird for you, messing around with another man and all, and if that's just one click too far on the bizarrometer, I understand." I started to sit up, but he took both of my wrists in one of his hands and pinned them back against the futon. I made a little mewling sound that I'd had no intention of making, and my cock twitched, which he had to have felt because he was still laying partially on top of me.

Brian kept my wrists pinned as he raised himself up and looked around the room, then pulled the belt from his jeans, which were slung over a nearby chair. He used the belt to bind my wrists together, and the speed with which he did so was both surprising and erotic.

I laughed self-consciously when he'd finished, and said, "Well, damn. And here I thought you might find this awkward."

"I prefer it, actually," he said with a grin. "This way, I know I'm the one setting the pace and controlling what happens." As he was talking, he pulled up my T-shirt and ran his fingertips across my bare skin. "Just so you know," he added, "in no way, shape, or form am I ready to have sex with you. But if you don't mind, I'd like to explore your body a little bit."

"Explore away," I said with a smile, shifting around and getting comfortable.

He did just that for the next few minutes, using his fingers and lips and tongue on my skin. A lot of time was spent on my nipples, which he caressed, then tugged and rolled between his fingertips until they were hard. He sucked them experimentally and asked if it felt good as he looked up at me.

I nodded. "They're really sensitive. I feel it in my cock when you play with them, as if they're all wired together."

At the mention of my cock, Brian's hand strayed below my waistband for the first time, lightly skimming my shaft through the fabric of my cotton sleep pants. I'd been rock hard since he tied me up, and his touch brought out a soft moan as my eyes slid shut.

He went in for another light pass, and then another, as if gradually acclimating himself to handling another man's cock. I murmured, "If you want to flip around, I'll suck you while you play with me."

"I'm supposed to be the one setting the pace, remember?" he said with a smile.

"I know. I just thought I'd make you feel good while you're on your little expedition."

"You *are* making me feel good." His hand came to a stop on my cock and his fingers gently wrapped around it through my clothing. I tried to fight the urge to buck into his hand, and failed. "Do you like what I'm doing?" he asked, and I nodded.

Brian began jerking me off, right through the fabric, his brows knit in concentration at first. But eventually he relaxed and found a good rhythm, and I joked, "You're a natural."

"I've been in an exclusive relationship with my left hand for the past few years. If there's one thing I know how to do, it's this."

I chuckled at that, rocking up into his hand slightly, trying to gain a bit more friction. "All that practice has paid off," I said, my breath coming faster as he stroked me. "You lose points for the cootie shield, though." He raised an eyebrow at me, and I flashed him a big smile.

"Even in the midst of a hand job, you're still a smartass."

"I offered you a way to shut me up. You declined."

Brian laughed at that, then rolled onto his side and sat up. He grabbed the cuffs of my pants and yanked them right off me, leaving me naked from the waist down. I gasped in surprise.

Using my precum as lube, he took hold of my cock and began to jerk me off in earnest. I moaned and bit my lower lip as he picked up his pace. His strokes were hard, demanding. Absolutely perfect. "Oh, fuck yes," I murmured. He flung his thigh across both of mine, pinning me down, and that spiked my arousal. "If you keep this up, you're going to make me cum," I told him as he worked me.

He chuckled at that. "Uh, yeah. That's kind of the idea."

Brian took hold of the hem of my T-shirt and pulled it up over my head, so that it was stretched behind my neck. I raised my head up and watched as the palm of his big hand swiped over the tip of my cock for more precum, then grasped me again and stroked me. His expression was one of sheer determination, and I probably would have teased him about that, if I'd been able to form words right then. Instead, I fell back against the sheets and moaned.

He pumped me rapidly, and finally drove me over the edge by leaning down and biting my nipple. I cried out and arched off the futon, thrusting into his hand as my orgasm tore from my body. It had been days since I'd cum, and I shot huge bursts all across my stomach and chest, some of it even hitting my lips and chin. He milked me right through to the end of my orgasm, gradually slowing his pace, bringing me back down.

When he finally released my cock, I was panting and shaking. After a few moments, I raised my lids and took a look at Brian. He was leaning against the wall with one arm draped across his lap, probably to disguise his very big, very obvious erection. He ran his eyes up the length of me slowly with a satisfied smile, and when we made eye contact I grinned and said, "Welcome to the pink side."

Brian threw his head back and roared with laughter. "You really are the most irreverent person I've ever met," he told me once he could speak again.

He began glancing around us, and I asked, "What are you looking for?"

"Something to clean you up with."

"I can just clean up in the bathroom."

"Nope. Then I'd have to untie you, and I have no intention of doing that."

I relaxed and smiled at him. "Oh? You're planning to keep me like this?"

"I am, right up until the moment you tell me you've had enough." He looked at me closely. "*Have* you had enough?"

"No."

"Good. Me neither." Brian ended up retrieving his discarded flannel shirt from the floor and using that to wipe me clean. He tossed it back where he'd found it when he was finished and settled in right beside me, sharing the same pillow. When I turned my head toward him, he looked at my mouth and grinned, then ran his index finger over my lower lip before sliding it between my lips. When I sucked it, I realized he'd fed me a missed drop of my own cum. A little purr escaped me and I sucked harder, turned on by how unexpectedly erotic that was. "God you're sexy," he murmured, watching my mouth intently.

When he finally slid his finger from my lips, I said, "Well, aren't you just the total revelation."

"How so?"

"For your first time with a guy, you're really surprising me. I wouldn't have guessed you'd be so bold and confident."

"It feels good to experiment with you."

"Is that what you're doing? Experimenting?"

"Not really. I'm giving in to primal lust. The experimentation is secondary."

"Before you keel over from terminal blue balls, maybe you should experiment with putting your cock in my mouth," I suggested. His erection poked into my thigh, even though he was trying to angle his body partially away from me.

"Let's just pace ourselves, okay? There's no hurry."

"Other than the aforementioned death by blue balls." He chuckled at that, and I added, "Plus, you have to admit that shutting me up must hold a certain appeal."

He scooped me into his arms and cradled me against his chest, my arms still bound above my head. "Just relax, Hunter. I can head off certain death later, when I'm alone in the bathroom."

"Now what man on Earth would possibly pass up a blow job in lieu of jerking off?"

"A man who thinks you need a night that's just about you, considering all you've been going through. Let me take care of you."

I knit my brows at that, but finally said, "Well, the offer stands if you change your mind."

"Noted." I kissed his cheek, then settled comfortably into his arms. After a while, he ventured, "So, how deep does this bondage thing run with you?"

"I'm not entirely sure. I've never really explored it in my private life, since as I said, I wouldn't let random strangers tie me up."

"Is this what you and your ex used to do?"

"No, never. Cole was very closed off, sexually speaking. He hid behind a wall of vanilla. I learned I liked bondage when I first started making adult films. It feels good…right, somehow."

"It doesn't scare you? The helpless aspect of it, I mean."

"When I'm tied up on set, there are at least half a dozen people in the room. Because it's supervised, I know it's not going to go too far, I'm not going to get hurt. And right now, I know I'm safe with you."

"Why do you put so much faith in me?"

"Just look at the way you're holding me," I said. He was curled around me like armor, cradling me carefully. "You're all about protecting me, keeping me safe. You wouldn't turn around and hurt me."

"You're right, I wouldn't," he said, then kissed the top of my head. "Not intentionally, anyway, and certainly not in this context."

"You think you'd hurt me unintentionally?"

"I know I will."

"How?"

He considered that for a moment, then reached up and tugged on the belt, freeing my wrists. I put my arms around him as he said, "I'm not proud of the fact that I take my anger out on those closest to me. I've been treating Kieran like shit ever since I got home from Afghanistan, and I hate that about myself. I might do the same to you if we got involved."

"We're already involved," I pointed out, nestling against him. "And unlike Kieran, who's one of the nicest people on the planet, I'll call you on it if you try to vent your frustrations on me. I'm really not afraid to tell you when you're being a dick."

He chuckled and said, "I believe that."

After a while, I ventured quietly, "I want to understand what was going on with you the day your brother brought Christopher home for the first time. How could you say those things to Kieran? How could you call him a faggot?"

"I don't want to try to justify it. I was a total asshole, and I feel really guilty about it."

"So, don't justify it. Just tell me what was going on with you," I said, reaching up and brushing his long, dark hair back from his face. "You already told me you resented Christopher for taking your brother away from you, but that can't be the whole explanation."

"It's not." Brian sighed quietly, and said, "I guess...I guess I resented both of them. I resented the hell out of my brother for going out and falling in love with a man. I mean, why should he be able to do that, when I—" He cut himself off abruptly.

"When you didn't feel you could?" I guessed.

158

He nodded, then rolled onto his back, staring at the ceiling. After a while, he said, "You're not the first man I've been drawn to. There was one other, and I gave him up, thinking he and I could never really be together. I thought my father and the rest of my family would disown me. I was so afraid of people finding out I was gay, afraid of what they'd think of me, that I let him go."

He continued, "I was so angry when Kieran brought a guy home. Why should he be able to have that, when I couldn't? I gave up someone who meant everything to me, and here was my brother, brazenly flaunting his newfound sexuality, not caring who knew. If I couldn't have Anthony, why the fuck should he get to have Christopher?"

Brian sighed and said, "I reacted like a schoolyard bully. I yelled at him and called him names, because I was so fucking jealous. I was pissed, too. I mean, here was my kid brother, showing me up, showing me he was twice the man I'll ever be by being brave and honest and open, by not trying to hide his relationship. I hated myself so fucking much when I saw the two of them together, and I took it out on my brother, just like I always took everything out on him."

"I think I get it," I said quietly.

"Like I said, in no way am I trying to excuse my actions. I was hateful, and hurtful," he said. "Earlier today, while you were doing your self-defense lesson, I tried to explain some of this to Kieran. I also tried to apologize. It's hard to talk to him, we both get really defensive. But I hope he at least heard the 'I'm sorry' in my botched explanation."

"Where's Anthony now?"

159

"He's dead, and it's my fault."

"How could it be your fault?"

"Anthony was a soldier like I was. We met in Afghanistan. He wasn't exactly out and proud, either. It's so hard to be openly gay in that kind of environment. He wanted to give our relationship a chance, though. He was coming to the end of his term and asked me to move to Boston with him after my stint ended, so we could be together. But even as much as I wanted him, I just couldn't do it. I couldn't imagine being openly gay. To me, it had always been this big secret, and I felt like I had to keep it that way. I was afraid, that was the bottom line. So, I broke up with him, and he ended up re-enlisting instead of going home to Boston. He was killed in the line of duty, four days after the start of his second tour."

"And you think you're somehow to blame for his death?"

Brian turned his head to look at me, his eyes tormented and his voice tight as he said, "Of course. If I'd agreed to move in with him, Anthony would have been apartment hunting in Boston, not patrolling that street in Sangin. That bullet never would have found him." He turned back to the ceiling.

I picked up his hand and laced my fingers with his as I slid a bit closer. "Aren't you going to argue with me?" he asked after a while. "Aren't you going to tell me I'm wrong to feel this way? That's what my therapist always did when I tried to talk about Anthony's death."

"His death *wasn't* your fault, but hearing that from me won't change how you feel. You need to learn to believe it for yourself." I put my free hand on his chest, and added,

"In here." He nodded and kept staring at the ceiling. After a while, I said, "So, you weren't willing to out yourself with that relationship, but you're not exactly trying to keep whatever's happening between us private. Why is that?"

"I like to think I'm not totally hopeless, and that I have the ability to learn from my mistakes. When Anthony died, it devastated me. I mourned him for years. And as I mourned, I kept thinking about the last thing he said to me, which was, 'I hope you're not going to go through your entire life as a fucking coward.' He was so pissed that I broke up with him." Brian rolled onto his side, facing me, our intertwined hands between us. "I hear that in my head all the time now. I've internalized it to the point where I'm forever telling myself, 'Don't be a fucking coward.' So, even though I honestly believe I have too many issues to really get involved with you, I'm still going to let myself touch you and kiss you and hold you, for as long as you'll let me, and I'm not going to be secretive about it. Because keeping it secret is what a fucking coward would do."

"So, all this time," I said, "I'd assumed you'd never been with a man. I really thought what you did for me a few minutes ago was a first for you."

"Oh, it was. Anthony and I, we never, um…consummated our relationship."

"Wait a minute. You were involved enough that he asked you to move in with him, but you never slept together?"

"There are all kinds of ways to be intimate with someone, Hunter. What you and I are doing right now for example, me opening up to you like this, is a form of intimacy. My relationship with Anthony was intimate as hell without being sexual."

"Well, okay. I still don't get why you never slept together, though."

"During the five months that he and I were involved, I was fighting my attraction to Anthony tooth and nail. I had such a hard time accepting my sexuality. From the time I was four, my father drilled the idea into me that it was wrong to be gay, that it was shameful somehow. I felt that I couldn't give in to it, that I had to push down those feelings and pretend they didn't exist." After a few moments, he said, "I couldn't deny the fact that I loved him though, and he loved me, too. But even still, our relationship wasn't physical, because I couldn't let it be. We'd kiss, and twice, I let him suck me because I was just too consumed with lust to stop it from happening, but that's it."

"Really?"

He nodded. "I fully realize how unfair I was, both to him and to myself, and how right he was to call me a coward. But all I can do now is learn from it, I guess, and not make the same mistakes all over again."

Chapter Eight

The next morning during breakfast, I announced, "I'm going to my production company today for a meeting with my manager. I want to brainstorm ideas for a publicity stunt that might draw my stalker out of the woodwork."

Everyone stopped eating and looked at me, and Christopher said, "I still think you shouldn't purposefully try to make this person come after you, Hunter. It's too dangerous."

"I appreciate your concern," I said, "I really do. But like I said yesterday, this has to end. That man needs to be in jail, and this might be our best shot at putting him there."

Brian frowned at me. "I hate this idea."

I turned to Christopher and asked, "Can I borrow a change of clothes? What little I brought from my apartment is in my locker at the gym."

"Of course, help yourself to whatever you want," he told me.

"Thanks." To Brian I said, "You can skip the bodyguard duty and wait here at the apartment. I'm just going to take cabs there and back."

"You're kind of missing the point of having a 'bodyguard.' Be sure to picture the air quotes that accompany that word, by the way," Brian said before taking a sip of coffee. I glanced at him, then bit my lip and focused my attention on the mug in my hands. "So, why don't you want me along?" he asked.

"Well, the lobby of Man-on-Man Productions is kind of…I mean, it's just not…."

He asked, "What's in the lobby? Posters of your films?" I nodded. "And you don't want me to see them?" I nodded again, still looking at the cup. "I'm a big boy. I can handle it."

"I know that. It's just—"

"They aren't going to change my opinion of you, Hunter," he said gently. "Besides, you already told me about the type of movies you make, so I know what to expect."

"But also, my manager tends to be really long-winded. You'd probably be sitting around for a good hour...."

"I'm coming with you." When I didn't say anything, he added, "I'll accompany you to the offices, and then I'll go find something to do in the neighborhood during your meeting. Text me when you're done and I'll meet you in the lobby. This is important, Hunter," he said. "Your stalker has hand-delivered letters to this place. No way do I want you going in by yourself."

He had a point. "Well, okay. Just don't say I didn't warn you."

*****

Man-on-Man Productions occupied an entire converted warehouse in San Francisco's South-of-Market district. That particular corner of SOMA was still trying to decide if it was upscale or sleazy, so a few reputable businesses were elbow-to-elbow with a strip club, and of course, my employer.

From the outside at least, the production company didn't look like much of anything. A small sign announced

164

it only as Bryer Enterprises. The sleaze factor didn't kick in until you stepped through the door.

I had never given much thought to the posters lining the walls of the spacious, high-ceilinged lobby, but I looked at them closely as I held the door for Brian. I was featured in more than half of them. They were mostly reproductions of DVD covers, but a few were publicity stills. I was naked in all of them, but, as my manager liked to put it, 'tastefully nude.' In other words, my junk wasn't actually on display. My ass was another story.

I did a quick count as the door swung shut behind us. My naked butt was featured in eleven of the nineteen posters hanging around the lobby. The worst of the lot was a ten-foot high publicity shot that hung right behind the reception desk. In it, I was upright on my knees against a white background, looking back at the camera over my shoulder with a serious expression. My arms were crossed behind me and bound with rope at the small of my back – high enough so they weren't blocking the view of my bare ass.

I sighed quietly, and Brian said, "Well, damn." A little, teasing grin played around his lips.

"Oh God."

"And all this time, I had no idea I was hanging out with the most famous, and apparently most photographed, butt in all of San Francisco."

I burst out laughing at that. Then I leaned down and kissed him, and said, "Shut up, Brian."

"Make me." He pulled me onto his lap and kissed me again.

When I came up for air, I said, "You know we have an audience, right?" There were seven or eight men seated in the spacious waiting area, and all of them were looking at us. That wasn't unusual. Most of the men who visited the offices were porn star wannabes, hoping for their big break. Virtually all of them recognized me.

"Yeah, I had actually noticed the fact that every single person in here is staring at us." Brian smiled at me.

"And you're okay with that?"

He just shrugged. "Why wouldn't I be?"

"It takes getting used to, being the center of attention like that." I tucked a strand of hair behind his ear and draped my arms around his shoulders.

He changed the subject by saying, "So, since we're fifteen minutes early for your appointment, will you do something for me?"

"Sure. Like what?"

"Tell me about some of these films." He swung his chair around and took us to a poster in a corner of the lobby, the one farthest from the prying eyes in the waiting area. In that particular picture, I was on my knees and naked, looking up at a big, naked, musclebound African-American guy. My head blocked the view of his junk, and my hands were on his big thighs.

"Why?"

"Because this is a part of your life," Brian said, "and you've banned me from actually watching any of them."

"So, what do you want me to tell you? There's not much plot, you know."

"Anything. What was it like making this movie? How long did it take to film? Did you like your costar?"

166

"Okay," I said, idly caressing Brian's long hair as I thought about my answer. "Well, most of my movies take one or two days to film, and here, my costar was Brock Brannen. That's his stage name, he's Jimmy in real life. He's a nice guy, and he's married to a sweet former model named Lettie. His wife has a baby on the way."

"He's…wait, what?"

"Jimmy's known for straight porn, but occasionally does crossover work. You know, gay-for-pay and all that? We've made five films together so far, and will probably make more because they're really popular. I think people like the fact that we're such physical opposites. The set-up for this particular film," I said, gesturing at the poster, "was that Jimmy was a personal trainer, and I played a new client at his gym. He had to…um, whip me into shape."

"Do you mean that he literally whipped you?"

"Yeah."

"I didn't realize your films were so hardcore S & M."

"They're not. They're fairly mainstream, actually. Man-on-Man does have a hardcore BDSM offshoot and an on-site dungeon, but that's not what I do. My films are the lighter end of that spectrum. I almost always get tied up, and at least spanked, sometimes a bit more, but that's it. My fans don't want to see full-on torture."

"You got whipped in this one, though." He tilted his head toward the poster.

"Well, yeah. But even when it comes to something like whipping, there are different levels. Jimmy used a fairly soft cat-o-nine-tails on me. It looked impressive on camera and it did sting a bit, but it only reddened me, it didn't raise welts or break the skin. As far as whipping goes, it was

167

really mild, and it was mainly included in this particular film because the director couldn't pass up the pun, 'whipping me into shape' at the gym."

"What were your feelings about being whipped?"

"Honestly? I thought it could have been a lot rougher," I said.

"And that would have been okay with you?"

"Some part of me takes pleasure in pain," I admitted. "Not that I ever wanted to cross over into the hardcore end of this business, or in my personal life, for that matter. But being spanked gets me so hard. I don't know why, I've never really understood that part of myself. And just like being tied up, it's not something I've ever been comfortable exploring with strangers."

Brian's blue eyes searched my face. "I'm glad you trust me enough to tell me this stuff."

"I'm an open book, especially in terms of my sexuality. Actually, most of my sexual development happened on-screen. When I first came to this company, I'd only ever slept with Cole, and like I told you, he'd been very closed off in terms of sexual exploration or experimentation. It wasn't until my ninth movie that the director decided to tie me up, and you can actually see my personal revelation on film if you're watching for it. The moment the ropes were put on my body, I went from pretending I was aroused and enjoying myself to the real thing. I came to life all of a sudden."

"Would you let me watch that film with you, the one where you're tied up for the first time? I'd love to see your sexual awakening."

168

I said quietly, "We talked about this, Brian. I don't want you to see me like that."

He looked at me for a long moment, running the back of his hand down my cheek. And then he said simply, "Okay."

I looked up at him. "Really?"

He nodded. "If you still don't want me to watch your films, then I won't." I hugged him tightly. After a while, Brian ventured, "So, hypothetically, if you ever got in a committed relationship, would you still continue in this line of work?"

That made me sit up and grin at him. "A hypothetical relationship with who, exactly?"

"Well," he said, breaking eye contact, "like…with me, for example."

"Have you been giving this some thought?"

"I mean, supposing I went back into therapy and got my shit sorted out," he mumbled. "Not that you'd want a relationship with me anyway."

I shifted my position so I was straddling his lap, tilted his chin up and kissed him deeply. When I finally pulled back and looked into his eyes, I said, "Oh, I wouldn't, would I?"

He raised an eyebrow at me. "You'd actually consider having a relationship with me? What are you, nuts?"

I chuckled at that. "Haven't I already made it clear to you, Brian?"

"That you're nuts? Yeah, pretty much," he teased, the start of a smile tugging at the corner of his mouth.

"That I'd want a relationship with you, you ass," I said with a laugh.

169

"Well, no, not really. You've made it pretty clear that you'd lower your standards enough to sleep with me, though." He gave me a big smile.

"So," I said, "if, hypothetically, we began a relationship, despite your ongoing protests that you can't and won't get involved with me, would you have a problem with my line of work?"

"Yeah. Big time. If you and I were really involved, then no fucking way on Earth would I share you."

"I mean, it's not really *sharing* me...."

"I believe in monogamy, plain and simple. I really can't begin to get why that Jimmy guy's wife is apparently okay with him going off and having sex with other people." I started to say something, but he cut me off by adding, "And if you're about to say it doesn't count because a camera's rolling and it's all just scripted, that's bullshit. If you were mine, you'd be mine alone. End of story."

"Hypothetically speaking."

"It's probably not just me. I'd think most guys would have a hard time with their partner having sex with other people. Do you really think, as long as you're in this line of work, that you'll ever be able to have a relationship with anyone?"

I felt self-conscious as I climbed off his lap and tucked my hair behind my ears. "Some guys like the fact that I'm a porn star. They think it's hot."

"But do they want to have a relationship with you, or do they just want to sleep with you?"

"Screw you, Brian," I exclaimed, crossing my arms over my chest and taking a step back from him.

"Hey," he said, "I'm not trying to be insulting. I'm just saying, this is a shitty career choice, for a lot of reasons. I don't think it's done wonders for your self-esteem, I think it makes men undervalue you, and I think if you ever try to have a relationship, your job is going to be a major issue. It doesn't matter if that's with me, or with someone else. Any guy that really loved you wouldn't want you doing this."

"Well, then it's a damn good thing no one loves me," I snapped. "Because, newsflash, Nolan. There aren't exactly a ton of awesome job opportunities out there for a stupid kid like me, so it's either porn, or a lucrative career in the fast food industry."

"You just called yourself stupid and used the word 'lucrative' in the same sentence. You're so much brighter and more capable than you give yourself credit for, Hunter."

"I'll be sure to include that on my resume: B-average high school graduate with work experience including unpaid farm hand, stock boy at Safeway, and porn star, but ready for a fast-track Fortune 500 management position because my vocabulary doesn't totally suck."

Brian smiled at me. "Don't forget to include a bullet-point about being a smartass."

I knit my brows and said, "You're not helpful."

"You're better than this, Hunter," he said, his expression turning serious as he gestured at the poster.

"See, that's the thing. I'm not. I'm lucky to have this. If I hadn't been discovered in that nightclub, I'd probably be working three minimum-wage jobs just to try to make ends meet in this crazy-expensive city. I'd be nowhere. I'd be *nothing*."

"You'll never be nothing, Hunter. Even if you had some crappy job that involved wearing a paper hat, even then, you wouldn't be nothing. You'd simply be this amazing individual that happened to have a shitty job."

I turned my back to Brian as my emotions welled up and I fought the urge to argue with him. *Of course I'm nothing*, I wanted to say. *Why can't you see that?* He came up right behind me and wrapped his arms around my waist, then rested his head on my back. After a moment, I wrapped my hands around his. Finally I said, "I don't want a job with a paper hat."

"It's not like those are your only two choices, porn or the golden arches."

I turned to face him and ran my thumb randomly over his thick eyebrow. "I have maybe three years left where I can make good money in this industry. I already look a bit older than twenty-two, and my specialty is playing sweet, little innocents, which is kind of an insane stretch after making nearly forty adult films, but my audience still buys it. My point is," I said, resting my hands on Brian's shoulders as his encircled my waist, "this career has a shelf-life, it's not forever. I haven't really thought about what I'm going to do when it ends, but I sure as hell know it won't pay as well as this. My two-year contract is ending in just a few weeks, and my manager's currently negotiating a three-year extension that'll pay me twice what I've been making. No freaking way would I pass that up."

"Not even for me?" He held my gaze steadily as he said that.

"For you? How many times have you told me you can't and won't begin a relationship with me?"

172

"But…what if I could?"

"What are you saying, Brian?"

"I'm saying don't sign that new contract. Please? Don't do that to yourself."

"That's not all you're saying."

"No," he said, "you're right. I'm also saying that I want you, Hunter. I want you so fucking much, and we already have so many obstacles to overcome. Please don't add another one."

Just then, the young, freckled redhead behind the reception desk called across the lobby, "Mr. Storm? Mr. Bryer is ready for you now."

I nodded at him, then turned back to Brian and looked in his eyes. There was such turmoil in them. I bent down and kissed him, then said, "I need to go to this meeting. And I'm not signing anything today, don't worry. I'll text you when it's over, in case you want to explore the neighborhood."

He nodded and cleared his throat, then said, "I think I will. See you soon."

I crossed the lobby and pushed open the connecting door to the offices, then glanced over my shoulder. Brian was right where I left him, watching me to make sure I was safe.

Brad Bryer, my manager and the man who discovered me, always looked like he'd just stepped off a golf course. He was in his forties, fairly well-built and a bit too tan, with highlighted brown hair and a terrible habit of wearing brightly-colored polo shirts with the collar turned up, as if it was still 1985 in his version of reality. "Hunter, sweetheart," he exclaimed, coming around his needlessly huge desk and taking me in his arms. He swooped in for a kiss, but I turned my head and it landed on my cheek. Somehow, the message behind that was lost on him, and he groped my ass as he said, "It's been way too long, sweetheart. I cleared two hours for us, so we can take care of business before we take care of business."

I wasn't proud of the fact that I used to let my manager fuck me. Truth be told, I used to let pretty much everyone fuck me. To me, it kind of went with the job. My audition two years earlier, after all, had taken place with Brad right in that very office, right on that desk as a matter of fact, with a little camcorder recording the whole thing.

He'd told me to undress, then stuck his cock in my mouth within ninety seconds of the start of the 'interview.' Ten minutes later, he was fucking me in every position imaginable. And naïve me, dumb little farm boy from Idaho, had gone along with all of it. I'd let him do anything he wanted to me, even though I'd been terrified and started crying halfway through. When he finally noticed the tears, he'd asked if I wanted to stop, but I'd told him no. I told him to keep going, because I desperately needed that job.

So, he did. He kept fucking me with that little silver camera pointed at us. As he fucked me, he kept telling me how beautiful I was, how famous I was going to be, how much money I was going to make. Actually, he delivered on all his promises. I did become famous, and the money was incredible, and after my fourth or fifth film, I stopped wrapping up each day on set by crying myself to sleep.

What never did stop was Brad fucking me any time he felt like it. He'd even do it right in front of people, and pretty soon, the crew got the idea that I was just this little

174

slut, there for everyone's use and entertainment. So, I'd spend all day getting fucked on camera, and then when filming wrapped, the crew would take turns with me.

I knew how that sounded. I knew I acted like a whore…and maybe that was all I really was. Maybe that was all I was good for.

It had been like that for two years. I'd never once turned Brad down when he wanted to have sex with me. So when the word *stop* came from me, small and unassertive, he totally ignored it.

I tried again as he lifted me onto his desk and began to undress me, pushing Christopher's hoodie off my shoulders with one hand while he reached for my belt with the other. "Stop," I said again, trying to put a little more force behind it.

His hands were all over my body. He'd be inside me in less than a minute. I didn't want that. *I didn't want him to fuck me.*

"Stop!" I yelled it that time, loudly, forcefully, and Brad pulled back abruptly, staring at me in confusion. He was shocked when I freed myself from his grasp, slid off the desk and said, "I don't want to have sex with you."

"Why not?"

"Because I belong to someone now." My answer surprised me. And it wasn't entirely true…although I wished it was. I should have just said, *because I don't want to.* I really didn't owe him any further explanations.

The truth was that I didn't want to have to go back out to the lobby and face Brian after letting my manager use me. Brian…who thought I was more than this, who looked at me like I was something special. He didn't want me, not really, and made excuses for why we couldn't be together. But that didn't stop me from wanting to try to become something better, someone worthy of him.

I tugged my clothes back into place as I said, "I need to talk to you about something serious."

"You're pissed at me," Brad guessed, adjusting his hard-on through his khakis and going back to his enormous chair behind his enormous desk.

"No, not at all."

"Is it because of the new contract? I told you I was trying to get Bart to up the dollar amount. He already approved a hundred percent raise while only requiring ninety films over three years, but I'm pushing for a hundred and twenty percent. I keep telling him you're worth every penny, and he's so close to agreeing."

Oddly, my manager not only shared office space with the company that held my contract, but that company was owned by his brother, Bart. Brad didn't work exclusively for Man-on-Man Productions, though. He placed and represented boys at companies throughout the U.S. He told me his brother got 'the pick of the litter,' but that wasn't really true. Bart really had to work for the boys he wanted, just like any other client, because Brad didn't believe in playing favorites. He believed in cold, hard cash.

"I'm not here to talk about the contract. I'm here because I need to arrange some sort of public appearance, and I need to do it within the next week or two."

"Well, a public appearance is easy enough. There are at least a dozen local clubs, adult shops and video stores that have been clamoring for you, though the dollar amounts they're offering have been far too low."

"No, that's not quite right. I don't want something with a lot of people filtering in and out, it'd be too chaotic. I need...I don't know, a seated audience or something."

Brad perked up at that. "An audience! Are you finally willing to do that live sex show I've been pitching to you for the last year?"

"That's not what I meant."

Again, it was like I hadn't spoken. "This is perfect timing," Brad said, swinging his monitor toward him and typing something into his computer. "I've been wanting a way to show my brother that you're still a hot commodity, and this'll be perfect! There are three private venues I've been looking at, my favorite is the Clarenden Club, lemme pull up the contact information for that place. We'll set a date two months from now and generate so much buzz that Bart will *have to* up your contract amount. And forget a hundred and twenty percent above your current contract, I'll be able to ask for a hundred and fifty! Your career's going to be on fire after I stage this event for you."

"You're not listening to me. I don't need an event in two months, I need an event *now*. And I told you how I feel about doing a live sex show."

He'd only half-way heard me that time, and muttered, eyes still on his computer, "No way can this happen quickly. We need to build the excitement, the anticipation. We need to milk this for all it's worth. It's all about generating buzz, you know. Besides, all these venues are going to be booked six to eight weeks out, at least in terms of the most desirable time slots, and—"

"Brad, will you shut up for a minute?" I yelled.

Finally he looked up at me, eyebrows knit. "Are you having some kind of diva moment, Hunter? Because that shit doesn't fly with me."

"You're not listening to me. You never have. But this is important."

He looked annoyed. "Fine. I'm listening. What's so important?"

"I need to organize an event that'll be a part of a police sting operation. I'm trying to think of a way to bring my stalker to me, so the police can arrest him. And I've told you a million times that I'm not having sex in public, so that's not what I'm talking about here."

"Your stalker? What does he have to do with anything?"

"Like I said, I want to draw him out so the police can catch him."

"Why?" Brad asked, pulling open a drawer. "He's just some jerk that likes writing letters. And speaking of which, I have the latest batch right here." He tossed a thick stack of white envelopes, bound with a rubber band, onto his desk. "I'm still saving them for your police detective, though I really think we should just throw this shit away."

"He broke into my apartment. And I found out this same person drugged and raped my best friend, and almost beat him to death."

Finally, I had Brad's attention. His expression grew serious, and he said, "Shit, I'm sorry. Is your friend okay?"

"Yeah. That actually happened a while ago, but we found out yesterday that it's the same man. He's really dangerous and elusive, and I want to help the police catch him, before he hurts me or someone else."

Brad mulled that over for a few moments, then said, "Okay, I get it. But you know, there's no reason why this can't be a two birds, one stone kind of situation. We plan some big public event, the police catch this psycho, and at the same time, we generate enough buzz to push your career into the stratosphere and get my brother to pay through the nose to renew your contract. Everybody wins."

I sighed at that, then said, "Whatever. The main thing, though, is that I need this to happen fast."

"Fast is problematic." Brad tapped his fingers on his desktop as he thought out loud. "Although, I could pull off a full media blitz in a short time frame, I could even hit some of the mainstream media outlets if we think of something big. But what and where?"

"Like I said, it needs to be in some sort of controlled environment. I don't want this guy slipping through the woodwork if we do some kind of big, public event."

"If we rent a theater, tickets will sell out fast. You're a big draw. Who's to say this individual will even be able to buy a ticket to the show before they sell out?"

"I bet he'd find a way to be there," I said. "He managed to break into my home and get my unlisted phone number, so I don't think something like sold out tickets would be much of a deterrent."

Brad lapsed into thought again. Eventually he said, "Maybe we need to announce something like a 'meet Hunter Storm' superfan event. We could say we're giving away tickets to the first fifty people that come to the offices, and the police can nab him when he comes for a ticket. After that, we can hold any kind of public appearance we want, we won't have to worry about this guy."

"That sounds suspicious even to me. If this man thinks it's a trap, he won't show."

We tossed ideas back and forth for a while, and finally I sighed and said, "We're overthinking this. Maybe we need to keep it simple, like signing autographs at a shop or something. An event like that would have crowd control in place, and the number of people entering the building at any one time would be regulated to avoid fire code violations. Maybe we don't need to do something big to bring him to me. Maybe he'll show up no matter what I do."

"You think so?"

"I have no idea," I admitted.

"Seems like," Brad said, "if you're going through all this trouble, and if you're getting the police involved, you should try to make sure he'll show up. If you do something outrageous, like a live sex show, that'll definitely draw him out. You told me before that he's very possessive, that he talks about your films as though you're cheating on him. So, if he knows a few big, hot studs are going to fuck you in front of a live audience, he'll be there, guaranteed. Don't you think?"

I narrowed my eyes at my manager. "And the fact that you've been trying to get me to do exactly that for over a year has nothing to do with it, right?"

"Of course not!"

"You're just thinking about how this'll benefit you, about how it'll earn you a fat commission if it boosts my popularity and gets your brother to sign off on a bigger contract. You're trying to take advantage of this situation."

"Since when do you talk to me like that?"

"It's way overdue. I've always let you intimidate me, Brad. That's why I never said no when you wanted to have sex with me. I have no problem talking back to other people, by the way, just ask Brian," I said with a little grin. But then I got serious and added, "With someone like you, though, or with my dad, I was always afraid to speak up."

Brad looked offended. "Did you just compare me to your father?"

"Just because you're both authority figures."

"How am I an authority figure?"

"You're twenty-three years older than I am. Plus, you hold the reins to my entire career, so I always felt like I had to shut up and put out. But I'm tired of that."

He watched me for a long moment, then said, "I never realized you felt that way. I wasn't trying to coerce you into having sex with me. I just thought…."

His voice trailed off, so I said, "What, that I was a slut who gave it up to anybody? I guess that's what I am now. I learned not to place any value on sex, or on myself. But you were only the second man I'd ever slept with, Brad, when you brought me in for my audition. I was twenty years old, and I'd only been in the city for two weeks. My boyfriend and I had just wiped out all our savings moving here and putting down first, last, and deposit on an apartment. On top of that, I was having serious second thoughts about moving in with him, and there you were, offering me a way out and an answer to all my money problems. Let's face it, you took advantage of an innocent

181

kid, fresh off the farm. It didn't come much more naïve than me back then."

He glared at me and said, "You could have said no, Hunter. You had every opportunity. I didn't force you to come here and bend over my desk, you did that of your own free will. And you said it yourself, you were twenty years old, you weren't a *child*. I resent the fact that, after all I've done for you, you now come in here and try to play the victim!"

"I'm hardly playing the victim! But I am finally saying what I've wanted to for years: you took advantage of me, and you and I both know it."

"Oh really? Tell that to your huge paycheck and luxury apartment."

"You profited plenty too, Brad. Your thirty percent cut is hardly the industry standard, only I was too dumb to know that back then. I know it now, though. You've made a fortune off me."

"What the hell happened to you?" he asked as I got to my feet. "Where is this coming from all of a sudden?"

"I don't know. Maybe I'm finally growing up, or finally learning that I matter."

"You're a spoiled brat, Hunter. I gave you fame and fortune, and this is my thanks!"

"Consider your thanks the dozens and dozens of times you got to use my body, no questions asked," I said as I headed for the door.

"Once you get over this diva shit, come back and we'll talk," he said as I left his office.

When I returned to the lobby, I realized I must look pretty flustered, because everyone was staring at me (and it was more than just the 'oh look, there's Hunter Storm' thing I usually got). I sat down for a moment in a quiet corner, pulled my phone from my pocket and sent Brian a quick message, letting him know my meeting was over. In less than a minute he replied: *I'm stuck next door. Stay put, I'll come get you as soon as I can.*

Okay, that was silly. It was broad daylight, and outside, the city street was crowded. I really didn't think my stalker was going to make a move in that kind of environment.

By 'stuck next door' I assumed he was having some sort of mobility issue, like maybe he'd maneuvered his way into a shop and couldn't back out again, so I went to see if I could be of assistance. I left the building and looked both ways. The production company's warehouse took up almost the whole block, but there were a few shops to the left of it, and I headed in that direction.

The business right next door was a men's hair salon. When I stepped into the cramped little waiting area, someone shrieked, "Look everybody, it's Hunter Storm! Brian wasn't kidding!"

A chorus of delighted cheers went up around the salon, and two seconds later, probably the most flamboyant man in the history of flamboyant men appeared at my side and linked his arm with mine. He was dressed in shiny black pants and a canary yellow dress shirt, and sported a full face of makeup, which was an interesting contrast to his short, gray hair. "Mr. Storm, welcome to Salon Viva! I'm Jason Winston de Vane, co-owner of the salon along with my husband Leo. It's an honor! I've seen many of your films, and may I just say, you're even more attractive in person. Tell me, who does your hair?"

"Um, Teddy at Salon 625."

He made a face at that. "Salon 625 is alright, I suppose, but you could get the same result here for half the price. No, *better*."

"For God's sake, Jasie, he's not here to talk about his hair, which is, let's face it, flawless," a second man said. He was a handsome Latino of maybe thirty, and he linked arms with me on the side opposite Jason. "I'm sorry, but Teddy Dane is a freaking genius, and you know it."

To me he said, "Please forgive Jasie, he's a star chaser. If you ever decide you're in the market for a new salon, we'd be honored to have you as one of our clients, Mr. Storm. But that's not why you're here. I'm sure you've come for Brian." The man beamed at me like a kid on Christmas morning, then said, "Oh, and I'm Leo, by the way. Pleasure to meet you. Now come and see!" With that, he clamped his hand over my eyes and propelled me forward, around the reception desk and into the heart of the tiny salon.

"Um, nice to meet you too," I mumbled.

We came to an abrupt halt, and Leo spun me a half-turn to the right, then yanked his hand away and yelled, "Ta da!"

There were seven men before me, four standing, three seated. All the men standing were wearing black Salon Viva T-shirts, and each was staring at me with identical looks of excited anticipation.

I blinked at them and said, "Sorry, I'm confused. What's going on?"

"Oh my God, he doesn't even recognize him," someone exclaimed, and they all laughed.

"Recognize who?"

"Who do you think?" That came from the man seated in the very center of the group with a big, black salon cape draped over him from the neck down.

I looked at the man who'd just spoken. Familiar blue eyes sparkled with amusement. "Holy shit, Brian," I yelled, and the room burst into laughter and applause as a couple camera flashes caught me off guard.

I went up to him, took his face between my hands, and just stared. He was clean-shaven, his dark brown hair was short and perfectly styled, and he was laughing at me. Finally he said, "I can't believe you didn't recognize me." He took one of my hands in his and kissed it.

"Look at you," I murmured, running my free hand over his hair. "I can actually see you now, you're not hidden behind that thicket."

"Do you think you could get used to this ugly mug?" His tone was joking, but there was real concern in his eyes.

"Ugly mug? What are you, nuts? You're so handsome, Brian. But then, I liked you even when you looked like Chewbacca." I leaned down and kissed him, and our audience applauded again.

"You know what I mean," he said quietly, and he traced my fingertips diagonally across his face. Only then did I notice the scars across his right cheek. They were very faint and the same color as his skin, but he was obviously really self-conscious about them.

"Is that what you were trying to hide with all that hair?" I asked gently. "I didn't even notice them until you pointed them out."

"Not really. I was just too lazy to shave and get a haircut," he said, trying to hide his insecurity behind a smile.

I would have kept reassuring him, but since we had an audience, I smiled too and told the assembled crowd, "I can't believe you did all of this in less than an hour. You're fantastic."

"We normally don't even take drop-ins," a young Asian man with a southern accent and hair to his waist pointed out. "But when Brian came in, we all stopped what we were doing and got to work. I mean, how often do you get a chance to do a total makeover like this? We took a before picture, and we'd love an 'after' with both of you in it, Mr. Storm, for our wall of fame, if that's okay."

"It's just Hunter," I said. "And as long as Brian doesn't mind, I'm game."

Brian agreed somewhat sheepishly. They plucked the cape off of him, and I leaned in so close that our cheeks were touching. A few photos were snapped, and when I handed them my phone, they took a couple for me as well. After that, the entire staff and the two other clients in the salon all took turns taking pictures with us in various combinations. Finally, Leo declared that we were being harassed and told his staff to knock it off.

"You got here just in time," Brian said with a grin as I returned my phone to my pocket and the little crowd dispersed. A couple of the stylists returned to their neglected clients (who seemed perfectly thrilled to have been witnesses to all of that). "Jules was giving me a manicure, and he was about to reach for the nail polish."

The Asian guy with the beautiful hair clicked his tongue and said, "Yeah, but just *clear*."

"See what I mean?" Brian said with a chuckle as we made our way back up to the reception desk. "So, what do I owe you?" he asked Leo as we reached the counter.

"Nothing," was his reply.

"What do you mean?"

"There's no charge. That was the most fun we've had in ages. I know we completely inundated you when all you asked for was a simple haircut, and you were such a good sport." He grew serious then, and added, "Besides, my baby brother is serving in Iraq right now, and I strongly believe our veterans deserve so much more thanks than they get. Consider this my way of saying thank you for your service."

"But it's too much. I can't accept it," Brian said, and started to reach for his wallet.

Leo came around the counter and took Brian's hand in his. "I can't do anything to help my brother or the boys serving with him," he said, his eyes slightly misty. "But I can do this for you, if you'll let me."

Brian softened a little at that, and said, "Well, okay. But when I come back, which is going to be every six weeks for the rest of my life, I intend to pay. You got that, Leo?"

The man patted the back of Brian's hand before letting go of him. "Well, if you insist. And I hope your charming and gorgeous boyfriend accompanies you on some of those visits." He beamed at me and said, "You two are such a beautiful couple, and I wish you every happiness."

Instead of setting him straight, we just smiled and thanked him, and then I held the door for Brian. He called out a big thank you, and everyone answered with a chorus of you're welcomes and goodbyes.

It took only a minute to hail a cab, and when we were settled comfortably in the back seat and on our way back to Christopher's apartment, Brian said, "I'm sorry about that."

"About what?"

"I didn't, you know, brag about being your boyfriend or anything. I just told them I was waiting for you to finish a meeting, and they jumped to conclusions."

"I'm glad they thought we were a couple," I murmured, resting my head on his shoulder.

"Do you like me better like this?" Brian asked hesitantly.

"No," I said, then tilted my head up and smiled at him. "I like being able to see your handsome face, of course. But I liked you even when you looked like a Yeti."

He chuckled at that. After a while, he said, "I'm not used to this. I look like I did when I was in the service, and it's weird."

"Do you miss the hair?"

"I'm not going to miss the hassle of it, that's for sure. It had gotten so long that it was a real bother. But I guess I kind of liked hiding behind it and the beard, which probably sounds stupid."

"What do you mean by that?"

"Before today, my outside matched my inside. It said clearly, 'I don't give a fuck.' People just had to take one look at me, and they'd know there was no point in asking anything of me."

"So, what changed?"

"You."

"Me?"

"Yeah. I met you, and all of a sudden, I wanted to stop hiding. I...."

"You what?"

He grinned at me. "Never mind. It's too corny."

"You've changed my life too, Brian," I said quietly, so the cab driver wouldn't overhear our conversation. "I'm different since I met you."

"How?"

"Well, for one thing, I didn't let my manager have sex with me today. I'm not going to do that anymore."

"You used to sleep with your manager?"

"Yeah."

"I take it by your expression that wasn't a good thing."

"It was never what I wanted," I whispered.

"Then why'd you do it?"

"I guess I figured after the first time, which got me the job at the production company, I was already a whore. I'd used my body to get a job, one where I was going to be fucked again and again by all sorts of strangers. Letting Brad fuck me, and taking that job, meant giving up a part of myself. It kind of felt like my body wasn't mine anymore, it was just this commodity. I signed a contract, I basically sold myself. So, by the time I'd done all that, by the time I'd debased myself that far, why say no when my manager came back for seconds? And thirds, and fourths? I was just a whore by then, I'd traded my decency and respectability

189

for money, and I deserved to be used by whoever wanted me. Like a whore was going to have standards and say, this stranger can fuck me because the camera's rolling, but that one can't because the camera's off?"

"Christ, Hunter," Brian murmured. "I wish you didn't treat yourself like that."

The cab came to a stop in front of Christopher and Kieran's building. The downstairs gallery was busy, and a few college students were carrying paintings in through the open double doors. A grand opening celebration was happening in a little over two weeks, and Christopher had invited several fellow students from his art school to show their work.

Brian paid the cab driver while I retrieved his chair from the trunk. We didn't go inside right away, though. Instead, Brian led me to the bench out in front of the building and took both my hands in his as I sat down across from him. He asked, his voice still low, "What's changed, Hunter? I mean, I'm thrilled that you're not letting your manager have sex with you anymore. But what brought on this change of heart?"

"You," I said. "I didn't want to come out of that meeting and have to tell you that I'd just had sex with someone I could barely stand. I was afraid of what you'd think of me, and I didn't want to let you down."

"Let me down?"

"You look at me like I'm something special, and I didn't want to see disappointment in your eyes."

"You couldn't disappoint me."

"I told him I couldn't have sex with him because I belong to someone now. I really wanted that to be true," I said.

"Oh," he murmured.

"Please take a chance on me, Brian. I don't care that it's going to be hard, or that we'll have a lot to deal with. This just feels so right."

He smiled at me. "This is a hell of a conversation to be having on a city street."

"I know. I'm sorry."

"I still don't know why you'd possibly want me," he said quietly. As he spoke, he placed both of my hands palms up on his uninjured hand, then traced my life line with his fingertip, focusing on that instead of looking right at me.

"Just trust that I do."

He glanced up at me from beneath his dark lashes. "I want to be with you too, Hunter. I want that so fucking much. I can list a million reasons why this is a terrible idea, but none of them change the fact that I'm completely drawn to you." After a few moments, he rested my hands on his thigh, pulled out his phone, and scrolled through his contact list.

"What are you doing?"

"If we're going to be together," he said, "you deserve so much better than this."

"Who are you calling?"

"I'm going to make an appointment with the psychiatrist I saw my first year back from Afghanistan. She's really good. I came back shattered and she pieced me back together. As bad as I am now, God, you should have seen me then."

"Really? You're going back into therapy?"

"I never should have stopped. I quit when my required twelve-month treatment plan was up, because I didn't have a reason to keep trying to get better."

"And now you do?"

He grinned at me and nodded.

Chapter Nine

The next couple weeks passed quietly. Brian and I kept living with Christopher and Kieran since I couldn't quite make myself return to my apartment, and he and I continued to grow closer. We moved slowly, spending our days talking and our nights wrapped in each other's arms. He was reluctant to jump into a sexual relationship though, so all we did was make out like teenagers.

There was no hurry. We were both getting to know each other, and Brian was working through a lot of personal issues. I knew that when the time was right, we'd take that next step.

He'd begun twice-weekly therapy sessions with Doctor Natalie Holbrook, the woman who'd helped him when he first returned stateside, and had also started physical therapy. "I want to give us a fighting chance," he'd said, and was really showing his commitment to getting better.

Since he took his bodyguard duties seriously, we were constantly together. I accompanied him to his appointments, reading People magazines from 2006 in the little waiting room at the V.A. while he met with the doctor. In turn, he went with me to the gym every day. We got him a membership and a personal trainer, and he built on what he was doing in physical therapy. Also, three afternoons a week, I met Kaia at a yoga studio in the lower Haight and took self-defense classes while Brian watched and learned along with me.

My stalker was absent during that time. There were no calls, no spray-painted messages, and according to my manager, who had texted me with an apology and was really making an effort to smooth things over (and not lose his most profitable client), no more letters had shown up at his office. It almost seemed like that person had lost interest, which made me let my guard down a little, while at the same time worrying that he was going to disappear before the police could catch him.

But maybe things were about to change. Brad had pulled together a short-notice public appearance at an adult store in the Castro, where I would be signing autographs. I'd pitched the idea of making the event a fund-raiser for a local charity that brought meals to people living with advanced HIV, cancer, and other life-threatening illnesses. I figured some good should come out of the evening, whether or not the stalker showed up and was arrested.

The S.F.P.D. had assigned three officers to work undercover. Detective Sanchez wasn't all that convinced the stalker would show, not in this kind of public, chaotic environment, so he'd been reluctant to pull a lot of personnel for the event. But the three cops would be placed strategically at every exit, so if the stalker came into the shop, his only way out would be through them.

I was nervous, especially about messing up and blowing the whole operation. If I saw him before any of the police officers did, it was vital that I didn't react. The stalker had no idea that I knew what he looked like. If my face gave something away, that would alert him, and he'd probably bolt.

The day of the event, I tried to burn off my anxiety with an extra-long session at the gym, including two advanced yoga classes and over an hour on the elliptical. Brian finished his workout after forty-five minutes, then stayed close, watching me. When I started to head for the treadmill after all of that, he caught my hand and said gently, "That's enough for now."

"I'm just going to run a couple miles," I told him. "I'm sorry, I know this must be boring for you. But I won't be much longer, I promise."

"You're wearing yourself out," he said. "I know you're nervous about tonight, but you're really overdoing it." He reached up and captured my left hand, which had been in my mouth. "And you're biting your nails again, Hunter. You're making yourself bleed."

I turned over my hands, which were in his, and saw he was right. I hadn't even noticed that I'd reverted back to nail biting. "Sorry," I murmured.

"You don't need to apologize," he said, drawing me into a hug. I put my arms around him and rested my head on his. "I just pointed it out because I know you do it unconsciously, and I hate watching you hurt yourself."

"I'm really a mess today," I admitted, stroking his short, silky hair as I held on to him.

"Just remember, I'm going to be right by your side tonight, you won't be alone. And if the stalker shows up, he's not going to try anything, not with that many people around. You'll be perfectly safe."

"You're right. I'm just being stupid."

Brian pulled back to look at me. "You're just being human. We all get scared, Hunter. Don't beat yourself up for it."

I bent down and kissed him, then whispered, "What would I do without you?"

He gave me a big smile. "Let's never find out."

When we arrived at Adam and Adam, the adult shop hosting my event that night, a crowd had already gathered. People were lined up down the sidewalk, even though the doors wouldn't open for another hour. The shop had hired private security for crowd control, and they'd cordoned off the front of the store. When I got out of the cab, the crowd cheered and applauded and several flashes went off. I stuck a smile on my face and waved, then retrieved Brian's chair from the trunk.

"That's a lot of people," he said as he got out of the cab. "You're more famous than I realized."

"Not really, not when I step outside the Castro."

A couple beefy guys with the word 'security' emblazoned on their billboard-like chests came up to us and ushered Brian and me into the building. Brad was already inside, all smiles as if nothing had ever happened between us, and he introduced me to the shop owner and a couple of local reporters. I had to hand it to my manager, he knew how to get things done. I did a quick round of interviews and tried not to sound like a total tool, then smiled for the cameras. A few more people were introduced to me. One worked for the company that distributed my films, and another owned a business that produced, according to him, "...high-end sex toys for the discerning, upscale gay." Um, okay. He really wanted me to endorse his products, and I smiled politely as he launched into a lengthy discussion about his company's innovations in dildo design. Good lord.

196

By the time seven p.m. rolled around and the doors were about to open for the event, I was already mentally exhausted. It was going to be a long night. I made my way over to a folding table that had been set up in the middle of the space. Racks of DVDs, sex toys, and other 'adult novelties' had been moved to the sides of the shop to make room for the event. Brian was already behind the table and had been watching the goings-on with an amused expression. When I took a seat beside him, I plucked a DVD from his hands and returned it to the display beside me.

"So, I have a question for you," I said.

"Shoot."

"If you're gay, how have you never seen any of my films?"

He burst out laughing at that. "I didn't realize they were mandatory viewing for those crossing over to the pink side."

"Really, though."

"I don't know. I don't tend to watch a ton of porn, because I like leaving some things to the imagination. And when I do, apparently I steer away from movies with bad bondage puns in the title."

I grinned at that. "They're not all puns."

"I know, but they're still pretty funny." He reached across me and started pulling DVDs from the rack and piling them on the tabletop. *"Bound and Determined. Fit to be Tied. Showing Him the Ropes. James Bound* – that's my favorite." With an English accent, he quipped, "Bound. James Bound."

I chuckled and said, "Stop it."

"Did you get to wear a tux and drink a martini?"

"I got to be naked, and tied to the hood of a Mercedes."

"*Crimson Tied*, that's pretty good, too." He was grinning at me wickedly, and I rolled my eyes at him. "How many movies have you made, exactly?"

"Thirty-nine."

"Holy shit, that's a lot."

"Well, like I told you, they only take a day or two to make. We're not exactly filming *Titanic* here."

"Ugh, thank God. That song makes me want to roll in front of a bus."

"Agreed." The shop owner pulled open the front door and the crowd surged forward, the first eager fans actually running toward the table. "Here goes nothing," I murmured, and stuck a smile on my face.

The event was scheduled to run for two hours, and it was nonstop. I was surprised so many people had turned out for it, especially since it had only been announced a few days earlier. It was so hectic that I didn't really have time to obsessively scan the crowd, looking for my stalker. The police officers on duty could handle that, they'd all studied his photo and knew who they were looking for.

I glanced at the cop by the front door. He should really have been wearing a black T-shirt labeled 'security,' because he was totally failing to blend in, and that would have given him an excuse for standing around awkwardly. He was dressed in a sweatshirt and jeans, but he might as well have been in full uniform, that was how uptight he looked. Couldn't they have found a gay cop or two to send

198

over? That one hadn't stopped frowning since the moment he arrived. I felt judged from clear across the room.

By nine p.m., the designated stopping point, my face hurt from smiling so much and I was seeing spots from all the camera flashes that had gone off in my face. But there were still some people in line, and they'd been waiting forever, so I asked the shop owner if we could keep going. "Hell yes," he said. "Sales are up four hundred percent. You can stay all night if you want."

"Let's hope it doesn't come to that," I said. The next eager fan was ushered forward, and I stuck a smile on my face again.

This particular gentleman was elderly, with shaggy gray hair that hung in his face, a mustache, bulbous nose, and glasses. "Hunter," he said, shaking my hand. "It's a real pleasure."

"Thank you for coming," I said politely. "I'm sorry you had to wait so long."

"Oh, I wouldn't have passed this up for anything," he said. The man paid the cashier to my right for a photo (all going to the charity I'd selected), then handed another shop assistant his phone as he came around to my side of the table. I stood up and smiled for the camera, and he put his arm around me as a flash once again blinded me. Then his hand actually slid down my back and caressed my left butt cheek before he let go of me. I bit back a surprised laugh. Grandpa had game.

He turned to Brian then. "Are you Hunter's boyfriend?" he asked.

Brian looked at me and smiled, then said, "I guess you'd have to ask him that."

I smiled, too. "Oh yes. He definitely is."

"You're one lucky fella," the old gentleman told him. "You've got yourself a real treasure there."

Brian was still smiling at me, and murmured, "I really don't know how I got so lucky."

"Neither do I," the man said, his voice dropping slightly. He then smiled cheerfully and bustled back around the table, retrieving his phone from the assistant. "A real pleasure, Hunter," he said before heading for the door.

Almost immediately, a gawky kid of about nineteen with thick glasses, braces, and greasy hair rushed up to the table. "Oh mah gawd, you're even more beautiful in person!" the teen exclaimed. "I've seen all your films. I love you, Hunter Storm! I'm Artie, by the way." He grabbed my hand and pumped it vigorously.

"It's nice to meet you, Artie. Thank you for waiting in that long line."

"I'd crawl over broken glass to meet you, Hunter Storm," he gushed.

"Um, thanks?" Awkward!

He said, "So, I've been thinking about breaking into the porn industry. Can we meet for coffee so you can give me some pointers?" Criminy.

"Oh. Well, I don't really have any pointers. You could just call the Man-on-Man offices and set up an appointment with a casting agent. That's pretty much all there is to it."

"I'd love to co-star in some of your films," Artie said, his gaze running down my body like I was a piece of meat. "I'd do you real good."

Brian tried to cover a laugh by coughing into his fist, and I said, "Yeah...so, you know, just call the offices."

"I'm calling first thing tomorrow! Bye, Hunter Storm!" Artie exclaimed, and headed to the exit without a photo or autograph.

"So, clearly we should have ended this at the designated time. All the weirdos come out after nine," I whispered to Brian. "Did you see that old guy feel me up?"

He burst out laughing. "No, but that's hilarious. And God am I glad I'm not famous. Being a celebrity sucks." He poured a cascade of little slips of paper out of the empty plastic cup in front of him and said, "But hey, on the bright side, twenty-eight men have slipped you their phone number. So if you get tired of me, look at all these options!"

I chuckled at that. "Why are you keeping those? I told you to throw them away."

"I want to see if you hit thirty. I mean, surely the most beautiful man on the planet could get thirty numbers in one night." He flashed me a big smile. He'd taken to poking me lightly in the ribs every time someone called me beautiful, and seemed to find the whole evening endlessly amusing. "I also want to see if you can make a dozen grown men cry, just from meeting you. You're at eleven. Good luck." He winked at me, and I grinned as I rolled my eyes and gave him a playful shove.

The next group finally approached the table. There were four of them, and they'd held up the line with a debate about which of them got to go first. They'd finally settled their dispute with a best-of-three rock-paper-scissors-lizard-Spock duel.

"Hi," I said. "So, I thought Spock beats lizard."

"No way! Lizard poisons Spock," the guy in the Doctor Who T-shirt explained. "Which, granted, is kind of misleading, since most species of lizard are totally harmless. In fact, only a few, like the bearded lizard of Mexico and the Gila monster are actually poisonous."

"That's totally ignorant. About a hundred species of lizard are venomous," one of his friends chimed in.

"Yeah, out of over *five thousand* known species of lizard!" Doctor Who told him.

"A hundred isn't a few."

"It is when you're talking about thousands of species in toto!"

"Then what beats lizard?" I interrupted, before they started brawling over reptile trivia.

"Scissors decapitates lizard," the guy in the Bazinga T-shirt explained.

"And rock crushes lizard," the African-American kid with a fedora added.

"What on earth are you talking about?" Brian asked me, and my fans and I did a quick demonstration. He tried and failed to make the Spock symbol, and we all had a good laugh.

"I just knew you'd be awesome," Doctor Who told me with a big smile. "I mean, not only are you the most beautiful guy ever—" (Brian subtly elbowed me in the ribs) "—but you're also totally cool."

It took a while to get photos with all of them, as a group and individually, on their various phones, iPads and miscellaneous electronic devices. They left with huge smiles on their faces. When they'd almost reached the door, kid-in-a-fedora doubled back and slipped me his number with a wink, then hurried after his friends.

"So close! Twenty-nine," Brian exclaimed, adding the slip of paper to the cup. "There are, let's see…five more people in line. I think you can get to thirty, fairest of them all. Oh and look," he whispered, "this next one's crying." I poked him in the arm as the fan slowly approached the table.

"Oh my God, I can't believe I'm actually meeting you in person! I've seen all your films a million times," the man gushed, tears streaming down his face. He was about sixty-five and reminded me of someone's grandpa, so that was a little awkward. "You're so gorgeous, Hunter. Oh my God!" After tearfully collecting an autograph and photo, he handed me a slip of paper. "If you call me, I will die a happy man," he said, before heading for the door.

"Yes!" Brian exclaimed, plucking the paper out of my hand and adding it to his collection. "That was a three-fer. Tears, phone number, and raving about your unparalleled beauty."

I grinned at him. "I'm glad you find it entertaining. A lesser man might have been threatened by all of this."

He smiled at me. "I already know you're gorgeous, baby, and my phone number's at the top of your call list. Just don't expect me to burst into tears at the sight of you."

"It's just the celebrity thing. It's not that I'm special, or even that I'm particularly attractive. The perception of fame just does weird things to people."

When the doors were finally closed and locked after the last person in line, I climbed up onto the table and stretched out flat on my back. "That was exhausting," I muttered. "My face hurts from smiling. Are my cheeks permanently upturned, like the Joker in Batman?"

"Yes. But don't worry, you're still handsome enough to make grown men cry."

I chuckled at that and turned my head to face Brian. "Thank you for being a good sport through all of that."

"It was fascinating, and highly educational."

"It was?"

"Sure. I never knew Gila monsters were poisonous."

I chuckled again, then slapped my palms to my cheeks. "Ow, stop being funny! If I smile any more, I'm going to break my face."

"Come on, Home Alone, let's get out of here before the bus pulls up with the rest of the Gay Nerds for Hunter Storm Convention."

"You're just jealous of the nerds," I said, rubbing my cheeks as I sat up and swung off the table, "because you're not cool enough to make the Spock symbol."

"Oh, believe me, cool is not the word you're looking for there," Brian said cheerfully.

After I thanked the shop keeper and the police officers who'd stood around all evening for nothing, I phoned for a cab. I then helped the clerks pull the racks of merchandise back into the center of the room. "You don't have to do that," the young, freckled guy that had been the cashier at my table said.

"This all got messed up because of me, so I should help put it back," I said. He seemed really surprised. That was the other thing about fame: people totally expected you to act like a douchebag.

"Hey, Hunter, do you have a minute?" a young African-American woman asked, sweeping long dreadlocks behind her shoulder. I'd noticed her come in about half an hour earlier.

"Sure."

"I'm Sadie Jones, from Lunch with Love," she said, shaking my hand. "This fundraiser of yours brought in a lot of money, and it's going to go a long way in our little organization. I just wanted to thank you in person for doing this."

"You're welcome," I said with a smile, then added, "You know, I expected you to be a lot older." I'd heard her name before, and knew she founded that nonprofit.

"I get that a lot."

"I really believe in the work you're doing," I told her. "If I can ever do anything else to help out, just let me know."

She handed me a business card. "If you're serious about that, we need all the help we can get. Call me any time, we'll figure out how to utilize your talents." I chuckled at that as I slipped the card in my shirt pocket, and she asked, "What's funny?"

"Well, you know what I do for a living. I can't imagine those talents would benefit your organization a whole lot."

Now it was her turn to laugh. "I'm guessing you have other skills, too."

"Cab's here, Hunter," Brian called from the front door, and I nodded at him.

To Sadie I said, "Thanks for coming down in person, it was nice to meet you."

"Nice to meet you too, Hunter."

As always, Friday night in the Castro was booming. And also as always, my appearance generated a buzz when we left the shop. It was ground zero for my fan base, the place where my fame reached its absolute zenith. A couple in their thirties approached me and asked for a photo (more smiling, my face would never recover), as did a group of club kids.

After that, I'd just about made it to the curb when someone called out, "Hunter!" Brian was on high alert during all of that, staying right at my side and watching the crowd closely.

He put himself between me and whoever had called out. But then, Trevor emerged from the crowd, his cheeks flushed, breathing rapidly. He was wearing the same threadbare cardigan he'd had on when I met him at Jamie's brunch. His hands were in his pockets, and his shoulders were slumped self-consciously.

"I was sure I'd miss you," he said. "I just got off work, and ran from the bus stop. Can I talk to you for a minute?"

"Now's not a good time," Brian chimed in. I glanced at him, and noticed a little frown line between his eyebrows.

I turned back to Trevor. "It's actually been kind of a crazy night. I'd love to talk, but can I meet up with you sometime tomorrow?"

"Yeah, if you want."

"I can come by your work, as long as Cole won't be there," I said.

"I don't want to trouble you."

"It's no trouble."

"Well, okay, if you're sure. I work the lunch shift until two. Cole's off tomorrow."

"Alright. See you around two then," I said, and he nodded, smiling shyly.

When we were in the cab and headed out of the Castro, Brian mumbled, "I wonder what that was about."

I turned to look at him. "So, you're okay with a couple hundred guys fawning over me, but then that skinny kid shows up and *now* you're jealous?"

"He's a good-looking guy."

"So were a lot of the men who came to my public appearance. But all you did was gleefully collect their phone numbers and make fun of me for being idolized."

"Well, yeah. But you don't like any of your fans."

"Sure I like them."

"I mean, *like* like."

"And you think I like Trevor?"

"I know you do," Brian said.

"Based on what?"

"You told me."

"I did? No I didn't."

"When I broke up that fight between you and Cole at Jamie's brunch, you admitted that you'd been thinking about hitting on Trevor. You're obviously attracted to him."

"Oh, that? Brian, before you and I got together, I thought about hitting on *everybody*."

He grinned a little and said, "That's not true."

"Pretty close, though." I slipped my arms around Brian and cuddled him.

"I've never understood what you're doing with me," he said, resting a hand on the arm that crossed his chest. "You're right that most of tonight didn't intimidate me, because the whole fame monster thing was bizarre, fascinating, and frankly, kind of funny. But someone like Trevor…I mean, he seems sweet, and shy, and he's so damn cute, and you guys are probably about the same age, and…I don't know. He seems like someone who'd be good for you."

"You're not exactly a hundred and fifty, Brian, you're only four years older than me. And guess what? You're all the things you just mentioned, excluding shy, but with extra emphasis on good for me."

"I might as well be a hundred and fifty. I feel like I am, sometimes. And no way in hell am I good for you."

"Let's not go back down that path. All I'm going to do is argue with you."

He was quiet for a while. Finally, he said, "When you break up with me, I'm not going to do what Cole did. I'm not going to blame you, or hate you. It'll make perfect sense to me."

I sighed and shook my head. "So, when that never happens, I'm totally going to say I told you so."

He chuckled at that and some of the tension left his body. "That doesn't make any sense. When exactly will you be delivering this I-told-you-so?"

"Every morning, from now on. When you wake up and reach for me and find me right there beside you, that's when I'll say it. I'll start each day with, *good morning, sweetheart. I told you so.*"

He laughed again and hugged me to him. "Because that won't get annoying."

"Hey, don't blame me. You brought it on yourself with this unfounded insecurity."

When we pulled up in front of Christopher's building, the downstairs art gallery was buzzing with activity. The next day was the grand opening celebration. I found my friend among the people rushing around doing last minute preparations, gave him a hug, and said, "The place is looking great."

"Thanks. How was your event?"

"Bizarre. And the stalker was a no-show."

"His fans literally lined up down the block," Brian chimed in.

"I knew that about the stalker. Brian kept texting Kieran with updates because he knew we were worried," Christopher said.

Kieran appeared beside us, dressed in full police uniform and carrying a cardboard box. I gave him a snappy salute and said, "Evening, Officer Nolan. Aren't you a little overdressed for the occasion?"

"Hi Hunter. And yes. I still haven't made it upstairs to change."

"Speaking of changing," I said, "I'm wearing your best outfit, Christopher Robin, and I'll bet you're going to want it for tomorrow night's grand opening. I'm going to run upstairs and put these clothes in the washing machine, and then I'll be right back down to help."

"Thanks," he said. "You don't have to help though, you must be tired. We'll be done here in another half-hour or so."

"Well, if I haul ass back here, let's see if we can shave that down to twenty minutes," I said. I gave Christopher a kiss on the cheek, then planted a second one on the top of

Brian's head before turning and jogging toward the back of the gallery.

"Hey, where's my kiss?" Kieran joked.

"Rain check," I called, flashing him a big smile over my shoulder.

When I got upstairs, I went straight to the tiny laundry alcove off the kitchen and stripped down to my briefs. There were a few other clothes waiting to be washed, and I loaded them in the machine, then went through the pockets of Christopher's dress shirt, pulling out Sadie Jones' business card and putting it on top of the dryer. I removed my wallet and Christopher's spare set of keys from the pants pockets, then found the business card of that guy that manufactured, what was it? Oh yeah, 'high-end sex toys for the gay.' What did that even mean? Were they like high-end sex toys for the straight, only rainbow-colored?

I pulled the belt from its loops and put it beside the other items on the dryer, then did a final sweep of the pockets. When I reached into the left rear pocket, I felt something smooth and square. I pulled out a little piece of paper, neatly folded, then stuck the pants in the washer and turned on the machine. I held the paper between my middle and pointer finger while I measured out some detergent and swirled it over the clothes, then closed the lid. Only then did I unfold the note, blinking at the small, tight handwriting.

It said: *I'm coming for you soon, my treasure.*

Chapter Ten

Kieran found me sometime later. Apparently, I'd sat down on the worn wood floor beside the washing machine, and I was still holding the note. "Hey Hunter," he said when he stuck his head in the laundry room. "There you are, we wondered what happened to you. Are you alright?"

I looked up at him and wordlessly held out the slip of paper. "What's this?" he asked, taking the note from me and turning it to face him. His expression went from cheerful to dead serious in an instant. "Where did this come from?"

"It was in the back pocket of the pants I just took off. It's from my stalker. I recognize the handwriting from some of his letters."

"Come on," Kieran said, holding a hand out to me. "Let's get you dressed, you have goosebumps."

I didn't move. "I'm just going to sit here for a bit." My voice sounded oddly hollow to me.

Kieran retracted his hand and watched me for a beat, then pulled out his phone and dialed a number. When someone picked up, he said, "Brian, could you come upstairs, please?"

Brian was so loud that I could hear him through the phone and downstairs as he exclaimed, "Is it Hunter? Is he okay?"

"Just get up here, but don't hurry. I don't want you to fall down the stairs."

"Screw that," came the reply, right before the line went dead. A moment later, I could hear a clattering sound on the stairs, and right after that, Brian appeared beside me as his brother stepped out of his way. He pulled me onto his lap, his big arms enveloping me as he asked, "Are you alright, baby? What happened?"

"I'm fine," I mumbled.

Kieran exclaimed, "That was surprisingly quick."

"Crawling on my hands and knees isn't pretty, but it gets the job done," Brian said. His eyes searched my face as he brushed back my hair. Whatever he saw made him knit his brows and ask his brother, instead of me, "What the hell happened, Kier?"

"He found a note from his stalker in the back pocket of the pants he'd been wearing."

"Holy shit," Brian whispered, all the color draining from his face. "But how? I never left his side, and I watched every single person that went in or out of that shop." He thought about it for a moment, then asked, "What are the chances that man has an accomplice?"

Kieran said, "It'd be pretty unusual. Most stalkers work alone."

Brian hugged me and kissed my forehead, then said gently, "Let's go to the living room, Hunter. You'll be more comfortable."

I got up and wandered to the living room, where I sank onto the sofa. The brothers were right behind me, and Brian crawled onto the couch and took me in his arms again.

Kieran grabbed a nearby blanket and covered both of us with it, then pulled out his phone again. "I'm going to call Detective Sanchez and let him know what happened. I'll go tell Christopher, too." He headed for the stairs as I put my head on Brian's chest.

"How could he have gotten that close to me?" I said quietly. "He was close enough to touch me, but no one saw him. How is that possible?"

"I don't know."

"*My treasure*. That's an odd expression," I mused. "Why do I feel like I heard it recently?"

"Because that's what the old man said, toward the end of the evening." Brian sat up a little. "He told me I had a real treasure in you."

I sat up too, and looked at him. "That was the guy who fondled me after we took a picture. I felt his hand on my butt, and the note was in my back pocket."

"Did anyone else touch you?"

"Plenty of people hugged me, but he was the only one who strayed that far south."

"So he must have planted the note. But why would some old guy be working with your stalker?" Brian asked.

"He said the same thing the note did, he called me a treasure, so maybe that was him. Maybe he disguised himself. I just don't get why he'd bother. He thinks I don't know what he looks like," I said.

Brian thought about that for a few moments before saying, "This guy has access to information he really shouldn't have, like your unlisted phone number and address. I'm just guessing here, but what if he somehow has access to police information? What if he knows they have a photo of him from that surveillance camera?"

"Aside from, obviously, a cop, who else would have access to that sort of information?"

He shrugged and said, "There are plenty of consultants who work for the police in various capacities."

"On top of that, are we saying he's also some sort of Hollywood-style makeup artist? That's pretty far-fetched."

"It doesn't have to be anything that elaborate. A wig, fake mustache and glasses are easily obtained. The only specialty piece would have been that nose, but even that wouldn't be hard to find."

"Really? You think you can just go up to the counter in Walgreen's and ask for a prosthetic nose?"

Brian pulled out his phone and tapped the screen a few times. Not thirty seconds later, he angled it toward me and said, "No. But you can get one for about ten bucks on Amazon. In fact, this big honker looks an awful lot like what that man could have been wearing."

"Christ," I muttered. "He sticks on a wig and a fake nose, and just walks right up to me. I'm so damn stupid. I didn't even sort of recognize him."

"Well, neither did I, and neither did anyone else, including the trained police officer at the front door."

We sat there lost in thought for a while, and then I said, "Here's another thing I don't get. I don't know this person. So, why did he use some kind of voice modulator when he called me a couple weeks ago? Why would he bother, if I couldn't recognize his voice anyway?"

"Maybe he just did that to mess with you. He obviously wants you scared, or off-kilter. This man is playing a game with you, that's why he made an appearance tonight and slipped you that note. That only accomplished one thing: freaking you out. So maybe the eerie, robotic voice synthesizer was meant to do the same thing."

I nodded in agreement. "I can see that. I guess he gets his kicks out of watching me unravel."

"He's pissed off at you," Brian said. "That's clear, based on his letters. When he watches your films, he thinks you're cheating on him, because he can't separate fantasy from reality. This is probably his idea of payback, a way to make you suffer for your perceived infidelity."

"You're probably right." I closed my eyes and slumped against the couch. But then, something else occurred to me, and I sat up quickly and turned to look at Brian. "What did he say to you? I met so many people tonight that it all kind of blurs together."

"He asked if I was your boyfriend, and you told him I was. It was the first time we used that word to describe our relationship, that's why it stands out to me."

"Oh God."

"What's wrong?"

"What if he turns all that anger on you, Brian? What if he decides the best way to punish me is by going after you? I'll never forgive myself if he hurts you."

Brian looked at me levelly. "I hope to God he comes after me, because then I can tear him apart for what he's doing to you, and for what he did to Christopher."

"This is no time for that Semper Fi, big tough Marine stuff. Maybe you should clear out for a while, just until this man is caught. Christopher said you and Kieran own a cabin in Tahoe, maybe you could spend some time there."

"And leave you unprotected? *Hell* no."

"I have a bad feeling about this," I said. "He focused a lot of his attention on you tonight, and we know he's seen us together before. You were with me when he called from that payphone, the day he was following us in the Richmond. If he gets totally wound up watching me with different men on film, what must it do to him to see me with the same man repeatedly, a man he now knows is my boyfriend?"

"Doesn't matter. I'm not leaving your side."

"Brian, think about it. This person is full of rage, but he's never directed it right at me. Instead, he hurts others. He's hurt boys who look like me, as if they're meant to take my place or something, and maybe he'd do the same to my boyfriend. He said he plans to make me suffer, and you know what would accomplish that? Hurting you, or going after Christopher again. You two might be in more danger than I am."

"I'm not going anywhere."

Christopher and his fiancé came upstairs, and as my best friend sat down beside me and picked up my hand, he said, "I called Dante after Kieran told me what happened. He owns this building, and I talked to him about upgrading security. It sounds like the stalker is stepping up his game, so we should, too."

"What did Dante say?"

"He wants to put his mafia connection to work and provide some security guards for tomorrow night's gallery opening. There are going to be a lot of people coming in and out of here, and after tonight's stunt, I wouldn't be surprised if the stalker tries to pull something. Dante also wants to upgrade the existing alarm system."

I nodded and said, "That's good. I couldn't stand it if something happened to any of you."

Christopher squeezed my hand. "We feel the same about you, Hunter. I'm going to make sure the gallery is all locked up, I'll be right back." He headed for the stairs with his fiancé right on his heels. Kieran obviously had his back, and that was reassuring.

"I feel like a jinx," I said to Brian as he took me in his arms. "All of you are in jeopardy because of me."

"You're not a jinx. You know what you are?"

"No. What?"

"You're Bound. James Bound," he said with a grin, and I chuckled at that.

"Only you could make me laugh at a time like this," I said.

"Glad to hear I'm actually good for something. Now do me a favor and go down and get my wheelchair, okay? I need to take you to the bathroom, and I'd rather not crawl."

"Why do you need to take me to the bathroom?"

"You look like you're freezing in that porn star-grade skimpy underwear, so I plan on sticking you in that huge tub and warming you back up."

I smiled at that. "Will you be joining me in the tub? It's big enough for two."

"It's big enough for *seven*. And no, I won't."

"Why not?"

He swung me onto my feet and swatted my butt. "Chair, please."

"I'm going." I jogged across the room and down the stairs, then lugged the bulky metal contraption up to the apartment. He was still using the electric wheelchair on loan from the hospital, since his sprained wrist wasn't back to normal, and it was quite a bit heavier than his manual chair.

I deposited it right beside him, and stepped aside. But before moving off the couch, Brian slowly ran his gaze down my nearly naked body. The 'porn star-grade' underwear, as he called it, left little to the imagination. It was basically just a skimpy black jockstrap. I looped my thumbs under the thin straps and pushed them down, and the underwear fell to my ankles.

As I stepped out of it, Brian asked, his voice a little husky, "Why did you do that?"

"I assume you want me naked in order to bathe me," I told him. "It also seemed like you might want an unobstructed view."

He looked me up and down again, the longing in his eyes absolutely intense. But then, he sort of shook it off and swung himself onto his chair. "You know," he said lightly, "your fans just might have a point. You may very well be the fairest of them all." With that, he pivoted around and headed to the bathroom.

I grinned at that as I scooped up my underwear and followed him. "None of them called me that. Only you."

"Well, then *I* might have a point."

Once the tub was filled and I was up to my neck in wonderfully warm water, Brian really did proceed to bathe me. His touch was so gentle, the entire experience as much about soothing and comforting me as it was about getting me clean. When there was nothing left to wash, I opened my eyes and sat up a little, then asked him, "And why aren't you in here with me, exactly?"

"You really want me in there?" he asked, and when I nodded, he shrugged and said, "Fine."

He took off the chambray shirt that he had on over a dark blue tee and tugged his belt from his jeans. Next he fished in his pockets and put their contents on a shelf near the sink. He then braced himself on the edge of the tub and executed a fairly graceful vault over the edge, depositing himself in the water.

I laughed in surprise, then said, "Um, you missed a couple steps."

"No I didn't."

"You're still wearing jeans and a T-shirt."

He smirked at me, his eyes alight with amusement. "Really? Thanks for pointing that out to me, because maybe I'd failed to notice."

"So...*why* are you still wearing jeans and a T-shirt?"

"Because I don't do naked."

"Everyone does naked."

"Let me amend that. I don't do naked around other people."

"I'm not 'other people.' I'm your boyfriend."

"I like that term," he said with a smile. "It makes this feel kind of official, don't you think?"

"Smooth subject change," I said, "but I'm not letting you off the hook just yet. Why are you wearing clothes in the bathtub?"

"Maybe naked is against my religion. Maybe I'm Quaker for all you know, and took a vow of modesty."

"Ok, A, you're Catholic. And B, Quakers don't take vows of modesty, because there's no such thing."

"There are too Quakers, and not just on the drum of oatmeal. Did you ever ask yourself why it comes in that drum, by the way?"

"There's no such thing as a *vow of modesty*. And your diversion tactics are starting to unravel at the seams," I told him with a smile.

"Totally up on Quaker doctrine, are you?"

"Brian. Tell me why you're fully dressed in a bathtub."

"Why do you think?"

"Because you think I'm enough of an asshole to get freaked out by your legs."

He knit his brows at that. "I hate it when you twist things around to make them your fault."

"Is that it? Are you afraid to let me see your amputations? Do you think I'm going to stop being attracted to you when I see for myself what I already know is happening under there?" He shrugged, and I said, "Give me a little more credit, Brian."

"Maybe it's all me. Maybe I feel ugly and self-conscious, not only because of my legs, but because of everything else that's going on under here. These don't stop at my neck, you know," he said, tapping the scars on his cheek. "The shrapnel tore into my body in a hundred places. And if all of that wasn't enough, I also have this lovely spare tire now, after three years of sitting in a chair eating pizza." His hands tapped his belly as he said that. "You add that all up, and you know what you get? The stuff of freaking horror movies, that's what."

"Brian, I fell for you when you looked like you were ready to play the lead in 'Jesus Christ, Superstar.' When are you going to stop thinking I'm completely shallow?"

He laughed at that. "How far back did you go for that reference, 1973? You're way too young to even know what that is."

I grinned at him. "My drama teacher in high school was a total hippie. He actually tried to get us to perform that play my sophomore year, but the local churches decided it was blasphemous and wouldn't let him bring it to the stage. Damn shame, too, because guess who landed the role of Jesus H. Christ?"

"You?"

"Yup, and my costume included a long, brown wig and huge beard, exactly like the one you used to sport."

He laughed at that. "I'll bet you looked awesome."

"Oh, I did, especially when you consider the fact that I didn't hit my growth spurt, such as it was, until eighteen. So at the time, here was this miniscule blond kid, wearing a beard that probably came down to my knees, belting out a rock opera while wearing a patterned bed sheet as a robe."

"That's quite the mental picture," he said with a smile. Then he asked, "Can you actually sing?"

"Yeah. I can act, too."

"Oh, I can imagine, Mr. Bound."

I laughed at that and splashed him. "That's not what I meant, though it did often take considerable talent to pretend I could stand some of my costars. I'm just saying I was pretty good in the high school productions. I was often cast as the lead, despite being so tiny that I was barely visible to the naked eye. Of course, there were only fifty-two kids in my high school, so that wasn't much of an accomplishment. And wow, did you ever steer us off on a huge tangent to avoid talking about your body issues."

"This is way more interesting. So, when you moved to California, did you have dreams of becoming an actor?"

"Oh hell no. If I had, I would have moved to L.A., not San Francisco. But that would have been insane."

"Why?"

"Do you know how many fresh-off-the-turnip-truck, or potato truck, in this case, naïve young boys inundate Hollywood every year? I would have wound up as just another statistic."

"Not necessarily. You're incredibly charismatic, not to mention strikingly handsome. You would have done well, I'm sure of it."

"You're biased. I mean, look at me. I would have been cast as the gay waiter, the gay roommate, or, if I was really lucky, the gay best friend. I think I was better off as James Bound."

"Come here, Mr. Bound," Brian said with a grin, holding his arms out to me, and I snuggled against his chest. He reached for the spigot in the center of the clawfoot tub and turned on the hot water for a few moments, warming us back up, then relaxed with his arms around me.

After a while, I asked, "Is that why you haven't had sex with me? Because you don't want me to see you naked?"

"There are a lot of reasons, starting with the fact that this is a really new relationship, and I don't think sex is something you just rush into. And then, of course, there's my total lack of experience with another guy."

"But you've slept with women before, right?"

"Uh, yeah."

"So, it's no different. Subtract the boobs, add a cock, and there you go."

He chuckled at that. "Have you ever actually slept with a woman?"

"Oh, hell no. I've been gay since I shot out of the womb, screaming *I'm never going back there!*"

Brian burst out laughing, then said, "So, despite your highly scientific explanation, you really have no basis for comparison."

"Well, that's true. But here's all you really need to know about sex with another man." I picked up his hand and rested it on my butt. "Fuck this."

He chuckled and said, "Thanks, Professor Sex Ed, I had actually figured that much out."

Instead of removing his hand, he began to caress my ass, then squeezed it gently and spread me slightly. His other hand slid down my body, and he ran a fingertip between my cheeks, grazing my hole. I gasped, then stretched up and kissed him. As his tongue slipped into my mouth, he kept exploring me, one fingertip lightly circling my rim.

I moaned as my cock snapped to attention, and he pushed a fingertip into me. I parted my legs as far as I could for him in the confines of the tub and kissed him again. When he met with resistance, I figured he'd end his exploration for the day. But instead, he withdrew his hand, ran his fingertips over the bar of soap, and went right back to my opening, his other hand still spreading me open.

His finger slid into me more easily that time, and when he was in about three inches, he whispered, "Is this okay?"

I nodded and said softly, "Do anything you want to me." I rested my head on his shoulder, my arms still around him, and he began to gently fuck my hole with his finger, going just a little deeper with each push until I'd taken him to his knuckles.

"You feel so good," he murmured, rotating his hand slowly and grazing my prostate in the process. I gasped, then reached behind me, taking hold of my right cheek and spreading it for him, just like he was doing with my left, opening myself further, giving him access to me.

"It's surprising," he said softly, "how passive you are in sexual situations. It's so different from the way you usually interact with me."

I raised myself up off his chest and looked in his eyes. "I can be anything you want me to be," I whispered. "If you want me to be more assertive, I can do that. I'll do anything you say."

The look he gave me was surprisingly sympathetic, and he asked, "Is this, right now, who you really are, Hunter, or is it just what you think I want?"

"This is me," I said, breaking eye contact.

Brian's hands left my ass and his arms came up to encircle me. When his lips found mine, the kiss was so sweet, so loving, and I just sank into it. After a while he asked me, "Did you like what I was doing to you?"

"I absolutely loved it. I love being penetrated."

"Do you promise to tell me if I do something you don't like?"

"Yes sir," I said softly, tilting my head down.

He smiled and said, "You would never call me that, not in a million years, if you weren't naked."

"But I *am* naked," I said with a little grin, glancing up at him from beneath my lashes.

He claimed my mouth with another kiss, that one deep and demanding, and my entire body responded. When he ran his fingers over the bar of soap again, I reached down with both hands and spread myself for him, giving him the most intimate part of me.

Brian penetrated me deeply, with first one and then two fingers. He paid close attention to my gasps and moans, using them to zero in on what gave me the most pleasure. His instincts were perfect. He quickly figured out how much stimulation I could take to my prostate, and when to back off and let me catch my breath. When he slid his hand between us and firmly grasped my hard, throbbing cock, I told him, "I'm not going to last long if you do that."

"So don't," he said with a grin as he began to stroke me. I moaned and put my head back on his chest, still holding myself open for him. He became focused on his mission, stroking me and finger fucking me roughly, and God was it good. I moaned and began to ride his hand, thrusting myself onto his fingers, the water sloshing around us.

I muffled my cries against his chest, grasping my butt so tightly I'd probably leave marks, trying to contain my thrusting so I didn't splash the water out of the tub. "Oh fuck yes," I yelled as he banged my ass harder still, twisting his wrist around, sending the most intense pleasure all through me.

It wasn't so much that I came. It was more that he *made me* cum, demanding it of my body, which obeyed him. My yells as I shot my load into the bathwater were wild, inhuman. I couldn't have controlled them even if I'd wanted to, any more than I could have held back that huge orgasm. I just came and came, still riding his fingers feverishly, yells turning to sobs as the intense pleasure overwhelmed me.

When my body finally had nothing more to give and that massive orgasm began to ebb, Brian eased his fingers from me, released my cock, and held me securely. I threw my arms around his shoulders and clung to him, shaking from the aftershocks for what could have been minutes or hours.

Brian reached down and pulled the plug, and the water drained from the tub. He grabbed a big, soft towel from the nearby rack and covered me with it like a blanket, then went right back to holding me. "I love the way you take care of me," I whispered, my voice raspy from yelling. His response was a kiss on the top of my head.

After a while, when my heart rate and breathing had returned to normal and I was no longer shaking, he said softly, "Get yourself dry and tucked into bed, baby. I'll join you in a couple minutes." I did as he said, climbing out of the tub and running the towel over my body. I was exhausted after that huge orgasm and almost on the verge of collapse.

I glanced back at him as I left the bathroom. He was reclining in the empty tub, his soaking wet T-shirt clinging to his broad shoulders, a satisfied grin on his face.

Not surprisingly, I dozed off the moment my head hit the pillow. But I awoke again sometime later, when the futon creaked slightly and Brian snuggled up beside me. He was dressed in a dry T-shirt and sweats, the fabric soft

226

beneath my hands as I slid my arms around him. "Hi," I mumbled.

"Go back to sleep, baby."

"No. Can't. It's too unfair. You made me feel so good, and I need to make you cum, too."

He stroked my damp hair and said, "Not tonight. You need to rest."

I shook my head, trying to push myself up on my elbows. "I can't leave you hanging."

Brian pulled me right back down to his chest, holding me securely as he said, "Don't worry about that. To be honest, I, um, took care of business after you left the bathroom."

I glanced up at him and raised an eyebrow. "You just jerked yourself off?" He nodded, and I frowned at him. "That's my job."

I felt him chuckle more than I heard it, his big chest rumbling beneath me. "Tonight, your job was to relax and forget your troubles."

"You're so good at that," I said as I snuggled against him. "You make me forget all the bad in the world. Everything just falls away, until all that's left is just you and me."

"That's exactly what I was going for." His big hand was rubbing my back, and after a while, it slid down and gently cupped my butt. "Was I too rough with you? I was, wasn't I?"

"There's no such thing as too rough," I murmured.

"But won't you be a bit sore tomorrow?"

"I hope so. Then all day, that deeply satisfying ache will be a wonderful reminder of the greatest bath of all time."

"You know, that didn't start out as my plan. I just intended to bathe you and tuck you into bed. I didn't know it would turn sexual."

"Well, yay to changing plans," I said with a grin, burrowing deeply into his arms, my legs straddling his right thigh.

"I don't know how you're still awake," he said as he returned to rubbing my back. "You looked like you were on the verge of unconsciousness after all of that."

"I had a nap while you were 'taking care of business.' You need a better euphemism for that, by the way."

"You're right."

"Incidentally, it turns out you need no instruction in guy-on-guy sex. That was masterful."

He chuckled and asked, "Was it?"

I tilted my head back and raised an eyebrow as I smiled at him. "Really? Because that cataclysmic orgasm seemed run-of-the-mill to you?"

"You were instructing me the entire time, you know. That's why the end result was so…explosive."

"I was instructing you? Did I black out during that part?"

"You're very vocal," he said, running a thumb over my lower lip. "You told me exactly what you needed and what you liked, with every gasp and moan and little purr."

"I did not purr," I protested.

"Oh, there was definite purring, kitten. And it was sexy as hell."

"Okay, I admit I have no idea what I was saying or doing. I just totally gave myself over to it. Actually, that's pretty embarrassing, now that I think about it. Your brother and my best friend probably heard every moment of that."

"They're adults, they can handle it."

"It doesn't embarrass you?"

"Honestly? I'm kind of glad they heard that."

"Why?"

Brian thought about his answer for a moment, then said, "I'm glad they know I take care of you, and that I make you feel good. They both think I'm a total asshole, and...I don't know. Maybe your cries of pleasure let them know I'm capable of giving, and that maybe I'm not the worst thing in the world for you."

"You're the *best* thing in the world for me."

"Hell no, far from it."

I stretched up and nipped his earlobe, and he let out a surprised bark of laughter. "Did you just bite me?"

"Yup."

"Why?"

"Negative reinforcement. Every time you try to tell me you're bad for me, I'm going to punish you. Eventually, maybe you'll learn to stop doing it."

"Interesting approach," he said with a smile. "There's only one thing wrong with it."

"What's that?"

"It kind of turned me on a little. So, that's actually *positive* reinforcement, and it'll never have the desired effect."

"You don't say." I smiled up at him as I ran my hand slowly down his stomach, stopping when it was wrapped

229

around his thick, partially erect cock through the fabric of his sweats. "Looks like you didn't take care of business as thoroughly as you should have."

"It wasn't enough to counteract snuggling in bed with the fairest of them all."

I laughed at that. "Oh my God! Quit it already."

"But it's so much fun to tease you," he said, flashing me a huge smile. I distracted him by massaging his cock through his clothes, and then I started to tug down his waistband. He caught my wrist and pulled my hand up for a kiss, then said, "Nope. Not going there."

"Do you want me to beg, Brian? Because I will if I have to."

"No, I don't want you to beg. I just need a little more time before I can even think about being naked around you."

I sat up and chewed on my lip for a minute, then said, "I have an idea. Want to hear it?"

"Does it involve me taking my clothes off? In which case, no."

"That's step three. Step one is tying me down, so you're totally in control of the situation. Step two is blindfolding me, so you can get used to being naked around me without any pressure." My hand had returned to his cock, and I felt it jump and swell through his clothing. I smiled at him. "So, you like that idea."

"I'd have to be dead not to find that completely arousing. But would you really feel comfortable with that? I mean, with all you've been going through lately, is now really the time to make yourself so vulnerable?"

230

"I'm safe here, Brian, in this apartment, in this bed, in your arms. Nothing's going to hurt me. You won't let it."

"You're right about that," he said, and kissed me deeply. Then he asked, "So, what do you propose I do with you, once you're tied up and both of us are naked?"

"Anything you want. But you might find it particularly enjoyable to put this," I took his hand and ran his index finger up his big erection, "here." I brought his finger to my mouth and licked it, then put it between my lips and sucked it, slowly, sensually.

"Holy shit," he murmured, his eyes going dark with desire. He sat up and looked around almost frantically. "We're going to need some rope or something."

I kissed him before slipping out of bed. "I've got that covered."

"You do?"

I nodded as I went to the door and confirmed it was locked (mostly for Brian's sake, that really wasn't the time for his brother or anyone else to walk in on us). Then I crossed the room to a chest of drawers near Christopher's easel. My back was to Brian, and I widened my stance before bending over, not at the knees, but at the waist, giving my boyfriend a good view.

He chuckled as I pulled the bottom drawer open and retrieved a little canvas grocery bag. "Subtle," he said.

"Oh yeah. I'm all about subtlety." I crossed the room to him and knelt beside the futon. "And speaking of subtle…." With that, I dumped out the contents of the bag and several sets of handcuffs clattered onto the floor.

"Holy shit, where did those come from?"

"I borrowed them a couple days ago."

"From who?"

I grinned at that. "Let's see, your brother's a cop, and my best friend is a former sex worker. Now who around here would have cuffs to lend me?"

"Oh man. Now they're going to go right back to thinking I'm an asshole."

"Why?"

"They probably think I'm going to get rough with you."

"Just because you tie someone up doesn't mean you're going to get rough with them," I pointed out.

"Do they know that?"

"You don't think those two engage in some light bondage occasionally?"

He laughed embarrassedly and said, "Wow, TMI."

"I mean, I don't *know* that they do. It's not like Christopher Robin discusses the details of his sex life with me. I'm just assuming, because really, doesn't everybody?"

"No, probably not."

"Their loss," I said, handing a set of cuffs to Brian. "So, do you know how to work one of these bad boys?"

"No."

"You don't?"

Brian dropped onto the floor in front of me, swung me onto my back on the area rug, and snapped a cuff onto my wrist, all in the span of about two seconds. Then he rolled his eyes at me. "Of course I do! Kier and I both wanted to be cops all our lives. You think we never practiced on each other with our dad's handcuffs?"

"Kinky," I said with a huge grin as I relaxed and placed both hands over my head. He chuckled and shook his head at that as he threaded the free cuff around the foot of the futon frame, then snapped it onto my other wrist. "I mean, there's no judging here. Did you follow up the cuffing with full-body pat-downs? You did, didn't you? And that's fine, it's not weird at all. I'm sure all brothers do that."

He laughed and said, "I'm so sorry I told you about the cuffs."

"I'm sure it was all perfectly wholesome," I said with a huge smile. "And the nightstick? Did you practice with that, too? I mean, just because it's shaped like a big dildo in no way implies anything."

He laughed again, then picked up a set of keys that were mixed in with the cuffs. They were on a small leather key fob, which he stuck between my teeth as he said, "Here, hold this."

I did as I was told, biting down on the little piece of leather, then said, "Yes sir. Though you're obviously just trying to shut me up." It came out sounding like dental-office-speak, 'shut me up' sounding more like 'ut ee uh.'

"Now, would I do that?"

"Totally." *Oh-ah-ee.*

"Okay, maybe."

"Why are we on the floor?"

"Because there's nothing to fasten you to up there." He indicated the top of the futon with a tilt of his chin, then retrieved a pillow and stuck it under my head. "Comfortable?" he asked, and I nodded.

He swooped in and kissed the tip of my nose, then removed the fob from my mouth before leaning in for a long, deep kiss. He tossed the keys aside, then brushed my

233

hair back from my face and said, "Now all we need is a blindfold. Then we can fully implement your brilliant plan."

"Can't wait," I told him with a big smile.

"So, do we need a safe word or something, since you're about to be totally at my mercy?"

"We're not going deep in the dungeon here," I told him cheerfully. "If you do something I don't like, how about if I just tell you? No point in going all secret password and all that crap."

"Well, you'd know about secret passwords, James Bound," he said with a big grin.

"Damn it! I don't even have any good insults to hurl at you in return, now that you've shaved off the Squatch Beard."

He kissed me again and said, "I'm sure you'll think of something."

"Speaking of thinking of something, there are probably a couple bandanas in Christopher's painting supplies, because he ties his hair back when he's working. They would do the trick."

"They would." Brian crawled across the room to the chest of drawers and returned a few moments later with a faded red bandana in his hand. I raised my head for him and he folded it into a strip and fastened it securely over my eyes, then tied it off at the side of my head.

"Thoughtful," I said as I relaxed against the pillow.

"What is?"

"Not making me lay on the knot. Most Doms don't think of stuff like that."

"Is that what I am, your Dom?"

"Right now you're my Dom, my master," the last two words were said with an English accent. "You're whatever you want to be."

I could hear the smile in his voice. "You just went Downton Abbey on me. What's up with that?"

"Oh no, we're not going Downton Abbey, we're going *downtown alley*," I said with a grin. "But I just can't say that word with a straight face. Every time I try to say it, I start channeling Dracula's Renfield. *Yes, maaahstah!*"

Brian burst out laughing. "You're both weird and fun. It's a great combination."

"Thank you, maaahstah."

"Bordering on certifiable."

"Well, as long as I'm only bordering." I smiled at him from beneath the blindfold.

"You're also so damn sexy that I can barely stand it." He began kissing and licking my earlobe as he took hold of my cock and began to stroke me.

"Danger, Spock!" I said, busting out my best Shatner impersonation. "Must...not...lose sight...of objective. Supposed to be pleasuring...self...not the bound...fucktoy."

Brian chuckled, then shifted around so that he was pressed right against my side. I felt him gently brush the hair back from my forehead as he asked, "Are you nervous, baby? Is that what's behind all this chatter?"

"I'm sorry. I'll shut up."

He pushed the blindfold up onto my forehead and looked into my eyes. "That's not what I said, Hunter. I asked if you were nervous."

"Nah. I mean, me? James Bound? Come on, I can handle this."

"Do you want me to untie you?"

"No!" That sounded desperate. I added softly, "Please don't. It'll just take me a minute or two to get used to it, that's all."

"Are you sure?"

"I'm fine, I promise. Please let me do this for you. As soon as we get hot and heavy, I'll be right there with you, you'll see." He watched me closely for a few moments. A little smile tugged at the corner of his mouth, and he leaned down and kissed me.

He revved me up slowly, first deepening his kisses, then caressing my body as his tongue flickered over mine. He ran his fingertips over my balls before cupping them gently, and I looked up at him and said, "Please don't just make this about my pleasure, Brian."

"I'm not, I'm going to do exactly what we talked about," he said, sliding his finger between my lips. "But it's not just about my pleasure, either. I'm going to make sure we both enjoy this." I sucked on his finger as he continued to stroke my balls, and when the palm of his hand skimmed up my shaft, I let out a soft moan.

He removed his finger and straddled me, rubbing his cock against mine through his clothes. One hand slid behind my head and he stepped up his game, taking my mouth in a forceful kiss. I moaned against his lips as I tried to rock my hips up and press my cock against him.

Wordlessly, he tugged the blindfold over my eyes, then raised himself off of me, but for only a moment. When he returned, the word, "Yes," slipped from my lips, almost a gasp. He'd removed his T-shirt, so we were skin-to-skin for the first time, and the contact was electric. "Oh God, Brian," I mumbled as he licked and kissed his way down my neck.

It felt like he couldn't get enough of me, and that in turn felt utterly, incredibly wonderful. His mouth and hands were all over my naked body, tasting me, exploring me, as my cock throbbed and leaked precum onto my belly. When he pulled off me abruptly, I made a little mewling sound and tugged against my chains, trying to grab him and bring him back to me.

Brian shifted around a bit, and when he climbed back on top of me, I realized he was completely naked. He rubbed his big, swollen cock against mine as his tongue pushed its way into my mouth and I moaned deeply. Next, he planted a row of kisses across my cheek. When he reached my ear, he nibbled and licked the lobe, and then whispered two words to me.

"You're mine."

There was nothing more erotic that he could have possibly said to me. "God yes," I murmured, rubbing my cheek against his because it was the only thing I could do.

"Say it," he whispered, then kissed the little hollow beneath my ear.

"I'm yours, Brian. Only yours."

"I'm yours too, Hunter," he whispered, his voice husky. I writhed underneath him, pulling at my chains, trying to get even closer to him, even though he was right on top of me.

Brian kissed and licked his way down my body, and when his warm, wet mouth surrounded my cock, I cried out. He sucked me greedily, hungrily, and I arched off the floor, pushing myself between his lips. Instead of complaining about that, he just sucked me harder and faster.

"Fuck yes," I ground out.

Brian shifted around above me, and when something brushed my lips, I stuck my tongue out eagerly. I tasted the tip of his cock and lunged up after it, engulfing it with my mouth, sucking him as quickly and desperately as he was sucking me.

Almost in unison, we began thrusting into each other's mouths. We were both totally lost to it, moaning, bucking, sucking like this might be our last chance ever to get off. I didn't know when I'd ever been so totally aroused, every part of me alive with sensation. There was only one thing that could make it better. And when Brian quickly licked his finger, then pushed it into my ass before going back to sucking me, it became total, absolute perfection.

Several minutes later, the first spurt of Brian's hot load filled my mouth. I moaned and kept sucking him, drinking him down, then came in his mouth a few seconds later. He swallowed eagerly, with no hesitation, and murmured, "Mmmm," around my cock, his finger reflexively fucking my hole. We were perfectly in sync, each of us nursing at the cock between our lips, slowing gradually, bringing each other back down, until finally we were both sated.

Brian eased his finger from my body, then went in for one more lick across the tip of my cock. "You taste fucking amazing," he murmured before swinging around and kissing my lips.

"So do you. And that was totally, mind-blowingly wonderful."

After he unchained me, he lifted me up and laid me on the futon. Then he climbed up beside me, stuck a pillow under my head again and pulled the warm blanket over us before clicking off the light. When he pushed the blindfold off my eyes, I grinned at him and asked, "Really? You're letting us sleep naked together?"

"It's dark and we're under the covers. Besides, I'm too damn happy to worry about a thing right now," he said. I could see his deeply satisfied grin in the dim light from a streetlamp that filtered through the curtains.

I cuddled up in his arms, and after a moment, smiled and said, "Would you take it the wrong way if I said you were a natural-born cocksucker?"

He burst out laughing at that. "Yeah? Did I do okay? I was so turned on that I really didn't give much thought to technique, to be honest with you."

"That was spectacular."

"Good to hear. And ditto, obviously. God I came hard. I thought I was going to black out for a minute there."

I grinned at that, then let my eyes slide shut and burrowed a little deeper into his arms. After a few minutes, though, I realized he was wide awake. When I looked up at him, his brows were knit, and he was chewing on his lower lip. "Regrets?" I asked quietly.

He met my gaze. "I thought you were asleep. And God no. Well, except for one." He reached behind him and flipped on the light. "I'm so scared of losing you, Hunter. I want you more than anything. But hiding from you, and living in fear of your rejection…well, that's not fair to either of us." Abruptly, Brian flipped onto his back and pulled the covers off his body. "So...this is me. I know it's not pretty. But the thing is, I'm kind of stuck with it." A solemn resignation settled on his features as he lay perfectly still for me.

I sat up and ran my gaze down the length of him. His torso was a maze of old scars which spoke of a history so violent that my breath caught in my throat. He'd been hurt *so terribly.* I reached out and lightly stroked a huge scar running all the way across his midsection. It was deep and jagged, and looked as if he'd almost been cut in half. "Oh God, Brian," I whispered, looking into his eyes, which were so sad. "You could have died. I could have lost you before I ever even had a chance to know you."

"I used to wish I *had* died," he said quietly. "I felt so ruined."

I couldn't even comprehend what all of that must have felt like, how he could have possibly survived so much trauma, mentally as well as physically. "Did all this happen at the same time? Was it all from the explosion that took your legs?"

"The majority of it."

I ran my gaze down his deeply scarred abdomen, over his unscathed genitals and thighs. His left leg ended just below the knee, and his right ended mid-calf. The amputations were smooth, rounded. Compared to the scars across his body, they actually spoke far less of the terrible violence that Brian had lived through. But then, of course, they were the work of surgeons. The rest was the work of war.

He propped himself up on his elbows. "Not this one, though," he said, pointing to a two-inch scar on his left shoulder. "I got that playing high school football." He looked down at himself, then touched a little circular scar above his left nipple. "And that one's from chicken pox when I was eight." He took another look at himself, then sighed and dropped back onto the pillow. "If you need to run screaming now, there's no fucking way on earth I'll blame you. The door's right over there. God knows I'd run from this shit too if that was somehow an option."

"I'm so sorry this happened to you," I said softly.

"Well, I was the 'lucky one.' Like I said, the two soldiers I was with died instantly. I was also lucky because there was this metal wash basin between me and the bomb. It was up on a little wooden stand, and shielded me from my crotch to my knees. If it wasn't for that, I could have taken advantage of the daily surgery special: free castration with every double amputation." He was staring at the ceiling again, and his voice was flat.

My hand lightly caressed the worst of the scars, running over Brian's midsection again and again as if somehow trying to soothe him. He turned his head to look at me. "You really don't have to pretend you can stomach this," he said, still in that detached tone. "I know this isn't what you signed on for, and I swear I don't blame you for what you must be feeling right now. I should have shown you sooner, before you got attached. That was unfair of me, and I'm sorry I kept this from you as long as I did. I wish you nothing but the best, Hunter. Really." He turned back to the ceiling.

I sighed and said, "Would you quit saying goodbye to me already? Do I look like I'm going anywhere?"

He turned to me with a wary expression. "Aren't you?"

I climbed on top of him, straddling his body, and pulled the blanket over both of us, then said, "If you want to know what I'm feeling, how about asking me, instead of jumping to conclusions?"

He considered that a moment, then said, "Okay. What are you feeling, Hunter?"

"Like I want to find whoever set that bomb and beat the living shit out of him. I'm not disgusted or repulsed. I'm fucking pissed."

His arms came up to embrace me. "I was too, for a long time. That doesn't get you anywhere, though. It just twists up your insides and makes it that much harder to heal." I reached over and turned off the light, then got comfortable against his chest.

After a while, he said, "You're a tougher man than me. The first time I saw my body, it was six weeks after the incident, and I'd just come out of a medically-induced coma. I actually puked. I thought it was the most disgusting thing I'd ever seen."

"It's not disgusting. It just makes me sad, because until I saw your scars, I really didn't know the extent of what you'd gone through. To find out someone I care about had to endure so much pain and suffering is heartbreaking."

He kissed the top of my head. "So...really? You're willing to be with someone who looks like he's been through a meat grinder?"

"Hate to tell you, but you're stuck with me."

"But, you could—"

I sat up quickly and pressed a finger to his lips. "Don't you dare say 'do so much better.' That falls under the heading of insulting my boyfriend, and you know I won't stand for that."

He kissed my finger before I pulled it away and settled back into his arms. After a while, he whispered, "Thank God that bomb didn't kill me, and Thank God I failed when I tried to kill myself. Thank God I somehow managed to stay alive long enough to find you."

"When did you do that?" I whispered, my heart stuttering in my chest at hearing he'd attempted suicide.

"It was during my first year back. I waited until Kieran went out to buy groceries and washed down a bunch of pills with a bottle of booze. Fortunately, I was completely incompetent and swallowed the wrong combination of substances. A few minutes later, it all came right back up. I puked into the toilet for about ten minutes."

"Oh God, Brian."

"It was such a selfish thing to do. As I laid there on the bathroom floor afterwards, I thought about my brother, about how he would have felt finding me, had I succeeded. I'd been too focused on my own misery to think about him beforehand, but once I did, I felt so guilty that I never tried it again. To this day, he doesn't know I did that. No one does, actually."

I clutched him to me fiercely, burying my face in his shoulder. Hearing he'd attempted suicide was more than I could bear, especially on the heels of learning the full extent of his injuries. After a moment he added, in an attempt to lighten the mood, "Though I did survive the bomb and the pills only to ultimately end up squished to death by my boyfriend."

I burst out laughing and crying at the same time, relaxing my hold on him slightly. I kissed him, and then I kissed him again, and again. "Don't you dare do anything like that, *ever again*. Do you hear me?" I told him between kisses.

"I won't, I swear," he said, holding me tight. "I'd never try to kill myself now. Not when I have everything to live for."

Chapter Eleven

We were awakened by insistent knocking the next morning. I sat up groggily, trying to get my bearings, and Brian stirred beside me. "Hunter!" a shrill, familiar voice called. "You in there? It's time to get up. Hell, it's past time to get up! Do you realize it's after ten a.m.? I don't have all day to wait around for you, you know! I'm due at the salon in half an hour!"

I grinned and pulled on the first thing I found, which was a pair of Brian's sweat pants. They were huge on me, but I cinched them up as much as I could with the drawstring, then opened the door to Nana. "Well, it's about time!" she exclaimed. "Hasn't anyone ever told you not to keep old people waiting? I could have been dead and buried by the time you got that door open."

I stuck my head out the door and looked both ways, then said, "I don't see any old people out here, Nana."

She grinned at that and bustled into the room. "Now you're just kissing up to me. But go ahead. You should, after keeping me waiting so long!"

"Good morning, Mrs. Dombruso," Brian said, sitting up in bed with the blanket pulled up to his shoulders.

"Oh," she exclaimed. "Christopher didn't tell me you had company, Hunter. And who is this handsome young man?"

"That's Brian."

"It's nice to meet you, Brian."

"We've met," he said.

"No we haven't. I'd remember a cute boy like you."

To me she said, "I hope I didn't interrupt some lovemaking.

245

Is that what was going on in here? Lovemaking? Is that why you couldn't come to the door right away? You can tell me. I'm not some old prude, you know. I'm fine with gay homosexual lovemaking. Ask anybody. Just make sure you use some of them rubber thingies. Wait, I think I have some." She started to dig around in her giant black handbag, as Brian did his patented cough-to-cover-a-laugh maneuver.

"Why do you have condoms, Nana?" I asked.

"Well, you know my great-grandson, Mikey Junior? He found them in his daddy's nightstand. This was news to me, that Mikey Senior was sexually active again after losing his young wife, God rest her soul." Nana stopped digging long enough to make the sign of the cross, then plunged her hand back in her purse. "Anyway, Mikey Junior, he comes to my house for pancakes the other day, and asks me if I know how to make balloon animals. He'd just been to a birthday party for one of his little school chums, I guess they had a clown. God knows why, they're such horrible things. Anyway, he asks me, 'Can you make balloon animals like that clown did, Nana?' So I said to him, if some creepy and in all likelihood drunk clown could make 'em, I supposed I could, too. I would just need some balloons."

She paused in the story long enough to fish out a huge pair of glasses and shove them onto her face, then peered into the bag. "And that's when he pulls out these." She held up a box of Magnum XXLs, then tossed it onto the bed beside Brian.

"Shouldn't you give those back to Mikey Senior?" I asked with a grin.

246

"Well, I was going to. But then, I can just buy him a new box. If you two are right in the middle of lovemaking, you need these more than he does. And honestly? I don't think he needs them anyway. I don't think he's seeing anyone. I think those are mostly for show, or maybe just in case he gets lucky. Like keeping a flashlight handy in case the power goes out, you know?"

As she was talking, Brian retrieved his shirt from the floor and pulled it on. Then he propped himself up with a pillow, the blanket draped over his bare lower half, and watched Nana with an amused expression. She turned to him and asked, "Are those the right size for you? If not, I guess I'll give them back to Mikey Senior. XXL though, I mean, that's pretty ambitious. I remember Mikey Senior's pecker from when he was a little boy and would run around with a Superman cape and no pants, and I can't imagine that little tootsie roll now requires an XXL rubber thingy."

That was almost too much for Brian. He turned red from the effort of fighting back a laugh, but finally managed, "Maybe it would be best if you gave them back to him."

"Oh," she said with a disappointed expression. "You got a tootsie roll, too?" After staring at him for a moment, she asked Brian, "Why do you look familiar?"

"Like I said, we met," he told her.

"Nah, that's not it. I'd remember. I'm not so old that my memory's going. You on TV or something? You a sports announcer? You look like maybe you play football, same as my grandson-in-law Charlie."

"Brian stayed at your house a few days ago, Nana," I told her. "We both did."

She looked at him again, then said, "Nah. That was some surly boy who looked like that big hairy thing from that movie my great-grandsons like. What was it called again? Oh yeah, Chewbacca. Plus, that fella was in a wheelchair. I kind of wanted to feel sorry for him for being in a chair and all, only he wasn't very nice. Not like this boy. You, I like," she said. Then she added, "Do you do the sports on Channel Seven? That's why you look familiar, isn't it?"

I changed the subject by saying, "Out of curiosity, why'd you come over, Nana?"

"Oh! Well, Christopher called Charlie last night, and then Dante and Charlie called over to my house looking for Vincent. He's downstairs right now, along with a whole team of his best men, installing a top-of-the-line alarm system. They're going to come up here and do the apartment next, so you might want to give back your sportscaster's pants so he can get out of bed. I came along to supervise operations, naturally. And, of course, to visit with you and Christopher Robin." She glanced at her dainty gold wristwatch, then exclaimed, "Holy Moses," and spun on her heel. "I'm going to be late for my hair appointment! I want to look my best for Christopher's big grand opening party tonight. See you in a few hours," she called, with a wave over her shoulder.

"Bye Nana." I followed her to the door and watched as she hurried out of the apartment, then closed and locked the bedroom door again.

When I turned to Brian, he looked at me gravely and said, "She's right, you know."

"About what?"

He held up the box of condoms. "These XXL rubber thingies will never fit on my tootsie roll." We both burst out laughing, and I fell into bed beside him, wiping tears from my eyes.

"God, I love her," I said, once I'd caught my breath.

"I can see why. It's too bad she hates me."

"She doesn't hate you."

"Well, she will once she realizes I'm Chewbacca."

"Aw, if only you were Chewbacca. How cool would that be? It'd be like having a boyfriend and a pet, all in one."

"What? Wookies aren't pets! They're kick-ass warriors."

"And you call me a geek," I said with a wink, rolling out of bed. "I need to find some clothes, you should do the same."

"Found some," he said, catching me around the waist and pulling me to him. He tugged down the sweatpants, then playfully nipped my rear.

"Hey now," I said, dropping onto his lap. "That's not going to get us downstairs."

"Nope. It'll keep us right here for some sweet gay homosexual lovemaking." I laughed at that, and he added, "Gay homosexual? Really?"

"She always calls it that. There's no point in correcting her, I already tried."

We got dressed and went downstairs, and found that the gallery was hopping. A few art students with a Crayon-box of hair colors were arranging and rearranging a cluster of black-and-white photos on one wall, bickering about 'balance' and 'composition.' They were an awesome contrast to the dark-suited mafiosos installing the upgraded alarm system. Since it involved cutting into the walls, the Sopranos were in turn wonderfully offset by a group of flannel-shirted Teamster types who were going around patching the drywall, while still more art students buzzed around, snatching paintings out of harm's way and complaining about the dust.

In the middle of the room, Kieran and Vincent were engaged in a deep discussion. Vincent was holding a little white control panel, gesturing at it with his long, graceful fingers. Brian joined them, and then Vincent glanced up and saw me. He barely reacted, just a little emotion flaring in his dark eyes, which he quickly pushed away.

He rejoined the conversation, and I watched him for just a little longer. He was such a beautiful man, and such a tortured soul. Whatever secrets churned in the depths of those dark eyes wouldn't be mine to uncover, though.

And thank God he'd pushed me away, because if he hadn't, I'd never have gotten involved with Brian. My boyfriend glanced over his shoulder at me, and gave me a playful wink and a smile. I beamed at him and blew him a kiss, then went off to find my best friend.

Christopher was out in front of the building. He and Charlie were standing side-by-side with identical poses and skeptical expressions, arms crossed over their chests, right hips slightly jutting out. "What are we looking at?" I asked, turning to face the building and assuming the same position the two of them were in. I tilted my head up like theirs were and said, "Ah."

"He's going to fall and crack his skull," Charlie said.

"Most definitely," Christopher agreed.

Charlie's husband Dante was hanging out of a second-story window, so far that it was surprising he hadn't already fallen. He was holding a pair of long-handled salad tongs, which in turn grasped a dripping wad of paper towels, and was trying to use it to scrub at something in the very front and center of the building. He kept coming up about two inches short.

"What's he doing?" I asked.

"He's trying to wash away some bird shit," Charlie explained.

"Ah. Why, exactly?"

"Because he takes his job as my landlord really seriously," Christopher said. "He noticed that huge seagull present and said it would never do, not with my gallery opening tonight. The hose wouldn't reach around the front of the building, and the stepladder was too short, so Landlord-of-the-Year Dombruso decided to approach it from above."

"He should have tried water balloons," I said. Then I yelled up to Dante, "You should have tried water balloons!"

"That's actually a good idea," Dante called down. "But I don't have any."

"I do," I called back. "Okay, technically, they're XXL condoms, but they'd do the trick. Your grandmother just gave them to me."

Dante started laughing, and dropped back inside the window, then stuck just his head out and asked, "Seriously?"

"Seriously!"

"Why did she do that?"

"I'm not sure, it was a long story. Something to do with tootsie rolls." I flashed him a big smile.

"Good lord," Dante muttered. Then he called, "I'm coming down. The salad tongs aren't working."

"Grab the giant condoms! They're on the futon in Christopher's studio!"

He joined us a minute later, box of prophylactics in hand, and asked, "Did Nana really give these to you?"

"She did indeed."

That obviously stirred up about fifty more questions, but after a beat, he just said, "Alright," and let it drop. He plucked a wrapped condom from the box and said, "You know, trying to wash off that bird crap with water balloons could actually work. But aren't condoms made specifically *not* to break?"

"Yeah, but they're also not made to hold a gallon of semen. And man, can you imagine such a thing? You'd have to have bowling balls between your legs. Anyway, get enough water in there, and I guarantee it'll rupture like a fat man's waistband on Thanksgiving." I gave him another big smile, and he chuckled at me.

"You're very jolly today, Hunter," Dante said.

"That's because he got some last night," Christopher said with a grin. "A lot of some, by the sound of it."

"Oh jeez. You heard everything, didn't you?" I asked.

"Nope, just the first moans of toe-curling ecstasy," he teased. "After that, Kier and I both put in these industrial-grade earplugs that he uses at the shooting range. They worked like a charm."

"Really? You didn't hear anything after that?"

"Well, okay, occasionally there might have been an orgasmic outburst that exceeded the earplugs' decibel rating." His grin got even bigger.

"I'm sorry for being such a pain. I really need to suck it up and move back to my apartment."

"No you don't," Christopher said. "And you really weren't that loud. Believe me, I've heard louder. Much, *much* louder." He shot a pointed look at Dante and Charlie, his former roommates, both of whom looked away quickly.

"Aw, how cute are you two?" I said, then took the condom from Dante's fingers, unwrapped and unrolled it. "You know, these don't really look much bigger than regular condoms. I bet they just print XXL on the boxes to make guys with tootsie rolls feel better about themselves."

"We should make a wager," Charlie suggested. "First one of us to actually hit the bird poop with a condom water balloon should win some sort of prize."

"Not so fast, Sporty Spice," I said. "Not all of us are jocktastic former football players like you, you know. To make it fair, you'd need some kind of handicap."

"I was a tight end, not a quarterback," Charlie protested. "I don't throw that well."

"Tight end," I camped. "Mmm mm mmm. God bless America and the game of football."

"We're not really going to do this, are we?" Dante asked. "Because there are a lot of people out here, and I for one could happily live my life without ending up on the internet in a viral condom-chucking video."

We all considered that for a beat, and then I said, "Okay, good point," and stuck the rubber in my pocket. "The bird shit lives to see another day!"

A few hours later, the grand opening prep was still frenzied. Brian turned to me and said, "Damn, you know what? I almost forgot that I have a therapy appointment in half an hour."

"That's okay. You have plenty of time to make it," I said.

"Yeah, but I need to accompany you to Jamie's bar, and I can't be in both places at once."

"Why?"

"Because I'm your alleged bodyguard."

"But why do we need to go to Jamie's bar?"

"You told that cute Trevor kid you'd meet him when he got off work."

"Oh hell, I'd forgotten all about that."

"I can go with you," Kieran chimed in. He was stretching his back a few feet away, arms up over his head. "I need to swing by Jamie's place anyway, because he's loaning us some chafing dishes for tonight."

"What the hell's a chafing dish?" Brian asked.

"Well obviously," Kieran told him, "it's a *dish* that *chafes*."

Brian chuckled at that. "You don't know either, do you?"

"No clue. Christopher said we needed them for the buffet, that's all I know."

"I thought a professional caterer was handling all the food for tonight's event," I said.

"Caterer, yes. Professional, not so much," Kieran explained. "Christopher hired the brother of one of his classmates, who's just starting out in the business. This is his first big job, and the guy's so excited." That sounded exactly like something my benevolent best friend would do.

A few minutes later, as Kieran drove me in his beat-up vintage Mustang (a restoration project in progress) I asked, "How's your back?"

"It's a lot better, it just stiffens up occasionally. Thanks for asking."

"*De nada.*"

We pulled up to a red light, and he glanced over at me. "So, you and Brian, huh? I would never have predicted that, not in a million years."

"Me neither when I first met him," I said with a big smile. He glanced at me again, and looked away, and I told him, "If there's something you want to say to me, don't hold back."

"I'm trying to figure out how to say it without sounding like an asshole."

"Let me take a guess at what you're about to say." I pivoted around to face him as much as the seatbelt would allow. "You're worried that I'm kind of a slut, and that Brian's just my flavor of the moment, right? You think I might get sick of him thirty seconds from now and dump his ass for the next pretty face that comes along. You're concerned about what that'll do to him, that he'll not only revert back to how he was, but he'll be ten times worse. How am I doing?"

"I wasn't going to call you a slut," he said embarrassedly as he rolled forward on the green light.

"I don't blame you for being concerned, Kieran. All you've ever seen from me is promiscuity. But this thing with your brother is different. It's something more."

"I'm glad." After a pause, he said, "You do understand what you're getting yourself into, though. Right? I mean, he's really happy right now, happier than he's been in years, and that's because of you. But underneath, he's still so damaged. He's been suffering from PTSD, depression, night terrors, trying to deal with memories too horrible to imagine, and that stuff doesn't just go away."

"I know."

"I'm not telling you all this to scare you away, Hunter. I just know better than anyone what you're taking on, and how overwhelming it can be. So, I guess what I'm saying is, let me be your support system, because you're going to need one. If you ever need to talk, or vent, or yell for a while, just know that I'm here for you. Okay?"

I reached out and squeezed his shoulder affectionately. "Thanks, Kieran. I really appreciate it."

"You know," he said after a while, "you're kind of a miracle worker. I tried for two solid years to get him back into therapy, and you got him to go in a matter of days."

"No I didn't. Brian did that on his own, he wants to get better."

Kieran glanced at me. "Wow, really?" I nodded, and he said, "He must be falling for you so damn hard. I mean, for him to proactively make changes like this, do you know how huge that is?"

"Yeah, I do."

We pulled up in the alley behind Nolan's, Jamie's bar and grill, and as we got out of the car, Kieran said, "Don't

256

forget what I told you. Just think of me as your 24/7 pressure valve, ready to lend an ear or a shoulder at a moment's notice."

I came around the car and gave him a hug. "That's really nice of you."

"Well, you mean the world to my fiancé, and now you're dating my brother. In my book, that makes you family, Hunter."

I smiled at him as we entered the building through the delivery door. "That's good to hear. It's been a while since I had one of those."

Once inside, we went in opposite directions, and he said, "I'll be in my cousin's office. Come find me when you're ready to leave."

"Will do. And thanks, both for the stand-in bodyguard duty and for everything else, Kier."

He grinned and gave me a friendly wink. "*De nada.*"

The lunch rush at Nolan's had been and gone, and the dining room was mostly empty. A couple lingered at a booth in the corner, and Trevor was working diligently, scrubbing down tabletops. I took a seat at the bar and ordered a coffee while I watched him.

He was obviously lost in thought. His expression was troubled, and there was a little crease between his dark brows. When he finally noticed me, it startled him so much that he knocked the salt and pepper shakers off the table he'd been cleaning. They rolled in opposite directions, and he lunged after them. By the time he returned them to the tabletop, Trevor was blushing furiously.

Finally, he hurried to where I was sitting. "I'm so sorry, I didn't see you come in," he said. "I didn't mean to keep you waiting."

"It's fine, go ahead and finish your shift."

"Oh. Um, it actually ended fifteen minutes ago. I was just tidying up a little."

Trevor stood there awkwardly, shifting from foot to foot, and I put some money on the counter and picked up my coffee. "Come on," I said, sliding off the barstool. "Let's go sit at a booth, so we can talk."

He followed me across the dining room and slid into a booth across from me, fidgeting nervously. "I didn't know how to get a hold of you," he blurted. "Jamie wouldn't give me your address, he said something about you having a need for security. Then I saw you were making that public appearance, only I got there too late…anyway, what I'm trying to say is, I'm really sorry for making you come all the way down here. I really didn't want to inconvenience you, Hunter."

"You didn't."

"Okay. Good." He hesitated, then reached out and took one of my hands, which had been resting on the table top. He turned it over and put something in my palm, then closed my fingers around it. "I can't accept this," he said quietly. I opened my hand to reveal a little bundle of twenties. They were still folded into the neat rectangle I'd made before slipping them in his pocket at Jamie's brunch.

"What makes you think I gave this to you?" I asked, trying to play it off.

"You did. After I found the money, I remembered the way you'd put your hand on my hip when we were at the buffet. At first," he said, looking down at the tabletop, "I thought you'd touched me like that because you were flirting with me. I guess I hoped that was the case, because I liked you, too. I mean, I *like* you. Not past tense. Anyway, then I found the money, and I was confused." He looked up at me from beneath his overgrown dark bangs. "Why did you do that? Why did you slip eighty dollars in my pocket?"

"Because I thought you could use it."

"But...why?"

"Please don't be embarrassed, but I saw you put some cookies in your pocket, so I figured money must be kind of tight for you. And, I don't know. I guess there's something about you that makes me want to take care of you, Trevor."

"*Oh.*" He looked absolutely mortified. "I just...I mean, they were for someone else, and...oh God, I'm so embarrassed that you saw that. What must you think of me?"

"I think you're a sweet guy who's trying to survive in a big, unforgiving, really expensive city. You think I never snuck seconds at a buffet? Hell, when Cole and I first moved to San Francisco, we used to take zip-top bags to this all-you-can-eat Chinese restaurant over on Kearny. We'd go home with pockets full of eggrolls. My point is, you do what you have to do to get by sometimes."

He grinned a little. "You didn't really do that, did you?"

"We sure as hell did, and got away with it twice. Our mistake was going back a third time. By then, they were on to us, and caught us in the act. Talk about embarrassing. To this day, both Cole and I are banned from Fu Wong's

Golden Delights Palace. Which is really a shame, because those eggrolls were freaking amazing."

"Well, I could go get you some." He was smiling now.

"Just don't forget the zip-top bags, that's key," I said, which made him laugh.

"You're so nice," he said. "I was surprised when I found out you're a big celebrity. Usually, you don't expect celebrities to be so kind."

"I'm not a celebrity in any real sense of the word. I'm just some guy that makes dirty movies."

"You're way more than that. They showed your public appearance on the news, and the line was down the block. They said you were raising money for charity. Which, again, shows you're a nice guy."

"Oh. Well, to be honest, the charity part of that was kind of an afterthought. That event was meant to serve another purpose. Only, the guy the police were trying to catch slipped right through everyone's fingers." I frowned and took a sip of coffee.

"Is someone trying to hurt you? Jamie alluded to something like that when he wouldn't give me your address."

"I have a stalker, and he's a complete psychopath. He hurt one of my friends, almost killed him, and might have hurt some other people, too. The police can't seem to find this guy, so I really hoped they'd catch him at that public appearance."

"Is there anything I can do to help?"

"Only if you have a bloodhound in your pocket."

"No. Just cookies." I looked up at him, and he smiled at me.

I smiled too and said, "Oh yeah. I definitely like you, Trevor."

He sat up a little straighter and seemed to gather his courage. Then he blurted, "In that case, would you go out with me?" His confidence waned as quickly as it had appeared, and he tacked on, "I mean, I know it's a total long-shot, but if I didn't ask, I'd never forgive myself."

I reached across the table and gave his hand a friendly squeeze. "I totally thought about asking you out when I met you, but since then, I've started seeing someone. Thank you for asking, though."

"I had to try."

I sat back and picked up my coffee again. "I have a counteroffer for you: let's be friends, Trevor. You're someone I'd really like to get to know."

He grinned at me. "I'd love that."

"So, judging by the fact that you just asked me out, I take it you and Cole are no longer an item."

"We never were. We just had that one date, and after he blew up at you in front of me...well, I guess he felt embarrassed. It was really awkward between us after that, and he never asked me out again."

"You should ask him out. Cole's a wonderful person, and you shouldn't judge him by that one incident. He's just really angry at me, and rightfully so."

"No," a voice nearby said. "Not rightfully so." I looked up at Cole, who stood a few feet away.

"I didn't think you'd be here," I told him.

"I'm not scheduled to work, but it's payday," he said, holding up the envelope in his hand. "Just came by for my check."

"This isn't what it looks like," I said, pointing back and forth between Trevor and me.

"I know. I overheard some of that. Sorry about eavesdropping." Cole took a couple steps forward, then stopped again, adjusting and readjusting his glasses. I knew that gesture so well. "Hunter," he asked, "are you okay?"

"Yeah. Why?"

"Because a police officer came to talk to me a few days ago, the same one who's back there talking to Jamie right now, actually. He said you have a stalker, and wanted to know if I had an alibi for when your apartment was broken into."

"I'm so sorry about that, Cole. I told him you didn't have anything to do with it."

"I can see why you'd suspect me. I've been angry for far too long," he said, fidgeting with the envelope in his hands.

"I really didn't suspect you. Kieran just wanted to be thorough," I said. "He's Jamie's cousin, by the way, and my best friend's fiancé, and he just wanted to talk to you informally. I'm so sorry he put you on the spot."

"It's okay. Really. I'm just…I'm sorry about what you're going through. It sounds scary."

"It is, but my friends are helping me through it."

"This person, he's threatened you?"

"Yeah. He says he's coming for me," I said.

"Oh God," Trevor murmured.

"I really am sorry. I would never wish that on anyone," Cole said.

"Not even your worst enemy?" I asked with a little half-smile.

"You're not my worst enemy, Hunter. You're just...."

"The guy who broke your heart," I said softly, sliding out of the booth and coming to stand right in front of my ex-boyfriend. "I know the words don't make it better or excuse what I did, but I'm *so sorry*, Cole. I know I hurt you terribly, and I'll never forgive myself for that."

His dark eyes were bright with unshed tears as he glanced at me, then quickly looked away. "Okay," he said quietly.

"Okay?"

"I accept your apology. And I'm sorry too, for all the horrible things I've thought about you over the last two years." He still couldn't look at me.

"I deserved it," I said.

"No you didn't."

"Sure I did."

He grinned, just a little. "Okay, you deserved *some* of it."

"Why the change of heart?" I asked him. "Why are you suddenly willing to forgive me?"

"It's not sudden, it's been two years in the making. Frankly, carrying all this hurt and anger around hasn't been doing me any favors."

"Still, though, just a few days ago, you were ready to beat me up."

"Well, here's the thing. After that cop came and spoke to me...okay, at first I was pissed. I was really insulted that you'd sent a police officer to question me, that you thought so little of me and would suspect me of something like that," he said. "But then, once I calmed down, I was just worried that you were in danger, and that's when I realized

I still care about you. I mean, yeah, I'm still angry and hurt, too. But I care about what happens to you, Hunter."

"I care about you too, Cole. I always have."

He grinned a little. "See, now my first impulse was to snap at you and say you have a weird way of showing it."

"You know why I ended it though, right? I couldn't go on fighting with you about absolutely everything."

"That's where we're different," Cole said. "I would have gladly kept fighting with you until we were two little old men in a nursing home, throwing our false teeth at each other." I chuckled at that, and he gave me a half-grin.

He grew serious and added, "The thing is, I grew up watching my mom and dad fight. They'd have these epic confrontations. We used to buy all our dishes at the thrift shop, because they never lasted more than a month. They'd just get all smashed up, and then we'd buy new ones. But despite all of that constant fighting, my parents loved each other more than anything. When my dad died in a car accident, my mom was *devastated.* She never fully recovered. So, I don't know. Maybe to me, that's what love is. It's screaming and yelling and breaking things, getting everything off your chest every day, and then curling up together every night and saying you're sorry, and knowing that no matter what, you still love each other."

"You never mentioned your dad," I said quietly. "Not in all the time you and I were together."

"I know. It's taken me a long time to come to grips with my relationship with him. He died suddenly, when I was twelve, and there was so much left unresolved. Anyway, I guess it's kind of a work in progress, like letting go of you."

We stood there awkwardly for a moment, and then I smiled at him and said, "Brace yourself. I'm going in for a hug."

Cole stiffened when I put my arms around him, but after a few moments he relaxed a bit and his hands came up to my waist. I said, "I know I'll always just be the asshole who dumped you, and I really don't deserve your friendship. But if you ever think to yourself, 'hey, I need more assholes in my social circle,' I'd love it if we could be friends."

He smiled a little as he let go of me and stepped back. "Baby steps, Hunter. This is the first time I've been able to be in the same room as you without wanting to throttle you."

I flung my arms out to the sides and said, "If it'll make you feel better, go ahead. I don't know what throttling involves, exactly, but I'm sure I have it coming."

Cole chuckled and lightly slapped my stomach with the back of his hand, which made me quickly retract my arms. Then he smiled at me, but I could tell he was withdrawing, closing himself off. He'd said a lot, more than he'd probably intended, and I could practically see him pulling his usual protective armor back into place.

He tried to sound cheerful as he said, "Still such a drama queen. So, look, I'm gonna go, before you and I find something to fight about. I'll see you around, Hunter." To Trevor he said, "See you at work tomorrow." Then he turned and left the dining room.

I called after him, "Don't forget: 1-800-A-S-S-H-O-L-E. No social circle is complete without one!" He gave a little wave as he disappeared through the kitchen door.

When I dropped back into the booth across from Trevor, I said, "That went well. But I'm sorry that we keep having these big, dramatic encounters with you as our audience."

"That's fine. It was nice to see you two doing something other than screaming at each other."

"This was pretty unprecedented. Screaming is much more our style."

"And that's why you broke up with him?"

"Yeah. Even though we loved each other, we were like gasoline and matches. All that constant fighting just really took its toll on me."

"I get it," Trevor said.

Just then, Kieran poked his head into the dining room. "You about ready to head out, Hunter? I want to get back and make sure Christopher's not completely running himself ragged."

I nodded at him, and he ducked back out the swinging door. To Trevor I said, "So, my best friend is having a grand opening celebration tonight at his art gallery." I pulled one of Christopher's new business cards from my pocket and slid it across the table. "Here's the address, you should come by. There'll be a buffet. Lots of cookies." I flashed him a huge smile, and he burst out laughing.

"Thanks, both for the invitation and for making light of that. I was pretty mortified, but you've made me feel better about it." We slid out of the booth, and Trevor walked with me to the back of the building.

"Life's too short to be embarrassed. Tell me you'll come tonight."

"I'll be there. I just have to run by the market first and pick up some zip-top bags." He grinned at me happily. His whole demeanor had changed over the course of the conversation as he became more comfortable with me, his body realigning as he stood a little straighter. I loved seeing him come out of his shell a bit.

I chuckled and said, "That's the spirit."

Chapter Twelve

The next several hours were total chaos, due in part to the impromptu demolition, installation and reconstruction brought about by the new and improved alarm system. I spent much of the afternoon on a ladder, pointing a blow dryer at wet plaster, so that Christopher could then come along and paint it. Meanwhile, Brian was upstairs in the kitchen assisting River, the surfer-turned-caterer who was in way, *way* over his head.

When Brian and I finally had a moment alone, I dropped onto his lap and said, "Hi stranger," then kissed him deeply.

"Hi baby." He wrapped his arms around me and hugged me like we hadn't seen each other in weeks. "How did your meeting with Trevor go?"

"Good. I invited him to come to the grand opening tonight. Still feeling needlessly jealous?"

"Nah. I've come to the realization that if I get bent out of shape every time someone's attracted to you, I'm going to be spending a hell of a lot of time that way. For example, that Vincent guy has a huge crush on you, but I'm not getting jealous. Instead, I'm thinking, well, who can blame him?"

"How do you know that Vincent has a crush on me?"

"It's so obvious. For one thing, just look at all he's doing with this security system. That's not for Christopher, it's for you because you're staying here. He put a bunch of other security measures in place, too, stuff I never would have thought of, all in the interest of keeping you safe."

"Like what?"

"I'll give you the run-down tonight, after this shindig. It's quite a list, all fueled by some kind of deep, unrequited desire."

I kissed him again and said, "Unrequited being the key word. You know he's not what I want. You are."

Brian smiled at me. "I'll try to keep my gloating to a minimum."

"Come on," I said, sliding off his lap. "Break time's over. Let's rejoin the frenzy."

"Okay, as long as you promise me one thing," he said, holding my hand.

"Anything."

"I'm dying for some one-on-one time with you. Can we go away this weekend? I don't care where. Any old hotel will do, just as long as it has room service and excellent sound-proofing."

I laughed at that and took his face in my hands. "It sounds like you're planning to make me scream again."

"Oh, I hope so, this time without worrying about my brother the cop breaking the door down and trying to come to our rescue."

I chuckled at that. "I think Kieran knows better."

"He does. But you know what I mean. I just want to spend forty-eight hours in bed with you with no interruptions, no worries, nothing but the two of us."

"That sounds heavenly. Let's leave first thing in the morning," I said.

"I was thinking we should leave tonight, after the grand opening."

"Okay. But only after we help with clean-up."

Brian grinned at that. "You're a good friend. I hope Christopher appreciates you."

"Oh, I do," Christopher chimed in, cutting through the little hallway we were in, boxes in hand. On the way by, he planted a kiss on my cheek, then said, "And you don't have to help with clean-up. You've already done so much, and I'm really grateful to both of you."

"We're helping anyway," I called after him as he continued down the hallway. To Brian I said, "This wraps up at ten, we can probably be on the road by eleven. It's not like we need to pack much. Just our toothbrushes and some handcuffs." I flashed him a big smile.

"And a really big box of condoms," Brian added, a mischievous sparkle in his eye.

My smile got even bigger. "Oh? You think we might be doing something that involves those, do you?"

"I think," Brian said, taking both my hands, "that I need to be inside you about as much as I need to breathe. I know I said I wanted to take this slowly, but I feel so comfortable with you that I'm revising my opinion. I don't need more time to get used to this, and us. I just need to be with you, in every sense of the word."

"Why wait? We can sneak upstairs right now."

He shook his head. "I don't want our first time to be rushed."

"Alright. Forty-eight hour sex it is, then."

"Come on," he said, turning and heading for the gallery, still holding my hand. "Let's go join your friends before I change my mind and take you right here in this hallway."

I followed him with a huge smile on my face.

*****

The grand opening was wildly successful. Christopher's debut art show several weeks earlier had been a smash-hit, generating a huge amount of buzz and publicity, and hundreds of people turned out for the gallery opening, even though he himself only had a couple paintings on display. Most of the wall space was taken up with the work of promising up-and-coming local artists and students from his art college. That was so like him, making sure the spotlight that had landed on him spilled over onto others as well.

The security team Vincent had brought along was efficient and professional. They set up an organized line and allowed only so many people into the little gallery at once. Their careful crowd control all went to hell though, when a white stretch limo pulled up out front and Nana and her entourage stormed the building.

The huge, meaty guy at the door must not have been a Dombruso, because he didn't recognize Nana and tried to direct her to the back of the line. Big mistake. She whacked him in the nuts with her giant black purse, and then she and her friends marched into the building while he dropped to his knees.

"Christopher Robin," she exclaimed, elbowing her way through the crowd. She stepped right in front of a reporter from the Chronicle and grabbed my friend in a crushing hug. "There's my favorite artist! Christopher, meet the girls. Girls, this is Christopher Robin Andrews. Remember that name. He's gonna be real famous, and you'll get to say

271

you knew him back at the beginning." The 'girls' were six tiny Nana clones, all with white hair, lots of jewelry, and giant designer handbags.

"And that," she said, pointing, "is his gorgeous hunk of a fiancé, Kieran. He's a cop, but we won't hold that against him. These two are getting married, but they refuse to set a date."

"I told you, Nana," Christopher said. "We wanted to wait until the gallery was up and running before we focused on the wedding."

"So, now it is, and I'm thinking the Fourth of July! Just imagine the fireworks! I got connections in Hong Kong, I can get the kind that ain't exactly legal, but they put on one humdinger of a show, lemme tell you." To her friends she said, "I already helped plan one gay homosexual wedding for my grandson Dante and his lovely husband Charlie. It was a winter theme. Just think what I can do with summer!"

"Actually," Kieran said, turning to look at Christopher, "a Fourth of July wedding might be fun. What do you think?"

"I've always loved fireworks," Christopher replied with a smile, and Kieran drew him into a hug.

"No illegal ones, though," Kieran told Nana over the top of his fiancé's head.

"See what I mean about him being a cop?" Nana told her friends. "Sucks the fun out of everything. I can forgive him though, because he makes my sweet Christopher so happy."

"The Fourth of July is in just over two months, Nana," Christopher said. "Won't it be tough to pull a wedding together that fast?"

"It would be for some people," she said with a dismissive wave of her hand. "But not for me." She spotted me then. I was a few feet away, working the bar for River, the novice caterer. "Hunter!" she yelled across the room. "What the hell you doing behind the bar?" To her friends she said, "Girls, that's Hunter Storm. He's famous. He makes that, you know, adult entertainment. Real racy stuff, from what I hear. Isn't he a handsome one?"

Then she yelled to me, "I hope you and that sexy brunet made good use of them rubber thingies I gave you, Hunter! I bought my grandson Mikey Senior a new box of rubbers and dropped it off at his house on the way here. Not XXL ones, because come on, who's he trying to impress? I just got him the regular kind, because I figure, you don't go from tootsie rolls to *grande salami*. Am I right?"

"You're right, Nana," I called with a smile.

"So what you got to drink? I'm parched over here!"

"There's beer, wine, and champagne," I called back.

"You should have said champagne first. I mean, who gives a shit about beer and wine when you got the bubbly?"

"Good point," I said as I began filling glasses for Nana and her friends.

River appeared beside me, looking completely flustered and carrying a big tray of stuffed mushrooms. I pulled an empty tray off the table so he had someplace to put them, and asked him as I went back to pouring champagne, "How are you holding up?"

"Dude, I'm minutes from a total nervous breakdown. Why did I think I could be a caterer? I'm not cut out for this." River's speech was an odd combination of southern drawl and California surfer. His appearance was disjointed, too. He was really tan, with long, sun-streaked brown hair pulled back in a messy ponytail, and he was wearing a stiff new chef's jacket along with board shorts and really beat-up Birkenstocks.

"Yes you are, your food's amazing. And now you know for next time: hire a wait staff."

"I tried to, but I made the mistake of hiring mah friends. They're a bunch of flakes, not one of 'em showed up."

A voice behind me asked, "Are you short on waiters? Because I'd be happy to help out."

I turned and flashed Trevor a huge smile. "You're an angel, you know that?" I introduced the two by saying, "River, this is Trevor. Trevor, River the caterer. He's trying to do this whole thing single-handedly."

"Oh no," Christopher said, coming over to the table and trying to get behind it. "It's bad enough that you're working, Hunter. I'm not going to put your friends to work, too. Just let me back there and I'll man the refreshments."

I held Christopher back by the shoulders and said, "Don't make me tell you again, Andrews. You're not pouring drinks at your grand opening. I'm just not going to let you!" I spun him around and tried to propel him back into the crowd. "Now go mingle. Or else!"

"This is all my fault," River said. "I'm so sorry, Christopher. Just so you know, I'm not cashing your check. This has been such a fiasco." He slumped against the wall in defeat, looking flushed beneath his tan, and stuck a stray lock of hair behind his ear.

"I'm happy to help," Trevor said. "I'll take some food out into the gallery, so you won't keep getting a bottleneck in front of the table." He pushed up his sleeves and quickly loaded an empty tray with little plates of appetizers, then hoisted it onto his shoulder and worked his way into the crowd. Even as shy as he was, Trevor was clearly the kind of person who'd always help out in a pinch.

"Wow," River said, watching my new friend maneuvering through the gallery. "That guy's awesome. Cute, too." His gaze lingered on Trevor another moment, before Nana seized his arm and yanked him out from behind the buffet table.

"Hi, cutie," she said to him, taking off her Chanel suit jacket and putting it and her purse under the table. "So, you're short-handed, ay? I overheard the whole thing. Don't you worry, me and the girls, we'll help you out. I owned a restaurant for years, I know all about pleasing a crowd. Now let's see if you can actually cook." She popped a stuffed mushroom in her mouth and chewed thoughtfully, then proclaimed, "Wonderful! You have the gift, Sonny. I would've added a hint more parmesan, but that's just me. Now you go do what you have to do in the kitchen, I got this."

Her girlfriends all went to work too, grabbing bottles from behind the makeshift bar. I was about to protest, but then they fanned out like a team of synchronized swimmers and began refilling glasses. "You're a miracle worker, Nana," I said.

"I know. Go take a break, sweetums, you look like you could use one." Someone started to reach for an appetizer, and Nana slapped his hand and told him, "Where are your manners? If you want something, ask nicely."

"Yes, ma'am," the man replied meekly. I recognized him as the arrogant big time art critic Christopher had been speaking with earlier. I was grinning ear-to-ear as I went off to find Brian.

*****

At the end of the night, right after the last stragglers had cleared out, we collapsed in the center of the gallery. Christopher was flat on his back, shoes off, head on Kieran's thigh. His fiancé was also on his back, and I was curled up nearby, on Brian's lap. Nana and her gang had departed a few minutes earlier, as had the security team. The night had gone off without a hitch.

"River, stop working!" Christopher called. "Come and sit down, the dishes can wait. You did an amazing job, by the way. Everyone raved about the food."

The caterer paused for a moment, balancing a big tray of dirty glasses. "They did?"

"Yup. And you damn well better cash that check I gave you, because you earned every penny. Three people asked for your number, by the way, and I gave it to them. Expect more work coming your way soon."

"The only way I'd ever take another catering job is if Trevor helps me again," River said. "I would have run screaming from the building about two hours ago, if it wasn't for him." He called to Trevor across the room, saying, "I'm payin' you for tonight, by the way, the full amount I was going to split between my three useless friends who didn't show up."

Trevor glanced up from the big stack of plates he was balancing on a tray and gave River a smile. "Well, if you insist."

As the two of them headed upstairs to the kitchen, I hopped off Brian's lap and found an unopened bottle of champagne, jettisoned the cork and brought my friends some glasses. "Let's drink to the most successful gallery launch in the history of western civilization." After I poured the drinks, I set the bottle on the floor beside Christopher and raised my glass in a toast.

"Not quite," Christopher said with a grin as he rolled onto his side and propped his head up with his hand.

"But pretty damn successful, though," I said.

"All of you had a hand in it, and I'm so grateful for your help," he replied, raising the glass I'd handed him.

There was a loud popping sound all of a sudden, and the champagne bottle suddenly exploded into a million pieces. My heart leapt in my chest as I dropped my glass and looked all around the room. It was strange how everything slowed down, how it seemed to take such a long time to realize someone had come into the gallery.

And that he'd opened fire.

Chapter Thirteen

Kieran was the first to react, throwing himself on top of Christopher, acting as a human shield. Brian went for the gun he'd been carrying in the small of his back, but the next bullet hit him and he lurched forward onto the floor, the chair rolling away from him. He wasn't moving. I screamed his name and lunged for him, but someone grabbed me from behind, hoisting me up off my feet.

I struggled wildly, then felt a sharp stinging sensation in my neck. A moment later, a big hypodermic needle fell onto the concrete floor with a clatter. As all of that was happening, Trevor ran down the stairs, yelling, "What's going on? Is everyone okay?"

As I screamed at Trevor to get back, the assailant raised his arm and tried to fire at him. I pulled and clawed at the arm holding the weapon, and the shot went off in some random direction. Trevor ducked down on the stairs, and then River appeared above him and dragged him back up, out of sight.

My vision was becoming blurry, my entire body giving out at once, going slack, my mind a jumble of confusion as whatever I'd been injected with took effect. I tried to fight it, tried to stay conscious. *Brian,* I thought, right before I sank into blackness, trying and failing to focus on his sprawled body on the floor. *Brian, please be alive.*

*****

I came awake slowly. It felt like swimming up through deep water, taking so long to reach the surface. The pressure was the first thing I noticed, something weighing on me heavily, making it hard to draw air into my lungs. And then I began to feel the pain. My body felt as if I'd been in a fight, dull aches pulsating from my face, my stomach, my chest.

As I awakened a bit more, memories flooded me. Brian, shot, hitting the floor. Oh God. Was he dead or alive? I wanted to cry out as terror seized me, but I didn't have enough control of my body yet to make a sound.

And Christopher, Kieran. Trevor and River. What had happened after I passed out? Did the assailant keep firing? Were my friends still alive? Had anyone survived that? My grief totally overwhelmed me.

When I was finally able to raise my lids, I blinked up at an unfamiliar, water-stained ceiling. And then I became aware of the stranger laying right on top of me, fast asleep, snoring. That was why it was hard to breathe. He was clothed, but I was completely naked. Oh God, had I been raped? I had no idea.

Sadness and hopelessness flooded me, tears trickling from the corners of my eyes, running back into my hair. I went to brush them away, and that was when I realized my hands were tied.

It's all over, I thought. *He got me. The stalker killed my friends, and he took me prisoner, taking me someplace no one would ever find me.*

I cried quietly for a while as the effects of the drug continued to wear off. My head was pounding and my mouth was so dry. I hurt, all over. I felt myself giving up. Giving up….

But then, I thought of Brian. My sweet Brian. He'd survived so much in his life. Maybe he'd survived this, too. Maybe….

I tried to hold on to that. Brian was a survivor, and not all gunshot wounds were fatal. Maybe he was alive. Maybe he was looking for me.

I stopped crying and raised my head up, just a little, taking in my surroundings. I was on a bed in the middle of a cluttered living room, inside what looked like an old, run-down trailer. It was dark out. The curtains were ajar on one of the windows, and I could see a moonlit forest outside.

A forest? Where had that man taken me? How long had I been unconscious? I took a few quick, shallow breaths as a panic attack rose up, threatening to engulf me.

No.

No!

If I was going to survive, I had to keep it together. No one was going to find me there. Getting away from that maniac was going to be up to me. My only chance was to stay calm, find my inner strength, and focus.

I forced down my panic, then tilted my head and took a look at the bindings on each wrist, tying me to a metal headboard. The rope had been tied quickly, sloppily. He'd been in a hurry to get to whatever he did to me. I twisted my hand around. The ropes weren't very tight, I could get out of them. I glanced down at the heavy, sleeping figure on top of me. I had to do that without waking him, it might be my only chance.

What felt like an eternity passed as I worked silently, my heart racing. Every time the man shifted a bit, I froze, fear coursing through me. But I kept going, picking at the knot on the rough ropes until my fingertips were raw.

Finally, *finally*, I freed my right hand, then reached over to my left, slowly, so slowly. If he woke up now, it was all over. It was easier to untie my left hand, since I had the use of my right, and soon I was able to slide it out from under the coiled ropes. I tested my ankles. They weren't bound. But how to get out from under this person?

He shifted a bit, and I quickly jammed my hands under the ropes, so it would look like I was still tied up. I let my body go slack and shut my eyes. If he thought the drugs were still working, maybe that would give me the element of surprise.

The man awoke, pushing himself up, probably looking at me. I felt his mouth on my body then, licking me. I fought back a shudder, willing myself to remain perfectly immobile. One of his hands slid between my legs, roughly fondling my genitals. His other hand grabbed one of my nipples, squeezing brutally. It was all I could do not to tense up, not to cry out. *Please*, I thought, *please let this be over soon.*

"You fucking whore," he mumbled, sitting up. I knew he was about to strike me by the low growl that came from his throat. It was almost impossible not to react when the hard slap connected with my face, whipping my head to the side, but somehow I managed it.

He grabbed my hair, yanked my head back up, and slapped me again. I dug my fingers into the ropes so my hands wouldn't be pulled free of the bindings. He was far too wrapped up in hurting me to notice.

When he dropped me back onto the mattress, my head landed turned to one side, my hair strewn over my face. He petted me gently as he whispered, "I don't want to hurt you, babydoll. But you gave me no choice by being such a dirty, unfaithful whore." The man pushed my hair back and kissed my cheek, then turned my head and kissed my lips. I smelled grain alcohol on his breath.

Throughout all of that, I remained perfectly slack, not reacting at all, drawing on every ounce of my acting ability to keep my expression blank. I was surprised that I had it in me to pull it off, especially since every ounce of me wanted to scream and cry and struggle.

Eventually, he got off me. I could hear him picking up something from a side table. After a moment, a clicking sound told me he was taking pictures. That infuriated me, every bit as much as his other violations of my body.

He did that for a few minutes. Finally, I heard him set the camera down. His hand returned to my genitals for another hard squeeze, and I fought the urge to leap up and hit him.

But then he let go of me and crossed the room, the trailer creaking with each step. I raised one eyelid a fraction of an inch, and saw he was headed to the adjoining kitchen. I closed my eye. The man took something from the refrigerator, and I could hear what I assumed was a beer can being opened.

He sat down, a chair creaking under him, and picked up some kind of wrapper, which rustled in his hands. Several long minutes passed as he ate and drank. I wondered when he'd start to get suspicious that the drugs hadn't worn off yet.

Throughout all of that, I was becoming more and more lucid, the drugs almost totally out of my system by then, replaced with a blinding headache. I kept trying to come up with some sort of plan. Part of me wanted to just leap up and attack him, but I knew that was crazy. He was much bigger than me, and I had no idea where his gun was. I decided it was best to keep pretending I was unconscious, then run for it when I got the chance.

That chance presented itself a couple minutes later. He finished eating, then walked down the hall. I risked a peek again and saw he was headed to the bathroom. He left the door open, his back to me as he used the toilet.

I slipped out of the ropes and bolted for the front door, trying to be as quiet as possible. I fumbled with the deadbolt, my hands shaking wildly, my heart trying to pound its way out of my chest.

I'd just gotten the second lock open when he grabbed my hair from behind, yanking me back ferociously. I spun to face him despite his hold on me, my hair twisting so painfully I was sure it'd pull right out of my skull.

And then I remembered. I thought of Kaia and all she'd taught me, and I lashed out, *heel, knee, palm.* Stomping on his foot didn't do much, since I was barefoot, but the knee to his groin made him let go of me, and the fleshy part of my hand shattering his nose made him scream and stumble back, clutching his face as blood ran between his fingers.

"You fucking whore, you're going to pay for that," he yelled.

But I was already out the door, sprinting into the woods. It was dark and cold and utterly unfamiliar. God,

283

where had he taken me? I was probably about to get lost in the forest, but that didn't really matter. All that mattered was getting away from that maniac.

In just a matter of seconds, I heard him pursuing me. I'd never known such overwhelming terror. Adrenaline propelled me forward, as fast as I could go, but it was tough to move very quickly in that environment. I kept tripping and stumbling, but I also kept moving.

A popping sound startled me, a tree immediately to my left splintering as I thought, *Oh God, he's shooting at me!* I hadn't expected that, I'd thought he'd want to keep me alive. But maybe he'd already taken what he wanted from me.

"This is how you repay me for all I've done for you, Hunter? For all I've sacrificed, just so we can be together? You broke my nose, you fucking bitch!" It sounded like he was some distance behind me as he yelled that, but I wasn't going to slow myself down by turning and looking.

A few minutes later, something cut deeply into the sole of my bare foot and I cried out, stumbling and falling to my knees. But I was back up in an instant, limping, pain shooting up my leg with every step. I tried to ignore it, focusing on running, on getting as far from that madman as possible.

"You can't escape me, Hunter!" he yelled. "Not today, not ever. No fucking way am I ever going to stop coming after you!"

Yet another cold jolt of fear raced through me at that, as I ducked under a low-hanging tree branch, then banked right. I could hear his heavy steps crashing through the brush, not far behind. He was closing the gap.

Minutes ticked by as I wove through the forest. A branch caught my forehead, tearing my skin. My vision blurred as blood ran into my eye. I tried to brush it away, but there was so much blood, and it just kept coming. A sob escaped me, but I dug deep and pulled out an extra burst of speed. I tripped and fell again a few seconds later. But I got back up. I kept going.

Abruptly, the forest gave way to a twisting, two-lane paved road. I skittered onto the blacktop and began running down it, limping severely, pain radiating from every part of me. A quick debate raged within me. On one hand, I'd be easier to shoot out in the open like that. But I could run faster there, and a car might come by, so I decided in a split second to stick with the pavement.

There were no cars though, no houses, nothing. There was just pain. So much pain. And there were the heavy steps of the man pursuing me, now slapping against asphalt. He was loping a bit too, but his limp didn't seem as pronounced as mine. One of us would give out soon, and I just prayed it was him.

Suddenly, a huge, black SUV rounded the corner, coming head-on at me. I yelled and waved my arms, and the vehicle skidded to a stop less than two feet in front of me. The doors to the SUV swung open as a shot rang out behind me. The bullet took out one of the headlights. I dropped into a tight crouch, and looked behind me for the first time. My stalker had stopped running, and pushed a pair of night vision goggles off his eyes.

He raised his gun, lining up his shot. I curled into a tight ball, my path of escape blocked by the big SUV, uselessly wrapping my arms around my head, as if the duck-and-cover drill I'd learned as a kid would somehow protect me. When a shot rang out, I braced for impact, waiting for the bullet to tear into my body.

But that never happened.

A moment later, arms were around me. I tried to fight them off, but then Brian said, "It's okay, Hunter. It's me. I've got you. Are you alright?"

I opened my eyes and looked into his face, beyond astonished. Then I sat up a bit and took in the scene around me. My assailant was sprawled on his back on the pavement, unmoving. Vincent was advancing cautiously on the stalker's prone body, gun drawn.

"Were you shot?" Brian asked me, and I shook my head. "Thank God," he whispered.

"But how?" I mumbled. "How are you here right now?"

"Vincent. He tracked you."

When Vincent reached the body, he kicked the gun out of the man's hand and checked for a pulse. He straightened up, turned to us and called, "He's dead."

I slumped in Brian's arms, clutching him with the last of my strength. "I was so afraid he'd killed you," I told him. "I didn't want to believe it. But I was so afraid."

"The bullet passed through the fleshy part of my upper arm," Brian said, pressing his palm to my forehead. I realized after a moment that he was trying to stop the bleeding from the gash above my eye. "When I hit the deck to avoid the next bullet, the wheelchair shot out from under me. I ended up whacking my head against the concrete floor, so hard that I passed out."

"What about Christopher and Kieran, and everyone else?"

"They're all fine, just worried about you. The first shot was meant for Christopher, but it hit the champagne bottle instead."

"Thank God you're all okay."

"I should text them right now, they're so worried." As he was talking, Brian shifted his hold on me, slipped out of his button-down shirt and draped it over me before going back to putting pressure on my forehead. With his other hand, he pulled out his phone and fired off a quick text, then dropped it into the pocket of his T-shirt. I noticed the ace bandage on his upper arm, bloody and tied hurriedly.

"I just called an ambulance. How is he?" Vincent asked Brian, coming up to us as he put his phone away.

"Lots of cuts and bruises, but no bullet wounds," Brian replied.

I looked up at Vincent and asked, "How did you find me?"

"I put a tracking device in your wallet. Didn't Brian tell you I'd done that?"

"That was part of the 'extreme security measures' I was going to brief you on after the gallery opening," Brian explained.

"I assumed the stalker would toss out your phone if he abducted you, so that wouldn't work as a GPS," Vincent said. "And he did just that."

"Thank you."

He brushed off my thanks by saying, "Unfortunately, the tracker's signal wasn't very strong. We lost it under the tree canopy, so we were only able to narrow it down to this general area. It's lucky you got free and made it to the road."

"Where are we?"

"The Santa Cruz Mountains, a couple hours south of the city," Brian said. "We called the police right after you were abducted, and once we tracked you here, they had every available patrol car combing the area."

Sure enough, a police cruiser rounded the bend a couple minutes later, and the officer quickly took control of the situation. She confirmed the assailant was dead and set up flares and yellow police tape, shutting down the road. Then she got on the radio, calling in the scene before her.

When the ambulance arrived, I tried to argue, insisting I didn't want to go to the hospital. The E.M.T. who assisted me was kind and patient as she triaged my head wound and then my feet, which were torn and bloody, and told me I would need stitches.

"It doesn't even hurt," I mumbled, a kind of heaviness settling on me. I began shivering, despite the big, warm blanket she'd wrapped me in.

"That's the shock setting in." She folded down the head of the gurney, which had been propping me up.

Vincent had been talking to the police while my wounds were cleaned and dressed, and he came over when the paramedic finished working on me. "I'm going to the station to fill out a formal statement," he said. "Call Nana if you need anything, and she'll get in touch with me immediately."

I looked up at him. He was stoic as ever, his dark eyes giving nothing away. I reached out and squeezed his hand as I said, "You saved my life, and I'll always be so grateful to you. I just wish there was some way I could repay you."

"There's no need. I'm just glad you're okay." That was all he said before turning and walking away. I watched him for a few moments, until my gurney was raised and loaded into the ambulance.

"Brian?" I called, propping myself up and looking around before they shut the doors. "Where are you?"

"I'm here," he said, wheeling into view. He was using a manual wheelchair that the E.M.T. had loaned him, since he'd left his behind in his haste to join Vincent and follow the tracker's signal. He'd been giving his statement to the police as well.

"Are you coming to the hospital?" I asked him.

He nodded. "I'll meet you there."

"You need to see a doctor for your arm," I said. "Make sure that bullet wound gets treated."

"I will."

I put my head back down on the gurney, trying to tell myself, *it's over. You're okay.* But I was still so scared and anxious. The fear just wouldn't go away. I wondered if I'd ever go back to the way I was before.

Chapter Fourteen

I was in the hospital three days. Once the shock wore off, my entire body hurt. The cut on my foot had gone all the way through to the bone, and had required surgery to mend it. Four other lacerations, including the one on my forehead, also needed stitches.

My body was a mass of bruises. The doctor examined me to see if I'd been raped, and the procedure was humiliating. I pressed my eyes shut as he instructed me to spread my legs, then visually examined me before using swabs to take samples for the lab, checking for semen. He determined that I hadn't been raped, which was a relief, though the exam itself felt like a violation.

Brian, Christopher, Kieran and Nana all came to the hospital the night I was admitted, but I asked to be alone. I needed time to process all that had happened. Once they left, I curled onto my side and cried, all the terror, the pain, the anxiety rising to the surface and overwhelming me.

I had to get it together the next morning, when the police came to speak to me. Local law enforcement was first, and they interviewed me for almost two hours. They had a dead body in their jurisdiction, and they wanted every last detail about what had led up to it.

Just as they were finishing up, Detective Sanchez and another member of the S.F.P.D. arrived, and I had to start talking all over again. At least Sanchez already knew the backstory, so he only asked about the last twelve hours.

When the detective finished his interview, I asked him what had happened to my stalker's body, and was told it was downstairs in the morgue. "Can I see him?" I asked.

"Why?"

"I never got a good look at his face, and I feel like I need to do that. It might help give me closure."

Sanchez frowned at me, but after a moment said, "Well, there's no law against it, though I don't think you'll be doing yourself any favors. I'll let hospital personnel know you want to see the body. They'll probably want to get it over with soon." I didn't ask why.

Just minutes after he left, a nurse showed up with a wheelchair. "I'm here to take you to the morgue," she said flatly. I sat up and swung my bandaged feet out of bed, sliding to the edge of the mattress. "Careful about standing," she said as she helped me into the chair. "You can put pressure on your heels, but avoid putting weight on the balls of your feet. That could rupture your stitches."

The nurse, whose nametag read Sue, wheeled me out of my room and onto an elevator, then down a long hallway and into the morgue. "We called ahead, the body's being prepared for viewing," she told me when we reached a small waiting room. "They'll call me when you're done, and I'll come and get you." With that, she turned and left me there.

The waiting room was windowless. Blue plastic chairs were lined up against the walls, and florescent lights were far too harsh and bright overhead. I thought about the people who must find themselves in that room, probably waiting to identify the bodies of loved ones. That cold, impersonal environment must have felt like hell to them. For me, it was different. It suited the task before me, the starkness setting the tone for what I was about to do.

Eventually, a young, red-bearded technician emerged and said, "Hey, how you doing?"

"Um, fine, thanks." I really didn't think he expected me to answer honestly.

"Alright. Well, I'm Chuck. I'll take you in now." He wheeled me into a small room, empty except for a gurney in the center. There was a body on the gurney, draped in a clean, white sheet. It felt surreal.

Chuck folded the sheet back, his movements fast and efficient as he revealed the face of my tormentor. I didn't look right at him at first. Instead, I glanced at the technician and asked, "Do we know his name?"

He went to the foot of the gurney and took a clipboard off a small metal hook. "According to the ID he had on him, he was Donald Alan Swensen," he read. "Age thirty-three. His address was in South San Francisco."

When I finally made myself look at Swensen's face, I asked, "Why is there a bandage on his head?"

"I put it there for your benefit," the man said. "The kill shot entered his brain mid-forehead. It was a very clean entry-wound from a large-caliber weapon. I assume he was brought down by a police sniper?"

"No." That clean, precise shot had been Vincent's doing.

"Oh. It looked like the work of a professional."

Now there was an eerie thought. I looked down at my hands, which were folded in my lap. "Could I have a minute alone with him?"

"I'm not allowed to do that, but I'll get out of your way," Chuck said, then stepped back to one of the corners.

I wheeled myself a little closer to the body and stood up. My bandaged feet throbbed in protest, but I ignored them. And then I took a good, long look at the man that had stalked and kidnapped me.

I'd never seen a dead body before. It didn't seem real, more like a prop in a Hollywood movie. He was pale, a little bloated, and his skin was almost waxy. It was really unnerving, but I tried to look past the indicators of death, focusing just on the man.

There was no doubt that it was the same person in Christopher's police sketch. My friend had remembered him in perfect detail. He was also the same person who'd been in the photo captured by the surveillance camera in my apartment building, minus the facial hair. I tried to picture him with a shaggy, gray wig and fake nose, and could see the old man from my public appearance as well.

I had needed to confirm all of that. I'd needed to see it for myself. It really was him. And he really was dead.

I stared at him a little longer. It somehow felt like he should be ugly, marked in some way, his dark interior reflected on his features, like the painting in the Picture of Dorian Gray. But he was just regular-looking. There was nothing unusual about him, aside from a little scar above his upper lip that looked like a backwards question mark.

I'd built him up to be larger-than-life. A monster. But he was just a man.

I sat down in my chair and rolled back a few feet, and the technician stepped forward and draped the sheet over the body. Then he said, "I'll call the nurse to take you upstairs."

"Was that man's family already notified?" I didn't know why it mattered to me. But I thought about him having a family somewhere, about them finding out their son was dead and finding out what he'd done, and it was depressing.

"I don't know. Someone else handles next-of-kin notifications," he told me as he wheeled me to the waiting room.

Seeing my attacker stirred up so many emotions that it was hard to sort them all out. And I was so far beyond exhausted that it was more than I could process. When I was taken back upstairs, I curled up in bed and shut my eyes. *It really is over*, I told myself.

But I didn't feel any different. Seeing him hadn't been the shortcut to closure I'd hoped for. I realized then that a long road stretched before me, and that healing, inside and out, was going to take time. Lots of it.

*****

When I awoke several hours later, Brian was in his chair beside the bed, watching me closely. "Hey," he said, his expression grave. "How are you?"

"I'm fine." It wasn't even close to the truth, but I couldn't bear the thought of talking about what had happened to me. It was still too raw, too terrifying. "How are you?"

He paused for a long moment before answering. Finally he said, "I've been better."

"Is it the bullet wound?" I sat up quickly. "Did you have someone look at it?"

294

"It's not that, a doctor patched it up." After another long pause he said, not meeting my gaze, "As long as you're okay, I, um…I think we both need some time to ourselves, Hunter. I'm going home to San Francisco. My house is repaired, and I'm going to be moving back in this afternoon. Christopher, Kieran and Nana are out in the waiting room. They'll take care of you and see that you get home safely."

Oh God, he was breaking up with me. That was what needing time to ourselves meant. All the drama had been too much for him. And obviously, he blamed me for what had happened. He should. He'd taken a bullet because of me. Here was a man with PTSD, and I'd gotten him *shot*, just for knowing me. No wonder he was leaving me.

All I could do was nod. If I tried to speak, I'd start crying, and I didn't want him to stay because he felt sorry for me. I turned my back to him.

Brian hesitated for a long moment, then left the room. I waited until he was out of earshot. Only then did I begin to sob.

Chapter Fifteen

For four weeks, I lived in Christopher and Kieran's apartment while my injuries healed. I didn't want to talk to anyone, but I couldn't bear the thought of being alone, either. My universe shrank down to the futon in their spare room.

I missed Brian terribly, but understood why he'd left me. Every few days, I asked Kieran about him, and the answer was always the same. He was fine, keeping busy, going to therapy and putting his life back together. He was much better off without me.

During that month, I was in a daze. I spent a lot of time sleeping, or just sitting by myself and processing all that had occurred. I met with a therapist once a week, but I didn't talk to my friends about what had happened. I just couldn't.

My therapist was trying to work through my guilt, but was making no progress, probably because I knew I *should* feel guilty. My loved ones had been shot at, because of me. That person, that sick individual, had been brought into their world. Yeah, I felt guilty, because it was *my fault*. If it wasn't for me, nothing would have happened to them.

And that man had done far worse things, because of his obsession with me. I just knew that was why Swensen had singled out Christopher and hurt him, because he and I were the same physical type. And then there were those two other young, blond boys who'd gone missing around the same time that Christopher was assaulted. When local law enforcement searched Swensen's apartment in South San Francisco and the trailer where I'd been taken, they didn't find any evidence linking him to the missing boys. All they found were hundreds of photos of me. So to the police, Swensen's case was closed.

They only had the word of a kid working in a soup kitchen that those two boys had even gone missing. No one had ever come looking for either of them. But I just couldn't shake the feeling that Swensen had hurt them like he'd hurt Christopher, maybe killed them, driven by his obsession with me. I couldn't even begin to grapple with the guilt and horror of that.

The police did learn a few things when they searched the apartment and dug into Swensen's past. His neighbors, like so many before them, described him as a quiet man who kept to himself. Typical. He kept odd hours and worked from home as a programmer, and had subcontracted on a job updating the police mainframe, so he'd been able to follow my case and find my contact information. Among other things, he'd also found out about the surveillance photos from my apartment building.

The police department was surprised that he'd slipped by, since they did background checks on their contractors and Swensen had a record. It turned out that the primary contractor, the one who'd brought Swensen in, had done so without going through the proper channels and had been paying him under the table, so Swensen never had to go through a background check.

My stalker had been arrested eleven years prior for making threats against an ex-boyfriend. The ex had let the charges drop though, and moved out of state to get away from him. Apparently, Swensen had secretly taken a lot of photos of his ex, which were confiscated when Swensen was arrested. Detective Sanchez reviewed the file, and mentioned offhandedly, "The ex-boyfriend looked a lot like you, Hunter. He was a slim, blond-haired guy in his early twenties." Sanchez suggested that the ex was at the root of Swensen's obsession with me. I didn't know what to think.

*****

Days passed. During my recovery, Christopher and Kieran were an amazing source of support. They made sure I ate, and coaxed me out of my room every night for a couple hours. They knew I wasn't up for talking, so they'd put in a DVD, and Christopher would just hold me while whatever random movie played.

I couldn't remember what we watched. My eyes were usually blurred with tears, my mind a million miles away. I only remembered my best friend's heartbeat, strong and steady under my cheek, and the feeling of his arms around me, so comforting and secure. Sometimes, it felt like his arms were the only thing holding me together.

Swensen's death had brought Christopher closure, helping him turn the page on that chapter of his life once and for all. I wanted to do the same, to learn from my best friend's example. But for me, it was still too raw, too fresh. Maybe that was why I still felt anxious and vulnerable and couldn't bear the thought of being alone. Closure was going to take time, apparently.

*****

My new friend Trevor visited me twice a week during that month, like clockwork. I'd tell him I didn't want company, and he'd simply say, "I know," before sitting beside me and putting his arms around me. He didn't try to get me to talk, and he didn't offer any advice. He just hugged me. It was better than therapy.

At the end of a month, when my feet were healed enough for shoes, he visited me one Saturday morning and said, "Come on. It's time you left this apartment."

"I don't feel like going out," I told him.

He rummaged through the suitcase that I'd been living out of and handed me a sweatshirt. "I know," he said. Then he waited for me to put it on.

"I'm serious, Trevor. I don't feel like socializing."

"That's not what we'll be doing."

I stared at him for a few moments, then sighed and pulled on the sweatshirt before sliding my feet carefully into a pair of sneakers. I pushed my glasses further up the bridge of my nose and asked, "Where are we going?"

"You'll see." He held my gaze steadily.

We rode a bus across town, then walked half a block to a small warehouse. The little white sign above the door said 'Lunch with Love.' I looked at Trevor and asked, "What are we doing here?"

"We're helping," he said simply, and held the door open for me.

There were four or five people inside, and everyone knew Trevor and greeted him warmly. He introduced me, then led me to a stool at the end of a long, stainless steel counter, which was loaded with supplies. "Since it's probably painful for you to stand very long, you can sit here and put the meal kits together. Like this." He pulled a few components from the various boxes, showed me how to assemble the bento-style tray and bundle the plastic cutlery in a napkin, and put the whole thing together.

"Yeah, okay," I murmured, and went to work. It was repetitive, but soothing in a way. I got into a good rhythm, and soon stacks of assembled kits lined the counter. I kept going until I ran out of supplies, then went to find Trevor.

He was in the big, industrial kitchen with Sadie Jones, sautéing vegetables in a huge skillet while she assembled green salads in little to-go boxes. Sadie smiled when she saw me, then came around the counter and gave me a hug. "Hi, Hunter," she said. "It's nice to see you again."

"You too. I, um, finished with the boxes," I said, gesturing over my shoulder.

"In that case, you can chop zucchini," Trevor said. "There's a barstool over in the corner, you can pull it up to the counter."

I did as he said. There were fifty pounds of zucchini to get through, and I washed it all in the sink, then stacked it up on the counter and sat before a big, scarred cutting board. I wasn't much of a cook, so I asked Trevor how he wanted it sliced. He came over to me and cut one up rapidly and efficiently. I picked up a knife and got to work, emulating his movements.

The next couple hours passed quickly. Two hundred and thirty hot lunches were assembled in the boxes I'd put together, then packed in special insulated carriers. Eighteen volunteers arrived around eleven-thirty and loaded up the meals into their vehicles, then headed out into the city, along with Sadie and a couple other people who'd been cooking.

Trevor and I worked with the remaining volunteers to clean the kitchen, and only when it was spotless did my companion finally pull up a chair and sit down beside me. "How do you feel?" he asked me.

"Tired, but good." I actually felt better than I had in weeks.

"Glad to hear it."

"How did you know I needed this?"

He shrugged and said, "It always makes me feel better when I volunteer here, so I was hoping it would do the same for you."

"It really did help. I've spent a lot of time dwelling on things lately, and this took my mind off...well, pretty much everything. It felt good to be helping other people, too."

"Do you want to come back tomorrow?"

"Tomorrow's Sunday. Are they open?"

He nodded. "Seven days a week, three hundred sixty-five days a year."

"I want to keep doing this," I said.

"I was hoping you'd say that."

"It's quite a coincidence that you volunteer at the same charity I chose for my public appearance."

"No it isn't." I glanced up at him, and he grinned at me. "That's how I heard about this organization. I've only been in San Francisco a few weeks and found myself with some free time after your event in the Castro, and so I looked into Lunch with Love. I've always enjoyed cooking, and I like what they're trying to do here, so this seemed like an ideal place to volunteer."

"You're a better man than me. I tend to just help out with my checkbook."

"That counts. It's not really an option for me though, so I give my time."

"Are you still working for Jamie?"

He nodded. "I'm still bussing tables, and hoping an entry-level position opens up in the kitchen. I've been doing a little work with River too, the caterer from Christopher's gallery opening. He's a brilliant cook, but kind of a disaster when it comes to running a business." Trevor grinned affectionately, in a way that made me wonder if there was something going on with the two of them.

"What brought you to San Francisco, anyway?"

He sighed, the humor draining from his features as he said, "I helped my underage cousin Melody run away from home when she got pregnant, to stop her dad from beating the crap out of her. We came to San Francisco to find my estranged father, hoping he'd help us, but we couldn't track him down. Meanwhile, my uncle, Mel's dad, is absolutely furious with me for helping her run away, so I can't go home again. Incidentally, he's the person who raised me, since my mother's been in prison for the last fourteen years. But that didn't stop him from swearing he'd hunt me down and kill me."

"Oh my God."

"Yeah, my family's awesome," Trevor said. He tried to keep his tone light, but there was heartbreak in his blue eyes. "Oh, and here's the kicker: three weeks after we got here, Mel met some guy and went off with him. So now here I am, waiting for her to come back, with about twelve dollars to my name."

"I can't believe she did that."

"Actually, I can. The way we were raised…well, Melody's always going to latch on to any guy who shows her a little affection, because there wasn't exactly a lot of love to go around when we were kids. It scares me to think about her future, about the jerks she'll end up with just because they throw some attention her way. I mean, she's only seventeen and pregnant already, and the baby's father is a complete thug. He was another reason we left Sacramento, and I hope to God he doesn't track us here."

"Sacramento? You didn't run very far."

"I know, we couldn't really afford to go much farther. Besides, we figured the best place to lose ourselves would be a huge city. It certainly worked for my father."

"I'm sorry about all you're going through, and I want to help. I wish you'd kept the money I tried to give you."

"I'm not really a big fan of hand-outs. That was nice of you, though," he said. "I managed to make rent on our crappy little apartment, I need to hang on to that so Mel can find me if and when she comes back. There's not much money left over for luxuries like food and electricity, but hey, I work in a restaurant, so I won't starve. That catering job with River holds a lot of promise, too. If it pans out, I'll be just fine."

"No wonder you were stealing cookies."

"They were for Melody, macaroons are her favorite. That was actually the day I came home and found a note saying she'd taken off with this guy she'd just met."

"You must be worried about her," I said.

"I am, but all I can do is wait for her to return. And I'm pretty sure she will as her due date gets closer. She was really scared about going through childbirth alone, and I promised I'd be there for her."

"Will she call and check in with you?"

He considered that, and said, "Well, she might try to call me at the restaurant."

"Why there?"

"It's not like either of us can afford a phone. But who knows if she'll think to call. Melody tends to be pretty wrapped up in Melody." He shook his head and added, "That was a really long and awkward answer to your original question. Sorry to dump so much on you."

"I'm glad you told me what's going on with you. And if you ever change your mind, my offer of help stands, whether it's money or a place to stay or whatever you need."

"I appreciate that, Hunter."

"You'd do the same for me."

"I would." After a pause, he changed the subject by saying, "Can I ask you a question?"

"Sure."

"Whatever happened between you and that Brian guy? Are you still together?"

"Oh…no. That ended." I looked down at my hands. "He left me."

"Why?"

"I assume he got sick of all my shit. I mean, he got shot because of me. He must have realized I was the last thing he needed."

"Wait a minute. It sounds like you really don't know why he left."

"Sure I do. I mean, in the short time he knew me, he had to put up with a lifetime's worth of drama. *Two* lifetimes. Why would he stick around?"

"That doesn't make sense. What did he say when he broke up with you?"

"Nothing much."

"No?"

"He just...didn't want me." Tears prickled at the back of my eyes, but I wasn't going to cry. I'd done way too much of that the past few weeks.

"I don't believe that."

I glanced up at Trevor. "Why not?"

"Because I saw the way he looked at you, Hunter."

"How did he look at me?"

"Like you were the most important thing in the world to him."

"But I wasn't, because he left me."

"It sounds like you have no idea why he left, or what was really going on with him. You two really need to talk."

"I doubt he'd want to see me."

"Go anyway."

I thought about it for a while, then said, "I guess I could do that."

"Good. I just don't buy the idea that he suddenly decided there was too much drama, especially after the situation with your stalker was resolved." *Resolved*...that was one way to put it. "Why would you accept the breakup without question, Hunter?"

I shrugged and said, "I guess it didn't surprise me that he didn't want to be with me, not after all I'd put him through. Plus, I was dealing with so much right at that time. I guess all I could do was accept it."

"Come on," he said, getting up and pushing in his chair. "Walk me to the bus stop. You need to go to Brian's house before you head home, so you can talk about whatever happened between the two of you."

"Yeah, okay."

Trevor and I hugged goodbye before we boarded buses heading in opposite directions. After I sank onto the lumpy vinyl seat, I pulled out my phone and texted Kieran, asking once again how Brian had been lately.

Fine, came his reply. *He's been really busy with physical therapy, counseling, and some house projects.*

When was the last time you saw him? I asked.

Actually, I haven't seen him since we got back from Santa Cruz, Kieran replied. *That's how busy he's been. But I text him a couple times a week.*

Something about that didn't sound right, and I frowned as I slipped the phone back in my pocket. I got off the bus in Noe Valley and walked two blocks, ignoring my aching feet, then stood on the sidewalk, looking up at Brian's house. My frown deepened. All the curtains were drawn, and a few old flyers stuck around the front door made the house look abandoned.

I went up the steps and knocked, and when there was no reply, I pressed my ear to the door and listened. "Brian?" I called.

Nothing. I decided to take my prying one step further and went to the edge of the little porch, leaned over the railing, and peered through a gap in the curtains. The living room was dark, but I could see right through the dining room to the kitchen, which was brightly lit with its wall of bare windows.

There was a body on the kitchen floor.

When I yelled Brian's name again, the figure didn't move. I ran to the door and rattled the knob, but it was locked. "Oh God," I murmured as I raced off the porch and around the side of the house. I had to scale a tall wooden fence to get into the backyard. It barely slowed me down. I tripped and fell as I took the back steps three at a time, and didn't bother to get back to my feet, scrambling the last bit of distance on my hands and knees. The back door was locked, too. I flung aside the doormat and grabbed Brian's spare key, the one he'd hidden there after the night we met and he'd locked himself out. I shoved it in the lock and twisted so hard, it was surprising that it didn't snap in two.

As soon as the door swung open, I dove for Brian's prone figure. "Please don't be dead. Please, please, please," I chanted as I grabbed his arm and rolled him over onto his back, then pressed my ear to his chest.

His heartbeat was strong and steady. And he reeked of alcohol.

I dropped into a seated position and stared at him as I tried to catch my breath. He was drunk off his ass at two o'clock in the afternoon, and he was a total mess. His clothes were stained and dirty, his hair was disheveled, and he sported a thick beard that was probably about a month old.

"Holy shit," I said to his unconscious form. "You've regressed right back to your former self." I leaned against the kitchen counter and watched him sleep it off for a while, then looked around me.

The kitchen was completely trashed, every square inch of countertop covered with takeout containers, beer cans, and liquor bottles. I pulled a receipt off the counter and frowned at it. "Really? There are liquor stores that deliver?" I muttered, then tossed the receipt aside.

I was still sitting there on the floor, watching him and debating calling Kieran, when Brian woke up suddenly. He'd begun snoring a little, and abruptly, he sat up with a loud, really flattering snort/snore combination. He looked all around him, obviously disoriented. When he noticed me sitting a few feet away, he just blinked a couple times, then looked around again and grabbed an almost-empty bottle of Wild Turkey from the floor.

He tugged off the lid and tossed it on the worn linoleum, then tipped the bottle back so he could guzzle its contents. "Oh, hell no," I said, lunging forward and grabbing the bottle out of his hands.

"Holy fuck," he cried out, scampering backwards until he hit the cabinets opposite me. "You mean you're *real*?"

"What the fuck did you think I was, a hallucination? And if you say yes, I'm shoving you in the back of a cab and driving you to the nearest alcohol treatment facility."

Brian was clearly still drunk, and he knit his brows as he tried to work out an answer. Finally, he came up with, "No?"

"No what?"

"No, I didn't think you're a loosination?" He slurred, holding my gaze as he said that, eyes open wide, like a little kid who was trying to get away with a lie.

308

I rolled my eyes and got to my feet. "You smell like booze and armpits. Come on, you're getting a shower."

"Why you mad?" he mumbled, trying and failing to pull himself into his wheelchair before giving up and sitting back on the floor.

"Because I grew up with an alcoholic father, Brian, and it fucking pisses me off to see you doing this to yourself."

"Sorry." He looked contrite.

"No you're not. And look, I know you were shot, and that probably totally exacerbated your PTSD and all that. But shit, turning to alcohol, Brian? You should be talking about it with your therapist, not drowning it in a bottle."

"Nope. No more ther'pist."

"What? Why not?"

"No point."

I knit my brows, then crossed the room to his chair and locked the brake. As I held it steady by the handles, I said, "Come on. Try again."

He climbed up onto the chair awkwardly, eventually flopping down onto the seat, and I pushed him down the hall to the bathroom. "No cold shower," he said when I parked him beside the tub. "I hate that."

I sighed and stared at him for a long moment, then muttered, "Fine." I put the stopper in place and began drawing him a warm bath.

When I turned toward him again, he tilted his head and said, "What happened to you?"

"What do you mean?"

"You never look like this. Just on the night I met you, but that's it."

"You know, you're in no position to judge people's appearances," I told him. "I bet I can guess every meal you've had this week from the stains on that T-shirt."

He looked down at himself, then said, "Gross."

"It *is* gross."

He turned his gaze to me again. "But you're so handsome. Why are you hiding behind the glasses and the messy ponytail and ratty hoodie? Where'd Hunter Storm go, with his designer everything?"

"Hunter Storm doesn't live here anymore. There's just Hunter Jacobs now, and he doesn't really give a shit." I turned back to the tub and watched it fill, then shut the water off and said, "Can I trust you to do this on your own, or are you so damn drunk that you might pass out and drown?"

"What a bad way to go, a grown man drowning in a bathtub," he said. "You'd hafta make up a story, tell 'em I went some cooler way, like skydiving or something."

I grinned a little at that, despite myself. "And who exactly would you be trying to impress with this fake skydiving accident?"

"I dunno. No one. Only you, but you'd already know I drowned in a tub."

"Get in, Brian, and try your best not to drown. I'll be right outside the door, make noise so I know you're okay."

"What kind of noise?"

"I don't know. Sing or something."

"I can't sing. I wish I could. Be cool to sound like Axel Rose. Woah a woah a woah!" The last part was sung so badly that it should have made the paint peel off the walls.

"Good lord," I muttered, stepping around his chair and setting the brake. "Come on, Axel, the soap is calling."

"I don't hear it."

"Oh, but I do."

Brian swung himself onto the edge of the bathtub and swayed precariously before finding his balance. Next, he looked at the water and murmured, "Needs bubbles." He then proceeded to dump an entire bottle of body wash in the tub and turned the water back on. Immediately, huge billows of white foam began rising from the water.

"S' better," he said, then peeled off his clothes and dropped down into the water. I turned my back to him as he did that to give him some privacy. Then I decided I really should stay in the bathroom in case he passed out, so I sat on the lid of the toilet, facing away from him.

After a few minutes, he muttered, "Shit. This is bad."

"What is?" I asked as I glanced at him over my shoulder.

"I'm starting to sober up. I need a drink." He looked around the bathroom, as if maybe he was going to find something in here. And then, to my astonishment, he pulled a half-empty beer can out from behind the tub and started to raise it to his lips.

"Oh, come on," I yelled, lunging for the beer. "That's *so* gross! How long has that been back there?"

"I dunno," he said, holding the can out of my reach. "But it's probably not, like, tainted or anything."

"Give it to me," I said, making another grab for the beer.

"No way. I told you I was sobering up, and that *cannot* happen. Especially not now, with you here."

He tried again to take a sip and I grabbed for the beer with both hands. "Don't do it, Brian!"

He yanked the can just out of my reach, and I went after it. That made me lose my balance and land in the tub on top of him. Water and bubbles sloshed everywhere. That still didn't deter me, and I tried again to grab for the can. His arms were a lot longer than mine though, and he held it up and back, over his head, while holding me down with his other arm.

"Shit," I exclaimed. "Fine. You want that nasty, probably toxic beer so damn bad? Be my guest. But don't come crying to me later when you're picking barf chunks out of your beard."

He looked at me for a long moment, and then he burst out laughing. "That's really disgusting."

"Oh, *that's* disgusting? You're trying to drink used bathroom beer."

Brian grinned at me. I could tell he really was sobering up. He'd lost some of that wide-eyed booze-buzzed expression. "I've missed you so fucking much," he said.

"I've missed you, too."

He dropped the can of beer, which landed with a clatter on the tile floor behind him, wrapped both his arms around me, and delivered a deep, long kiss that I felt from my lips to my toes. I wove my arms around his neck and returned it passionately.

But after a while, I pulled back and said, "We shouldn't be doing this. You're drunk, and you're going to regret this once you sober up."

"The only thing I'd regret is not kissing you while I had the chance." His lips met mine again and we made out wildly, for so long that the tub started to cool. But Brian just reached over and added more hot water, stirring up the bubbles again, then slid his hands under my waterlogged sweatshirt and held me to him, kissing me like his very existence depended on it.

"God I've missed you," he said again. "Every single minute of every single day. I drink to forget, but it doesn't really work. Nothing could make me forget you, or this." He kissed me again, and I completely gave myself over to it.

"I don't get it, though," I said, next time we came up for air. "You broke up with me, you didn't want to be with me anymore. I don't get why you'd still want to kiss me."

"Didn't want to be with you?" he repeated, shaking his head. "I wanted to be with you more than anything in this world, Hunter. But I just couldn't face you anymore, not after what I did to you."

I sat up a little and asked, "What did you do to me?"

"I completely failed you. I let that maniac take you from the gallery, and I will forever be so fucking sorry."

"You didn't fail me! No one could have predicted he'd strike like that, in a room full of people. None of us were ready for it, there was nothing we could do."

"I could have gotten to my gun and shot him. Then he wouldn't have been able to take you."

"But I'm okay, Brian."

"He hurt you, though. The sight of you naked and bloody, limping down that road, is seared into my memory forever," he said, his eyes pools of agony. "You trusted me to keep you safe, to protect you, and God, how I failed."

"That's why you broke up with me? Because you think you failed me?"

He nodded. "I don't deserve you."

"It wasn't your fault, Brian. There's only one person to blame, and he's dead."

"I should have stopped him. I was your bodyguard and your boyfriend. It was my job to protect you."

"You have to stop blaming yourself." I took his face in my hands and looked him in the eye. "I survived, I got through it. Yeah, he took me, but I got away. And you're part of the reason I found the strength to escape. I wanted to get back to you, more than anything. You're what kept me going."

"I was?"

"Yes. But now, we've both gotten so bogged down with guilt and blaming ourselves that Swensen is getting what he wanted all along. This is driving us apart, and I don't want that, Brian."

He knit his brows. "Why are you blaming yourself?"

"Because of his obsession with me, that man hurt Christopher, and maybe other boys too, and shot you, and—"

"No!" Brian sat up in the tub, taking hold of my upper arms. "Don't you dare blame yourself for any of that! Swensen was a sick individual. You didn't make him that way."

"But my films fed his sickness."

"If you'd never moved to California and never made those movies, what do you think would have happened with him? Do you think he would have ended up healthy and normal?"

"Well…no."

"Exactly! If he hadn't had you to obsess over, he would have found something else. That man was deeply, deeply disturbed, and that has absolutely nothing to do with you."

I rested my head on Brian's chest and thought about that for a while. Slowly, a little of that message was seeping in. "You're better than my therapist," I said quietly.

"I've always said the same about you."

"So, you really believe that man was going to snap no matter what. That it really didn't have anything to do with me."

"Absolutely."

I sat up and looked at Brian, straddling him with my hands on his shoulders. "Well, then the same goes for you. If I can't blame myself for that man's actions, then neither can you."

He shook his head. "It's not the same thing. I could have prevented him from taking you, if only I hadn't messed up so badly."

"How did you mess up?"

"I knocked myself out when I hit the deck, when that fucking chair shot out from under me."

"And you're blaming yourself for that?"

"I should have focused on getting to my gun, not diving for cover."

"Someone was shooting at you! Diving to the ground was the only thing that made sense in that situation, otherwise the next bullet could have killed you! So you hit your head and got knocked out. Good! That meant you stopped moving, making Swensen think you were dead. If you hadn't, he probably would have emptied his clip into you!"

"But—"

"The fact that you got knocked unconscious is the best thing that could have happened. You probably would have been killed otherwise. I could have lost you forever. As it is, I almost lost you anyway, because we were both so overcome with guilt. We let it get in the way of this, of us. But we have to stop doing that. We already lost the last month, and I don't want to lose even one more day. I want you, Brian, I want to be with you. But that can only happen if we both stop blaming ourselves for things that weren't our fault."

He stared at me for a long moment. And then, Brian's face lit up in a smile. It was beautiful to see, and it made me smile too. "What?" I asked.

"I was just thinking it's a damn good thing I've sobered up, because that was a hell of a speech, and it'd be a shame if I missed it."

My smile got wider. "It'd be a downright tragedy."

And just like that, the mood shifted, just enough of the fog of the past clearing away to reveal the path ahead. Yes, we both still had a hell of a lot to deal with. There were no quick fixes or easy answers for any of it. But I knew, right then, that we'd be dealing with all of it together from that point forward, and that made it all seem so much less daunting.

I stripped off my wet sweatshirt and T-shirt, reached over and deposited both in the sink to drain. I shifted around and pulled off my wet sneakers and socks, dropping them on the tile floor as Brian turned on the hot water. It

316

was hard to shimmy out of my wet jeans, but eventually I freed myself from them and my underwear. When I pulled my phone and wallet from my pockets, I said, "Damn."

"Nice one." Brian grinned at me.

I tapped the dark screen on the phone and murmured, "Oh well," then tossed it in the sink with the rest of my wet things.

"You know, you could have just let me drink that beer," Brian said. "You didn't have to commit cellphone suicide."

"Yeah, that was *not* going to happen."

"It wasn't going to kill me."

"It might. For all I knew, you were one sip away from alcohol poisoning. Plus, ew! Used bathroom beer. That's so nasty."

He chuckled at that, then said, "Come here." When I slid between his thighs, he took my glasses off and put them on the floor outside the tub, then carefully untangled the elastic band from my ponytail. With one arm behind my shoulders, he dipped me down into the water, wetting my hair. He then put me on his chest and proceeded to shampoo my hair, so gently.

"That feels good," I murmured, letting my eyes slide shut. "But I should really be doing that to you. You need a lot more TLC than I do right now."

"I think we both need a lot of TLC, and you can do me next."

"You know," I said, sliding an arm around him, "you've sobered up really quickly."

"I have a high metabolism. Plus, I wasn't that drunk."

"Like hell. You were passed out on the kitchen floor!"

"I wasn't passed out, I was sleeping it off. There's a difference."

"That was not sleeping it off."

"How do you know?"

"Because you were face down *on the kitchen floor*, that's how!"

"It's as good a place as any to sleep off a bender," he said.

"Right. Like you'd purposefully pick the floor, and not your bed."

"I can't even get to my bed right now, that's how messy my room is. I've been sleeping on the couch. Or, you know. Wherever."

"Is that how you spent the last month? On one long bender, living on the couch?"

"And the floor."

"Wow, when you fall apart, you really fall apart," I said.

"Oh, I know."

"Kieran thought you were being super productive, going to therapy, fixing up the house."

"It's easy to lie to him, especially in a text. I just had to be sober enough to keep the typos to a minimum. He bought all that stuff because he wanted to believe it, and I just didn't let him see how much breaking up with you affected me." Brian tilted me back then and rinsed the shampoo from my hair.

"My turn," I said. I proceeded to shampoo his hair and wash every inch of him, and when there was nothing more to wash, we got out of the water and wrapped each other in towels. He sat on the lid of the toilet and brushed his teeth,

318

and then I put on my glasses, lathered his face, and shaved him, slowly and carefully.

"I've never done this to anyone before," I said as I slid the blade over his skin.

"I've never let anyone do this, either. Obviously."

"Why obviously?"

"Because this takes a ton of trust. I have to believe you're not going to mess up and slice my jugular. Usually, I'm not so big on trusting people. Only you."

I bent down and kissed his forehead, then said, "I trust you, too. Now stop talking. I don't want to nick you." A minute later he slid his hand behind my head and pulled me in for a kiss, leaving me with a muzzle of shaving cream.

"That's a good look on you," he said with a grin. "Makes you seem slightly rabid, but it's a good look nonetheless." I smiled at him and ran the corner of a towel over my face.

When we'd finished cleaning each other up, we wove our way to the living room. There was barely enough room for his wheelchair to maneuver. "Wow," I said, tossing a pizza box off the arm of the sofa. "I see you've been busy. But that's okay, I've been needing a project since I quit working, and cleaning the hell out of your house is going to be really therapeutic."

We settled in on the couch. As Brian pulled a blanket over us and I nestled in his arms, he asked, "You quit working?"

"Yeah. I'm now the only thing worse than a porn star. I'm a washed-up ex-porn star."

"You're not washed up, you chose to walk away. Right?"

"I did."

"Why is that, exactly?"

"Two reasons. First of all, after that nightmare with Swensen, I'm really not so eager to keep putting myself out there for whoever will have me."

"What's the second reason?"

"You. Even though you broke up with me and I thought you didn't want me anymore, I still…well, I still felt like I was yours, Brian, and making another film would have felt like I was cheating on you."

"Really?"

I nodded and said, "It's kind of problematic, actually, because I'm required to make one more movie under my current agreement. If I don't, my studio's going to sue me for breach of contract and take all my money. I don't quite know what to do about that."

"I'm sorry."

"Well, I kind of brought it on myself."

After a pause, he said, "It's surprising that you'd feel like you were cheating on me, even after we broke up."

"Breaking up with me didn't change what was in my heart."

"I shouldn't have done that. I should have stayed so we could talk about all of this, like we're doing today."

"You know what, though? It would have been too soon to try to talk," I said. "You were right about needing time. We both had a lot to work out for ourselves."

"We still do. Our personal issues haven't just evaporated."

"I know," I said. "But I'm better now than I was a month ago. And next month, I'll be even better, especially

320

now that you and I are back together. I mean, let's face it. We're both disasters on our own."

"But two wrongs don't make a right. If we're disastrous separately, who's to say we won't be disastrous together?"

"We won't be."

"You sound pretty sure of that," he said.

"Oh, I am."

Brian rubbed my back gently, and after a while he asked, "So, what's the plan now that you've left the world of adult entertainment?"

"Poverty, I'm assuming, and probably a glamorous job in the fast food industry. I've been practicing by asking everyone I meet, 'would you like fries with that?' I think I'm a natural."

He chuckled, the laughter rumbling in his broad chest. I'd missed that sound. "I doubt that's your only alternative."

"We'll see. At least I have some savings, since I always knew my porn career wouldn't last forever. I can probably keep the paper hats at bay for a few months, at least until I lose it all in that inevitable lawsuit."

"You'll figure out a new career. I suppose I will, too." I glanced up at him, and he grinned a little and added, "Not that my career as a professional drunk wasn't going swimmingly. I think I had a real future in round-the-clock inebriation."

"You had a real future in liver poisoning."

"That too. Hey, maybe there's a job we can do together."

"Like what?"

"I was a brilliant ventriloquist as a kid. You could be my cute, blond dummy."

I grinned at that. "Such a terrible, terrible idea."

"Yeah, you're right. You'd totally steal the spotlight, and I'd be forced to trade you in for a less adorable assistant."

"I hope you're kidding about doing ventriloquism as a kid. Because that's kind of creepy," I teased.

"Oh, just for that, I'm going to introduce you to Mr. Wiggles. He's still around here somewhere." Brian sat up a bit and looked around.

I shuddered dramatically and said, "Oh lord, you'd better be kidding. You don't really have one of those horrifying dolls around here, do you?"

"And now you've hurt his feelings," he said with a big grin, laying back against the arm of the couch.

I burst out laughing. "Oh my God, you really need to shut up."

"Make me." Brian flashed me a huge smile.

"Okay." I leaned in and kissed him, softly, gently.

"I have an idea," I murmured against his lips after a few minutes of kissing. "Let's never break up again."

Brian kissed me once more, then said softly, "I'm so fucking sorry I did that to you."

"I know," I said, looking up at him and running my fingers down his cheek. "But it's behind us, where it belongs, along with all those other bad things. Our job now is to look forward, instead of back."

"Do you really think it's possible to put the past behind us?"

"Absolutely."

"Okay. So how do we do that?"

"We do that," I said, "together."

Chapter Sixteen

"I can't believe I agreed to this."

"Just go with it," I whispered to Brian. It was a couple weeks later, and we were in my apartment because we'd been summoned by Nana. When she found out I hadn't spent a single night there since the break-in, she decided it was high time to eradicate the 'bad juju.' I'd actually been spending every night at Brian's house lately, not because of bad juju, but simply because that was where Brian was.

She was determined to do the cleansing for me though, despite being busy planning Christopher and Kieran's Fourth of July wedding, which was in just over three weeks. She'd called us a couple hours earlier and announced we'd be performing the ritual that afternoon. Apparently, she'd roped in the Wiccan granddaughter of a friend of hers to help.

But Nana was running late. Brian and I, along with Christopher and Kieran, sat on my living room floor, waiting for her. Sarah Meier, the granddaughter in question, sat with us, an e-reader on her lap and a Trader Joe's shopping bag beside her. Not to stereotype, but she didn't look much like a Wiccan. I'd kind of expected long, flowing hair and long, flowing skirts. Instead, Sarah was a soccer mom with a short, no-nonsense bob, jeans, and an L.L. Bean fleece jacket. Her attitude was no-nonsense, too. As far as she was concerned, she was there to perform a basic public service. Never mind that that service fell under the heading of witchcraft.

Finally, about fifteen minutes after the designated start time, Nana rang the buzzer. When I opened the door to the apartment, I had to smile. She, unlike the actual Wiccan, had dressed for the occasion.

Nana and her six clones burst into the apartment, chattering excitedly. Each tiny eighty-year-old wore a Chanel suit in a cheery Easter egg color and carried a handbag big enough to smuggle a Thanksgiving turkey. And each sported a tall, black, pointy witch hat.

"Seriously?" Sarah Meier muttered under her breath. She was not amused. But I sure as hell was.

"Sorry we're late," Nana said. "You know how hard it is to find witch hats this time of year?"

"That really wasn't necessary," Sarah told her.

"Sure it was. What fun is doing witchcraft otherwise?" Then Nana asked, "Where's yours?"

"I don't have a hat like that," Sarah replied haughtily.

"Oh, no problem," Nana told her. "We got extra."

She produced a stack of hats out of a big shopping bag and plopped one down on Sarah's head, then did the same to Brian, Christopher, Kieran and me. Sarah started to take the hat off, but I shot her a look and whispered, "I really wouldn't do that if I were you."

"Why not?"

"Because no one crosses Stana Dombruso," I told her ominously, fighting back a smile. Sarah thought that over for a beat, then left the hat in place.

"Alright," she muttered, "let's get this over with."

She fired up her e-reader, and I asked, "What's that for?"

"All my spells are in here," she said. Gotta love twenty-first century witchcraft.

For the next half hour, chants and prayers were said, trinkets were utilized, and various substances were burned. I tried to take it seriously, but kept sneaking glances at the clock. I didn't believe the ritual would actually accomplish anything, but at least Nana was having a good time. She'd put on her huge glasses, the ones that made her look like an owl, and paid rapt attention, participating enthusiastically whenever the ceremony called for group involvement.

Finally, some kind of conclusion was reached. Sarah plucked the hat off her head and announced unceremoniously, "Okay, that's it."

The little Nana clone in the bright coral suit exclaimed, "Mazel tov!" All the ladies leapt to their feet, and someone popped the cork on a bottle of champagne. Nana pulled out her phone and pushed a button, then yelled into the receiver, "It's done, all the bad juju is gone! Come on up!"

"Who were you talking to, Nana?" I asked as she hung up the phone.

"Everybody!" She bustled across my apartment and swung open the front door.

In less than a minute, people began filtering in by the dozens. Trevor and River led the way, carrying huge trays of food. "I hired 'em because I wanted more of those stuffed mushrooms," Nana said. "Only now, River knows to add a touch more parmesan. He's gonna be a top-notch caterer, just you wait and see. Especially now that I've taken him and his business partner under my wing."

"Business partner?" I asked.

"That'd be me," Trevor said with an embarrassed smile, as he hoisted a big tray onto my kitchen island.

"Oh! When did that happen?"

"Yesterday," he told me, peeling back layers of plastic wrap and revealing some great-looking sandwiches. "Nana wants to help River launch his business, but thinks he shouldn't go it alone. She suggested we team up, which sounded like a good idea."

"That's awesome."

"It is."

"So, how've you been," I asked, "and have you heard from your cousin Melody?" It had been four days since I'd last seen him, during a volunteer shift at Lunch with Love.

"I've been okay, and I haven't heard a word. I still think she'll show up sooner or later, though."

Dante appeared beside me with a bulging canvas shopping bag draped over his arm. "Hey, Hunter," he said. "Congratulations on ridding your home of all the bad juju." His amusement was unmistakable. "We didn't know what to bring to an impromptu post-Wiccan-cleansing house party."

"But then we thought, booze is always the answer," his husband Charlie finished for him as he stepped through the gathering crowd, took the bag from Dante and handed it to me.

"Thanks," I said with a smile, depositing the tote on the kitchen counter. "Um, do you have any idea who all these people are?"

"Well, let's see." Dante looked around, then pointed out various groups around the room. "That'd be most of my extended family. And that's Nana's Ma Jong group. That man over there is her hairdresser, Mr. Mario, along with what I believe is the entire staff of his salon. Oh, and that group, I'm pretty sure, is from Nana's gun club. The camouflage is kind of a tip-off. Beyond that, no clue."

"Well, okay then."

Brian appeared beside me, already eyeing the sandwiches. "Those look damn good," he said.

Nana overheard him and exclaimed, "Like I said before, that cute little River boy has a gift." He was arranging a big tray of desserts a few feet away and grinned embarrassedly. "That's why I'm getting him to cater Christopher and Kieran's wedding," she said. A momentary look of panic crossed River's face, but Trevor shot him a reassuring smile.

"I still don't think that's a good idea," River said.

"Sure it is," Nana insisted. "Good ideas are the only kind I come up with."

As Trevor continued to set up the food, he said, "This is an amazing apartment, Hunter."

"Thanks. I'm probably going to have to sell it, though. My agent informed me this week that my production company is suing me for breach of contract, because I quit the industry before making one last film for them."

"Didn't that schmuck call you?" Nana asked me, hands on her hips. She still wore the two-foot-tall witch hat.

"Which schmuck, exactly?"

"Your agent. He was supposed to call and let you know the lawsuit's being dropped."

My eyes went wide with surprise. "It is? Why?"

"Because I went and talked to him after you told me you were being sued. I convinced him that your last film should be a retrospective, made from clips of all your films. The Best of Hunter Storm. Only, he'll probably give it a

328

racier title. That way, you don't have to get in front of the camera."

"And he agreed?"

Nana grinned at me. "You say that as if he had a choice."

"Did you threaten him?"

"See, that's a common misconception people have about those of us in the family business," she said. "We don't threaten. We *persuade*."

"Well, thank you, Nana. I really appreciate your help. I wish there was some way to repay you."

"There is," she said. "I seen all of them posters of you they got down at that production company. That's some caboose you got there. Me," she said, slapping her bottom with both hands, "I got no caboose at all. So I'm thinking, maybe you can come to the gym with me and show me a few exercises. I mean, don't get me wrong, I can turn heads just fine like this. But I figure, if I work out a bit, then I can get me some of them designer jeans and really make the cougar hunters swoon."

I smiled at her and said, "What does Mr. Dombruso think about you turning the young guys' heads?"

"That man was dumb enough to stray once. It serves him right to keep him on his toes." She had a point.

Later on, when Brian and I were curled up in a relatively quiet corner, I relaxed against his shoulder and watched the crowd. Everyone seemed to be having a good time, with the exception of Vincent. He was standing off to the side, hands folded in front of him, looking like a pallbearer at a funeral. Nana must have coerced him into coming. It was so obvious he'd rather be anywhere else.

Suddenly, Vincent was in motion. I wondered what had set him off. In one fluid movement, he caught a big tray of glasses that Trevor had been about to drop. I watched as the two of them had some sort of one-sided conversation, which I could have sworn ended in Vincent very nearly smiling.

"Did you see that?" Brian asked. "Good ol' Vinnie just may have a new man-crush."

"You think?"

"He's been staring at Trevor all night. Boy, those two are a weird combination."

"Weird is good. It works for us."

"That it does," Brian said with a grin.

"And if Trevor can coax a smile out of him, then maybe he's the perfect person for Vincent."

"Vincent didn't actually smile," he pointed out.

"No, but he *almost* did. Trevor gets points for coming close, like in horseshoes."

Brian chuckled at that. "Like in horseshoes? What does equestrian footwear have to do with anything?"

I grinned and said, "The *game* of horseshoes, city boy. You know, where you chuck horseshoes at a stick and call it entertainment? You get points even if you miss."

"Ah, okay. Now I get it."

I returned my head to his shoulder and watched the crowd. "You know," I said after a while, "I wasn't convinced that the Wiccan ceremony was going to shake the cobwebs out of here, but this party is doing the trick. It's nice to see so much positive energy filling this place."

"Speaking of this apartment," Brian said, "I have something I want to ask you."

330

"What is it?"

"When Kieran and Christopher get married, I want to sign the house over to them as a wedding present. So I wanted to ask if I could stay here with you until I find an apartment."

"Of course. And wow, that's huge! Are you sure you want to do that? I mean, you grew up in that house."

"Kieran did too, and after all he's done for me, I feel like I want to say thank you in a big way. He always loved that house, and I think it would be a really nice gift for him and Christopher as they begin their lives together."

I kissed him and said, "You're a sweet man, Brian Nolan."

"Shhh." He pressed a finger to my lips. "Not so loud. You're going to shatter my reputation as a straight-up douchebag."

I wrapped my arms around him and cuddled a bit closer. "You don't have that reputation."

"Anymore."

"Anymore," I repeated with a big grin. "So, we have a little over three weeks to finish fixing up the house. I think that's doable."

"I think so, too." Then he added, "If you'd rather not have me stay here, it's fine to say no, by the way. I can figure something else out until I find a place."

"We haven't wanted to spend a single day apart since we got back together," I pointed out. "Why on Earth wouldn't I want you here with me? I don't even think it should be temporary, you should just move in."

"That's crazy talk," he said with a smile.

"I know. But still."

"I want to take you up on that, which proves I'm just as crazy as you are. But it's way too soon to talk about moving in together. I mean, we haven't even...you know...."

"Consummated our relationship?" I wiggled my eyebrows at him playfully, and he chuckled.

"Yeah. That." While we'd certainly messed around plenty over the past few weeks, we hadn't actually progressed beyond oral sex.

"It'll happen when we're ready."

"I was thinking," he said, "That maybe I *am* ready. So, you should let me know when you are."

I sat up and looked at him. "Really?" He nodded, a little grin playing on his lips. "Well, I'm definitely ready, too."

"Would it be rude to pull the fire alarm and clear all these people out of here?" His grin graduated to a big smile.

I laughed and said, "Oh, so you're ready *now*."

"Well, okay, we don't have to do it right this very minute. I can wait a couple more hours."

"You sure today's the day? This is a big deal to you, and we shouldn't rush into it."

"How could this possibly be construed as rushing?"

"I just want to make sure you've given it some thought."

"Oh, believe me, I've been thinking about it plenty. I even went so far as to have an STD test last week when I went in for my physical, just to make sure we were all systems go." He flashed me two thumbs up. "It all came back just peachy."

"Peachy, ay?"

"Yes. Peachy. That was my official diagnosis."

"Coincidentally, I got tested a couple weeks back. I actually do that routinely, every three months, even though I've always played safe. My diagnosis was also peachy. If you still want to use condoms though, that's understandable."

Brian raised a brow. "You're fine, I'm fine, and we're in a monogamous relationship. Why would you think I'd want to use condoms?"

I broke eye contact and began picking at some lint on my dark jeans. "Well, you know what I am."

"You practiced safe sex in all your films. I'm not worried."

"I don't mean the part about me being in porn, though that's certainly bad enough. I mean the part about me sleeping with half of San Francisco." After a pause, I said, "I wish I had more to offer you. You deserve better than some dumb slut who thought he could make people love him by giving his body to them."

He pulled me into a hug and buried his face in my hair. "That's not what you are, Hunter."

"It is."

"You're completely wrong."

"Then what am I?"

Brian pulled back to look at me, his arms still around me as he said, "I'll tell you what you are. You're a fascinating, complex, intelligent individual. You're a wacky sense of humor with the face of an angel. You're my reason to wake up every morning. You're sweet and sexy and nurturing, and a million and one good things. You're the man I love, Hunter." My eyes went wide, and he grinned at me. "Don't you dare look surprised at that. You know I love you, even if it's taken me a while to actually say it."

"I love you too, Brian."

"Okay, see, you don't have to say it just because I said it. I mean—"

I cut him off with a long, deep kiss, and when I finally pulled back a few inches, I grinned at him and said, "Let's try that again. I love you, Brian."

"So, I get that it would seem awkward to leave my declaration of love just hanging there, but still, it's not like you're obligated to—" I cut him off with another kiss, and when we came up for air the next time, he was smiling. "I have absolutely no incentive to stop my insecure ramblings. Not if you shut me up with a big kiss each time."

I smiled too. "You're a total dork, and I completely love you."

"I completely love you, too." After another kiss he asked, "Can we pull that fire alarm yet?"

"Nope."

"Damn. Don't these people have homes? What are they still doing here?"

"Having a darn good time, by the looks of it."

Brian sighed and said, "Don't they understand that I *need* to be inside you? That I've waited weeks and weeks, and another couple hours just might kill me?"

My cock throbbed in response to that, but I said lightly, "No. I'm pretty sure they don't understand that."

"Maybe they'd take the hint and leave if I tied you naked to the buffet table and started rimming you."

"Nah. They'd probably just take out their camera phones."

"Probably. Bunch of degenerates."

"I love the way your eyes sparkle when you're amused," I told him.

"Oh man. This is what it's going to be like now that we've declared our love for one another, isn't it? We're going to turn into one of those sappy couples who are all like," he raised his voice a couple octaves, "I love your nose, and I love the way you chew your food, and I love the way you squeeze the toothpaste from the center of the tube." In his normal tone of voice he added, "By the way, I don't love that. Normal people squeeze it from the end. Were you raised by toothless chimpanzees?"

I burst out laughing. "I love the way you're a colossal pain in the ass."

He beamed at me. "Thank you. And right back at you."

"Maybe that's why we're perfect for each other."

"No, that's not why. This is." Brian swung me across his lap, tipped me back, and kissed me for all he was worth. Lust and heat and love and desire shot through me as my lips parted and I gave myself to him.

"Oh that's right," I murmured, and then I went right back to kissing him.

Chapter Seventeen

"I thought they'd never leave."

"Great party, though," I said.

"It was," Brian agreed. "Nobody knows how to throw a spur-of-the-moment Wiccan ritual/house party like your adopted octogenarian mafia grandma."

"This is true."

"Speaking of the ritual, whatever the Wiccan was burning made this place smell like a Renaissance faire," he said as he helped me make my bed.

"I'm pretty sure that was a combination of sage, rosemary, and weed."

"Like I said. Renaissance faire."

I grinned at him. "And you know what a Renaissance faire smells like because...?"

"I'm just speculating."

"No you're not, you totally went to one. Did you go dressed as a knight? Please tell me there are photos."

"Not a knight, and the photos have been destroyed."

I burst out laughing. "Oh my God. Next time I talk to Kieran, I'm asking him for details. I bet he knows all your deep, dork secrets."

"Do you mean dark?"

"No. I mean dork."

Brian was smiling as he tossed a pillow on the bed. "There. Clean sheets. Which, by the way, doesn't make a lick of sense, since we're now going to completely trash them." His smile increased a few hundred megawatts.

"We are. But it'll be nice to at least start with them fresh." I ran my palm over the sheet, smoothing out a wrinkle, then admitted, "Okay, so the last time I was in this bed was the same night I met you. I brought some guy home. I didn't even know his name. He was just some random person who picked me up in a club."

"I see."

"It seems like a lifetime ago. I don't even feel like I'm the same person anymore."

"You're not. Neither of us are," he said gently.

"Anyway, hence the clean sheets."

"Got it," he said as he rolled around to my side of the bed. Suddenly, he scooped me up and tossed me onto the mattress. "Now let's get them dirty."

"Yes sir." I smiled and held my arms out to him.

Brian climbed on top of me, parting my legs with his knee, and kissed me voraciously. As I rubbed him through his 501s, he untucked my shirt. He then took hold of my hem and yanked it in opposite directions. Buttons flew everywhere as I let out a surprised bark of laughter.

While one hand massaged my hard-on through my jeans, the other worked on my belt, then my button and zipper. As soon as he got my pants unfastened, he pulled them and my underwear to mid-thigh, then just devoured my cock. His hands slid around to my ass as he sucked me, kneading my butt as he took me down his throat.

"Oh shit," I murmured, arching off the mattress. "Bri, if you keep doing that, you're going to make me cum."

Brian looked up at me, still sucking my cock, and gave me a playful wink, which I took as a go-ahead. He reached up and gave me his finger to suck, then slid it into my ass as his lips and tongue continued to work my shaft. His free hand moved to my balls, rubbing and squeezing them. I liked the fact that he wasn't dainty about it, that he handled me like he was asserting his claim on my body. It was exactly what I wanted.

I didn't stand a chance of holding back, not with all he was doing to me. Within a few minutes, I was yelling, "Oh fuck, Brian," as my cum filled his mouth and he finger-fucked my hole relentlessly. He drank me down before finally releasing my cock from his lips and licking it gently.

He climbed off me as I laid there panting and went right back to undressing me. "I couldn't resist," he told me with a smile as he pulled off my shoes and socks. "You just looked good enough to eat."

Soon we were both completely naked, and he traced his fingertips down my body before grinning at me. "Oh look," he said. "You're a natural blond."

I laughed at that. He was stroking my wispy happy trail, which had begun to grow in since I no longer had a need for full-body waxes (and wow, was I ever *not* going to miss those). "What, you didn't think I was?"

"I wasn't sure. I thought maybe you had some help in that department."

"I only added highlights. I was already blond."

"So I see." Brian kissed my stomach, then dotted a row of kisses up my chest before reaching my mouth. He climbed on top of me again, tangling his fingers in my hair as our lips met, and I wrapped my arms and legs around him as he rubbed his cock against mine.

When he sat up with me on his lap, his big hands caressing my back, I whispered, "I love you, Brian."

"I love you too, Hunter. More than anything." He wrapped his arms around me and held me securely, and I burrowed against him as he nibbled my shoulder.

"So, obviously we should forego the handcuffs," he said softly after a while.

"Why?"

"I can't imagine you'd be comfortable with that, not after...well, you know."

"I want you to tie me up before you fuck me. It's important to me."

"It is?"

"Yeah. It's a part of me, and it's a part of us."

"But—"

"Swensen took a lot from me, my confidence, my sense of security, my peace of mind. Slowly, I'm rebuilding those things, but still. He took so much, and I don't want him to take this, too."

"I don't know, Hunter."

"He was the last person to tie me up, and it was terrifying, because it was against my will. But now I want to reclaim it, make it ours again. I want to prove to myself that he didn't break me, that he didn't shatter my ability to trust."

Brian chewed his bottom lip and watched me for a long moment. Then he said, "I have an idea. Where are your cuffs?"

"I don't actually own any. Remember how I said I never did this in my private life? The ones we borrowed before are still at Christopher's apartment, so we'll have to improvise."

"Okay. Then bring me something to improvise with."
He smiled at me sweetly.

"Be right back." I jumped out of bed, hurried to my walk-in closet, and looked around. When I returned, I told him, "This is such a cliché, but it's all I could think of." I put a little pile of black silk neckties beside him.

"That'll work."

"Where do you want me?" I asked, and when he patted a spot on the mattress, I started to climb up onto the bed. But then I exclaimed, "Oh wait, one more thing," and rushed off to the bathroom. I was back a few moments later with a little container. "You'll need this." I pulled the plastic seal off the lube and tossed it aside before handing the bottle to him, and he smirked at me as he tucked it under the pillow.

"I did actually know we needed that. This may be my first time having sex with a man, but I'm not completely clueless."

I grinned at him as I crawled up on the bed again and kneeled in front of him. "Never said you were."

"It was implied."

"Then maybe you should punish me for my brattiness." I flashed him a huge smile.

Brian chuckled at that. "Maybe I should. But for now, give me your hands." I stuck them out, palms up, and he got on his knees in front of me and kissed the inside of each of my wrists in turn. Then he put my hands together and held them in one of his while he untangled a necktie from the pile. As he wound the silky strip of material around my wrists, he asked, "Why would anyone own so many black ties?"

"They're all different."

"No they're not," Brian insisted. "They're all black."

"But some are skinnier, some wider, some shiny, some matte, and some are textured. And I actually own way more than that. I just didn't bring them all to the bed."

He chuckled again. "You and I are from different planets. You know that, right?"

"Why? How many black ties do you own?"

"Zero."

"Really?"

"I only own one tie, and it's dark blue. I bought it at Target for my high school graduation."

Now it was my turn to chuckle. "How does a grown man only own one tie?"

"I only have the one neck." As he said that, he cinched the tie around my wrists, then knotted it. He looked up at me and smiled as he said, "Okay, try to escape." I tugged lightly on my bindings, and he rolled his eyes. "Try harder. You don't want it to come apart mid-fuck, do you?"

At that, I really tried to bust out of my bindings. They held firm, and I shot him a big smile. "Well done."

"So, I thought maybe this was a good middle-ground, tying you up, but not tying you down. You're still bound, but you aren't helpless. I thought that might help you ease back into it."

"It's perfect. Thank you."

"Alright," he said, scooping me up in his arms. "Time for your punishment. Which is a bad word for it, since you're obviously looking forward to it." At that, he tossed me into the air a few inches, flipped me over so I was face-down, and put me across his lap.

"Mmmm," I murmured, rubbing my cock against his thigh, my arms stretched up over my head. I'd been rock hard ever since he began wrapping the tie around my wrists, and so was he. Right now, his big, thick erection was pressed snugly against my hip, and I made sure to rub against it as I gyrated on his lap.

He reached for the lube and parted my legs as he said, "I'm going to prep you as I spank you. I have a feeling neither of us is going to be able to hold out for long after this." He popped the top with his thumb, then drizzled a cool stream between my cheeks.

When he slid a finger into me and began working my hole, I moaned with pleasure and said, "You're right about that."

He kept fingering me deeply as he brought his other hand down on my ass. I moaned again, bucking harder against his lap, and he chuckled and said, "Oh yeah. Definitely not punishment." He slapped my ass again, and it elicited the same response. "Fuck, that's hot," he murmured, then began spanking me rapidly.

Brian established the perfect rhythm, each slap accompanied with a thrust into me with two fingers. It was so intense, the pleasure/pain such a rush, that it cleared everything from my mind, leaving only pure, primal lust. Finally, Brian swung me upright so that I was straddling his lap and sat me on his cock. I threw my bound hands around his neck, moaning as I took him to his balls.

He grabbed my ass with both hands, bouncing me up and down on his shaft while thrusting up into me. "Oh fuck," he ground out, throwing his head back as he took me forcefully. We were both so turned on that it only lasted a few minutes. I came first, shooting all over his chest and stomach, and then he came inside me, claiming me yet again as he yelled incoherently.

Brian tipped me onto my back, still inside me as we both gasped for breath. He was propped up slightly on his knees and elbows, being careful not to crush me, and I wrapped my legs around his waist as he kissed me, deeply and lovingly.

He looked into my eyes and smiled at me, and I said with a grin, "That was amazing."

"I have to agree with you there."

"So, first time having sex with a guy. What's the verdict?"

"I'll let you know when I'm done."

My grin got even wider. "You're not done?"

"Oh, hell no. Just taking a short breather." He looked happier than I'd ever seen him, and I pointed that out to him. "Well, of course I'm happy," he said. "I'm currently inside the man I love. That's the best place in the entire world."

I craned my neck and kissed him, then said, "I love you so much, Brian."

"I love you too, Hunter." His lips met mine again, and he kissed me passionately. After a couple minutes, he began moving in me again, thrusting slowly. His erection had barely diminished after he'd cum, and I felt it swell and grow, filling me.

The first go-round had been quick, almost frantic, driven by lust. The next one was different. Brian took his time, thrusting deep into me while holding my gaze. I smiled at him and stroked the back of his head with my bound hands. He reached up and brushed my hair back from my face, then caressed my cheek tenderly. When he traced my lower lip, I caught his finger between my lips and sucked on it for a moment, before letting go and kissing him again.

Brian wrapped his arms around my shoulders as his thrusts became more forceful, gearing up slowly, the intensity building and building until he was pistoning in and out of me, his body slapping against mine. He reached between us and took hold of my cock, stroking me in time to his thrusts. I really didn't know if I had a third orgasm in me, but he built me back up, took me right to the brink, and held me there for several minutes as he fucked me.

Moments before he came in me again, he began working my cock rapidly, insistently. And when he cried out and began shooting in me, I came too, my cries mingling with his, filling the quiet apartment. "Oh God Brian," I ground out as my orgasm peaked, my entire body shaking.

He eased out of me carefully when we'd both finished, then rolled onto his side and held me to him. His heartbeat thudded against my chest. I threw my head back and laughed. It was probably a weird reaction, but I was just so happy in that moment.

He smiled at me and said, "So, did you enjoy that?"

"Are you kidding? That was epic. I can't even believe you pulled that off, cumming in me twice! Do you know how rare that is?"

"Well, you only get one first time. I figured I should make it count." He had a huge, satisfied grin on his face.

"You're a pretty amazing guy, Brian Nolan," I told him.

"You're pretty amazing yourself, Hunter Jacobs." He leaned in and kissed me lightly, but soon deepened the kiss, and I parted my lips for him. We kissed for a long time, his big hands splayed out on my back, holding me to him as warmth and contentment flooded me.

Finally, he rested his forehead against mine and let his eyes slide shut. "I'm yours," I whispered, and that made him smile.

"And I'm yours, Hunter."

"I have an idea," I whispered. "Let's stay like this forever."

"Absolutely. We're both right where we belong."

I'd never felt so certain of anything in my entire life.

The End

\#\#\#\#\#

Thank you for reading!

For more by Alexa Land, please visit alexalandwrites.blogspot.com

Trevor takes center stage, Hunter and Brian's relationship continues, and Christopher and Kieran get married in Salvation, the fifth book in the Firsts and Forever series. A brief bonus excerpt from Salvation follows. Enjoy!

Sneak Peek

Salvation: Book Five in the Firsts and Forever Series
Beginning of Chapter One

Focus, Trevor.

Okay, that'd be a lot easier if the insanely gorgeous man in the corner stopped staring at me. Who was he, and what was he doing at this party? He certainly wasn't here to have fun. He was more like a sentry, expressionless in his dark, expensive suit, every black hair in place. And there was an air of danger about him, like maybe he was in the FBI, or a hit man or something. Silent but deadly.

I had to fight back a laugh at that. Oh man, I was totally losing it. What was I saying about focusing? I dragged my eyes away from SBD and gathered a few empty cans and glasses from the furniture, lining them up on the heavy tray I was awkwardly balancing on my left hand.

About ten seconds later, I snuck another look at him. He was still watching me. It actually would have been slightly unnerving, if I didn't find him incredibly sexy.

Aside from his silver, wire-framed glasses, SBD kind of looked like a younger version of an actor whose name escaped me, a tall, hunky Italian who had played a part in a movie I'd seen recently. The movie was Magic Mike...what was the character's name again?

Oh, right. Big Dick Ritchie. At that, my gaze flickered involuntarily to the man's...area. When I realized what I'd just done, a blush crept up in my cheeks. God, what a spaz.

I turned my back to the man in the corner and pulled a dish cloth from the black apron tied around my hips, busily wiping up a water mark to hide my embarrassment.

I swung around to head back to the kitchen, and tripped over a stair I not only knew was there, but that I'd reminded myself earlier not to trip on. The tray swung precariously to the left, then the right as I flailed wildly. It was like some sort of comedy juggling act, only I wasn't laughing. This was my second catering job ever, and I was about to smash all of my host's glassware to bits. That was so not good.

A big hand clamped down on the edge of the tray, stabilizing it instantly. *Don't be the hottie, don't be the hottie, don't be the hottie,* I thought to myself as I straightened up and pushed my overgrown bangs out of my eyes.

It was the hottie.

SBD's gaze was even more intense close up, his dark eyes beautiful and piercing at the same time. I felt another blush warming my cheeks. God I hated that about myself, the fact that I blushed like a southern belle at a cotillion every time I got embarrassed, and I got embarrassed *a lot.*

Right now, for example.

Don't start rambling, don't start rambling, don't start rambling. "Wow, you got over here really fast," I rambled. "Kind of like that scene in Twilight where he stops the van." *Oh my God, I'm talking about Twilight! Someone kill me!* "I mean, not that I've seen it, or anything. Well, okay, I'm lying. Obviously I've seen it. Otherwise, how would I know about the van scene? I just didn't want to admit that I'd seen it. Actually, I saw it three times. I was totally team

Edward." For the love of God, *shut up!* "And you did get over here really fast. But instead of saving me from a van, you saved me from the cans." I picked up an empty soda can from my tray and rattled it, then set it back down. Then I almost dropped the tray again. SBD's hand shot out and steadied it. Was I imagining it, or was there the faintest trace of a smile on those full lips?

"Okay. So, I'm just going to go to the kitchen and die now," I said. "Enjoy the party. Which, you know, you'll stand a better chance of if you don't go back to that corner." I turned and fled, my face most certainly Santa suit red.

"Wow, dude, what happened to you?" River, my new friend and business partner, asked when I returned to the kitchen.

The huge apartment was an open floor plan, so I was still within sight of…okay, I had to stop calling him SBD. The Italian Secret Service, that was better. I was still in sight of ISS, but kept my back to him and the rest of the party as I asked, "What do you mean?"

"I was watching you out there. You were having some kind of conniption."

"What's a conniption?"

"You know, like a conniption fit? Some kind of spazzy little breakdown? Don't ya'all say that out here?" River was originally from Louisiana, but he'd lived in San Francisco almost five years. His speech was now a weird mash-up of southern slacker and California surfer.

"I thought a conniption fit was when someone got really angry and started waving their hands around."

He considered that for a moment, then said, "Okay, maybe. I thought it also meant, like, a spaz attack, but I could be wrong. Anyway, what were you doing out there? And please tell me that Italian mobster stereotype was not hitting on you."

"No. But funnily enough, apparently Nana's family really is in the mob. I just found that out."

River's brown eyes went wide. "No shit. And here she's offering to help us with our catering business. Next thing you know, we'll be money laundering and running numbers on the side."

I grinned at him and asked, "Do you actually know what either of those things involve?"

"No clue." River turned to the stove and pulled a pan off the heat, then said, "Seriously, though, that guy looks like trouble with a capital W.T.F. If I can make a suggestion as your new friend and business partner, it would be this: stay the hell away from men that look like Tony Soprano's much hotter younger cousin."

"I wonder who he is." I snuck a glance over my shoulder. He was back in his corner, those dark eyes still on me. Embarrassingly, certain parts of my anatomy liked the fact that he was watching me, and I surreptitiously adjusted the front of my apron.

"He rode in the limo with Nana, that's all I know." River raised an eyebrow at me and exclaimed, "Oh mah gawd. Has he gotten your lady parts all hot and bothered?"

"River, I'm a dude. No lady parts."

"I know. I'm teasin' ya. But if you did have lady parts, tell me this. Would they be wet now?"

I laughed at that and threw a dish towel at his head. "There's really something wrong with you."

"I know. And you were dumb enough to go into business with me. Speaking of which, how long do you think it'll be before everyone discovers we're not real caterers?"

"We *are* real caterers, and we've got the bill from the restaurant supply store to prove it."

"Yeah, gawd, don't remind me. This gig will almost pay for half of it."

"The job next Saturday should pay for the rest, if we manage to keep costs down."

"Check you out, with your natural-born business sense and all. This is why it's good that we've teamed up. I hate thinkin' about stuff like money and expenses. I just want to make food that tastes awesome."

"And you do that very well." I'd been unloading glasses into the dishwasher as we were talking, my back still to the party, and I asked River, "Is he looking over here now?"

"No."

"He isn't?"

"And you're all disappointed! Yes, of course he's still lookin' over here. That is one smitten Soprano. By the way, how totally fifth grade was that question? Do you want me to pass him a note? 'Do you like Trevor? Check the box, yes or no.' For fuck's sake, T!"

"Sorry. I'm just not used to scorchingly hot guys noticing me. Hell, I'm not used to *any* guys noticing me."

"What're you talkin' about? You're cute."

"I'm not. I'm shy and awkward. Oh and also, kind of a spaz. That guy's probably staring at me because he can't believe how dorky I am. Do you know what I did when I had a chance to talk to him? I started rattling off about Twilight."

River looked stricken. "Please tell me you're joking."

"I told him I'd seen it three times, and that I used to be team Edward."

River tried to hand me a huge chef's knife. "There's just no coming back from humiliation like that. Ritualistic suicide is the only option left to you."

"Don't I know it." I added detergent to the dishwasher and shut it, then pushed the on-button. "It's really no wonder that I'm a twenty-year-old virgin."

"Okay, so that's what your problem is."

"The fact that I need to get laid?"

"No, the fact that you have a chronic case of TMI. People don't need to know that about you, Trev. And the Man in Black over there certainly didn't need to know you have the cinematic taste of a fourteen-year-old girl."

"*Nobody* needs to know that."

"Exactly my point!" River exclaimed as he stirred the sauce he'd taken off the stove, then refilled a decanter on the buffet. "Oh, bad news," he said. "Nana just said something to MiB, and he's headed for the door."

"Damn it, really?" I snuck a glance across the apartment and confirmed that River wasn't just yanking my chain. "Aw. Goodbye, Big Dick Ritchie," I murmured. The guy left without looking back.

River laughed at that. "You have x-ray vision or something?"

"What? Oh, no. He just reminded me of a character in a movie."

"A porno movie?"

"No. Never mind."

"Hey, don't get all sulky now," he said as he moved to a cutting board and began chopping things to replenish the crudité platter. "You didn't want that guy anyway."

"I didn't?"

"Hell no. Innocent little virgin like you? You'd be better off dating a great white shark than that straight-up gangstah."

"I'm so sorry I told you I was a virgin."

River shot me a big smile, his dark eyes sparkling. "I know."

Made in the USA
Middletown, DE
21 June 2019